NO FADE-OUT

This isn't happening, Megan tried to tell herself, as the clothes were ripped from her body by brutally strong hands. *It's a nightmare.*

But it was happening. She looked up. There stood Bir-Saraband. He was laughing now, smirking as he unzipped his trousers and came closer. Closer.

Megan shut her eyes very slightly. Maybe if she couldn't see him, it would be better. But she did not close them fast enough. For behind him she saw the other men, waiting their turn, some already rubbing themselves in anticipation.

Megan belonged to the world of the TV news screen. But this was a different world. A world where horrors did not stop after a sixty-second news clip. A world where horror went on and on and on. . . .

THE
PANTHER THRONE

The Best in Fiction From SIGNET

*Price Slightly Higher in Canada.

†Not Available in Canada

THE
PANTHER
THRONE

A novel by
Tom Murphy

A SIGNET BOOK
NEW AMERICAN LIBRARY
TIMES MIRROR

PUBLISHER'S NOTE

This novel is a work of fiction. Names, characters, places, and incidents are either the product of the author's imagination or are used fictitiously, and any resemblance to actual persons, living or dead, events, or locales is entirely coincidental.

**This book is for the Atkinsons—
Tom, Ulla, and Dane—with love.**

Copyright © 1982 by Ganesha Properties, Ltd.

SIGNET, SIGNET CLASSICS, MENTOR, PLUME, MERIDIAN AND NAL BOOKS are published by The New American Library, Inc., 1633 Broadway, New York, New York 10019

First Printing, November, 1982

1 2 3 4 5 6 7 8 9

PRINTED IN THE UNITED STATES OF AMERICA

Dallas, Texas: August of Next Year.

High in the black tower that is the corporate headquarters of Revere Oil, Bradford "Bradboy" Shane peered irritably into the clear blue eyes of the young geologist who stood unflinchingly on the other side of Shane's enormous desk. Perry Carlton's services were much in demand and Bradboy knew it. Carlton took no crap from anyone, especially not from one who so greatly enjoyed the sour pleasures of intimidation as Bradboy. Bradboy, who had inherited his uncle's money and meanness and voting shares of Revere Oil, but not the old man's brains, was uneasy around people he didn't own or couldn't buy. He needed Carlton and hated himself for it.

"Wadi Darr?" The Arabic name stuck in Bradboy's throat.

"It's the sorriest little oasis you ever saw—two palms and some scrub acacia and a few rocks. And more oil than anyone's found out there since the big Saudi strikes in the 1950's."

"How big, exactly?"

"Big. You know we can't tell exactly, Bradboy, not yet. But take my word for it. You get those Kassanian drilling concessions renewed—and at just about any terms. It'll be in October, won't it?"

"The fifth." Bradboy shifted uneasily. The Kassanian oil-lease concessions were the foundation of Revere's foothold in OPEC. For fifteen years they'd run along with the usual escalator clauses, filling thousands of tankers with that pure sweet Kassanian crude. Filling Revere Oil's annual report with ink blacker than oil. But now the original lease was up. Up for grabs, maybe, even though old King Nayif El Kheybar seemed friendly. Seemed. How could you tell, for God's sake? Those hooded dark eyes. Face like an old leather saddle. And a thousand years of silent desert pride behind it all. Some Arabs you could buy. Bradboy knew that for a fact, because he'd paid the bills. But that didn't work with old Nayif. Bite your hand off if you tried. And the King of Kassan was old—pushing eighty, although nobody knew for sure.

1

"Thanks, Perry," said Bradboy, feigning a sort of good-old-boy camaraderie. "You all come back soon, hear?"

Perry smiled, not bothering to hide his contempt. He turned to leave the huge vulgar office, then paused. After all, Shane was paying him, and paying him damn well. He owed it to this obscene joke of a man to tell him about the rebels.

"One more thing, Bradboy—don't count on the stability of the Panther Throne. There are rebels out there. One rebel in particular: Bandar Al Khadir. He means business. He's got more support than the establishment would like anyone to know. I think he's dangerous."

Bradboy ran his thick forefinger over his chins. It was a long journey. His breath came out slowly, like air escaping from a ruptured tire. "Hadn't heard about them. Them rebels. Oh, hell, Perry, we got rebels right here in old Dallas—don't make no nevermind."

"Just what Batista used to say. Not to mention your pal the Shah. Well, I just wanted you to know. With your permission, I'll brief T.R. Kalbfleisch, and I'll be back in Kassan by next week. Winding up the wildcat part of it. So long, Bradboy."

"Take care, Perry. Don't let them rebels get you!" Bradboy's laugh was slow, like gurgling oil. There was no humor in it.

"Thanks. Get the concessions renewed, Bradboy."

The geologist was out of the big room as fast as he could move without running. Bradboy's office didn't really smell. It just felt that way.

The door had hardly closed when Shane picked up the phone. "Mary? Get me Washington, honey. D.C. The Secretary of State. *Pronto!*"

New York City: An Evening In August of Next Year.

Megan entered the room on David Crane's arm, conscious of the impression they made together. The youngest of this group, by far. David, sleek as a seal in his dinner jacket, just this side of being too handsome. And if she did say so herself, she looked all right in the new lavender sheath from Hanae Mori. It was part of her journalist's training that made Megan acutely sensitive to how she looked, to the vibrations in a room—or anyplace else. She hadn't gotten to be the fastest-rising television reporter at INTERTEL by sticking her head in the sand. *Then why don't you feel more secure, Megan?* she asked herself. *Why do you always think someone's going to find out you crashed the party, that you're just a little Irish girl from Queens, that you don't belong here at all?* Waves of fear came over her. She smiled, knowing it was a dazzling smile, very nearly a famous smile, too. It helped only a little.

This was David's world. His friends. His boss, Gordon Langstaff, was giving the party. Langstaff of Langstaff, Hillyer, and Langstaff. If God were contemplating some heavenly merger, the chances were he'd work it through the Langstaffs. If they'd have him.

Forty-two floors above Park Avenue, waist-deep in antique wainscoting, their cultured voices muted even further by the ancient Flemish tapestries, the worn Oriental carpets, the velvet gone almost threadbare because it had been woven—by hand, in Venice—three hundred years ago. David's people. David's world. It would be her world too, if she married him.

Not yet, David darling, she thought, smiling more brightly. *You're very dear and you're dynamite in bed, but please, not yet.*

David knew precisely what he wanted, and Megan was part of it. The rest of his all-too-perfect picture included the predictable old farmhouse in, probably, Greenwich. Kids, of course, and large dogs. A few horses, more likely than not. A picturebook life for a picturebook lover.

If Megan felt trapped in that picture, it wasn't because the picture was anything less than perfect.

Like the excellent dancer he was, David guided her through the crowd to their host. Gordon Langstaff beamed and bent elegantly to kiss her hand. He twinkled as only very rich men over sixty can twinkle.

"You're looking ravishing as ever, my dear," he said. "She's much too good for you, Crane, much too good."

David laughed. It was all so easy, so familiar.

"Megan, dear, stay with us a minute, you'll be interested. We were just talking about Kassan."

"What's Kassan?"

Megan had never heard the word before. It might have been a person, a place, or the latest upper-crust parlor game.

Langstaff's aristocratic eyebrows arched just slightly. Megan could feel his pleasure at finding at least one subject on which she wasn't well-informed.

"Kassan, my dear girl, is a wart upon the thigh of Saudi Arabia." Then Langstaff's attention veered from Megan to a new arrival. He was obviously pleased. Megan followed his glance: a trim suntanned man, yachtsman, she guessed, no beauty, but with character. He'd photograph well, she thought, expertly scanning the planes of the newcomer's face. *Bill Holden's younger brother.*

Langstaff's voice cut gently through her appraisal. "Jeb," he said, "so glad you could make it. Megan Mcguire, David Crane, meet one of our brightest young architects: Jeb Stuart Cleaver."

Megan smiled conventionally, trying and failing to place the name. She put out her hand and he took it in his. For a long beat Cleaver said nothing. He just looked at her.

Port Kassan, Arabia: September of Next Year.

The white Rolls-Royce limousine moved through the thronged streets of the old town with the whispering grace of the wind. Crowds parted. Goats, camels, and chickens scattered. The huge car was a familiar sight in Port Kassan. Like most of the royal conveyances, its passenger-compartment windows had been replaced with one-way mirrors which were, not incidentally, bulletproof. In the shaded silence, the Crown Prince of Kassan sat staring straight ahead as though the familiar, elegantly uniformed back of his driver could answer some riddle.

There seemed to be too many riddles now, and too little chance of answering them.

Selim did not want to go to this reception at the American embassy. A boring party with boring people. But his father, King Nayif, was off hunting again, playing the Bedu chieftain in the desert with a few old cronies and his thoroughbred falcons. Sometimes his eldest son and designated heir thought that the king cared more for the falcons and the hunting than for himself. Role-playing, that was what Selim hated. And it was his only real job in Kassan, crown prince or not. His father would hear nothing of a real position. Selim filled in on occasions like the forthcoming reception. Selim took his father's place at tiny unimportant ceremonies. Stood at the right of the Panther Throne on ceremonial occasions. Boring, boring, boring.

Selim El Kheybar was thirty-nine years old and handsome. The oil wealth of Kassan would have assured him of international celebrity if he were ugly as a toad. But women had always been drawn to Selim, even women who had no idea in the world who he was or what he would one day inherit. That had been fun, years ago, at Harvard and later in Paris. But fun can be boring too, and now Selim was firmly settled in Kassan, a married man at that, and a father, trying too hard to do his duty. If only there were some real duty to do!

Selim had been to a thousand such parties. He tried not to think about how many more receptions he might have to attend should Allah spare him and give him long life. The Arabic sense of hospitality was deeply ingrained in him. In all Arabs. Here Selim was the host, no matter whose party it might be according to the invitation. Here Selim must be unfailingly polite, gracious, at ease. It was very hard work sometimes, just to stay awake.

He sighed, looked at the thin gold wafer of a wristwatch that Fawzia had given him on his last birthday, calculated how briefly he could linger with the desiccated Wilfred Austin and his sad vodka-drinking wife. Anything less than an hour might constitute an international incident. What rot it all was!

The Rolls-Royce joined the small procession of official limousines pulling into the driveway of the huge, ugly Arabian/Edwardian mansion that served as the American embassy. Rumor had it the Americans were about to build a new one. It could hardly fail to be an improvement.

The car glided to a stop and the crown prince climbed out without waiting for his driver to open the door. Let the man linger in the mercifully air-conditioned Rolls. Why should they both suffer?

Selim stood for a moment in the harsh sunlight, illuminated as though by a thousand flares, dazzling in a suit of the whitest silk. He blinked against the glare and walked briskly toward the embassy.

New York, the offices of Kuniyoshi & Cleaver, Architects: Early September.

Jeb looked at the aerial photographs of the site. There were three sets, each set taken from the same perspective but at different times of day: early morning, high noon, and late afternoon. To the highly trained eyes of Jeb and his partner, Oscar Kuniyoshi, the moving shadows as revealed by these pictures told tales of infinite meaning. Even when they designed buildings for small urban spaces, they did shadow studies, tracking the shadow that would be cast by their design to be sure no aesthetic damage was done to the neighboring structures by simple deprivation of sunlight. It wasn't strictly necessary. No laws required such consideration. But by caring more, and stretching their collective imaginations to deal with such problems, the firm had won a great and growing reputation.

The photographs that absorbed Jeb and his partner now were of a hilly site in northern California, in the wine country above Marin County. Sonoma. And their assignment was a dream: to create an entire town! Sonoma Hills. The assignment had just come to them. The photographs had been supplied by the developer, and they'd arrived only this morning. Jeb stared, fascinated. But what he saw was more than hills and trees and rock outcroppings.

He sat transfixed. The image of Megan Mcguire kept floating in and out of his head as though the lovely redhead were the result of some strange new drug washed down with Jeb's morning coffee.

"Who is she, Jeb?"

The soft mocking voice of Oscar Kuniyoshi cut into Jeb's reverie.

"Who's who?"

"That's what I'd like to know. Whoever she is, she must be

something. I haven't seen you in a trance like that in . . . well, in a long time."

Not since Hillary, Jeb thought, and snapped right back into the bright brutal present. *Not since the split.* Five years. Plenty of women to fill in the dark places. The hurt still throbbing. And then, at Langstaff's, of all places, Megan. *Megan!*

Jeb looked up and grinned. You could not fool old Oscar. Not that you'd ever want to. Oscar was fifteen years Jeb's senior, and measured by the size of his worldwide reputation, even further away than that. And there was something paternal—avuncular anyway—about his relationship to Jeb. It had been a dazzling moment for Jeb, nearly ten years ago now, when Oscar had picked him out of a dozen eager young architects who had entered a competition for a rural hospital in Minnesota. Jeb's design hadn't won the competition. It was too radical for that. But it won something far more important. It won Jeb the attention and the respect of Oscar Kuniyoshi. And that led to a partnership. The partnership had led to increased success for the firm—its capacity more than doubled now by the synergy of their relationship. It had led to a lot of very welcome recognition for Jeb Stuart Cleaver.

Maybe the pressures of his busy job had helped deepen the cracks in his relationship with Hillary. Maybe. Jeb tended to blame himself for anything that went wrong in his life. That the marriage had cracked and then shattered in horrible cutting fragments must have been his own fault. At least fifty-fifty. She drank more when he was away, and he was away a lot. And to hell with it. He'd raked over that particular set of coals much too often. And still they burned him. The memory of what he'd had with Hillary in the beginning made the end that much more bitter. It made the self-condemnation that much more intense.

Jeb blinked and looked up. "You got it. Oscar, let me ask a personal question."

The silver-gray eyebrows of his partner made small Oriental arcs above Oscar's gold-rimmed eyeglasses.

"Do you watch television?"

Oscar laughed. "A secret vice. Yes, Jeb. Sometimes I do."

7

"She's on television. A reporter of some kind. I don't even know what station."

"The lady's name?"

"Megan Mcguire."

"INTERTEL. Channel 1. A very well-designed red-headed person, if I am not mistaken."

"You are not mistaken."

The photographs lay on the big drawing table between them, waiting. Jeb had just begun to focus on them again when his secretary walked in. She was carrying a big creamy-white envelope with a crest engraved on the back.

"I thought you'd want to see this right away, Jeb," she said.

Jeb accepted it and looked at his name, handwritten on the thick paper.

Then he looked at the crest.

"The Secretary of State" it said, "of the United States of America."

Port Kassan, Arabia, a Side Street in the Old Town: Night, September of Next Year.

The street was very dark, but Bandar knew it by heart. It was narrow, like all the streets in the old quarter, the tall houses almost meeting at the top, more tunnel than street. The jutting balconies and protruding upper stories made cool shadows by day. And a nearly impenetrable blackness at night. Bandar counted on that darkness. He wore it like a cloak. Like a shield.

Majid, as ever, was at his side. Second-in-command of the People's Army of Kassan. Of which Bandar himself was general, founder, prime mover. The People's Army was still half a dream. But starting tonight, the dream would be written in blood.

What reason and rallies and pamphlets couldn't achieve, open revolution might. If the new Kassan must be built from bricks made of ashes and blood, so be it. Hadn't the Prophet himself led an army? The new Kassan had waited long enough.

Bandar was very specific in what he wanted.

A Kassan of, by, and for its people. Not the greedy El Kheybar and their even more greedy relatives, the maggots that clustered about the Panther Throne, but Kassan for Kassanians, down to the lowest goatherd. Theirs—his!—would be a true socialistic democracy, like Iraq's. With elections. A parliament. A true and fair judicial system. Police whose sworn obligation would be to help people and to uphold the law, not to persecute, torture, and kill innocents for the greater glory of a monster like General Bir-Saraband, who ruled not only the army but also the secret police, ADDAK—the most feared and dreaded organization in all Kassan.

Bandar could see ADDAK headquarters clearly from where he and Majid stood in a deeply shadowed doorway. Hidden, like the dark activities it spawned. Just down the street to the left, four old houses had been cleverly gutted on the inside while their crumbling facades remained, to the unsuspecting eye, precisely like the neighboring houses. Well, not precisely. The cluster of powerful antennae on the roof gave the show away. And the fear in the eyes of the neighbors. Inside, there were torture cells, sophisticated communications equipment, and soundproof rooms where unspeakable things were the order of the day.

Rumors hovered about the place like carrion birds.

If ADDAK came in the night—it was usually in the night—and took you away, only Allah could help you. ADDAK informers were everywhere, and there was no fighting them. No court to hear the other side of an accusation. Just fear. Fear, and now revenge.

ADDAK patrols roamed Kassan. They issued from this viper's nest across the street, burly men in ill-fitting Western-style suits driving gray Mercedes-Benz sedans. They were notorious. Tonight Bandar would attack one of those patrols.

It was Majid's idea to begin a quiet program of eliminating these patrols. Majid, who even as a schoolboy had been marvelously clever with a knife.

Bandar looked at his watch. The ADDAK patrols were not run with anything like true military precision, but every night of their vigil, two men had left at just about midnight, give or take ten minutes.

It was eleven-forty-five.

The trap was ready.

No traffic moved on the narrow street. Now, rattling and growling, a gray Mercedes lurched around the far corner and stopped in front of ADDAK's doorway. Two men got out and went in. Bandar knew what would happen now. In a few minutes two other men would come out and drive off in the direction the car was pointing. He nudged Majid. They slid out of the doorway and up the street. It curved as it climbed, and before they had walked twenty yards, ADDAK was almost out of sight.

Majid waited here, to give the signal. Bandar went on to the next intersection and gave a low whistle. There was a pause, and then another, softer whistle came in reply. The boy was ready, then. The timing must be precise. They had rehearsed the maneuver twice.

Bandar watched Majid. The night was so still he could hear his heart beating. His dagger was ready and he knew just how to use it. Bandar tried to ignore the fact that he had never killed anyone before. Majid raised his hand and slowly let it fall. That meant the ADDAK men were in the car and moving.

Bandar whistled: twice in quick succession.

From the street above the intersection there came a muffled rumbling.

The gray Mercedes wasn't in any hurry. Even if it had been, the incline and curve of the hill would have slowed it. The dusty gray sedan moved steadily up the hill, low beams cutting through the darkness. Just before ADDAK's car gained the intersection, there came a loud rumbling, a muffled shout from the driver, and the screech of badly lubricated brakes.

A runaway ox cart came lumbering across the narrow street. It jolted to a halt at a crazy angle in the middle of the intersection, effectively blocking the Mercedes' progress.

The ox cart was unattended. Cursing, the passenger climbed out of the Mercedes and crossed the intersection to investigate. The driver sat glowering, drumming his fingers on the steering wheel. Majid was on the other man the instant he moved around to the far side of the ox cart: one strong hand clamped the ADDAK agent's mouth shut just as he opened it to scream. The scream never came. It was cut in half by Majid's dagger, which sliced the man's throat so deeply the head was almost severed. The driver hadn't seen this, but he called out. Majid replied, calling for help.

Quickly the driver turned off the engine and leaped out of the car, drawing a .45-caliber automatic pistol as he moved. Bandar was behind the driver, moving softly as a shadow. The driver paused by the left-front fender of his car, tensed, and raised the pistol in his right hand, supporting it with his left.

Bandar's hand sliced out of the darkness before the driver could shoot. His pistol wrist crashed into the very solid fender of the Mercedes and the gun clattered to the cobblestones below.

The driver turned, forming a scream. Bandar's other arm coiled around the man's neck. The man twitched and struggled. Bandar's arm only drew tighter. Bandar could see the fear in his eyes now, bulging in the darkness. He thought of ADDAK, what it was, what these men undoubtedly did in the course of their jobs every day. Every night.

Bandar's knife was ready but he didn't use it.

He tightened his bicep and lifted his knee into the base of the man's spine, pushing outward with the knee as he pulled back with his long wiry arm.

It seemed to take forever, but in fact only a few seconds passed before Bandar heard the driver's neck snap, the sound of a dry stick breaking. Suddenly the fear drained out of the man's eyes. Bandar could see that happening too, as the driver went limp and sagged against him. There was a sickening intimacy to it.

Bandar was still holding the corpse when Majid crept up beside him.

"Well done, General Al Khadir," he said, only half in mockery. They quickly stuffed the bodies into the back of the car, pulled the ox cart back to where it belonged, and retrieved the lad who had helped them. Then they drove off to a secluded wharf Bandar knew. The night's work wasn't quite over.

The next morning a large, neatly wrapped cardboard box was found on the doorstep of ADDAK headquarters. The first reaction of the officer in charge was to summon the bomb squad. He had no illusions about ADDAK's popularity in Kassan. The bomb squad came with their steel nets and their truck. The package was taken out into the desert, where, very carefully, it was opened.

Inside were the severed heads of the two ADDAK agents and a pamphlet from the People's Army of Kassan that bore the rebels' slogan: "FAKK RAQABA!" *Lift off the yoke*.

The rebellion in Kassan had begun in earnest.

Port Kassan, a Chamber in the Cellar of ADDAK/HQ: September, Next Year.

The general was not amused. He looked down at the man whose arms and legs were strapped to the stainless-steel table and derived none of the usual pleasure from the man's utter helplessness. The man would die, and no matter. Probably he was a rebel. Certainly he had been found with a cache of rebel posters in his room.

The man was beyond screaming. Twice he had fainted. Ibn Bir-Saraband waved away the first team of inquisitors. His own men. Brutal, of course. Effective enough in most cases. But not today. Now it was important that the man on the table live at least long enough to tell what he knew. If he knew anything.

There was blood everywhere now. Especially from the raw places where the man's fingernails had been. Rebels!

At the beginning—three years ago now—the so-called People's Army of Kassan had seemed useful to the general. He watched its bumbling start with a certain amusement. A touch of rebellion fitted his plans handsomely. Kassan in rebellion would have to be rescued. A strong man would be needed. Not the old king, surely. And even more surely not his heir. Not Selim. No, it would be the general himself who would do the rescuing. Who would demonstrate beyond questioning and for all the world to see that he, Ibn Bir-Saraband, was the rightful occupant for the Panther Throne of Kassan.

Ibn's plan was simple. It had been years in the hatching.

12

Twenty years. Starting with his marriage to the king's daughter. Which meant that his sons were royal, the old king's grandchildren. Their claim to the Panther Throne was clear, logical. He would merely be a sort of regent for the boys.

First, of course, King Nayif must be persuaded to see the logic of it. Made to see Selim for the weakling he unquestionably was. Made, perhaps, to abdicate publicly in favor of the general.

It had all seemed so easy at the beginning.

Key to the plan was keeping a tight check on the rebels, orchestrating their growth in ways that could be subtly managed. But suddenly things had gotten out of hand. Ibn was too clever not to recognize that. Where previously he had watched the strutting rebels and privately mocked their skinny leader, Al Khadir, now the general was hunting them desperately, with all the resources he could command.

But they eluded him. They were *jinn,* vanishing into the desert like the wind, striking first here, then there, taunting him. The People's Army was attracting notice. Worse, it was having the opposite effect from what the general had anticipated. Instead of making him emerge heroic, the People's Army was making him look foolish, incompetent.

And if there was one thing in the world that Ibn Bir-Saraband could not tolerate, it was to be humiliated.

The new team arrived, mercenaries trained in Algeria. There were two of them. One was tall, graying, rather scholarly in appearance. The other was all muscle. These were scientific practitioners, well versed in the uses of drugs and sophisticated electronics. They didn't believe in brutalities like lowering a naked man into a bathtub filled with scorpions.

The taller man carried a gray metal box with three knobs protruding from it and a fan-shaped white gauge ruled off in fine black lines. Two wires snaked out from this box. One terminated in a three-pronged plug. The second wire was separated into two strands of copper encased in blue plastic, with several inches of bare copper wire protruding at the end.

Fastidiously slipping on a pair of surgical latex gloves, the smaller of the two approached the table.

Gently, deftly, he wound the first of the two copper wires around the man's left testicle, three twists, not too tightly but tightly enough to hold through the convulsions. He repeated the procedure on the other testicle. Then he stepped back, bowed to the general, and signaled his partner that all was in order.

The tall man flicked the first of the three knobs on the gray box, then turned the second knob carefully to the right as though he were tuning a sensitive radio. Intently he watched the red needle as it crept along the fan-shaped gauge.

From the naked man on the table came a howling such as Bir-Saraband had never heard. The man's back arched galvanically. *He is having sex with a spirit creature*, thought Bir-Saraband, smiling a little at the thought. But for the wide leather straps holding him down, the general's guest might have levitated. The high-pitched wail reached a crescendo, peaked, and subsided into a low moan.

The man at the controls looked at Ibn.

"You may want to ask him something now."

The general's voice boomed in the small chamber. "Your only hope is to tell me where Al Khadir is!"

The man's lips moved silently, as if in prayer. His reply was what it had been. What it would always be, the general realized now, and the knowledge burned in his gut like a knife wound. "Nothing, please Allah, I know nothing!"

Bir-Saraband nodded at the inquisitor. His hand moved to the dial. Again, the arching back, the unearthly scream. Ibn didn't stay for the end he knew was approaching swiftly. He lifted his heavy body and walked out of the chamber, down the hall, and into the little elevator. A few minutes later he was in his cool and spacious office on the fourth floor. He sat in the oversized leather-covered desk chair and toyed with a silver panther that served him as a paperweight.

His brother-in-law had given him that sculpture. Selim El Kheybar, heir to the Panther Throne. Unless something— someone!—prevented it. Ibn stroked the little panther and thought about the throne. The glittering throne that was rightfully his own. The cold silver statue warmed under the general's caress.

It was fitting. It was as Allah must have wished it to be:

that he, a Bir-Saraband of the purest stock, should attain that throne at last. *It would be nothing more than righting a wrong that had been done to the Bir-Saraband more than a thousand years ago.*

1

Somewhere in the Desert Between the Persian Gulf and the Foothills of the Burujurdi Mountains: 800 A.D.

The falcon was ready.

Selim could feel the bird's tension even through the thickly padded leather tube that sheathed his left arm from wrist to elbow, the falcon's perch, Selim's protection. But the peregrine, Selim knew, would never harm him. Selim had trained the bird from a nestling, fed it with his own hand, fashioned the hooded cap that brought the falcon into sudden darkness at its owner's whim. With the darkness came peace, for only then did the falcon's hard, dark-yellow eyes cease their restless scanning. Nothing that moved in the desert was safe from the peregrine's questing eyes. And much more there was, moving in the desert day or night, than most men's eyes could see.

Selim sat tall on his camel. He had ridden—it was his right and his custom—a little ahead of the rest of his party. The five other falconers clustered behind their leader, to his left. Selim urged the camel gently, with a subtle pressure of his knee. Slowly the camel mounted the dune and paused at its crest, waiting. They had all played this game before: the bird, the camel, the rider.

Sometimes on these hunts Selim felt that he was one with the falcon. For Selim El Kheybar shared many qualities with

17

his favorite peregrine falcon. Like the bird, Selim was lean and quick and eager. Like the bird, Selim was young. Too young, it had been whispered, for Selim to be headman of the tribe. Together with his falcon, Selim had learned many lessons from this hot, harsh land. He had learned to watch. He had learned to stalk. He had learned when to wait and when to strike. Like the bird, Selim could, when it was necessary, kill swiftly and without fear. Without remorse. He could outrun the wind, catch a wild stallion and break it and turn it into a most respectful ally. Selim could find water where other men saw only burning sand and baking rock. When he spoke, men old enough to be his grandfather listened carefully. For these reasons Selim had been chosen headman of all the El Kheybar.

For a long moment Selim sat on the crest of the great dune, his eyes scanning, scanning. To a stranger, one dune might seem much like another: great ripples of sand with here a clump of sage or acacia, there a rock or a blighted tree. The dunes rippled like god's mockery of water, each flowing into the next all the way to that far purple haze that marked the ending of Selim's world and the beginning of the legendary Burujurdi Mountains, home of panthers and jackals and angry *jinn*. Men who ventured to cross those mountains did not come back.

But the dunes that Selim regarded with such intensity were no more alike than people or animals. Each had its own charms and weaknesses, its obstacles and opportunities, promises and tricks. Here one might find water near the surface. There, an innocent-seeming stone might shelter death: a desert adder coiled and ready. Selim's eyes roved, registering a thousand impressions, making and rejecting small decisions. The sun burned, but he did not feel it. There was a small movement in the air, the ghost of a breeze.

It was a fine day for falconing.

Selim smiled: falconing was one of the things he liked most. Then he felt the peregrine stiffen. Instantly Selim followed the falcon's gaze.

There! Just this side of the horizon a black speck was moving, moving slowly, small enough at this immense distance to be indistinguishable from some desert insect. Only the faint smudge, a pale blur of dust, told Selim's well-trained eyes that here, perhaps two days' journey from where he sat on his camel, an entire tribe was on the march.

He watched the moving speck impassively for a moment.

Beyond doubt, the Bir-Saraband were on the move again, and may they find no luck in the quest. *What a pleasant place this desert might be,* he thought, *if only the El Kheybar could share it with the wind, with each other, with the sun and their falcons and their game.*

But Allah had sent them the Bir-Saraband instead! Selim laughed, a short and scornful sound. The Bir-Saraband were an irritant, to be sure. They grazed and overgrazed, they were careless about the cleanliness of the life-giving desert wells, they were soft and scheming, the men more like women than real Bedu, traders, not hunters or herdsmen.

For as long as anyone could remember, the two tribes had roamed this same stretch of desert. Warily, seldom meeting, distant rivals, the Bir-Saraband and the El Kheybar avoided each other as oil avoids water. From time to time there were incidents. One hunting party, for example, might skirmish with another. Thefts were suspected, night raids alleged. Twice each year the tribes met to trade. The Bir-Saraband, who lived by trading, came to the El Kheybar for camels, for horses, and for falcons. What they offered in exchange were spices from the far lands beyond the mountains, objects in metal: steel knives curiously wrought, needles, ornaments. The Bir-Saraband even had perfumes and silk, and thin white bowls and pitchers fancifully decorated in blue, glazed with the smooth shimmer of glass itself, and—to hear the smooth-tongued Bir-Saraband—almost beyond price.

Such trading was necessary and brief. The moon had waxed and waned eight times since last the two tribes gathered. Soon it would be time again. Selim stirred in his saddle. One day, he knew, there must come a reckoning. One day an incident would loom too large to be brushed off as incidental. And then blood would flow in this desert. Selim did not seek such a conflict. But if it was in Allah's plan, then Selim would be ready, and all his tribe with him.

He watched the black speck that was the Bir-Saraband. In the short time since the movement had come to his attention the tribe could not have moved a quarter-mile. They were passing Selim's position, west to east. They might be headed toward the gulf. In any event, he thought, shrugging, the Bir-Saraband were—for once—not intruding upon the grazing land of the El Kheybar, nor on their wells.

Selim looked at his falcon and smiled. He reached out with his right hand and stroked the bird's sleek, mottled back. The peregrine shivered with pleasure. He loved being stroked. The bird looked at his master alertly, inquiring. *Yes*, thought Selim, *it is time.*

He raised his left arm. Quickly, precisely, he loosened the soft leather thong that constrained the falcon's curved-needle talons. The peregrine blinked once, quivered, and shot upward. Up and up he went into the cloudless desert sky. High overhead now, the falcon swerved, extended his wings to their fullest, and hovered on some unseen current of air. The falcon was circling very slowly, but from below it looked as though he was frozen in time, imprisoned in the infinite silence overhead.

Selim knew better.

The bird circled, angling now, riding the wind. In his mind, Selim imagined that he was up there with the falcon, soaring, looking down—unseen!—on the Bir-Saraband, watching, waiting for the kill. If only it were that easy.

Suddenly the falcon pumped his wings furiously and dived. Selim couldn't see the bird's target. His eyes raced ahead of the plummeting falcon. A lean desert hare, brown as the sand, ran darting and leaping across the face of the far dune. Frantic, spotting a bit of thin cover in a scraggly, burnt-dry acacia bush, the hare leaped valiantly for the dubious protection of the twigs. The falcon struck its prey in mid-leap. As always, the peregrine went for the hare's neck, breaking it cleanly with the sheer impact of his dive. The hare shuddered and fell. He would not, Selim knew, have felt pain.

Selim urged his camel down the back face of the dune, calling to his companions as he moved. The falcon waited for his master, sitting astride the dead hare, proud and protective. There was a drop of blood—but only a drop—on the falcons' beak. A taste of victory, but just a taste. The bird had been too well-trained to do more damage than that.

Selim dismounted, knelt close to his falcon, and slipped the bird back onto the leather perch he wore so effortlessly.

Again Selim stroked the bird, and the bird responded with a low murmur of contentment.

The sun was lowering now.

It had been a good day's hunt: Selim alone had accounted for five hares and two bustards—the fat desert hens that would taste so fine and juicy tonight, gutted and spitted and roasted over the gently perfumed coals of an acaciawood campfire.

He greeted his friends, laughing at some small joke. The six of them rode off to their camp. As Selim passed the crest of the dune, he paused and looked to the place where he had seen the moving dot that must be the Bir-Saraband.

There was no speck of blackness now. Some trick of the undulating landscape had swallowed the whole tribe. Allah might have stricken them all, erased them from his great plan. Selim smiled. He believed in luck. Luck had come easily to Selim El Kheybar, many times. But luck, like everything in this desert, required vigilance. It would be unwise to trust luck too far. And Selim knew that the Bir-Saraband would not simply vanish, however much he might wish that they would. Selim spurred his camel to move faster. Soon it would be dark.

The six hunters rode in silence for a time. Selim chose not to mention the sighting of the Bir-Saraband. Why stir up emotions? He watched the desert sun, falling with the swiftness and mystery of a coursing falcon. Now it was only a red target on the western horizon.

Then the mountains seemed to swallow the blazing star whole. The shadows were blue for a time, then purple, then black. The six camels moved quietly. A glow far ahead signaled Selim's camp. In the gathering shadows, he reached out one more time and stroked the smooth feathers of the peregrine's back. The bird murmured in its sleep—if it was sleeping in that false night, under its hood—and Selim wondered what dreams it might have. Of fat hens and juicy hares, no doubt. Selim smiled in the darkness. Not the smile of the headman of the El Kheybar. It was the quick grin of a seventeen-year-old boy who, just for a moment, has become the thing on his arm.

There, in the dark, Selim became a falcon. He soared high over the desert, swooped close by the luxurious tents of the

Bir-Saraband, heard their schemes, and made schemes of his own.

It always came down to this. The El Kheybar and the Bir-Saraband, roaming the land, sometimes colliding. Always uneasy.

The camel jogged over a stretch of rough ground. Selim blinked. Reality was all around him. The dream had slipped away. He could smell the acacia smoke on the soft night air. Soon the hares and the hens would be roasting. There would be a feast in camp. Not every day were they so lucky in the hunt.

They rode into camp, dismounted, gave their day's catch to the cooks, and sat near the fire sipping a thin concoction of yogurt and well water laced with dried mint.

Selim stared into the flames and wondered what the Bir-Saraband were doing this night.

Ibn Bir-Saraband stood in the open flap of his great black tent and watched the sun sinking down and down. The noises of his camp were dense in the air. It was only a journeying camp, quickly erected, to be struck as quickly at dawn. Still, as ever, the headman had seen to his comforts.

Ibn's tent was larger than any other, and more splendidly furnished. It was only fitting. He had earned his position, and he relished the power and the worldly goods that came with it. With voracious eyes, he guarded his privileges.

He walked slowly into the darkened tent, his fine linen robe loosened against the warm evening. A brazier glowed in a corner of the carpeted space, fragrant with cedar. A dish of dried, sweetened pomegranates was at hand. Ibn lay back on the soft cushions and from time to time indolently reached for a dried fruit and slid it into his mouth, letting it dissolve slowly, sensually. Now he smiled, thinking of the girl who would soon be with him. But first there was business. Urgent business.

Soon there was a rustling at the entrance, and the trail scout Ali-Jain slipped in. The guards had orders to admit no other man, and the girl only later, when Ali-Jain had gone. Ibn looked at his visitor: Ali-Jain might be any age. His skin had been turned to leather by the desert sun. On a horse or a camel Ali-Jain moved with an almost lyrical swiftness, a creature of the dunes. On foot he scuttled like a crab. *But,* Ibn thought, *such a useful crab!*

Ali-Jain came close to his master and smiled, bowing.

Ibn Bir-Saraband favored the man with a smile in return.

"It is," said Ali-Jain softly, in a voice dry as the desert wind, "as you hoped. The young headman is off in the desert, falconing. We should arrive at their camp before he returns."

"Good."

The boy was a threat, possibly a deadly one. That was why Ibn planned to acquire the power and fealty of the El Kheybar by negotiation, not by force of arms.

This meeting with the El Kheybar would be more than the usual trading session. In the time since their last meeting, Ibn had developed a plan. For years—for as long as the oldest grandfather could remember—the two tribes had lived in a state of mistrust that was never quite warfare and never an alliance.

It was wasteful. And what Ibn Bir-Saraband hated most was waste, to see a chance for profit and pass it by.

In the El Kheybar, Ibn saw a great chance for profit.

The strengths of the El Kheybar—and they were significant—could complement the assets of the Bir-Saraband, United—under Ibn Bir-Saraband—there was no end to what they might achieve. The El Kheybar were hunters, breeders of superb livestock. The Bir-Saraband knew that life did not end at the gulf, that there was a rich and fascinating world beyond the Burujurdi Mountains. But the Bir-Saraband were soft. They loved luxury. Hand-to-hand, in the desert, they would be outmatched by the El Kheybar. This alone was reason to conquer the El Kheybar with words rather than with warfare. And if any man alive could achieve this unheard-of feat, Ibn Bir-Saraband was he.

He smiled, thinking of the possibilities that awaited him as chieftain—no, king!—of a people suddenly doubled in size and more than doubled in strength. Ibn reached for a date and slipped it into his mouth.

The curtain rustled and the girl came in.

She was very young, not yet twelve. He preferred them that way. The girl entered, a smile trembling on her well-formed lips, the mask of awe and of gratitude. Her father had assured Ibn that the child was virgin. Her father was ambitious.

"Come closer," he said softly, smiling. She moved to the place where he lay on the many pillows, and stood there, trembling a little, saying nothing. Ibn stood up then, the height and the bulk of him towering over her. He smiled and reached out with both of his hands to touch her shoulders. They were delicately boned, the bones of some songbird more than the frame of a girl who soon would be a woman.

He slipped off the thin black cloak that covered her. Still she said nothing. She wore a thin shift of ivory-colored cotton, obviously her best dress and seldom worn, for it barely reached her calves.

Gently, slowly, Ibn slid the dress over her head. She was elegant as some wildflower, unformed, not a hair on her body.

She regarded him gravely with enormous dark eyes, not knowing what was expected of her. Swiftly, still smiling, Ibn took off his own robe and stood before her in the throbbing immensity of his lust.

The girl gasped. Ibn took this as a compliment. He encircled her with his arms and drew her close. Then he lifted her easily in one arm, stroking his sex with the other hand, and knelt, easing the child onto the waiting pillows. She squirmed uneasily.

Ibn knelt beside her, stroking her smooth little belly, caressing the insides of her thighs, touching her in places where she had never been touched before. He whispered to her now, soft words of endearment. She wiggled like a minnow under his touch, and her face was a mirror on which reflections of unsuspected delight intermingled with the shadow of fear. Then, suddenly, still caressing her with words, Ibn thrust himself inside her. One hand cradling her buttocks, he drew her closer, at the same time thrusting in. Ibn was careful to keep his full weight off the girl, knowing that might suffocate her. It was work, but he kept thrusting, pushing himself inside her, wondering when she'd begin screaming.

They always screamed, sooner or later.

The girl looked up at him, her eyes darting left and right with the desperate urgency of a bird in a snare. There was fight in her, he had to admit that. She would not scream. Ibn thrust deeper, driven now by an uncontrollable need to master her absolutely, to make her completely his. There was blood now. He had expected that. It was a much-needed lubrication. They struggled in silence now. He had abandoned the pretense of affection. Ibn was sweating, pushing deeper and deeper. The crimson of the girl's blood mingled with the deep red of the pillows, smeared his hairy stomach, and coated the child's fine-grained skin with a warm, sticky richness: the juice, Ibn told himself, of victory. Suddenly the girl began trembling. He smiled and thrust deeper still, thinking that he had given her this first knowledge of pleasure. She quivered with the taut resonance of a lutestring and then went limp. He looked at her face. The eyes were glazed now.

They were focused on some infinite distance far beyond the tent of the headman of the Bir-Saraband. And they saw nothing. The girl shuddered and was dead.

Slowly he drew himself out of her, not believing what had so obviously happened. He lifted the girl to the floor. There was a jar of water. Ibn washed himself thoroughly and put on his robe.

Suddenly it seemed chilly in the black tent. He found a rag and cleansed the girl's body. Then he dressed her. He rinsed his hands and dried them.

Ibn knew that his servant would be alert at the entrance of the big tent. Therefore he went to the back of the tent and carefully untied one of the flaps. He looked out into the darkness. The camp was sleeping. It was impossible to tell how much time had passed. There was—a blessing from Allah—no moon. Ibn had ordered his tent pitched on a rise at the far end of the camp. Behind the tent was a narrow ravine.

He went back into the tent and picked up the girl's body. It was still warm. Carrying her in one arm, he slipped through the flap at the back of the tent. The intensely black night was both a help and a hindrance. Probably no one would see him, but it was difficult going on the unfamiliar ground. He made his way slowly, following the narrow ravine from its uppermost rim, perhaps two hundred yards away from the camp. The ravine was at its deepest here.

He paused and hurled the girl's body out into the

blackness. There was a long moment before the body crashed onto the rocks below. Ibn walked very carefully back to the tent. His story would be a simple one; that was always the best way. He had pleasured himself and fallen asleep. If she had run out into the night and tumbled into the ravine, that could hardly be Ibn's fault. Pity. Ibn walked carefully, because he knew that he had more to fear from desert adders than from the girl's father. She had been merely a child, a girl-child at that.

And her father was very ambitious.

Selim and his five friends made their camels trot as they climbed the last steep rise before the base camp. It had been a fine hunt, but Selim was restless now. There would be much to do after five days.

As he usually did, Selim had chosen the campsite himself. It was an old favorite, less than a day's ride from the sea, on the banks of a stream that in springtime flowed freely but was now—in midsummer—only a trickle. Still, a drop of water was to be cherished, and the stream provided enough for all their camels, horses, and sheep.

Selim took the lead, urging his camel to go faster.

At the top of the rise he halted and raised his hand to the others, warning them.

Something was wrong in the camp.

It had doubled in size. The El Kheybar had unannounced visitors! Selim cursed himself for a fool, having seen the Bir-Saraband on the march and not suspecting their destination.

Only Allah himself knew what mischief they might be up to.

Still, the double encampment seemed peaceful. Typically, the Bir-Saraband had camped on one side of the little stream only. Selim's own people had regrouped on the other side. He smiled. It was the old story. Selim supposed it always would be.

He spoke briefly to his companions. Then they all rode down into the camp. For all that he was their chosen headman, Selim El Kheybar continued to live modestly in the tent of his grandfather. His own parents had died long ago of the yellowing sickness. Grandfather was not to be seen at their home tent. Selim dismounted and tended to the camel himself. His grandfather kept two herdsmen, but it was and always would be Selim's rule to feed and groom and train his own animals, be they falcons or horses or camels or the sleek coursing hound that greeted him now: his beloved Saluki, a breed trained in hunting by the ancient kings of Persia. The dog yelped with delight and leaped at Selim, greeting him with both paws on Selim's slender chest. The dog was called Jinn, after the legendary sprites of the desert, all fire and mischief. Too old to hunt now, the graceful short-haired animal had been Selim's companion for six years.

He stored his gear, and just as he was coming out of the tent, his grandfather appeared, a tall old man, wrinkled but unbowed, his eyes bright as a falcon's.

The old man embraced Selim. The boy—of whom his grandfather was tremendously proud—was all the family he had left. He beckoned his grandson into the tent.

"I have just come," said Selim's grandfather, "from the council."

"You called it in my absence?"

Selim bristled, not at his grandfather, but at the implicit insult: the council of the elders meeting without their chosen leader!

"It was agreed—mutually—when we heard what Bir-Saraband was up to."

"Which is?"

The old man frowned. "It may be that I am losing my faculties," he said gently, "for even though I have lived all my life mistrusting the Bir-Saraband, as did my father and his father . . . well, what Ibn said has some sense to it."

"Grandfather " Selim laughed. The old man would ramble on. Soon he'd be telling the tale about that summer when the panthers came down from the hills and began raiding the camps.

"Please," said Selim, gently, "tell me."

"Ah. What he wants is simple. How he proposes to achieve his goal, there's the problem."

"What goal?"

"Ibn Bir-Saraband has come to us with an outrageous suggestion, Selim. He wants nothing less than to unite the Bir-Saraband and the El Kheybar. To make one tribe—one nation, as he calls it."

Selim shot to his feet, seething.

"Under the command of fat old Ibn himself, I've no doubt "

"More subtle than that, my boy. He left the decision up to us—and his own council, of course. We are to vote, an equal number of the Bir-Saraband elders and of our own."

"I'll fight first, Grandfather. Even to the death."

"I know that. And that is why I am pleased to be part of the council just now. To prevent bloodshed. That must be first in all of our minds, Selim, and in our hearts."

Selim turned, flushed, then turned back to this wise old man. He thanked Allah for sending him such a grandfather.

"And what must I do—or Bir-Saraband, either?"

"You must wait. It will not be long, perhaps tomorrow. Three days we have been in council. We . . . well, you know us, Selim. But the others are men of goodwill. Their leader . . . Who knows, truly?"

"Grandfather, I think you're all going soft. I wouldn't trust Ibn any further than I can throw a camel. Don't think it was coincidence that they appeared when I was off hunting."

"You are angry. That is easy to understand. But think, Selim. Think what could be. We spend our lives in useless squabbling with the Bir-Saraband, when—admit for a moment it could be possible—we'd be stronger if we joined the two tribes."

Selim frowned. "Joined with a nest of adders!"

"You judge them harshly, Selim. Ibn Bir-Saraband may not be an honorable man. Still, he is clever, there's no denying that. And whatever his failings may be, surely they are not shared by the whole clan."

Selim felt the hot anger rising. *Couldn't they see?*

"The day Ibn can be trusted," said Selim, "is the day camels can fly. If he comes to rule my people, I must go far away."

Selim knew that leadership in his tribe was earned, not inherited. Young as he was, Selim had earned his position and by the light of Selim's keen eyes, Ibn Bir-Saraband was a menace. Selim knew him but little, but Ibn's reputation had spread across the desert with the dark persistence of a bloodstain.

His grandfather reached out and touched the boy on the

shoulder, partly in benediction and partly in warning. "Think, Selim," he said. "If Allah wills it, you could lead these two tribes. It could be. Promise me that you will do nothing in haste. Wait until the council has come to—as I pray it shall—a just and honorable conclusion."

Selim looked at the old man, and his head swam with a mixture of love and loyalty, of doubt and fear.

"I promise," he said at last. "Only because you ask it of me, and I can refuse you nothing."

The old man smiled then. "Come," he said. "We'll have tea. Tell me of your hunt."

The next day, Selim had many things to do. There were disputes to be resolved, decisions to be made. All morning he received callers in his grandfather's tent, as was his custom. Some brought Selim real problems. Others merely wanted relief from the quirks and twistings of their own human nature. A wrinkled grandmother who was absolutely sure lustful men were trying to sneak into her tent at night. A boy caught stealing chickens. Two men who had gotten to gambling, each accusing the other of cheating. Selim gravely assured the old lady that her tent would be watched in the future. He could easily see that the young chicken thief was starving and that a foster home of some sort must be arranged. As for the gamblers, Selim had little sympathy: both men were trouble-makers. It was possible that both had been cheating. He threw their dispute out of his court with a warning to both never to pick up a pair of dice again. That injunction, Selim knew, would last—with luck—until sundown.

The morning was crowded with appointments, but still Selim could feel the time dragging. He gave his full attention to every supplicant, but in the intervals his mind roamed far. What was happening, right this moment, in the tent of the council of the elders?

It was time for the noonday meal, but Selim could not eat. He walked the length of the camp, keeping as far as he could from the tent of the council. The dog Jinn went with Selim, scampering playfully at his heels, eager for a romp in the desert, for a hunt. But it was not a day for romping. Selim wondered where Ibn was right now, and what he was thinking. Cooking fires smoldered in the camp. Women grinding wheat in round stone mortars looked up at Selim and smiled in greeting. Children laughed and played. But Selim could feel the tension in the clear dry air, the sense of waiting, and for what?

When he got back to the home tent, his grandfather was there, sipping sage tea. The old man regarded his grandson gravely. Then he spoke.

"It is done, Selim. They have gone to fetch Ibn. Then they will come for you."

"And then . . ."

The young man's voice was taut with concern. Who were these old men, this council, to decide his fate? Selim had always made his own way in the world, trusting his strength, his wits, and his instinct for men and animals and the fickle ways of the desert. This independence was a power in him. It was what made him a leader of the tribe even at the age of seventeen. And now, it seemed, that independence was being taken away from him. Selim didn't like that at all. Still, with the deep well of respect for his elders that had been bred in him, he awaited his grandfather's reply.

"I am sworn to say nothing until both headmen are together and before the council. But . . ."—the old man smiled—"Allah is wise, my lad. I think you will not be disappointed in our decision."

Selim frowned, but he knew better than to pressure his grandfather. He poured half a cup of tea from the copper pot that was steaming on the coals of the old iron brazier.

Before Selim's tea was cool enough to drink, the messengers had presented themselves at the tent's entrance.

Selim walked with them, his grandfather at his side.

Ibn Bir-Saraband was waiting, bedecked in a ceremonial robe, a gilded sword at his side, arrogance in his demeanor. Selim never thought about how he was dressed. This day he wore what he normally wore: a simple cotton robe that had once been white but was now worn and faded to the color of old ivory. A short, keenly sharpened old hunting dagger was sheathed into Selim's plain leather belt. Otherwise he was unarmed. He looked at his tall, heavyset rival as Ibn stood proud and glittering in the hot sun of noon. Selim bowed. Ibn nodded.

The leader of the council appeared, an old man that Selim

did not recognize. He had been chosen, by all, from the elders of the Bir-Saraband. The old man spoke simply.

"Selim El Kheybar and Ibn Bir-Saraband, you know why you are here. Three days and more we of the council have debated the wisdom of Ibn's proposal. And we have agreed that it should come to pass that our tribes unite."

Selim looked at Ibn. He was glowing with pride, fairly gloating. The old man resumed speaking.

"But who will lead this new tribe of tribes? This is not an easy thing to decide. In an election, obviously, pure numbers win, so no election can be a fair one. Many possibilities have been suggested. One involved a throw of the dice. And another was that we have two—or more—leaders. There cannot be two leaders. A man cannot have two fathers. So, because it is, in the end, from the desert that we come and from the desert that we must live, we have decided thus: that no man or group of men can choose who will lead the combined tribes of El Kheybar and Bir-Saraband."

The old man paused, partly to regain his breath and partly to judge the effect of his words. A crowd had gathered now, and they listened intently. Selim was puzzled. Bir-Saraband flushed, whether with pride or with indignation, it was impossible to tell.

The old man continued.

"The desert will decide," he said, and paused again. Selim looked at his grandfather. Grandfather kept his face impassive, but Selim thought he could detect a quick twinkle of mischief in his eyes. But what did this mean?

"It is the only fair way, and—perhaps more important—it is the only method of choosing that all of the council agrees to. Tomorrow morning, two caravans will leave this camp. Each will include men from the tribes of Bir-Saraband . . . and from El Kheybar. In one caravan will be Ibn, and in the other, Selim. They will ride for three days, one to the north and west, the other to the south and west. Both will end in the foothills of the Burujurdi Mountains. The distances will be equal. Both of our headmen will be unarmed but for their hunting daggers. They will have no food and no water. They will have neither camel nor horse. And whichever of these men first returns to this camp, he will be leader of the united tribes, and his sons after him. So we have determined in the council."

For a moment both headmen stood silent, awed by the enormity of what they had just heard.

There could be no backing out now.

The council had been duly elected. The council had made its decision, and both Selim and Ibn must abide by that decision or slink away in disgrace.

There was no question in Selim's mind that he would take up the challenge. The desert was his friend, for all its dangers and mysteries. He knew the dunes, the hills and dry plateaus, even as he knew his grandfather's wrinkled face or the bark of his dog Jinn. If it was Allah's will that he lead the two tribes, Selim was ready. If not, he would die trying. It was not even a question of making the decision. That decision had been made for Selim by forces he did not understand and did not question, long ago.

Selim looked at Ibn Bir-Saraband and tried to imagine that date-and-honey-stuffed bulk, those rich robes, that overelaborate sword dragging on foot across the broiling sands.

Slowly Selim began to smile. Then he caught Ibn looking at him with frank hatred in his eyes, and the smile vanished. Ibn Bir-Saraband was a man who would stop at nothing.

Selim began to wonder if the desert would be the most treacherous enemy he'd have to face in the coming ordeal.

There was nothing more to say.

The listeners were silent, but as Selim and his grandfather walked back to their tent, the whispering started. Selim knew that until this strange ordeal was resolved, all the old rivalries between the tribes would be intensified. He wondered if the council would have the strength to keep the two neighboring camps at peace until his return. If he returned.

Selim faced that possibility calmly. Through all the quickening seasons of his young life he had always striven to excel: to win the footrace, to tame the wildest falcon, to coax obedience out of the most reluctant camel. He was as ready for the ordeal in the desert as he possibly could be, and now, suddenly, he found himself looking forward to it. Whatever the outcome. At least, the great question would be resolved as to who, finally, was best suited to lead.

Only when they were back in the shaded quiet of their tent

did his grandfather ask the inevitable question. "Well, Selim, what do you think of your council?"

Selim laughed. "I enjoy my life, Grandfather. I do not court death. There is something out there—in the vastness of the desert, when I am alone under the enormous sky—that speaks to me. I don't know what. I don't know why. The desert calls me. So I accept the council's challenge. It will be with Allah now, not between men fighting. If my blood is spilled, it will be with a jackal at my throat, not Ibn Bir-Saraband."

"Be careful, Selim. Ibn is a jackal, and worse."

"So I suspect. I will be careful, Grandfather. Of that you may be very sure."

They ate their simple evening meal alone, just Selim and the old man. Then the visitors began arriving. They dropped by with various excuses because they well knew that to visit Selim on this of all evenings was an intrusion. People drifted in and drifted out, accepted the old man's offer of tea, lingered and left, almost every one with the ancient traveler's blessing: *May Allah be with you on your journey.*

The visitors had come, Selim knew, to say good-bye. And even though they would have died rather than admit it, he could see in their eyes that most of them thought this would be the last time they would set eyes on Selim El Kheybar in the world of the living.

Selim was courteous. He tried to make these farewells casual. Not an easy task. Finally the last visitor had gone.

Selim walked out of the tent and called to his dog. Jinn appeared out of the darkness, eager, sniffing the night air. Together with the Saluki, Selim walked to a rise behind the camp. He could see it all now, his own people's tents and campfires and, across the little stream, the Bir-Saraband. Selim stood still in the quiet night. Jinn nuzzled his legs and Selim reached down and stroked the dog's long, sleek head.

There was a quarter-moon. Selim looked down at the dog's eager face. Good old Jinn, a one-man animal. The dog did not trust everyone who came by. But Jinn trusted his master absolutely. Selim had raised Jinn by hand, from birth, with affection and insight, as he had also done with his falcons, his horse, and his camel.

Selim thought that if Jinn knew of the challenge waiting

for his master at dawn, the dog would be prepared to wait forever, sure in the expectation that Selim would never let him down. *And may Allah grant that it be true!*

Suddenly, there on the hillside beyond the camp, it became very clear to Selim El Kheybar that he must do anything, undergo any hardship, in order to fulfill the hopes of his people.

In the mindless trust of the dog Selim could see the expectations of all the El Kheybar: from the half-mad old woman who had come to him just this morning to the joy of children yet unborn. Selim thought of his grandfather, whose pride in Selim was unspoken but solid as rock. He stroked the dog once again, drawing strength from his communion with the animal—with all animals.

And Selim felt a new strength growing inside himself. He felt more ready here, alone with his Saluki in the night, than he had ever felt.

He spoke softly to the dog. "Remember me well, Jinn. I wish you could be with me. For out there, tomorrow, I too must be *jinn*, quick and clever and able to find magic in the desert."

Then Selim turned, patting the dog, and walked swiftly back to his grandfather's tent. The old man was asleep. Selim took off his robe and lay down on the carpet. Jinn curled up at his master's feet. Selim slept deeply. What would be, would be.

In the camp of the Bir-Saraband, Ibn was busy. There were preparations to make, and some of these must be secret. He doubled the guard on his tent, made visits to several unexpected corners of the camp, and once he ventured into the desert itself and returned an hour later with a mysterious leather sack.

Then he washed, changed into a fine light robe for the evening, and supped splendidly and alone, and drank sweet wine. Only when Ibn was sated with the rarest delicacies his cooks could command did he send for the one visitor he desired to see this final night before his ordeal.

The visitor was the trail scout, Ali-Jain.

Ali-Jain came to Ibn, drank tea, and listened to the plan that had been forming in Ibn's mind ever since he had first heard the awful pronouncement of the council.

For more than an hour Ibn spoke. Ali-Jain nodded, grinned, drunk with the opportunity that lay before him. Ali-Jain's bright beady eyes danced in the light of Ibn's brazier.

Finally the scout left, but only after having repeated, in the most discreet of whispers, his leader's instructions.

Then Ibn had one more glass of wine and slept.

Dawn found both camps vibrant with excitement.

Never had such great events touched the El Kheybar, nor the Bir-Saraband either. It was all the more thrilling because the excitement was laced with danger. The two small caravans set off just as the first red rays of daylight thrust across the desert. Six camels in each, five escorts in each, and Selim on the sixth camel of the north-bound caravan and Ibn with the group that headed south.

Selim turned back only once, to watch the men of El Kheybar and of Bir-Saraband as they stood on a low rise, utterly silent, watching the two little caravans move briskly into the desert. For a people given to chatter and gossip and quick exclamations, the silence was all the more impressive. Everything, or so it seemed to Selim, had been said.

Now, for the tribesmen, would come the time of waiting.

What would come for Selim, he had no idea.

The motion of the camel underneath him was familiar and somehow reassuring. Now, for a brief reckless moment, the boy in him deposed the man he soon would be, and his heart rose up in joy at the prospect of another fine hunt. He felt like singing, and quickly rejected the idea. Behind him, still as statues, the tribesmen watched and waited.

Both camps knew it would be six days or more before even the luckiest and most skillful man could make the distance across the desert on foot.

The caravans took a long time to vanish from the sight of the tense men who watched.

Finally they were gone.

Still people stood transfixed, watching, wondering what in the world would happen now.

No one wondered more than the elders of the council.

It had seemed like such a good idea. It had seemed to remove the possibility of armed conflict between the two mutually hostile tribes. Now, as the old men who had set destiny in motion looked about them, they were no longer so sure. Some of them were not sure at all.

Quietly, led by the old men, the watchers dispersed.

They walked slowly back to their various tents, still in a strange pervasive silence.

Now would come a time of testing every man's patience.

They left Selim in the foothills near a tall rock that stuck up out of the rolling hills like a finger. Selim said his farewells quietly, then stood tall and watched the camels out of sight.

The last thing his escorts had done before leaving was to search him, to make sure he had no water, no food, and no weapon other than the hunting dagger that had been agreed upon by the council. Thus, too, would Ibn Bir-Saraband be searched. Witnesses from both tribes watched gravely as Selim stripped naked and handed his robe and headcloth to the caravan's leader. Embarrassed, the leader quickly shook out the light cotton robe and the even lighter headcloth and handed them back.

Then the escort bowed in formal leave-taking and mounted and left. Selim had never felt so entirely alone before.

He also felt a curious sense of relief.

The great adventure was beginning. Now there would be no more waiting and no time to wonder what tricks Ibn might get up to.

Selim watched the little caravan until he could see them no more. If the wind stayed down, their tracks would be a path in the sand that he could easily follow. But even without tracks he could navigate by the sun, and even by the stars. For most of his walking must be done at night. The sun was a thief. It could steal a man's strength, squeeze all the juices out of him, leave him dead and dry as a raisin, hardly a fit meal even for jackals. Selim had come upon such a corpse once. What had been a man was now turned to bones wrapped in skin mummified into leather by the sun.

Selim forced himself to sit in the shadow of the finger rock. The shadow slowly moved as the hours passed. Selim moved with it. Sleep eluded him, but he willed himself into immobility, sitting like a statue in the shade, eyes closed, waiting.

Only when the shadow was very long and the day had exhausted the sun's deadly powers did Selim rise, stretch, and begin the long trek whose ending was known only to Allah.

Selim followed the caravan's tracks in the fading light. The trail was clear, five mounted camels and the sixth, riderless, leaving lighter tracks.

He walked steadily but not fast. Every resource in him must be metered out like grains of gold. If he covered the distance he hoped to during the night, there might be no shade tomorrow, no escape from the relentless sun. And by the second day, Selim knew, he must find water or perish.

The moon rose. The enormous sky was dotted with stars. Grandfather had many stories about the stars. Gods lived up there, and the jinn of the skies, and sacred animals. Selim smiled as he remembered some of the old legends, and felt less alone.

Far away, from behind him in the foothills, he heard a mournful wailing. It might have been a soul in torment, but Selim knew the jackal's song. He imagined the greedy beast tearing at its kill. Or, more likely, at someone else's kill, a panther's prey, a falcon's leavings. The jackal cried once. The silence after that was as big and as deep as the sky.

Selim lost all sense of time passing. He walked on the pale moonlit sand, calm and vigilant, for there might be other creatures abroad in the night. The air was cool now, almost chilly.

Selim walked for hours, never pausing. South and east, south and east. The caravan's track was visible in the moonlight. South and east. Selim tried not to think about the hunger pangs when they came. Lean and wiry, Selim was no stranger to hunger. On a hunt, with bad luck and a sudden windstorm, he had once gone nearly two days without food. But then he had water, and a horse.

South and east, south and east.

The pain in his gut had been sharp at first, a knife thrust of hunger. This passed. Now the pain was a dull ache and easier to bear. Selim had walked carefully, his eyes studying the trail before him. The desert came alive at night. In the cool and the darkness, many creatures prowled, crept, and slithered. Some of them harmless, some fatal. The desert adder, pouring itself sideways with every thrust forward, was nearly invisible even in daylight, buff-colored as the sand, and deadly. And there were scorpions whose sting could kill a weak man and leave a strong man writhing for days in fever and in pain.

Still Selim walked steadily.

A bird flashed through the sky, cackling loudly, and was gone. Selim looked in its wake. There, somewhere, would be water. But the bird had flown north-northwest. He must go forever south and east. He sighed and moved on. He could feel the chill weight of the desert night lifting even before the eastern sky grew pale.

Now a faint wash of blue was seeping into the sky at the edge of the horizon. All night Selim had walked down through the foothills. The slopes were less steep now, the rock outcroppings fewer. This was the edge of the great desert that lay between the foothills and the gulf. And in the desert there would be no shelter but what he might make, no water but what he might find, and no mercy, ever, from the eternal sun.

He came to a ledge of rock still cool from the night and touched it to see if by some good fortune a few drops of dew might linger there.

It was dry as bones.

Soon the sand would make itself into great dunes. And sometimes a great dune would catch and keep the far-spaced desert rains, soaking the sand and releasing some few brackish gulps of the precious fluid to a skillful and lucky digger.

Selim picked up a few small, clean, rounded pebbles from the desert floor. He wiped them on his robe and slipped them into his mouth. It was an old Bedu trick. He could feel the saliva coming. The pebbles felt good in his mouth. It was almost as though he had something to eat. He straightened up and kept walking, east and south, south and east, into the rising sun.

Before long the character of the land changed entirely.

There were no rocks now. This was the kingdom of dunes. Selim studied the dunes as he walked. On the northwest side of one special dune he might, with luck, find what he sought: a dry acacia bush or two, whose roots could point to water.

The fifth dune was lucky. There on the northern slope, three small acacias struggled against astonishing odds for a slender chance of life.

He knelt close by the largest bush and began to dig. Selim

probed the dry sand with his dagger and scooped with his hands. He worked as he had walked: deliberately but without undue haste. Conservation guarded his every motion. He would not spend one drop of sweat unless he had to.

One foot below the dry surface, the sand grew noticeably cooler, significantly heavier. The coolness and the weight of it were moisture. Selim made his hole wider as he deepened it. This burrow must serve him twice: as a shallow well, if water would come to it, but even more importantly as a cave to shelter him from the murderous rays of the sun.

The hole was nearly two feet deep when Selim paused to rest. The sun was higher now. He could feel the growing heat even here on the shaded side of the dune. When Selim looked back into his hole, he found that Allah had left a small blessing there. A thin glaze of water had formed over the deepest part! He watched, fascinated, hardly daring to move. The film of water was slowly spreading, deepening. Quickly, carefully, Selim removed his headcloth. He tore off a strip of the white cotton and laid it on the wet place at the bottom of the hole. Thirsty as its owner, the cloth soaked up the water.

Triumphant, but taking great care, Selim lifted the dripping cloth in both hands, threw back his head, opened his mouth, and slowly squeezed every drop into his parched and eager throat, the sweet taste of hope.

By the time he had savored the first clothful of brackish water, more had formed in the hole. Three times Selim repeated the gesture: dipping, squeezing, drinking. Then he lowered himself into the hole, forming his lean and wiry body into a ball, draping the damp headcloth over his head and face, smiling at the coolness of it. Selim knew that it would not outlast the hour. He knew, too, that the water he'd drunk was barely enough to sustain him through the day. Even so. One day of the ordeal was past. He was alive and he had made progress.

Selim closed his eyes and fell into a deep and welcome sleep.

Ibn Bir-Saraband walked through the blistering heat of afternoon, cursing Selim every step of the way. But for that impertinent whelp whom the El Kheybar were so foolish as to name headman, he, Ibn, might be back in the camp, in the comfort of his tent, making real plans rather than having to keep his eyes open to be sure he didn't miss the cache.

That there would be a cache, Ibn had no doubt at all.

His talk with the scout Ali-Jain had assured that.

All afternoon he walked, in the trail of the caravan, scorning the heat as beneath the consideration of one who soon would be king of the desert.

The shadows were lengthening when Selim awoke.

He blinked, reached up and removed the covering headcloth, and slowly opened his eyes. Something was wrong. Some quick instinct told him not to move a muscle. Then he saw the unwelcome visitor with whom he had shared the cool of the burrow. A shuddering fear ran through him.

A thick desert adder lay half-coiled, resting, its head not six inches from Selim's left leg.

He had slept with death.

Moving his right arm more subtly than any serpent, Selim eased his dagger gently from the sheath at his belt. He drew in his breath slowly, slowly, as though by taking in more air he might also gather strength. The first blow must kill: there would be no second chance.

Selim raised himself on his left elbow, raising the knife at the same time, still not breathing.

The adder's tail twitched, then lay still.

In the instant before he struck, Selim studied the serpent. The adder was thick, muscular, engorged with the flesh and blood of creatures it had stalked and killed, its geometrically perfect armor of scales flowing in chevron patterns mottled tan and lighter tan, its blunt head flat, heart-shaped, and deadly.

Selim's arm flashed. A blur of shining steel, a spurt of blood, a lashing. The thick evil head lay apart from the still-thrashing body. Selim kicked sand over the head and stared, fascinated, at the long thick body as it danced and writhed and finally subsided, jerking and lashing into reluctant death.

Now Selim smiled and breathed deeply again, the relief refreshing him more than any oasis or cool water.

He reached for the snake's body. It was smooth and dry, almost cool to the touch. In five swift motions Selim skinned the beast and sliced its white flesh into bite-sized chunks. He put a piece of snake meat into his mouth and chewed it slowly, sucking out the juices, pulverizing the tough, pungent flesh, carefully removing the segment of backbone and rib with his fingers before throwing them away. To spit would be a luxury beyond dreaming. He ate one more chunk of the adder, then wrapped the rest in a spare bit of cloth and tied it at his belt.

Then he rose, stretched, and set off on the next leg of his journey. The taste of the snake's flesh lingered sweetly.

There had been no wind. The caravan's track was still visible. Selim walked as he had walked last night—slowly, deliberately, scanning the ground as his eyes became accustomed to the lessening light: the adder might have had friends.

Selim walked far that night, keeping to the crests of dunes. Had he been forced to move in daylight, he would have kept to the valleys between the dunes, to shade and concealment. The moon rose clear. The night grew chill. South and east, east and south, Selim walked into his destiny.

Bir-Saraband frowned. Surely the scout could have chosen a better quality of dates than these! Dry as dust, and coarse into the bargain. Still, the cache was there, clearly marked with the pattern of stones they had agreed upon, and with more than enough nourishment to get Ibn Bir-Saraband through the next day. To the next cache. He finished off the dates and the goat's milk cheese and washed this rough meal down with one of the three leather flasks of water that had been included. The other dates, coarse as they were, and the rest of the water must be saved for tomorrow. If, thought Ibn, the knave had only included some wine! Still, Ali-Jain had done well, considering the need for speed and for secrecy. Ibn stood up, rubbing his unfilled belly. Well, the scout would be rewarded. Yes. The headman of Bir-Saraband smiled. The scout would be rewarded beyond his expectations.

On the third day, Selim dug a hole at the northwestern base of a great sand dune and found nothing but dry sand. Still, as he had done before, he covered his head and curled up in the hole to sleep.

Seventeen years old and half-dehydrated and more exhausted from his trek than he would have dared to admit, Selim nevertheless slept only fitfully as the day grew hot, and hotter still. But he kept his eyes closed, and his mouth, and breathed slowly. Conservation. Selim dozed, dreamed of his dog Jinn, of his grandfather. He dreamed of all that he might never see again.

He woke unrefreshed, his eyes burning, throat dry as sand, and forced himself to eat the last two bits of adder meat. It was dry now and going rancid, an evil, sour, cloying taste. He ate it anyway, slowly, sucking out whatever nourishment might be left.

The night was clear and cool, as the other nights had been. Selim walked until dawn, accompanied only by the stars and the transient moon. Sometimes in the silent night he would hear a brief scuttling in the sand, or a distant cry of pain or victory. The desert, going about its business, oblivious of the two-legged intruder on his impossible journey.

But Selim would not despair. He walked steadily onward.

On the morning of the fourth day Selim dug and found water, much as he had on the first day. The water saved his life—for the moment—but it was barely enough.

He slept well, awoke with the setting sun, ate nothing, and began walking south and east.

Selim had been walking less than an hour when the scorpion struck.

He must have stepped on the thing.

He felt the quick sharp sting in his ankle, the sting and the burning. And he could see the little monster, half-crab, half-spider, dancing backward in the moonlight, its slender, deadly tail arched forward in the attack position, ready. Selim made no move to confront the scorpion. It scuttled backward and to the side, and was gone.

Quickly Selim sat in the sand and drew his throbbing ankle toward him. He unsheathed his dagger, wiped it, and made a shallow X-shaped incision. Then he bent and sucked the flowing blood, sucking and spitting, wondering if he was getting the poison out, wondering, too, how much of his own precious body fluid was going with it. He repeated the sucking and spitting until the blood ceased to flow freely. Then he bound the wound with a strip of his fast-diminishing headcloth, stood up, wincing at the pain and alert to the dizziness that the effort of rising had cost him. He took one step forward, then another. To move at all was contrary to everything Selim knew about scorpion bites. You were supposed to lie flat while people brought you broth and dates and much water.

He smiled, and moved painfully on.

Selim struggled onward. He thought of the good luck he'd had in his short life. It had been a fine bit of luck, for instance, to wake and see the adder two days ago, before the adder saw him.

To step on a scorpion was not uncommon.

And it was only children and the very old who were likely to die of scorpion bite. But there would be great pain, and fever, and these things Selim knew might turn the balance against him. Still he pressed on, favoring his bitten leg. The moon rose. The stars were glorious. But Selim did not look up. His every effort was focused on the next step forward, and the one after that.

When the fever came burning into his head, Selim tried to take no notice of it. Perhaps, like an unknown and ferocious dog, it would simply snarl and back away if he ignored it steadfastly. It did not back away.

He could feel the flush of it, the fire inside his head, his throat burning. He could feel his ankle too, swelling, throbbing. But the pain in his head was worse, and the burning, burning in his throat. He walked slowly onward.

It was raging now, burning behind his eyeballs, making his head swim. From time to time would come flashes of clarity and calm, and he would wonder if he'd lost course, and remember to check the moon, the stars. He was on course. Perhaps he would die on course.

When he fell in his tracks, he was beyond knowing it.

He sank to the sand, his legs folding beneath him, useless. Selim lay on his back in the sand, one arm flung out, gasping, defenseless.

On the fifth day, Ibn Bir-Saraband was more pleased with himself than ever. It was not for his physical abilities that he had been chosen headman of Bir-Saraband. Surely he could ride and hunt and do all things the Bedu prized in a man. But his heart was an indoor heart. In his dreams Ibn lived in a city, high in a palace such as he had heard the caravan riders describe in Bagdad. Inside, all would be cool and shining. There would be gardens and fountains and music. And women. Many, many women. This was his dream, and when he was king, he would make it more than a dream.

In the meantime, Ibn walked on through the blistering afternoon. It was hot and hard going, but there was water at his side and another cache waiting. And the night would be cool. In two days he would be back. In two days he would be king.

Selim's grandfather walked on the hill behind the camp. At his side was Jinn. The old man walked slowly. His body was still strong, but his thoughts weighed on him.

What had they done, he and the other old men of the council?

For more than a week he had watched the tension building in both camps. Both tribes were restless, used to wide-open prowling lives. To be thus cooped up, waiting for what fate they knew not, was almost too much to bear.

In the camp of El Kheybar the men of the council kept to themselves, not by any arrangement but simply because the waiting seemed a little less hopeless that way. In the camp of the Bir-Saraband, the old man knew, the men of the council had gathered in one tent for their vigil.

He looked across the little valley made by the trickling stream. It was the eleventh day since the caravans had set out, the fifth day of the two headsmen's long trek back to camp.

With luck, one of them might achieve the march in six days.

Tomorrow might tell.

But what pressed in on all of their hearts was an enormous and implacable dread of what might happen if neither Selim nor Ibn came back. And this, the old man feared more with every passing hour, was a likely thing.

Selim lay where he had fallen. From time to time he moaned softly. From time to time his poisoned leg would twitch a little, as though it were trying to toss off the pain. A tiny desert mouse came hopping by, its grasshopper legs balanced by the long whip of a tail, the tail plumed incongruously like an artist's paintbrush. The little creature regarded Selim with huge black-button eyes. No danger there. The mouse hopped away into the darkness. Selim moved against the cool sand. He tried to form words, but his tongue was parched dry. It lay in his dry mouth like a dead thing.

The moon was waning.

Selim's eyes were closed in a fevered sleep.

He did not see the huge and fearsome creature that was stalking down the face of the dune.

In the camp of the Bir-Saraband, five old men sat silent in their tent. The chessboard had been abandoned in mid-play. A brass kettle of herbal tea was cooling near the brazier. And the brazier itself was guttering from lack of attention.

It was late afternoon of the fifth day. And although the men of the council respected Ibn, they feared that out in the wasteland he might be at a disadvantage compared to the young hunter Selim.

Yet it had been their decision that had sent him there.

The burden of that act was no less weighty for being invisible. At the happiest of times these were not talkative men. Now they wore their silence like armor. The air in the tent was dense with unspoken fears.

The old men had given orders that they were not to be disturbed other than in a grave emergency.

There was a commotion at the tent flap, a moaning sound.

Five heads turned as if they were on one pivot.

The tent flap opened and in staggered a dirty and bedraggled figure, lurching like a drunken man and in the end falling.

He fell and writhed on the tent floor for a time, moaning incoherently. Obviously it was not Ibn. Equally obviously, this poor creature was near death. There could be no harm in him.

One of the men got up, went to the trembling figure on the floor, knelt, and gently turned the man over.

"It is," he said softly, "the scout Ali-Jain."

Ali-Jain, perhaps awakened by the sound of his own name, seemed to recover himself. He sat up, tried to rise, and gave it up as a losing battle.

But he spoke. His words were broken, barely understandable, punctuated by many sighs and pauses. Someone gave him tea with sugar in it. He spilled half of the pale liquid in trying to raise the cup to his lips.

"I come," said Ali-Jain, "to ask your forgiveness. I am a dead man. Two adders have made a meal of me not an hour ago. Two. They were a punishment. For my sins."

"What sins, Ali-Jain?"

"Before he went into the desert, Ibn . . . Ibn Bir-Saraband, our revered leader, summoned me to his tent. Many times, in the past, I had done . . . things . . . for him. Now he wanted a great thing done. And great, said he, would be my reward."

The scout paused, went into a fit of trembling, and clutched his swollen, reddened right arm.

"Quickly, man," said an imperative voice from the back of the tent. "What did Ibn ask of you?"

"That I follow the caravan which would take him into the hills. That I keep myself secret, hidden from all, following the caravan on a separate, parallel track. That my camel be well-loaded with food and with water. That I make secret caches of this food and water at an easy day's march, each from the other, all the way back here. And this I did. Ibn said he would reward me richly. That I must not wait for my reward. He told me precisely where to find it. That in his tent is a small iron treasure chest. He handed me the key and dismissed me. It would," Ali-Jain continued, his frail voice touched with wonderment, "have been so easy to betray him. But I did not betray my leader. Carefully I stalked the caravan. More carefully I hid the food and the water, marking each cache with an arrangement of stones, as we had agreed. Finally I made my way back, circling, arriving from a completely different direction. Just hunting, I said, and not much luck at it, either. Ha!" His laugh was not a pretty thing to hear. "Straightaway I went to Ibn's tent. He had shown me where the chest would be . . . the treasure chest. It was as he promised. The key fit perfectly. I turned the key and lifted the lid and quickly reached in without looking. As he knew I would do. In the chest were two desert adders. Angry, of course. And here I am, gentlemen of the council. And death is my reward. May Allah forgive me . . . and the tribe. . . ."

He died then, with one final shudder.

The old men looked at him, blank with horror.

After the body was taken into the desert for burial, the men of the council of Bir-Saraband talked long into the night.

They were men of honor, and their honor had been shattered. It was agreed, without dissension, that should Ibn return to the camp—soon or late—he must be publicly denounced for his treachery and publicly tried as a murderer. But, given the tense relations with the neighboring camp of the El Kheybar, it was also agreed—and also without dissension—that they must say nothing whatsoever until Ibn did in fact return. For there was always the merciful hope that he might not come back.

The light in the brazier was a lingering red memory when the old men of the council took themselves off to their separate tents to sleep.

Each of them knew, come what might, that the treachery of Ibn Bir-Saraband had altered their future irrevocably. Had he been there in the terrible moment of their discovery, old as they were, they would have hesitated not one instant before tearing him limb from limb.

Darkness fell mercifully on the double encampment.

Selim moaned and turned his head in the sand. Dimly, through the fever and pain, he could feel something warm and wet caressing his cheek. And then something cold and damp. He was being licked and nuzzled by an animal. A big animal. Many times had his dog Jinn thus wakened him.

"Jinn?"

Selim spoke his dog's name reflexively. Then he reached out and touched the thing that was nuzzling him so gently. And then he opened his eyes. The biggest panther Selim had ever seen or ever would see was bending attentively over him. The beast was snow white in the moonlight. One huge paw was pressing gently on Selim's chest while the great cat continued its attentions to Selim's parched cheek. A low rippling growl came from somewhere deep within the white panther.

It was a friendly sound, but with the resonance of distant thunder.

Selim touched the beast's paw. He could feel the softness of the fur, the hard-packed muscle. The contented rumbling in the panther's chest took on a new urgency. *If he wanted me for his supper,* Selim thought, *I would be dead now. And it could be that I am dead and this is some spirit come to lead me . . . where?*

Slowly, taking care not to anger the huge panther or alarm him, Selim sat up. He had forgotten his fever and the pain in his leg. He had forgotten that there is no such thing as a white panther, especially not a white panther more than twice the normal size. Sitting, Selim was still not on a level with the panther's awesome head.

The panther tossed its head, and Selim noticed the collar.

It was gold and curiously wrought. It glittered in the pale moonlight, sparkling with rubies and magic. Awestruck, Selim decided that he was dead or dreaming. Without a moments' hesitation he gave himself up to the dream.

Once more the panther tossed its head. *He wants me to follow him,* thought Selim, rising to his feet with some difficulty.

Selim rose and took an unsteady step toward his visitor.

He reached out and stroked the panther's back. He scratched behind the panther's ears. In fact he caressed the enormous beast just as he might have stroked Jinn. Selim was beyond fear. He abandoned himself to the magic. The panther edged closer, rubbing his snow-white fur against Selim's chest. And once again the splendid white head tossed impatiently.

Then the panther knelt.

He wants me to ride him, thought Selim, easing one leg over the panther's back, which was nearly as big as the back of a small pony.

The panther growled reassuringly and gently rose to its feet. Selim had been an intuitive rider since earliest boyhood. With a gentle pressure from his calf muscles he indicated to the panther that he was ready. He reached forward and lightly gripped the golden collar, pleased to discover that it was not rigid but finely wrought of great flat links. Two gold knobs protruded from the panther's collar, just at the back.

Wound around these knobs was a length of golden rope, flexible as any hempen braid but wrought of pure gold. *Reins!* Selim was so thoroughly enchanted that he forgot to wonder who might have the skill to work gold so magically well. He unwound the golden rope and held it lightly.

And the panther seemed to fly.

The great white cat moved over the dunes with such a graceful surge of power that they seemed to touch the sand only occasionally.

Selim threw his head back and laughed for sheer joy.

If the fever was still on him, he couldn't feel it, nor the scorpion's sting in his ankle.

Selim could feel the panther's great muscles surging beneath him. He could feel the cool night air rushing past. Selim's throat was still dry, but thirst had been left behind him with the pain. Somehow he had melded into his mount. Selim and the white panther were one now, moving over the dunes with the swift inevitable flow of pouring water, the great white cat and its rider, also in white. They coursed through the pale moonlight.

The panther knew his destination, and Selim did not trouble to think what that might be. If this was death, it was an adventure, and it would be presumption to ask for more.

Selim had never thought of death, nor feared it.

Death to him and to all of the Bedu was merely an ending, some longer night.

Selim closed his eyes and gave out a great soaring battle cry. It was consumed by the empty night. Then the panther cried out. Selim had never heard a sound like it: at the same time haunted and triumphant, angry and sad. A voice from another world.

Now, flying through the night, he seemed about to enter that world. He smiled. The panther raced on. There was no sense of time passing. The dunes passed beneath the panther's soaring bounds. It might have been a dream, but Selim knew that the rope between his fingers was solid and real and of immense value. He knew that the curiously gentle monster underneath him was real too, that the panther's tongue could lap blood as easily as it could soothe a fevered cheek, that beneath the silky white fur lay claws whose lethal curve would, by contrast, make a peregrine's cruel beak seem soft.

They soared, and Selim's heart flew high as the stars, swifter than laughter. He knew that if these were his last moments of life, they were all the more to be treasured. And Selim knew that if he lived to be older than the desert itself, he could never forget this night, this panther, this dream that soared without wings.

The panther leaped over the crest of a great dune that, in the climbing, seemed no different to Selim from a hundred others they had crossed with similar ease. But on the other side of the dune a small oasis lay sparkling in the moonlight. There were date-palm trees and grass. There was a small lake. And it was absolutely deserted.

The panther kept up his pace all the way down the far side of the dune and to the very edge of the water. Then he paused, growled a little, and turned his head to Selim as if asking a question.

Selim slid off the panther's back, first coiling the golden rope on its two gold knobs.

He came to the beast's head and spoke softly to it. "Thank you, white panther," said Selim gravely, for it was his habit always to treat animals as though they were deserving of the same respect he might extend to his own grandfather. "You have saved my life and perhaps taken me into a new one. I will not forget your kindness, nor your strength."

The panther rumbled his response, a deep and contented sound. Then he rubbed himself affectionately against Selim much as he had done earlier. Together they walked the short distance to the lake.

Selim knelt and scooped up a double handful of water.

It was clear and pure as the dawn sky. He lowered his dusty face to the water and drank deeply and long. The panther at his side drank too. At last Selim was thirsty no more.

He took off his robe and walked into the lake as far as he could go, laughing, splashing like a child. He swam, dived beneath the surface and came up again, and looked to the shore. The panther was nowhere to be seen. Then Selim heard the familiar rumbling. The panther had swum out into the lake! He was swimming slowly, deliberately, in circles around Selim, rumbling his low greeting, the well-remembered sound of thunder far away.

He has been sent to protect me, thought Selim. *But by whom?*

Then Selim dived beneath the water and came up behind the panther and climbed on its back. Together they swam back to shore. Selim dismounted, thanked the panther for the ride, and went to look for his robe. There was a robe, neatly folded, on the spot where Selim had casually dropped his old one. But this was not his. It was new, and very fine, white cotton so sheer it could almost be seen through, embroidered at the edges with deep blue and gold. Real gold. There was a belt, too, and a dagger. But they were not the belt and dagger Selim had discarded on the bank. The belt was worked from the softest leather and intricately stamped with gold in a design of laurel leaves. The dagger was sheathed in gold, the gold set with rounded stones of bloodred and deep blue and a green that danced with blue fire. The blade was Damascene steel, the handle a rope carved in ivory, butted in gold, the butt set with one huge ruby. A caliph's ransom was in those stones. Selim wondered what he had done to deserve them.

He stood naked in the dawn, still dripping from the lake. The desert air dried him quickly. He slipped on the robe, knowing that it would fit perfectly. And so it did. He fastened the belt and sheathed the dagger, then turned to find the panther close by, watching. The beast gave a little nod, approving, or so it seemed to Selim El Kheybar.

Then the panther came close, knelt, and motioned for Selim to mount. In an instant they were off again, moving faster than Selim remembered them moving in the night. But that could have been because now he could see the desert and how quickly they moved over it, where last night everything had been one swift blur of enchantment.

The new robe was so fine, it seemed weightless. He might have been wearing the wind. They rode all day and into the night. His thirst slaked, Selim felt no hunger.

At last, just as the full moon had risen, the panther paused at the crest of a high dune. The white beast stood absolutely still. Selim could hear his breathing: deep, steady, and even. The panther seemed to be waiting, listening. Selim looked about him as best he could in the moonlight. Wherever they had been, however far they had traveled, this landscape looked familiar. Selim felt they were not far from the double encampment by the stream. He wished he had a way of asking the panther such a question. The white panther stood still, waiting.

Finally Selim saw what the panther was waiting for.

A figure made its way over the crest of the sand dune just beyond the one on whose crest the panther and its rider stood waiting.

Ibn!

Even at that distance, even in the moonlight, Selim could spot that arrogant bulk.

From the panther's chest came a new and ominous rumbling.

The panther shook its head from side to side and slowly knelt. Selim knew this was a signal for him to dismount. He had no choice. Selim slid off the panther's back, rewound the golden reins, and stood close by the beast's head, one hand lightly stroking the back of its neck. The panther turned its head to Selim and regarded the young man steadfastly for a long moment. The growl deepened.

Then the panther was off, a white streak of vengeance in the night. He flashed over the sand, a blur of speed paler than the pale sand. It seemed only seconds until the panther reached its prey, but those seconds would last forever in the mind of Selim El Kheybar. Ibn didn't even have time to scream. It was over very quickly. Selim was too deeply stunned even to feel a sense of victory.

The panther screamed then, and all the trumpets of Allah could not equal the horror contained in that one long wailing cry. There was joy in the panther's scream, and there was death in it too. Selim felt himself shuddering, even though he was as certain as he would ever be about anything that this strange white beast meant him no harm. Once again the panther let out his dreadful cry.

Then, magically, he was back at Selim's side.

And for the second time that day Selim thanked him.

They rode quickly over the next dune. There, just beyond, lay the camp. The panther knelt and Selim dismounted. This time Selim kept the golden reins. He stroked the great shining white head and spoke soft words to the panther. And then Selim led the panther into the camp of El Kheybar.

The guards took up the cry of alarm and then fell silent

when they saw this extraordinary spectacle walking confidently toward them.

Selim paused in his own camp only long enough to greet his grandfather. A great shout of triumph sprang up as he passed by the tents and the campfires. He responded only by nodding gravely. He kissed his grandfather affectionately, never letting go of the golden rope that held the great white panther. Then Selim turned and crossed the little stream into the camp of the Bir-Saraband. It was real, then. He hadn't dreamed the panther.

The elders of the council of Bir-Saraband were waiting in their tent.

Selim entered, the panther with him.

The elders said nothing, and so it fell to Selim to speak first. He spoke quietly. There was no trace of triumph in his voice.

"I am here," said Selim El Kheybar. "Your king has returned to you."

He turned and left them then. There was nothing more to say.

And from that moment down through all the ages, the sons of El Kheybar have ruled their desert land from the Panther throne.

2

By noon of the day after the Langstaff party, Jeb had made a date with the Secretary of State and been turned down for a date by Megan Mcguire. It was Wednesday. His luncheon in Washington was scheduled for Friday. He determined to call Megan again on Monday at the latest. Maybe sooner.

In the meantime there was no shortage of things to keep him busy: five ongoing projects and now Sonoma Hills to develop from scratch. They'd have to fly out to the site one day soon, maybe even next week if he and Oscar could twist their busy schedules to allow for it. The aerial photographs were a useful tease. The U.S. Government Survey maps that detailed the elevation in ten-foot increments were precise but cold, lacking in soul. No map could tell you where the breezes came from or what the most interesting view would be.

Jeb's feet fairly itched to walk the site. To get the feel of the land, figure how to put houses for three hundred or more people on four hundred acres while preserving whatever was wild and beautiful on the site. It would be some sort of cluster arrangement, that was almost a foregone conclusion. With great sweeps of open land and maybe a small lake if they could find enough water to feed it.

Other questions came bubbling up to the surface of Jeb's day, problems to solve, questions to ask and to answer.

Thank God for work. Work was the great cosmic pain reliever. Work took his mind off what the rest of his life might be. Might not be.

Megan Mcguire had hit Jeb hard. Struck without warning.

How long had it been since a woman had affected him so strongly and so soon? There had been many women in the five years since his divorce. More than he liked to think about. More than he could count.

All the wrenching pain of leaving Hillary had forced Jeb Cleaver to form a turtle's shell around the bruised remains of his capacity for love. At the advanced age of thirty-nine Jeb had slid into a cynical style he had never wanted: take it where you find it and don't think too much about tomorrow.

Jeb found a lot of quick affection, easy consolation in the long empty nights. He learned about the minefields in his memory, the quicksand pits, the things it didn't pay to drag out for inspection. And he managed. Managed very well, considering. It always came back to work. To the firm, the challenges, and to Oscar.

Oscar was a friend, adviser, patron.

If there had been no Oscar in Jeb's life when his marriage fell apart, almost anything might have happened. There was no way to thank that man enough except by doing what Jeb knew Oscar wanted him to do: create better and more imaginative buildings as each opportunity came along.

Jeb came early to the office on Friday. Just time enough to go through the mail, review a concept that one of his assistants was working on—and to call Megan Mcguire.

She was out of the office.

At nine-thirty Jeb was in a taxi heading for the Eastern Airlines shuttle out of La Guardia. It was warm for September. Jeb had stopped thinking about what the Secretary of State might want. Maybe an assignment—but what kind? Maybe to ask his opinion about some project. Whatever it was, there was no way to find out in advance. No way to second-guess the situation. Sure as God made apples, the Secretary wasn't having him down to talk about the weather. Flattering. But flattery didn't mean much to Jeb Cleaver. He'd had good luck, recognition, money. Jeb wasn't rich, not as he counted rich. But the firm was doing well, and even with the divorce and all the expenses of psychiatric care for Hillary after her time in that fancy drying-out place, Jeb knew he could always count on living very comfortably.

Comfortably, maybe. But alone?

He eased himself back in the taxi's worn vinyl seat and closed his eyes and thought about Megan.

How could you love a woman who wouldn't even go out with you? Whom you couldn't even reach on the phone? Jeb smiled, contemplating a life on hold.

God, she was attractive. Something in her glowed. Megan was conventionally very good-looking, no doubt about that. But Jeb knew dozens of beautiful women. This one had something else, an extra measure of vitality that sparkled from deep within her the way a gold nugget might glimmer out of base rock.

Hell, she was probably all tied up by that smooth young lawyer—what's-his-name. Jeb had asked about what's-his-name while still at the Langstaffs'. Everyone knew him there— David. Rising young lawyer, and rich in the bargain. Of course. Probably the football captain and an incredible stud to boot.

Maybe he should just forget about Megan.

Fat chance.

The ten-thirty shuttle was only about half full. The eager beavers would have crammed into the early ones. Jeb took a window seat and looked idly out at the rolling landscape of New Jersey, Pennsylvania, and Delaware. A little too early for the leaves to turn.

Jeb closed his eyes and eased the seat back as far as it would go. A daydream formed itself uninvited in his head. It was a dream of Sonoma Hills. The town newly finished, the cool hill country fragrant with mingled aromas of fresh-sawn redwood, new paint, and autumn. Jeb was on foot in his dream, walking up a hill to the first house of a cluster. It had a front door of bittersweet red. The door opened before Jeb had a chance to knock. And there stood Megan. But she wasn't a housewife. Megan held a microphone. Behind her was a television crew, their camera aimed at him.

"Is it true, Mr. Cleaver, that you've already made a mess of one marriage and you're still dreaming of another?"

There was a sickening lurch as the pilot lowered his flaps for the descent into National Airport in Washington. Jeb blinked and sat up. The daydream obligingly vanished.

Forget Megan. Sure.

A few minutes later Jeb was in a cab moving past the

familiar monuments of central Washington. A very mixed bag. Strange emotions always stirred in Jeb when he visited here. Part pride. Partly a sense of opportunities missed. Nobility and squalor cheek by jowl. An elegant Jeffersonian vision unevenly realized. The ragbag of bureaucratic styles was an unintentionally amusing reflection of America itself, the best and the worst of it. At least, thank God, they'd managed to preserve the sky. Whoever thought that one up had done the nation a great service: the Victorian law that in Washington nothing could be built taller than the Capitol dome had been a landmark in good preservation thinking. And totally neglected elsewhere in America for nearly a hundred years.

Five minutes later Jeb was in a small elevator being whisked silently up to the Secretary's office on the fourth floor of the new State Department Building. The car stopped of its own accord and its doors opened automatically.

He stepped out into a foyer that might have been lifted intact from some fine old New England whaling captain's mansion of the eighteenth century. The corridors of power were parquet, old and gleaming, softened here and there by splendid antique Persian carpets. The furniture and paintings were old, too, and of museum caliber.

A young man was waiting. He introduced himself and led Jeb down a hallway to a large door that was itself an antique: wonderfully faded mahogany with massive brass hardware. The young man knocked.

The door opened and there stood Hardy Leighton, all six-four of him, white-haired, square-jawed, and movie-star-perfect for the role life had given him: Secretary of State of the United States of America. Jeb smiled and extended his hand and found himself thinking: *Too perfect, maybe?*

His voice was rich and easy. "Mr. Cleaver, I'm so glad you could make it. Can I show you around a little? Then we'll have lunch."

Hardy Leighton knew his stuff. The formal reception rooms were stocked with the finest obtainable American antiques, donations, mostly, Jeb learned. These rooms and the White House had the same curator, Clem Conger by name, and by the look of the objects he had assembled here, something of a genius. The tour was a quick one. Jeb could almost feel an invisible taxi meter ticking off somewhere inside the Secretary's well-barbered head. Soon the tour ended back at the Secretary's own suite of offices. A small round pedestal table had been laid for two in an alcove. Settings of pistol-handled silver, fine linen place mats, old Imari plates, and heavy crystal wine glasses with triple twists of air imprisoned in their stems. Copies of something they'd dug up at Williamsburg, Leighton said.

"I took the liberty of ordering for you, Mr. Cleaver," said Leighton as they sat down. Instantly a waiter appeared holding a bottle of white wine for the Secretary to taste. He did so with a wine lover's enthusiasm, swirling the pale liquid in his glass and sniffing deeply before tasting a few drops. A quickly lifted eyebrow was the only signal the waiter needed to pour a glass for Jeb.

"Estrella chenin blanc," said Leighton happily. "One of my favorites. To your very good health, Mr. Cleaver."

Jeb smiled and lifted his glass. *Why did the toast sound ominous?*

The food was excellent. A soup appeared: chilled bisque of mussels and scallops with a hint of curry in it. While Hardy Leighton talked knowingly and charmingly about the world in general—small talk when you considered where it was coming from—the waiter came and went, keeping their wine glasses discreetly full, taking the soup bowls and replacing them with lobster salad in a fragrant tarragon mayonnaise. Dessert was sliced peaches in fresh raspberry puree. At least they're spending my tax dollars well, Jeb thought, knowing he'd have been disappointed if Leighton had offered a ham sandwich. Small plates of cookies were passed, and espresso.

And only then did Leighton say what was on his mind.

"My doctor," he said with a finely tuned man-to-man grin, "says I can't talk business at the table, on pain of ulcers. But now we're finished, Mr. Cleaver, you may have guessed I didn't ask you down here to talk about the weather."

"That figures."

"In fact, the computer asked you, Mr. Cleaver."

For one startled moment Jeb wondered if his last year's income-tax return had been in good order.

The Secretary cleared his throat, a little preface to what Jeb imagined must be his main thrust. "I have to caution you,

Mr. Cleaver, that this is all very confidential. More than top-secret, in fact."

"I understand," said Jeb, who didn't understand at all. *Computer? Whose damn computer?*

"I can see," said the Secretary with a hint of mischief, "that you're maybe less than flattered to have been asked to lunch by a computer."

"Puzzled, is more like it, Mr. Leighton."

"Puzzled. As why shouldn't you be? Well, we're puzzled too, Mr. Cleaver. May I call you Jeb?"

"Of course."

"Does the name Kassan mean anything to you, Jeb?"

The word hit Jeb like falling bricks. Of course. But why in the world. . .? He sipped his coffee deliberately before he spoke.

"You've got yourself some computer. Yes, Kassan I went to college with a member of their royal family: Selim El Kheybar. We were—still are—friends. Although it's been quite a while since I've seen Selim. Years—maybe five, six."

Kassan. Don't let yourself think about Kassan.

"How familiar are you with the oil situation in the Middle East?"

"Only what I read in the papers—which isn't a lot. I'm not really a very political person, Mr. Leighton."

"The reason—to make a very long story short—that we are interested in you, Jeb, is that we're very interested in Kassan. You know, of course, that Kassan has oil. Not as much as the Saudis, but a great deal of it. For fifteen years Revere Oil has been lucky enough to hold a drilling-and-exporting concession from the king. King Nayif. In just about a month—the fifth of October, to be precise—that lease will expire. It will be subject to renegotiation. That sounds simple enough, but it might not be. For various reasons I won't go into, oil is hot again. A new and potentially enormous discovery has just been made in Kassan—a find that'll more than double their production. Everyone wants that oil. The Russians. The Germans. The Japanese—you name it. We have determined it's vitally important for our own stability that we secure the Kassanian leases. And the situation in Kassan is a treacherous one. There is rebellion. There are various factions in the establishment who are perhaps scheming, wanting a little bigger share of the pie. And most importantly there are the Russians. They want the oil. But they also want Kassan."

"You mean they'd take over?"

"It could happen. And if it does, it won't be another Afghanistan, Jeb. It'll be war. Because we won't sit back and let 'em do it. Not this time. Not to Kassan."

Jeb sat stunned. He was as puzzled as he was surprised. *What in the world did they expect him to do about it?*

"I guess I understand what could happen. But I don't see where I fit in."

Hardy Leighton smiled. "It boils down to this, Jeb. The CIA has screwed up again. Our intelligence on Kassan is next to zero. Oh, we do have an ambassador over there, but he's not quite up to giving us the real picture. Basically he buys whatever the palace is selling that day—by way of information, that is. What we need—urgently—is a clear vision of whatever the hell's going on over there. Are the rebels a real threat? Where does your pal stand—the crown prince? How's the king's health? All that, and much more."

Jeb frowned. He understood the problem, but he was just as puzzled as ever. "So I just drop in on Selim and play spy for a while? I couldn't do that—wouldn't. I'm very busy, to begin with. But aside from that, I don't spy on friends, Mr. Leighton."

The anger had been building. Now it was very close to the surface. *What kind of creep did these people think he was, anyway?* Jeb felt cheapened by the thought of it. His feelings for Selim were deep and true and they went back more than twenty years. If it had been only twenty minutes, he still wouldn't want any part of an espionage setup.

"Easy, Jeb." The Secretary's smile had a fine metallic edge to it. "I made it a rule long before I got to Washington never to ask a man to do a thing I wouldn't do myself. The fact is, your pal's in big trouble. He's the heir to a throne that might not exist this time next year. And by all we know, which I admit isn't a lot, he doesn't even realize it. Prince Selim is pretty standoffish, the way I hear it. The army in Kassan is small and, putting the best light on it, untested. Ceremonial, really. If the People's Army—the rebels—really get their act together, the country could blow up. And quickly. And if it does, that's setting the stage for the Russians to come marching in. They want access to the Persian Gulf so badly they can taste it. Can you see what might happen? They go into Kassan—allegedly to restore order, maybe at the invitation of one of the rebels—we go in to stop them. Somebody gets too hot under the collar. Zap. You've got World War Three, just as easy as that."

"You really believe that can happen?"

"I really do. And I'm not a bit sure you—or anyone else—can prevent it, Jeb, but I'm goddamned if I won't try. And I'd hoped you might be . . . well, willing to give it a try yourself."

Jeb took a deep breath. Suddenly he had the feeling he was drowning in unreality. A sort of dreamlike distance seemed to have come between him and the rest of his life—the office, Megan, all that seemed very far away, shimmering faintly like a mirage.

"But what, precisely, could I do?"

Hardy Leighton laughed. It was gallows laughter. "If I knew, as you put it, *precisely*, Jeb, you wouldn't be here. Sometimes these dicey situations can be saved—completely turned around even—by a few words in the right ears at the right time. What we hope—pray—will happen is just that. All peaceful and quiet and behind the scenes. We have reason to believe King Nayif is friendly to the United States. Well, so was the Shah friendly, if you take my meaning."

Jeb took his meaning. And still didn't know what the man wanted of him.

"I have a job for you, Jeb, if you'll take it."

"A job?" Jeb was beginning to feel like a Martian, lately landed. He didn't quite understand what these weird people were talking about.

"In the last ten or so years Kassan has grown and changed dramatically. It is one of the five or so world centers of petroleum, just for starters. A generation ago Port Kassan was a backwater. A little pearl fishing in the gulf, shipping a few dates. Nothing. Our embassy reflects that. It's like something out of Somerset Maugham. Well, we're going to change that. Build a new embassy. A real showplace. Money—within reason—is no object. How would you like to build that embassy, Jeb?"

He sat transfixed. An embassy! Oscar would do cartwheels

from here to Sonoma. That was certification. Instant fame. Worldwide recognition. An embassy.

The pause resounded in the elegant room.

"Your firm does take overseas assignments?"

"Oh, yes. Yes we do."

"It's perfect, then, Jeb. Not like spying at all. To do the embassy—which, need I say, we feel you are eminently well qualified to build—you'd have to be in Kassan for months. It would be the most natural thing in the world for you to renew your old friendship. All we'd ask is that you keep us informed. Of any developments that happen to attract your attention. You can be sure we'll have other people in place, trying to do the same thing. Kassan is suddenly our number one priority around here. But nobody we could send there— or that we have there already—has your connection with the Panther Throne."

"I don't speak the language."

"Nobody does. That's been one of our problems. But you have eyes. Ears. And a lot of brains. And—correct me if I'm wrong—no special personal ties that would keep you from going."

"No. Nothing like that."

Hardy Leighton stood up then, a sure signal that their meeting was over. Jeb rose too. Then the Secretary was walking him to the elevator, one arm congenially around Jeb's shoulder. *We're old chums already*, thought Cleaver. *Isn't it grand?*

"Jeb, I know I've thrown a lot at you today. I don't expect you to make up your mind in five minutes. But your friend is in trouble—I can't overstate how much trouble he'll be in if this rebellion catches fire. And the architectural opportunity is a splendid one. I'm sure you understand that. But most of all it's a chance to do your country a real—and vitally important—service."

Jeb looked at him. Speaking of facades.

"If I do it, Mr. Leighton, just how will it work? I mean, the timing, all that?"

"We'd send you somewhere for a week or so of very intensive briefings. Then up and over. The sooner the better. Of course, you can come and go. If there's something urgent in New York, or wherever . . . well, Kassan has quite good jet connections. We are prepared to be extremely generous about all the arrangements connected with the new embassy—rent you a villa and all that. Servants, car of your choice. It wouldn't be a painful assignment, Jeb."

"I'll think about it. Thanks for lunch."

They shook hands.

Jeb's head was swimming as he rode down in the Secretary's personal elevator. A limousine was waiting. Kassan. Selim. Tamara, for God's sake. *Don't kid yourself, Cleaver, she's probably a fat Muslim housewife with five kids and a mustache by now.*

But Selim's sister Tamara was inextricably a part of Jeb's memory of Kassan. Of the one magical summer he'd spent there between freshman and sophomore years at Harvard. Of meeting Tamara and discovering, for the first time and at age eighteen, the infinite possibilities of love.

So long ago. Jeb thought of her often, but Tamara was like part of a dream. Lovely, gentle, a dream with the fine sweet scent of jasmine to it. He thought of Selim too, elegant even as a boy, strong and quick to laugh. Selim had cut a swift golden trajectory through Jeb's much more earthbound existence at college. It had been a glorious flight, and Jeb was grateful to have been taken along for even a short part of it. At the end, both of them had always known, the Panther Throne waited, glittering. *Selim in trouble?*

The black State Department limousine moved silently through Washington. They were at National Airport in less than ten minutes.

And before the Eastern shuttle jet took off, Jeb knew the answer to Hardy Leighton's proposal.

There was no way in the world he could refuse to go to Kassan.

3

Port Kassan lay baking in the heat. On a side street which led from the old town into a newer section of the city, three dark figures moved in single file close to a faded stucco wall. They walked slowly, stooped under their burdens, the ageless, endless hauling and lugging that is the heritage of Arab women. These three wore the distinctive robes and masks of Harasi women: black gowns to the street, long black head-cloths, and masks cut from stiffened black cloth with slits for eyes and ending in a strange birdlike beak.

An immemorial tradition. A perfect disguise.

Bandar Al Khadir was the tallest of the three. He carried the biggest burden—a bundle of dry twigs—and he stooped the lowest to disguise his height. Bandar had long since ceased being afraid for his own safety. But still he was cautious. The revolution couldn't afford to lose him. Not now. Not yet. General Bir-Saraband had a price on his head: ten thousand Kassanian pounds. A fortune to the very people who were Bandar's main support. Which one of them would be tempted?

He trudged on down the dusty street. It didn't bear thinking about: there was too much else to do. They came to an arched gate set deep into the wall. The door was thick: wooden planks studded with iron nailheads. It hung from iron straps wide as a man's arm. In the center of the door was cut a small round window, four times barred.

The door swung open as Bandar lifted his hand to knock. The young man who had been awaiting them was dressed in a dark blue suit, crisp white shirt, a necktie the color of mildewed prunes. He bowed and ushered them in. The door closed behind them with a deep solid thump, followed by a grating noise as an iron bolt was drawn shut.

It could, of course, be a trap.

Bandar was betting the entire future of the People's Army that the man upstairs needed him more than he needed the gratitude of King Nayif for capturing the most wanted political criminal in Kassan.

They set down their bundles just inside the gate and stood, stretching, glad to be relieved of the load. They were in the garden of the Soviet embassy to Kassan.

Everything here was green, shaded, and cool. There were lemon, orange, and almond trees and a thousand carefully tended flowers. A long reflecting pool held several jets of water that splashed musically in the silent, shaded air.

For communists, thought Bandar, *they managed to live very well.*

Bandar had no illusions about the Soviets, but he needed what only they could give him: sophisticated weapons and money. A chance to shift his revolution into high gear. A chance to move from occasional small-scale raids to total warfare—if that was what it would take to topple the El Kheybar.

The blue-suited aide led them through the cool garden into the embassy itself. Across a marble foyer. Up a wide marble staircase. The interior was chilled to the point where Bandar was grateful for the black robes he wore.

Nikolai Kurakin's office on the second floor was predictably grand. Bandar had met the man just once before: at night and in a back alley of Bandar's own chosing. This visit marked a change in their relationship—a new degree of trust. If such a word could be used in connection with the Union of Soviet Socialist Republics. The USSR had long fascinated Bandar. He had studied their history at the University of California at Berkeley. Bandar had, in fact, been a history major at Berkeley. Subsidized by the man he was sworn to overthrow. How long ago that seemed! It had been only five years.

The aide knocked at Kurakin's door and was bade to enter. The ambassador sat behind a huge rosewood desk of the most extravagant French post-Napoleonic design, all curving legs encrusted with gilt bronze. Kurakin was sleek, a man of medium height and studied grooming. A thick solid gold Rolex wristwatch gleamed from his left wrist. His cufflinks too were of gold, and a golden chain restrained his opulent necktie.

"Welcome, Bandar Al Khadir," he said, smiling from ear to ear. "You seem to be setting a new style in revolutionary costume."

So *charming*, thought Bandar, so polished. So dangerous. It was a thing he'd have to get used to if the revolution really came off. To deal with men whose lifework it was to feign good fellowship. Bandar wondered if it would ever be possible for him to look a man in the eye and tell lies. Perhaps. Perhaps in the end, everything was possible. He managed to smile.

"You have not, I think, met my lieutenants: Majid and Falih?" Bowing and smiling and shaking each of them by the hand, Kurakin asked them to be seated. Tea was brought, offered, and drunk.

"Let us," said Kurakin, "come right to the point. You need help. We are prepared to give it. It is our crusade—and our pleasure. To topple decadent aristocracies wherever they exist. But you know that."

Soon, thought Bandar, *he'll say what he wants in return. But still, he's taking a risk. If it were to be known that Kurakin received us here, it would be worth his job. Surely he'd be expelled in disgrace. If you can disgrace a Russian.*

"You know, Bandar Al Khadir," said Kurakin smoothly, "that we have watched the progress of your revolution with both interest and admiration. You have come a long way, and with few resources."

"Thank you, excellency. We can, I think, go all the way to the Panther Throne, given better equipment. And money."

"Of course. Of course. And we are prepared to . . . But let me show you precisely what we are prepared to do." With that Kurakin raised his right arm and snapped his fingers. Someone must have been watching the entire performance, because in that instant the big double doors that led from Kurakin's office to the hall outside swung open.

In walked two burly men, blue-suited and wearing ties, but

men of a different type than the aide who had let Bandar and his men into the garden. The two men were struggling with a large wooden crate. They deposited it in the middle of the thickly carpeted floor and went back for the next crate. Soon there were three. Despite the fact that it was a staged performance for his benefit, Bandar felt his pulse racing. Whatever was in those crates was more—much more—than the People's Army had in the way of weaponry.

Slowly, like the master of ceremonies he was, Kurakin got up and walked to the nearest crate. He prolonged their agony for a moment, then bent and lifted the top of the heavy box. He might have been a child at Christmas, so intense was his delight as he picked up the rifle and held it triumphantly over his head. The three Arabs watched transfixed in spite of themselves. It was glistening with the rust-preventive lubricant the factory used to coat their new weapons. And this was the newest of the new: a deadly Belgian K22-V Fromentor automatic with night sights.

Kurakin looked at Bandar as if for approval. Bandar smiled, nodded—and waited. Kurakin dived for the next crate, anxious to please. But first he gave the rifle to Majid, who held it reverently before passing it on to Bandar. Bandar glanced at it. His face remained impassive. He set the rifle down on the crate it had come from.

Now Kurakin held up a grenade: small and globular and dark green in color, it had the expected ring-pin and two less-expected buttons set cunningly into its side. "French," said Kurakin happily, "and with the newest time-delay switches. You can drop it into a truck, say, and the truck won't blow up for fifteen minutes."

Bandar looked at Majid. Majid was staring at the grenade. Bandar could imagine what thoughts were racing through his friend's mind, for very similar ones were coming to Bandar.

The future of Kassan was in those crates. It took more willpower than Bandar knew he possessed not to jump up and shout his delight.

Now the show was over. Now would come the time of paying—of promising to pay. Pay with what? Blood? Oil? The Panther Throne itself? Arabs were supposed to be master traders. That was about like imagining that all blacks could tap-dance and play jazz trumpet. Bandar quickly prayed he'd be up to the challenge that was most certainly coming. To get the weapons—money, too. To keep his revolution intact. To keep his honor as a Kassanian and as a man.

Kurakin went back to where he had been sitting.

He cleared his throat.

"There are ten dozen of the Fromentor rifles in the embassy right now. One thousand and twenty grenades. Some of the latest plastic explosive with special radio-activated fuses and the radio transmitters to set them off. And, of course, hard cash. And, should you need it, other types of assistance—advisers, technical people ..."

"You are too kind," said Bandar softly. "We can use the weapons, as you know. And the money will be appreciated, so long as you understand, excellency, that it is to be a loan."

"Of course! From one great revolutionary government to another."

He stood and walked to his desk and opened the top middle drawer. And produced a paper.

Of course, thought Bandar. *He wants it in writing*.

"I have here a treaty—the beginning of a treaty at any rate," said Kurakin. "All official, drawn up in both Russian and Arabic—do you read Russian, General Al Khadir?"

He knows I don't. "No, alas."

Kurakin beamed as rich uncles have beamed from the beginning of time. *I won't trust him*, thought Bandar, *any further than I can throw the central mosque. Yet we need what he's selling.*

"What do you want of us, excellency?"

"We want you to win! We want the People's Army to triumph! We want you on the Panther Throne—or, better, melting it down for ingots if that's your pleasure. Your regime would be—we hope—more sympathetic to the goals and ideals of the Union of Soviet Socialist Republics than is the present one."

"May I read your document?"

Kurakin handed it over. Bandar read quickly. It was less a treaty than a statement of intention and shared ideals. Only at the end, buried in rhetoric, came the hard part. The part that said the People's Army of Kassan would tender to the Soviet Union first-refusal status when it came to negotiating the oil-lease rights to Kassan. Bandar looked at it once, then again. No mistake. None was possible, not in those terms. In his head he knew the immense value of Kassan's oil. But oil was so far down on Bandar's list of priorities that he sometimes forgot how very central it was to the ambitions of others. Well, so be it then. If oil was a weapon, he'd use it like a knife or a gun.

"Why," he asked gently, as if to a naughty child, "didn't you simply tell me you wanted the oil?"

Kurakin's jolly laugh was stretching a little thin now. "My dear general," he said too quickly, "everyone wants oil. Everyone."

Bandar's reaction was quick and startling.

He shot up out of his chair and stood tall. All six feet and three inches of him. Even in the slightly comical black female robe, he dominated the room utterly. He could sense a physical fear building in Kurakin now. Kurakin was clever—clever and powerful too. But Kurakin was soft. He liked gold watches too much, and Italian suits, and who knew what other pleasures of the society he was pledged to destroy.

Bandar spoke evenly, not letting the anger show.

"If my birthright is to be for sale, excellency, then it is surely my duty to seek out the highest bidder. Perhaps the People's Army can obtain more favorable arrangements elsewhere. From the Americans, for instance. Or from the Japanese."

Kurakin could barely believe what he was hearing.

There were several things he could do right now, not the least of which was to blow the whistle on the whole thing, to turn in Bandar Al Khadir and his silly friends. But that would be only a short-range victory and Kurakin had early on learned the benefits of playing for the long pull. And the long pull indicated that a revolution in Kassan could be both pleasing and profitable to the USSR. By a supreme effort Kurakin masked his outrage.

"Come, come, General: surely you mistake me. If there is anything on that paper that upsets you, it will be changed."

Bandar turned to his men and signaled them to rise.

"Shall we continue this discussion when the weapons and the money have been delivered, excellency? We must leave now. The revolution won't wait."

"No," said Kurakin heavily, "it won't."

There was a pause in which Bandar felt almost anything might happen. Kurakin recovered himself and said, "If you'll just tell us where you want the shipment and when, all will be arranged, General."

Smiles. Handshakes all around. The young man in the blue suit reappeared by magic and led them out of Kurakin's office and down the wide staircase.

Kurakin went to his window and watched the three grotesque black-robed figures as they resumed their burdens and left his garden. Such was the future of Kassan. The El Kheybar were madmen when they brushed aside this Bandar person. Madmen. And it would cost them the Panther Throne one day. One day soon.

Kurakin thought of October 5. Of the renegotiation for the oil rights of Kassan. If King Nayif were still on the Panther Throne, it seemed a foregone conclusion that the leases would remain where they had been—with the damned Americans.

Kurakin watched his visitors leave, then picked up the paper Al Khadir had rejected. It had taken guts to do that. However grudgingly, Kurakin admired the gesture. Al Khadir would get his weapons, his money. Maybe there would be another piece of paper one day. Maybe not. Change was in the air today in Kassan. Kurakin sensed it with the quivering accuracy of some finely tuned barometer. It was a talent that had taken him far in the KGB. It would take him further still. If he played his cards cleverly in Kassan, it might take him all the way to the Politburo itself. Not beyond imagining.

In the street, Bandar grinned behind the flat mask. Even small triumphs were to be cherished these days. And he had, in one bold unplanned gesture, turned the tables on Kurakin. He had risked much and achieved much. For himself. For the People's Army. Kurakin would never again take him for granted—or assume that he was cheaply for sale.

The weapons would be delivered tomorrow, as they'd arranged. And the money the day after.

Bandar savored the moment. How Kurakin had wilted, like some wildflower in the hot Kamsin wind, when he'd threatened to go to the Americans! The Russian must want that oil more desperately than anyone had guessed. *Why?* It was a question to ponder. To use. To use again and again.

Oil. An accident of nature. Some called it a gift. A most dangerous gift, thought Bandar. One day the oil would run dry, and then where would Kassan be?

The king would have his falcons. The white Rolls-Royce would still jam traffic in Port Kassan. And the people?

The people would be nowhere unless he, Bandar Al Kahdir, did something to change their lot.

The three black-robed figures moved slowly, slowly toward the labyrinthine streets of the town.

Toward the future of Kassan.

4

Megan walked briskly up the limestone steps and into the Fifty-ninth Street door of the Plaza Hotel. *Focus, Mcguire, keep your alleged mind on your meeting with Freddie F.; David can come later. Or go later.* It wasn't every day that Megan got invited to breakfast with the most famous television anchorman in the world. Frederick Franklin had been a household word since before Megan was born.

She could remember him from so far back she was afraid to tell Freddie about it. About being a poor little girl with a drunk of a father, about feeling trapped and hopeless and seeing the TV news with Frederick Franklin. In a way, she had used that flickering black-and-white image as a substitute father. There was something gentle about Freddie's delivery, gentle and strong and wise and all the things Megan's own father could never be. It had been her image of Freddie Franklin that first interested Megan in journalism. He seemed to come from a world where everything was interesting and alive. Where even the bad parts—Freddie F. never tried to disguise the fact that there were bad parts—could be turned to good. Somehow.

Because of Frederick Franklin, Megan had waited tables through NYC, managed a scholarship to Columbia Journalism School, gotten her first job at WBAY-TV in Boston. After a couple of years there her searching coverage on racism in the North End caught the attention of someone at INTERTEL. And the crown jewel of the INTERTEL news department was none other than Frederick Franklin. They all called him Freddie. And no matter what else might be going crazy or falling apart in the weird world of INTERTEL news, Freddie was a rock. Freddie could be relied on. Freddie had long since left behind any sort of ego trip. Freddie gave advice only when asked for it. Twice in the three years that Megan had been at INTERTEL he'd sought her out and made a point of praising her work. Megan cherished those compliments more dearly than rubies. She worked like a lake full of beavers, a hive filled with bees. And she got more assignments. Two specials with her own byline. Three raises. It was all coming, she could feel it.

Too bad it wasn't coming a little faster.

The doorman smiled at her. Megan smiled back. She basked in the recognition. On camera, she was remarkably at ease. She imagined that she was talking to just one person. Very often that person was Freddie F.

Why has he invited me to breakfast today?

Megan caught a glimpse of herself in one of the Plaza's many gilt-framed mirrors. Not bad for a nervous wreck. The lightweight heather tweed suit set off her copper hair, her creamy skin. The headwaiter of the Oak Room smiled. Megan returned that smile, special delivery, and walked on past him.

There at his usual round table sat Frederick Franklin. Megan felt the usual quiver at the idea of actually being in the private company of such a legend. If there were any more room on Mount Rushmore, they'd carve Freddie's head up there in a minute. Poll after poll named him as the most respected man in America. *How the various presidents must hate him,* she thought as he rose to greet her.

Freddie F., the world's favorite uncle, kissed her on the cheek. At Megan's place a tall glass of freshly squeezed orange juice awaited her, regal in its silver urn of crushed ice.

"I leave the rest to you, my dear," said Freddie, "but it is a sin not to drink fresh orange juice."

"You're ruining me, Freddie," she said, trying to match the playful tone of his famous voice. "I think I'll go completely to hell and have the eggs Benedict. I love 'em here. And coffee, please." He poured from a large pot at his elbow. The waiter came and went on silent feet. Megan could feel the other people in the big room stealing glances at Freddie. At her for being with Freddie. *And to hell with them*, she thought. *I've worked for it.*

He came right to the point.

"You know I admire you, Megan. At least I hope you know." *What's he leading up to? Is he going to sack me? Make a pass? The sacking, she knew, was unlikely. That ugly task would be the lot of Lucas B. Lucas, the much-dreaded head of programming for all of INTERTEL. As for the pass, that was even less likely. Such things happened, but not with Freddie F.* She started to speak, changed her mind, and said nothing. She just looked at him expectantly.

". . . and, well, I didn't want you to get this from the rumor mill. I'm finally doing it, Megan. After the first of the year, I'm leaving INTERTEL."

"Freddie . . . no!"

It came like a physical blow. That hard. That fast. Megan had heard the rumors. INTERTEL was a nest of rumors. Megan gaped. She liked to think she had imagination. But it was hard to imagine INTERTEL without Freddie.

He laughed. "I'm seventy, Megan. The old warhorse is tired. I've been working my ass off since I was twelve. And I've loved almost every minute of it. But when Becky died last year—I guess you didn't know my wife—well, it hit me very hard. Not just losing Becky, though that was bad enough. But it gave me a sense of diminished time. Of how little I might have left myself. There's so much I want to do. And it's time to start doing it—before they ship me out of INTERTEL in an oak overcoat."

He paused, sipped some orange juice, winked at her with the audacity of a mischievous boy. "I just wanted you to hear it from me first. Before the rumormongers get hold of it."

Her eyes were tearing up. Megan blinked fast.

"I appreciate that, Freddie. It's just that . . . well, I'm stunned."

There was a pause. Megan sensed he was leading up to something, but she couldn't imagine what.

"The job," he said, speaking so quietly that it was like a whisper, "isn't mine to give. I'm kind of a lame duck already. But I want you to know I think it could be—and should be—yours."

Megan felt her stomach churning. The room seemed to be

churning a little too. First the one shock, then this. This! It was almost unthinkable. Even in her wildest and most ambitious fantasies she hadn't dreamed of stepping into a spot like Freddie's. But someone would. If Freddie thought she could do it, maybe he was right. He'd been right often enough before, God knew.

"Freddie!"

"That's exactly what I told Lucas yesterday, right in this room. "Don't try to clone me, Lucas," I said. "Don't get yourself another elder statesman. Maybe people are getting bored with elder statesmen. Do something different, fresh, unexpected. Do Megan. Well," he went on, "who knows how deeply that sank in, if at all. It's hard to tell with Lucas—and I've been studying him for some time. But I thought you ought to know how I feel, Megan. I think you're terrific. And I think you're just what my anchor spot needs right now. So go get it!"

She managed to laugh.

She reached across the big table and took his hand in hers.

"Freddie, if you say one more word, you're going to have teardrops in your orange juice. I'll never forget this, no matter what happens. You . . . you're a dear, dear man."

Then she got up and kissed him on his freshly shaven cheek.

Heads turned in the famous old room. She could imagine more rumors starting right then and there. She asked him about his plans, asked if there were anything she could do.

He smiled shyly, as though there might be.

"I want to learn how it feels to travel someplace—even across the damned street!—not on assignment. To be able to talk to someone without him imagining that whatever he says will be all around the world on INTERTEL the next morning. To wander, really wander. To linger, if I feel like it. To be lazy. Those things are unimaginable luxuries, Megan. And I'm going to try them all."

"I, personally, give it about six months. Then you'll be back beating on the door of the newsroom, foaming at the mouth to get your hands on a story—any story."

"I'd kill to get a good obituary, as the saying goes. Maybe you're right, my dear. It does get in your blood. I'm sure it will be a shock, for a time, to look at my watch without imagining a deadline. But I'm damned well going to try."

"You really think I could do it, Freddie?"

"Of course I do." He fixed her with the gaze that had made kings tremble and terrorists cringe. "If you dare. And I'm betting you'll dare."

"What—if I can dare to ask—did Lucas think of all this? I mean, it probably surprised him as much as it did me."

"Like the old song Chevalier used to sing—he didn't say yes, but he didn't say no."

Freddie drank some coffee. One reason he liked the Oak Room was that the tables were spaced far enough apart to make it reasonably certain you weren't being overheard. "Let's hope there aren't any lip-readers in the room," he said softly, grinning.

"I'll talk to him today. While the iron's hot." Then she said, as much to herself as to Freddie, "What can I lose but my job?"

"You won't lose that, Megan, and if you ever do, you promise to let me know about it, okay? Even if I'm in a hammock on Pago Pago, where I firmly intend to be."

"It's a deal." Megan looked at her watch. She had hardly touched the eggs Benedict on her plate. "Freddie, this is terrible, but I've got to get to the office. Will you excuse me?"

"It goes with the territory, Megan. Actually, I've got to run also." He waved for the check, and it materialized as if by magic.

They walked out together. The stares of the other diners were frank with curiosity now, alive with speculation.

Megan walked past them in a happy daze. The chances of her really getting Freddie's spot must be, conservatively, a million to one. But wasn't it beautiful that he thought enough of her even to suggest it?

He caught a cab at the Fifth Avenue entrance to the hotel and gave Megan a lift down Fifth to Fifty-fourth Street: IN-TERTEL was just two blocks west on Fifty-Fourth. Again, she kissed Freddie lightly on the cheek.

"Freddie, you have made my day—my year! Thanks again."

"Go for it, Megan. Call Lucas this morning if you can."

The taxi slid out into the stream of downtown traffic. Megan walked briskly toward the building they all called

Wonderland. The nickname was based on the fact that IN-TERTEL's architect had covered the entire skyscraper in mirror glass. Like a TV image, it was there and it wasn't. And crazier things went on behind that looking glass than Alice had ever dreamed of.

Megan's office was on the Fifty-fourth floor. She walked in, ordered coffee from her secretary, glanced at her desk while reaching for the phone. Lucas B. Lucas was in conference. She asked for an urgent—repeat, urgent—meeting as soon as his schedule would permit.

Her desktop was paved with notes, file folders, news summaries, and other miscellany. The rubble that had accumulated in one afternoon away from Wonderland. Methodically she worked her way through it all, making notes on some items, discarding others, relegating still others to her nonurgent pile. The three pink call slips that told her Mr. Jeb Cleaver had called and would call again were put, firmly, on the nonurgent pile.

Megan had to restrain herself from jumping when the phone rang. As always when she was in her office, Megan answered it herself.

"Reception, Miss Mcguire. You have a florist's delivery they want you to sign for in person."

"I'll be right out."

More puzzled than annoyed, Megan walked around two corners to the big slate-floored, Bauhaus-furnished foyer.

There, holding the biggest flower box she'd ever seen, stood Jeb Cleaver. Grinning.

"Special delivery for Miss Mcguire," he said. "Three dozen yellow roses, one for each of my poor unreturned phone calls."

"Jeb. Are you crazy?"

"Just determined. It's sort of an architectural trait. First you dig the foundation, see? Then you plant the girders, then you pour the concrete . . . it's really quite simple."

"You are crazy. But thanks."

The last time Megan Mcguire had felt truly flustered was at least ten years ago. She felt flustered now. And by this weirdo she'd met only once. Jeb held out the big white box. She had to accept it. One rose each to every secretary on the floor. Or find some nice gangster being buried today.

"Jeb, really, you shouldn't have."

"I thought you reporters tried to avoid cliches. But I forgive you, Megan. Have dinner with me tonight."

"Jeb, I'd love to . . ."

"Then do it. I don't bite. Unless seriously provoked."

"But . . ."

"You're otherwise engaged, right? Headache, maybe? Gotta stay up with a sick friend. Of course. I should have known. How about tomorrow?"

She didn't know whether to throw the damned flowers in his face, or scream, or laugh. Something about the expression on his face made Megan decide on the latter.

"Tonight. But I've got a taping at seven, won't be done till eight at the earliest."

"Can I watch? Where is it?"

"Right here—Forty-eighth floor, news studio eighteen. I'll let them know you'll be there. . . . Wait—you need a pass." Megan went to the young man behind the big black reception desk. "Herbie, could you write Mr. Cleaver a pass for News 18 at about seven? Thanks."

She handed Jeb the buff-colored cardboard ticket that would admit him to Wonderland after five.

"Thanks," he said, grinning. "You have made me a very happy architect."

"You really are crazy," she said. "But thanks."

"See you tonight," he said softly, in a tone that made her understand he wasn't crazy at all.

Back in her office again, Megan opened the box. The roses were immense, beautiful, probably shockingly expensive. She kept one for herself and asked Louise, her secretary, to give away the rest.

Now she looked at her desk in earnest, reappraising every assignment in the works and upcoming. Thinking how they'd fit into whatever plan she cooked up to try for the brass ring. For the anchor spot on the seven-o'clock news, the Freddie Franklin spot.

From all the papers on her desk Megan chose a slender manila file folder marked with the letter K. K for Kassan. She'd opened the file the day after first hearing the word Kassan at Langstaff's party. INTERTEL's usually excellent

research staff had come up with very little: a brief ency-
clopedia-type history that was probably years out-of-date—it
listed the chief industry as pearl fishing. A sketchy history of
the ruling family, the El Kheybar, mention of the Panther
Throne itself—nothing more. But just yesterday afternoon
Megan had been in Washington interviewing an Undersecretary of Defense about the upcoming missile controversy in
Congress. They were going at it fast and furiously when the
gentleman's phone buzzed urgently.

"Please excuse me," he said. "This must be a hot one."

He picked up the phone and listened. Very attentively.
Glanced at his watch in response to something that was being
requested at the other end of the line.

"That's right, sir. I'll get on it immediately. Absolutely.
Thank you, sir."

He hung up the phone. Megan was reviewing her notes,
expertly taken down in shorthand.

"Damned Kassan!"

The Undersecretary said it so quickly, so entirely without
thinking, that for an instant Megan felt sorry for him. What
a pain it must be to have reporters in the room!

Then he remembered who his guest was and grinned.
Sheepishly. "You didn't hear that, Miss Mcguire."

"Hear what?"

Megan had a kind of radar about news stories. It was the
extra sensitivity that separates great reporters from merely
adequate ones. Instinct honed by a wide-ranging mind, polished by all the most up-to-date information, it amounted to
the most sophisticated kind of hunch. Megan's hunch was
that the next hot spot in the world was going to be Kassan.
There was only one item in her file that indicated trouble
brewing in the desert: it had appeared in a British paper, the
Manchester Guardian, a month ago. It said that the office of
General Ibn Bir-Saraband, commander in chief of the Kassanian Army and security forces, vehemently denied that the
so called People's Army of Kassan was more than a band of
young idlers. They were not, nor had they ever been, a threat
to the internal security of Kassan.

Megan knew all about official denials.

She had sharpened her claws on Watergate, and before
that she had studied many a minor incident in which official

denials had a way of melting before the white heat of emerging truth.

Megan was still reading the file when her phone rang. Lucas B. Lucas would see her in ten minutes. It might just be the most important interview of her career. She could think of no special way to prepare for it. Instead, her mind kept roaming back to Jeb Cleaver. It was only coincidence that she didn't have a date with David tonight. David was out of town, in Chicago to straighten out some corporate hugger-mugger. Not that David minded when she occasionally had a date with some male friend or other. Perfect in all things, David was perfectly understanding, too. Sometimes Megan found herself wishing David would screw up in some important way, just to find out how he'd react. She decided not to hold her breath until that happened.

Lucas B. Lucas was the Wizard of Wonderland, the man behind the scenes who structured the programming, playing established hits against untried newcomers with the ingenuity of a chess master. Lucas did all the important hiring and firing. Lucas approved every new show and every actor on it. Lucas decided whether new shows prospered or perished. It would be Lucas' decision, subject to the approval of the board of directors, as to who would replace Freddie.

In the elevator riding up to his offices on the sixtieth floor, Megan tried to count off how many times she'd actually met the man. Few, too few. A dozen, tops, in five years. Yet Megan, like every other writer, reporter, and actor who worked for INTERTEL, had an unsettling feeling of being watched. Lucas sat up there on the sixtieth floor like a spider in his web, seeing everything that INTERTEL and all the other networks programmed. Pulling strings, making a hundred decisions every day that might affect anyone. Everyone. It was awesome, this much raw power concentrated in the unassuming presence of Lucas B. Lucas.

The elevator slid open on the sixtieth floor. Here was the absolute pinnacle of success at INTERTEL. It was very quiet. The rest of Wonderland hummed with activity, galvanized by tension, by the never-ending pressure of deadlines and air dates, by the pulsing, tingling need to fill the eternal darkness with light. The enormous dark void extended itself every second. There was no catching up to it, no getting ahead. The darkness was out there, hungry for news, for entertainment and game shows, for soap operas and documentaries, for sports and thrillers.

All of INTERTEL throbbed with the need to fill this ravenous void. But on the sixtieth floor there was a calm like some great cathedral. The decor was equally hushed: all muted grays and ivories.

The receptionist had been chosen to match the color scheme: she wore gray flannel and her hair was sculptured ivory. She buzzed Lucas' secretary. Megan was bidden to enter the sacred portals.

Men like Lucas lived and died by the rating system. In a few thousand houses across America, allegedly ordinary families were paid to have small black boxes affixed to their television sets. These boxes recorded to which station the set was tuned in, and when, twenty-four hours a day. And from these data came a program's ratings. And from the ratings came the amounts of money that a network could charge for a unit of commercial time. Life and death, the ratings, and no one in the world knew who actually watched. For all Megan or Lucas knew, a clever pet cat had turned the dial that killed the promising new show. To manipulate the ratings even adequately took genius. To do it very well and consistently was magic. Lucas B. Lucas had that magic. INTERTEL was number one in the ratings and had been for years. It was a continuing struggle, naturally. Part of the trick was getting the prime-time audience early and holding them.

And the foundation of INTERTEL's prime-time supremacy had always been the seven o'clock news with Frederick Franklin. All of this information was churning in Megan's brain as she walked into Lucas' office.

He was sitting at his enormous white marble table-desk, talking into a white telephone. He smiled and waved Megan in.

Three monitor television sets flickered eerily, the sound turned off. On one of them a housewife, grinning catatonically, was pulling something out of a brown paper bag in a crowded supermarket while two female friends gazed at her in reverent interest, obviously about to learn the elusive mystery of vanquishing waxy yellow buildup. On the middle screen a grave, spectacularly handsome young intern stood watchfully at the hospital bedside of a young woman whose bust measurements might make Jayne Mansfield rise from the grave in envy. On the third monitor screen a furious mob of bearded men was protesting something, screaming silently, gesticulating wildly, some waving placards, others waving guns. In the background a large fake-Palladian building was in flames. Megan shuddered a little at the thought of how many places in the world this particular scene might be happening at any given moment. India? Iran? Chile? Detroit? All mobs, she had long since decided, are the same. *Give me a nice simple avalanche any day.*

Lucas hung up. "I'm sorry, Megan," he said in his curiously soft little voice, "it was Paris, and I just couldn't get him to stop yammering. You're looking gorgeous. What's up?"

Megan hadn't rehearsed a speech. The few times she had tried that she'd ended up forgetting the carefully planned phrases anyway. *He's just a man,* she told herself, *he can't behead me or have me beheaded in the public square.* He could, of course, destroy her career with one phone call—two phone calls. But somehow Megan knew it wouldn't come to that, even if she didn't catch the big brass ring.

"I had breakfast with Freddie today," she said, diving right into the shark-infested water.

His eyes flicked from the television riot to Megan's blue-green eyes.

"Then you know."

"I know."

"He told you about our little chat?"

"He told me he'd suggested me as his replacement. I'd like a shot at it, Lucas."

"I'm sure you would, Megan . . . and you *shall* have a shot at it."

Megan felt a quick hot rush of pleasure at these words. It was almost sexual. She looked at him, a slender balding man in owlish gold-rimmed eyeglasses. quite unprepossessing to see. Until you understood who he was and what he could do. Or not do.

"I realize I haven't been around all that long . . ."

He laughed. "Megan, you've been around long enough to score—and to score big. I hope it doesn't sound . . . well, sinister or anything, but we've been watching you." With that he gestured toward the three monitor screens as though Megan might not have noticed them. She wondered who "we" might be. *Got a mouse in your pocket, Lucas?*

"And we like what we see, Megan. We like your style, we like your thoroughness—the way you dig to the bottom of an issue. By our standards—considering how big we are—your progress has been spectacular. I hope I won't offend you by adding that your success is even more remarkable since you're a woman."

"I try," she said softly, burying the resentment, smoothing over the impatience that made her want to scream; "The job, dammit, tell me about Freddie's job!"

"You certainly do. Freddie noticed it, and so have plenty of other people up here. The fact is, we haven't come to a decision about filling Freddie's spot as yet. I can say that without any fear of contradiction."

He smiled. *You sure can say it, Lucas,* she thought. *Only God himself could contradict you, baby, and then not on prime time.*

"Lucas, if I am in the running, do you mind saying against whom?"

"Ah. Against the memory of Freddie, I'm afraid. That's what we're all running against. We've got to face up to the fact that Freddie may truly be irreplaceable. That is, by any one person—however talented."

He paused to let this sink in. It sank, all right. Like a corpse with cement overshoes. Megan felt her stomach sinking too.

"What can I do, Lucas, to improve the odds?"

"Everything you've been doing—only more so. You've been building interest—I hardly have to tell you that. It's getting so we can advertise a Megan Mcguire special and people will tune in, no matter what the subject. Your interview with the Pope was marvelous. Just marvelous. So warm. You're becoming . . . well, bankable, as our friends on the West Coast like to say."

"Then bank on me. Give me Freddie's slot."

Again the smile came curling across his thin lips.

"You're so impetuous, Megan. It's youth. It's also part of

what makes you such a good reporter. You go where angels fear to tread."

She waited, looking at him with an unwavering stare.

"Your name has come up in connection with the job. This will be—I know you understand—a board-level decision. And boards tend to be conservative. It's their function, really."

"What are you getting at, Lucas?"

"Just this. Certain voices—not necessarily my own, mind you—wonder if you've really had enough experience, Megan. One thing the directors love is a . . . well, a track record."

"I'm twenty-eight, Lucas. It's been a pretty short track."

"I know that, of course. Freddie's concept of going an unexpected route with his replacement is a very appealing one. I just wish that there were one spectacular coup we could point to. Something like your series on the corruption in the old people's homes—only more so. Isn't there some special project you'd like to do—something that'll really impress the directors? I'll back you to the hilt, Megan. And there is time—Freddie's not leaving until January."

"When will you make your decision?"

"Well, there's no saying for sure, but I hope by the middle of October."

"Kassan," she murmured.

"Pardon me?"

He thought I sneezed.

"Kassan, Lucas, is a wart on the thigh of Saudi Arabia. It is also the next big trouble spot in the Middle East—maybe in the whole world, if my guess is right."

"And you'd like to do a series on Kassan?"

"Blow it right out of the water. And before anyone else gets there first. Kassan is hush-hush right now, Lucas. But it won't be for long, you can bet on it. I'd like a first-class crew and at least three weeks location. It won't be cheap—we'll need desert vehicles, an interpreter, drivers—my usual crew if they're free."

"They will be. I like the way you take me up on this, Megan. Kassan it is, then, and good luck to you. Get whatever you need—this'll be a no-budget situation. If you get any flak from the bureaucrats, leave 'em to me. And God bless you."

"Thanks, Lucas. You won't regret it."

Megan walked out of his office on a cloud. That lasted all the way to the elevator. But as she descended to her own floor, she felt a sinking sensation that had nothing to do with the steel cable that was lowering her through the bowels of Wonderland.

What have you gotten yourself into this time, smarty? Suppose there isn't any damned story in Kassan? What're you going to do, make up one? You can't speak Arabic. You don't know beans about that part of the world. You are one dumb risk-taking broad, Miss Mcguire.

But by the time she regained her office, Megan's doubts evaporated. She quickly flipped through the Kassan file. Then she asked the invaluable Louise Russell to step in.

"Red alert," said Megan. "In about one week I want us to be en route to the Middle East. Full crew, the works. Jerry, Philo, you—we'll need an Arabic interpreter. What are those British cars that go anywhere?"

Louise's pencil was flying. "Land Rovers. Or Range Rover, that's the fancy version."

"Great, rent us three—equipped for everything we'll need in the desert. And tell the crew to arrange backups for all their equipment. We'll need three minicams and three backups, battery packs and backup battery packs—Milo will get it. But to be taken from here. No chance of renting on the spot—too risky."

"Megan, hang on," said the unflappable Louise. "Where in the world are we going, and for how long? Sounds like the moon."

"Might as well be, darling: we're going to a little-known— at least it is right now—place on the Persian Gulf called Kassan. Just down the road a piece from Kuwait. Oil country. Pure Arabic. While you're at it, get research to pull out all stops—discreetly. We don't want to make too much noise right now. Ask corporate travel to make reservations in someone else's name—definitely not mine."

"Clandestine operations?" Louise smiled. She was a twenty-two-year veteran of INTERTEL, and nothing surprised her. Or fazed her.

"If word gets out that we're mounting a major shoot in Kassan, we mightn't be the first—and that's important."

"Got it. Anything else?"

"There will be, but that ought to do it for today. Any questions, refer 'em straight to Lucas. And we want to get going just as soon as we can. The State Department should be contacted—at a fairly high level—and you should see about passports, shots, all that. We're all human pincushions by now, but maybe there's some local thing you have to be vaccinated against."

"I'm off, then."

"Thanks, Louise. It might even be fun."

Louise grinned. "Yeah. Catch myself one of those sheikhs."

Megan sat back and took a deep breath before digging into the paperwork on her desk. Wouldn't you know this'd be the night she'd let herself be talked into having dinner with Jeb Cleaver? Well, she decided, it would be a very quick dinner.

Jeb had never been in a television studio before. His pass was checked at the ground floor of INTERTEL and again on the forty-eighth floor. He was directed down a very long hallway lined with studios. Number 18 was about halfway along the way. He pulled open a thick door with a glass window in it and found himself in a small control room. There was a row of low couches close by a huge plate-glass window. Behind the couches was an immense electronic console bigger than the cockpits of two jumbo jets side by side. There must have been a thousand knobs, lights, and dials of various kinds. Toggle switches, microphones, levers. Ominous red and green flashing signals. Five video monitors. Two men sat behind the console, playing it like some enormous organ, their faces reflecting the colored lights below. They nodded at Jeb and motioned him to sit down.

Outside the big picture window was a stark modern setting that featured two very modern swivel chairs and a low glass table in between. Behind the two chairs was a large screen where location footage could be shown.

Megan was sitting in one of the chairs interviewing a fat man who was obviously uncomfortable. He was the traffic commissioner of the city of New York, and Megan was raking him over the coals in an especially incisive manner. Her voice had a low, almost husky quality that carried very well without ever needing to be raised. Her manner was easy, conversational. But the questions she asked decimated the squirming commissioner with one torpedo after another.

"Then what you mean to tell me, Mr. Randall, is that you see no hope at all for relieving the congestion in midtown Manhattan?"

"Well," he said, sputtering with repressed anger, "it's not a clear-cut, thing, you see, we've had these cutbacks . . . it's like more and more people are bringing their cars into town and . . ."

Megan turned to the camera.

"Excuse me, Commissioner Randall. Our time is just about up. It has been a very illuminating experience having you here on INTERTEL Channel One News. Thank you so much for coming."

The commissioner sat there puffing, looking the image of outraged incompetence.

Jeb was watching the monitors now, fascinated. There were three cameras trained on Megan at all times. She looked lovely on every one of them. Part of the job the men at the console were doing was to edit, fading angle into angle, cutting to close-ups here and distance shots there, melding the rather static interview situation into something visually fluid. He thought it must be over now. He was wrong. Megan shook hands with the commissioner and he left. An aide was waiting to escort him off the set. Megan turned briskly to the control room, spotted Jeb and waved, then said, "Jeff, can I do about a minute-and-a-half wrap-up? Can we squeeze that in somehow?"

"You got it, honey," said one of the two men at the console. A woman came scurrying out from nowhere and patted Megan's face with a powder puff, rearranged a strand of hair, peered at Megan with a mother-hen sort of scrutiny, and walked off the set. Megan endured it stoically. She sat down in her former place and turned to the camera.

"Can you put up the Forty-seventh Street gridlock footage?"

There was no reply. The screen behind Megan filled with a shot, taken from some high angle, of the worst traffic jam Jeb had ever seen.

The monitor picked up a medium shot of Megan with this

clearly visible behind her. She waited for some invisible signal, then spoke.

"The commissioner of traffic earns sixty thousand dollars a year. He has the use of a city limousine. He has four aides who earn more than forty thousand dollars each. The entire department employs nearly two hundred people. This is three times as many people and four times as much tax money spent on salaries as ten years ago. And New York traffic, I hardly need to tell you, has never been worse. As we've seen, the commissioner is long on excuses and short on answers. I put it to you—to the mayor and to the chief of police—that if something doesn't get done quickly, this city will be one huge gridlock from 125th Street to the Battery. Thank you. This is Megan Mcguire for INTERTEL News."

She stopped and waited. *It has to be over now,* Jeb thought, looking at his watch. Seven-forty-five. But it wasn't over. Megan heard a playback and wasn't satisfied with her reading. She did it one more time. Then the acoustics specialist in the booth picked up a funny buzzing noise—a mechanical noise—on the tape. Megan went through her spiel again. It was five past eight before they left.

"Hi, Jeb," she said casually as she walked into the booth. "Was it hideous?"

"It was great."

"Let's go upstairs: I've got to pick up something from my office."

She said good night to the men in the booth and they went down the hall. Jeb felt the electricity building. In the four days since he'd met Megan, Jeb had flicked his television to Channel 1 several times without catching her.

"You really let him have it—the commissioner."

She laughed and looked up at him. "I was kindness itself. He's a political hack of the lowest order. Couldn't organize his way out of a paper bag. It really makes me seethe—and, Jeb, he is one of thousands in the city government alone. Not to mention what goes on in dear old Washington."

They got out of the elevator and walked down another long hallway. Jeb noticed a forest of tall yellow roses sprouting from desk after secretarial desk. Couldn't be a coincidence. Was this walk to her office Megan's way of telling him how lightly she regarded the gift? Seventy-five damned dollars' worth of roses!

"You made a lot of hardworking girls very happy with those, Jeb—I do thank you."

"There was really only one I had in mind."

Her answer was a low chuckle. Megan's office was larger than most of the others they'd passed, but still quite compact in size. One L-shaped desk, two small chairs, and the desk chair—and one of Jeb's roses in a Perrier bottle. Megan picked up a briefcase, turned to Jeb, and smiled.

"I am starved, Jeb. Where are we going?"

"Do you know Il Nido?"

Megan did a lightning-fast double-take, thinking about how many times she'd been there with David.

"I love it. My favorite Italian place in New York. You architects have good taste."

They walked the six blocks east and one down.

Megan shone in the dimly lighted restaurant. The headwaiter knew them both, and Jeb's table was a rounded banquette in the front room, really a table for four. A privilege to be given that place when you were only two.

Megan ordered white wine and Jeb asked for the same.

"I hope, she began, "that you don't think I was avoiding you, Jeb—I was out of town yesterday and I really would have called back."

"I'm delighted you'll see me under any circumstances. I'm not really the joker those flowers may make me seem. It's just that it's been a long time since I've been hit with the old baseball bat quite the way I was at Langstaff's the other night."

"I'm flattered. And pleased."

David, she was thinking, *would never be so outspoken.* Megan suddenly found herself wondering about this funny stranger at her side. Almost against her will, she liked Jeb Cleaver. He was older than David—David was thirty. Jeb must be nearly forty. But such a nice forty.

"Tell me," she said when their wine came, "about Jeb Stuart Cleaver."

He lifted his glass.

"To the most beautiful reporter on all television."

"I'll bet you never watch television. I'll bet you'd never seen me before the other night."

Jeb laughed, but he felt the incisiveness of her thrust. "You have some instinct, there, Megan," he said. "I guess I was the only person at the party who didn't instantly know who you are."

"What a relief. You haven't seen all my clinkers."

"Judging by tonight, they're few and far between."

"Not as far between as I'd like—sometimes when we're shooting live, it gets pretty hairy. Doing retakes the way we did tonight is a luxury."

Jeb listened attentively, thinking: *I could watch you do retakes until the sun freezes over.*

"But," she went on," you didn't answer my question. About the life and times of Jeb Cleaver."

He sipped the wine. "Born in a humble log cabin in Greenwich, Connecticut. Family moved around a lot. My dad was a roving troubleshooter at IBM. Three high schools in four years. Harvard. Harvard for architecture, too. Married, divorced, no kids. Partners with Oscar Kuniyoshi. Forty on my next birthday. Unaccustomed to being on my own. Smitten with Miss Mcguire of television fame."

At least, he thought, I made her laugh. He remembered a fake-quaint sign his uncle had in the guest bathroom. "The maid who laughs is half-taken." God should be so kind.

"Very incisive, you architects," she said. "First you dig in the pilings, right?"

"We try. Depends what we're digging into."

The waiter came with menus. They split an order of the restaurant's famous tortellini with four-cheese sauce as an appetizer. She had broiled bass, he had grilled shrimp. More white wine. Already Jeb felt an intimacy, a sense that she was on the same wavelength. *She must feel it too—that or she is one hell of an actress.* The meal ended too soon. They had espresso.

"Jeb," she said, stirring half a cube of sugar into the steaming black brew, "I really enjoyed this."

"I did too. I felt like an idiot—those flowers and all. I'm a little old for sophomoric pranks."

"I loved those flowers. So did all the girls on my floor."

"Look, Megan, I don't mean to snoop, but—"

She held up one hand with a small but eloquent gesture of warning. It could have stopped a freight train.

"Not yet. I'm here, okay? Free, freckled, and twenty-eight. You don't see any chains because there aren't any. I'm a maiden lady, Jeb, so to speak."

"Have supper with me Thursday? I'm going out of town for maybe a week on Friday."

"Thursday's fine. Thanks. Where are you going?"

"You'll think I'm an idiot, but I don't know yet. It's a bunch of briefings on a new assignment, and they don't seem to have set that up yet."

The check came and he signed it. They walked to Third Avenue and caught a cab uptown. "Maybe on Thursday you'll come and see the architect in its lair—actually it's another architect's lair, a loft I'm subletting on Broome Street."

"You're on," she said, kissing him on the cheek as she stepped out of the taxi. "Call the office about where and when."

Megan lived in a small cooperative apartment on Fifth Avenue at Sixty-eighth Street. The doorman opened the glass door to the lobby. She checked her mail: two invitations to parties, four bills, five bits of junk mail. On the way up in the elevator she thought about Jeb Cleaver. All during dinner she'd been fighting the image of David. Then, without realizing it, Megan had just stopped thinking about David and begun enjoying Cleaver. Nothing profound. She hadn't been aware of any trumpets sounding—but fun. Good, easy, interesting fun.

She showered, set out her clothes for tomorrow, brushed her hair and her teeth, and slid into bed.

What have you gotten yourself into this time, smart-ass? she thought, as sleep came in a cloud of yellow roses.

5

Port Kassan: September 7.

The dark green Mercedes-Benz 600 limousine of General Bir-Saraband pushed through the clogged traffic of Port Kassan, its horns blaring. The crowds melted away, for they knew the huge car by sight. In the back seat Ibn Bir-Saraband rode alone and in silence. The car was a portable fortress: the tires were puncture proof, with a core of solid foam. The glass was bulletproof and the steel panels had been doubly reinforced to the fifth level of NATO armament for passenger vehicles. The car had, as part of its communications system, a Swiss encoder/scrambler that enabled the general to speak normally to a receiver at ADDAK headquarters, where the message would arrive in a code whose cipher was changed daily. Ibn doubted if the American President himself had a more sophisticated arrangement.

Until lately such measures were more for the general's entertainment than to fulfill any real function in Kassan.

But now all that had changed.

Only one month remained until the time when the oil leases must be renegotiated.

It made a convenient timetable for the general's plan to seize for himself the Panther Throne. The broad strokes of his coup were already firmly fixed in the general's mind. It only remained to fill in the details. *Step one*: stage the kidnapping of King Nayif and make it look like the work of the rebels. *Step two*: kill Prince Selim and his sons. This, too, could be made to look like rebel mischief. *Step three*: persuade Nayif to abdicate in his favor—and kill the old he-goat if he refuses. It would be very simple. Logical. Easy.

Only two complications seemed likely, and one of these had come to pass already. Selim's wife and the twin boys had left the country for an indefinite stay in Paris. Paris operations were a bit beyond ADDAK. Ibn wouldn't risk an operation in Paris. Not yet. So it was only a question of attending to Princess Fawzia and the eight-year-old twins when they returned. Perhaps some accident could befall the royal jet. As for Selim himself, there were several possibilities. The reason Ibn was going to the old palace was to check up on one of them.

As for King Nayif, he was scheduled to leave on a hunting expedition in the desert very soon. Perfect. The old fool insisted on hunting unescorted but for his servants, a falconer, and a few friends. Easy targets. Child's play.

Ibn smiled. The car inched forward, nudging untethered goats, prodding pedestrians, grazing the occasional camel. He thought of his meeting with Kurakin. That, too, was a part of the plan. For when Ibn's coup took hold, he would need the support of major foreign powers. As long as Wilfred Austin was at the embassy Ibn could be sure of the American side of the equation. The Russians were, as ever, quite another matter. Yet Kurakin was friendly—more than friendly, he was downright eager to weld a closer bond between his government and the new occupant of the Panther Throne. Why else would he have tendered the document that Ibn had signed just this afternoon? Why, if Kurakin weren't absolutely sure of Ibn's success, would he go so far out on a limb?

The general leaned back against the opulent seat. The Americans versus the Russians—all competing for his favor! Not to mention other possibilities, other rich and powerful countries. It was a promise of infinite wealth for the ancient house of Bir-Saraband. Wealth that would make his present huge fortune look like a heap of camel droppings! Ibn could see it plain. How Selim had played into his hands over the years—first by absenting himself, then, once he had come back, by keeping himself aloof. By the Prophet's beard, Selim could have demanded the army, the construction industry, the

Petroleum Ministry, the lot! Surely Ibn would have seized such things were he in Selim's shoes. Selim's isolation made him vulnerable. Made him a perfect target.

There was, of course, Tamara. Selim's sister, Ibn's wife, Nayif's daughter. Ibn loathed his wife for the way she looked at him these days—had always looked at him, even from the first. But at the beginning it hadn't mattered that she disliked him. She was an Arab wife and she did her duty. Four sons' worth of duty. Tamara filled a vital function in her husband's plans. She was an impeccable connection to the Panther Throne. Her children carried the blood royal in at least half of their Bir-Saraband veins. When Ibn's eldest son sat on the Panther Throne, it would not seem as though the boy had appeared out of nowhere. Especially not with his father acting as regent.

The palace sat on a hill at the edge of the old town. It was not one structure but rather a collection of forts, houses, stables, barracks, and a small mosque all encircled by one high wall of dun-colored native brick. A town within a town, immense but quite shabby on the outside, spectacularly luxurious within. Ibn preferred his own new palace at the edge of the desert, all gleaming white marble with walled gardens and pools and the most modern stables in all of Kassan. There was even a small private airstrip.

King Nayif's palace was like the king himself: frozen in tradition. Even now, the king's backwardness enraged the general. Ibn dreamed of F111s and Fairchild A10 Thunderbolt jet fighter-bombers specially fitted for desert combat, potent with bombs and missiles. But the king's reality was six helicopters for official visitors and surveillance, plus two old Cessna trainers. Ibn hadn't even been able to persuade the king to set up an official Kassanian airline. Every self-respecting Middle Eastern country had its own airline. It was a disgrace. The king suffered from an underdeveloped sense of his own dignity, of the importance of symbols.

Nayif ran Kassan as though it were a Bedu camp in the old days. He still held the weekly audience in person, exposing himself to all manner of riffraff, dispensing justice on the spot. The king's majlis, for so the audience was named, would be one more bit of excess baggage to be stripped away under the new regime.

THE PANTHER THRONE

The general's Mercedes pulled through the Portal of the Dawn into the palace courtyard. As ever, the great space thronged with petitioners, layabouts, the ragtag of the souk, and even the occasional red-faced foreign businessman in an uncomfortable dark suit. Ibn eased himself out of the Mercedes and adjusted his general's cap, its stiff black brim encrusted with golden laurel leaves in imitation of a victorious athlete's crown in ancient Greece.

The king, he knew, was making himself ready for the hunt. Precisely where Selim was, the general didn't know. This was what he had come to find out. The white Rolls-Royce had been seen leaving the palace earlier in the afternoon. Probably going to the reception at the American embassy. Ibn had decided not to attend: he had more important things to do and his relations with the ambassador were as good right now as they were ever likely to get. Ibn sought out Selim's secretary and asked three questions. As usual, the answers were vague to the point of uselessness: no one knew when the Princess Fawzia and the boys would return. Selim was at the American embassy, but his plans for the evening were unsettled. The only positive answer, Ibn knew already: that Nayif and two friends were setting out tomorrow to go hunting.

He left Selim's wing of the palace and admitted himself to the central reception area. Here Ibn walked down a long deserted hallway until he reached a large wooden door with old iron fitments. He pushed this door open swiftly, and just as swiftly slid inside, closing it after him with a quickness that was almost furtive.

Now he was alone in the throne room.

It was a big rectangular space, its ceiling lost in dimness perhaps forty feet overhead. The only light was from a double row of slender windows topped by pointed arches. These windows ran down both sides of the big room, and the late-afternoon light came streaming in in slices. As though the sun itself had been carved by a scimitar's blade.

Ibn's glance was riveted on a strange and vibrant object at the far end of the chamber. There, elevated on three stone steps, was the Panther Throne of Kassan.

The room was plainly furnished. Rows of benches for supplicants, a central aisle carpeted in fading red, the carpet leading toward the throne. But the Panther Throne made up in dazzle for what the rest of the big dusty room lacked.

It had been crafted in the seventeenth century by some itinerant goldsmith, probably trained at the Moghul court. The throne was a huge chair, so tall it needed a footstool. The throne and its attendant stool were built of solid silver. Its arms, legs, leg braces, and the finials of the back were deeply encrusted with a carved frieze of panthers wrought in three colors of gold. These beasts disported themselves in play, in love, in hunting, and just in the pleasure of panther-dom. They writhed, stalked, wrestled, leaped, crouched, ran: one even slept in the branch of a silver tree. Each of these beasts wore a collar of diamonds and each panther had eyes of polished unfaceted rubies. The effect was one of constant movement. The panthers seemed alive. The seat of the throne and its back were upholstered in wine-red velvet. The back of the seat was embroidered in thread of silver and gold with the royal symbol: a rampant panther crowned with the crown of the El Kheybar.

Ibn looked at the throne with naked lust.

The panthers of Kassan would have a new master, and very soon! The chair was only cloth and metal—however precious—yet it radiated a strange power. Ibn had never yet dared to sit on the throne. Just seeing it was enough. Enough for now.

He stood transfixed, then turned to leave the throne room, then turned back for one last glance at the object of his most deep and cherished desires.

Perhaps it was a passing cloud, or even a flock of seabirds. But as Ibn looked, something moved across the shaft of sunlight that lit up the throne like a searchlight from heaven. For a few seconds the Panther Throne was in shadow. Then the sun came out again and all was as it had been. Or was it? Was someone watching?

The general prided himself on being without the useless superstitions that hobbled so many of the older generation. Nevertheless, he was sweating now in the cool room. He felt a chill of senseless terror running down his spine. He shuddered, gained control of himself, and walked firmly out of the throne room and down the empty corridor beyond.

6

Jeb paced his sublet loft as though he were measuring the place for carpeting. Damn stupid thing, asking her up here. She'd see right through it. He felt like an adolescent on his first date. That anxious to make a good impression. And what would Megan think of a forty-year-old who could barely fry an egg? Thank God for Dean & Delucca, the famous charcuterie where he'd bought supper. And what did it mean anyway, with him going off to Kassan for nobody knew how long? Dumb time to start up something when you knew perfectly well you couldn't finish it.

The hurt of losing Hillary still burned in Jeb's memory. And no matter how many times he told himself—or listened to friends telling him—that it wasn't his fault, he felt responsible. What could he have done differently to avoid that mess? What turning had he taken that took him so very far away from the girl he'd married?

Nothing he could name or put his finger on.

The apartment, at least, was worth seeing. Fred Hauser was brilliant—he'd done a magnificent job on the huge old loft. Now Fred was building an entire city in India—luckily for Jeb, he'd be away at least a year longer. Living quarters were just one more decision Jeb hadn't made since his divorce. He'd gone from sublet to sublet like some kind of well-heeled vagabond.

It seemed that committing to a permanent home would be boxing himself in somehow. And Jeb felt boxed in already.

Boxed in and too much at loose ends: it might have seemed like an amusing paradox if it happened to anyone else.

Jeb set the goat cheese out to soften and opened the wine. Let it breathe. If he had to serve a picnic, at least it'd be a fancy one. Megan was probably always on a diet anyway, although you'd never know it from the way she'd gobbled up the tortellini the other night.

Jeb stood in the immense living room of the loft. Four huge columns defined the windows. Fred had painted the whole place ivory, stripped the old factory floors down to the original clear pine, then lacquered that a dozen times with polyurethane until the mellow wood shone like water. The furnishings were overscale and simple: three big leather couches, a black slate coffee table you could dance on, and several big ficus trees in ivory wood tubs. The kitchen was an island off to the left somewhere in the shadows. There was a deep alcove for sleeping and one completely separate room which Fred used for his drafting table and files. *Neatly done, Hauser.*

Half an hour until she was due. *You are turning into a creature of impulse, Cleaver,* he told himself: taking the Kassanian assignment just like that, now making such a play for Megan. Maybe it's one of those middle-age crises. Maybe you've finally slipped your tether.

Kassan.

Tamara. That had been another kind of madness. The Jeb of today could forgive the Jeb of twenty-one years ago for falling into some kind of wacky romantic trance. Kassan, then, had been some cosmic movie director's idea of *Arabian Nights* exotica. Selim? Well, Selim was there; the Selim Jeb knew as a roommate in Cambridge, Massachusetts, wasn't all that different on his home turf. Crown prince or no crown prince, the Panther had a sense of humor that wouldn't quit, and a fine ironic perspective on the whole place. But Tamara was something else again, an ivory-skinned princess with haunted eyes who walked in a kind of innocent yet very seductive beauty such as central casting never dreamed of.

After that one quick dreamlike month that he'd spent in Kassan during the summer of his eighteenth year, Jeb had never been quite sure how much of his feeling for Tamara had been real and how much was the product of his highly active imaginaton. No doubt there was a mixture, fermenting, fermenting in his brain. In his heart.

Part of going back to Kassan would be confronting that dream. He didn't like to think what twenty-one years of being an Arab wife might have done to her. Maybe that slender girl had become fat and familial, reverting to some medieval Islamic dream of a woman's role in the house—palace—of a rich man. General Something-or-other. Jeb had seen Selim several times since college. The last few had been in the company of Hillary, and something there, some unspoken tension, had prevented his asking Selim about her. *She could be dead, and I wouldn't know it,* he thought, and dismissed the thought. More stupidity.

Jeb had stayed at home last night just to watch television. Megan's interview with the traffic commissioner had been featured on the seven-o'clock news. The replay was even better, somehow, than the taping Jeb had seen from the control room. Megan was a girl who could go anywhere in the television business: this was apparent even to Jeb, who barely watched a program a week.

Why would a woman like that give him the time of day? Megan probably devoured kings and prime ministers for breakfast. Jeb didn't want to admit, even to himeslf, that he was scared. Scared of a new relationship that was anything more than a one-nighter. Scared of making himself vulnerable again.

The doorbell rang. Right on time. He smiled. Vulnerable? He hoped she'd never know just how deeply vulnerable he was at this moment.

Megan stood in the doorway, glowing. Her hair looked polished. If she was wearing any makeup beyond a little eye shadow, Jeb couldn't see it. Fresh and radiant and looking young enough to be his daughter. If he had a daughter. In her hand was a bouquet of daisies.

She kissed him lightly on the cheek. Sisterly. Old-pal-ish. Nothing sexual in it. Damn. "I couldn't manage lots of yellow roses, Jeb, but here."

"My favorite flower," he said, wondering if anyone had ever brought him flowers before. Any woman. She was wearing a shirtwaist dress of fake suede in a deep amethyst color. She carried a lightweight raincoat. Jeb took the coat and looked for something to put the flowers in while Megan walked around the loft.

"Very nice," she said. "Whose is it?"

"Hauser's—Fred Hauser. He's an architect. In fact, we went to school together."

"I've been learning about architects," she said. "For instance, I know what bright young man won the Louis Sullivan Award in 1978."

"Who told you that?" The Louis Sullivan Award was given each year to one architect. Many people in the profession considered it to be the most prestigious award in America. Jeb had won it that year, 1978, for a chapel he'd designed at the University of Oregon.

She smiled. "I'm not a reporter for nothing, buster. One phone call to INTERTEL research got me a file on you that's thick enough that I only had time to skim it. I mean, a girl has to know who she's visiting, right? To be sure I don't wake up in a freighter bound for Shanghai."

"With that in mind, can I offer you a drink?"

"Got any soda water?"

He poured her some soda water and poured a glass of white wine for himself. Then he led her to the leather couch. The cheese and some crackers were on a cutting board on the table in front of them.

"I'm glad you came, Megan. Last night I caught your interview—the one you taped Tuesday. It was dynamite."

"Thanks. We got some calls. Including a furious one from the mayor's office. That's the part I love—sticking it to 'em."

"You stuck pretty good. But I'm at a disadvantage, Megan. Here you've been doing all this homework and I don't really know a thing about the work you do. The other night was the first time I'd ever been in a television studio."

"And we know you never watch the damned thing. Well, it's basic: I'm a reporter . . . and I report. On all kinds of things. The traffic commissioner was fairly run-of-the-mill. If you're lucky, they give you special projects. Sometimes even a whole show to do by yourself. Although nothing in television is really by yourself. The most important thing is to have the right backup support—the best cameramen, the right editor . . . all the logistic stuff is vital. Or else you look—and sound—like a turkey. Like the whole turkey farm, sometimes."

"You don't look like a turkey."

"Thanks," she said, regarding him over the rim of her soda glass. "Neither do you." She sipped. "Jeb, you never told me where you're going—have you found out yet?"

"Virginia. Williamsburg, luckily. Can't think why."

"Can you talk about it? I mean, do architects get into deep corporate secrets, things like that?"

He laughed. "Not usually. Some companies are a little secretive by nature—don't want people to know just how much a project cost, for example. But generally it's pretty straightforward. This is something new to me, though—a government project. An embassy, to be exact."

"Jeb! That's great. I mean, it's a big honor, isn't it? To do a whole embassy? Where?"

"A place nobody's ever heard of. Kassan."

She set her glass down very carefully, as though it might be filled with some specially volatile explosive. "Say that again."

"Kassan. It's in the Middle East, right down the Persian Gulf from Kuwait. An oil country, mostly."

"You aren't going to believe this. I almost don't believe it myself. In about one week I'll be in Kassan, Jeb. Doing a special. Of all the hundreds of countries in the world, how about that?"

"I think it's swell. I'm not sure just when I'll get there, but it'll be soon. They want to start—almost too soon. I get a few days' briefing, then it's off to the races. How long will you be there?"

"As long as it takes. More than a week—maybe two. Maybe more, if things develop the way I think they will."

"Can I ask what that means?"

She grinned. "Hunch. Kassan seems to be popping up in a very select bunch of conversations these days. Please, Jeb, if you have friends in the news business, don't mention Kassan to them. It hasn't hit the news yet. It will—and I want to be there first. Firstest with the mostest."

"But what do you think you'll find besides a bunch of camels—or Rolls-Royces, more likely these days?"

"I think Kassan's in line to be the next Arabic domino.

The next kingdom to fall. I think Kassan's ripe to explode, and nobody knows about it—or is willing to talk about it. For fifteen years Revere Oil has been very hand-in-glove with the ruling family. They've quietly taken out uncounted amounts of the sweetest grade of oil. Their leases expire in a few weeks. Nobody knows just what the oil king will do then. I mean, everything's changed so much since that first concession lease was sighed. And then there are the rebels. Nobody talks about them, but they're there. And there's a large Russian presence—not to mention all the usual playmates that gather around the honeypots in that part of the world—Libyans, the ASSAD, the PLO, you name it. Things could get very lively very soon over there. Your embassy better have nice deep bulletproof cellars, Jeb."

"It will. Nobody forgets Iran. There never will be an indefensible embassy built anywhere overseas after that. But I hope I'll be able to make it much more than a bunker."

"The man who built the Oregon chapel? The man *Time* says is one of America's ten best architects under fifty? Of course you will."

"Thanks." Jeb got up to refill his glass. Megan had barely touched her soda water. Coincidences seemed to be popping up all over. Jeb and Selim being roommates at college. Megan and this possibly wacky idea of hers. Wacky like a fox, though. The lady did have a killer instinct for a story.

As he walked the short distance back to where they were sitting, Jeb began to think how very difficult it might be to have her in Kassan. On any terms. He'd already seen the way Megan went after a story. And suppose she went after something the State Department or Selim didn't want known? It could get very dicey over there. Probably *would* get very dicey.

And there was nothing he could do to stop her.

"You really think Kassan's going to blow up?"

"I'm sure it *could* blow up, Jeb. And I wonder just how that'll affect our foreign policy. How it'll affect the balance of the entire Middle East. If this rebel is another Gaddafi, it could literally blow up."

"Rebel?"

"Al Khadir. Bandar Al Khadir. He's sort of the Fidel of the situation, lurking in the hills most of the time, pulling raids whenever he dares, spouting propaganda like crazy. You never know whether they really are crazy, of course, until they've got the power."

"And then, if they are crazy, it's too late."

"Sometimes. Tell me about Richard Nixon."

Jeb dodged that one.

He got up and put the quiche into a low oven to warm. The butter was out, softening. The long loaf of French bread was crisp and only a few hours old. Jeb put a thick slice of country pâté onto a big serving plate with a bowl of small sour pickles and a jar of mustard. He brought it to the table, then the bread and butter, then the red wine and wineglasses. Megan was still talking about Kassan, and the more she talked, the more apprehensive Jeb became.

He sat down and served her some pâté, then poured the wine. His voice was quiet when he spoke.

"You really want that to happen? For Kassan to blow up?"

Megan tasted her wine, then put the glass down. *You are coming on too strong, Mcguire*, she told herself. *This guy is definitely of the still-waters-run-deep variety and you just don't know what might be lurking under that all-American surface.* In the hour she'd been in the loft Megan had found Jeb more and more attractive. More and more of a paradox.

"Well, Jeb, you know—it's what I do. I hope you're not one of those people who think the media are always manipulating the news. We don't make it happen—we just work like donkeys to get the word out. Of course I don't want Kassan to blow up. But if it does, I intend to be there—cameras and crew and everything."

"I guess," he said, eating some pâté in the meantime, "that I got a little whiff of ambulance chasing."

"Touché. There is that. Nobody ever made headlines because Mrs. O'Leary milked her cow. It's when the beast kicks over the lantern and burns down Chicago that it begins to get interesting."

He laughed. "And the first thing a smart dictator does is muzzle the press. What's the Arabic press like?"

"Muzzled. Very muzzled in the few remaining kingdoms—places like Saudi Arabia. And all over the lot elsewhere. Not reliable except in the broadest sense of seeing who's feeding what to whom. Whole wars can be fought and monarchs tumble and you'd never know it to read the local papers. In Kassan, for example, there has been no mention at all of the rebels. Someone thinks that if you don't talk about them they'll go away."

"What attracted you to Kassan?"

I could ask him the same question, she thought, *but not right this minute.* "Gut instinct. I keep my ears open. The name began popping up in the kinds of places where it has to mean something special. I'm going to find out why."

Jeb sipped the wine. Calon-Segur 1971 and worth every penny of the twenty-three bucks it had cost him.

Then he smelled the quiche—not quite burning but on the brink. "Damn!" he said, leaping up. He pulled it out just in time and set it on the counter to cool a little. "Very well-done quiche, if you'll forgive me, Megan. I shouldn't be allowed near a kitchen."

"You do very well." She smiled. "Shopping well is nearly as hard as cooking well."

Megan ate a little of everything but only sipped the wine. Dessert was a bowl of fruit from Balducci's. She was eating her third grape when Jeb leaned over and kissed her. Megan smiled, knowing she'd wanted him to do exactly that. Then her arms were around Jeb's neck and she was pressing him to her, kissing him back, letting go. It was as natural as it was sudden, and without taking his lips off hers, Jeb lifted Megan in his arms and carried her to the far end of the loft and around the corner to the alcove where the big double bed was set into its own niche. It was gentle and fierce, a discovery and a sharing. They felt at ease, free to enjoy each other, generous and abandoned. When he had time to think, later on in the long night, Jeb felt better than he had with any other woman. Comparisons weren't fair, but this had been beyond comparing. He looked at her in the blue-gray light of dawn. Radiant. Warm. Glorious. He kissed her cheek. Megan stirred but didn't wake. Then he dozed off again.

Jeb woke to the sound of water running. Megan was showering in Hauser's spectacular circular glass-brick shower stall. He got up then, threw on some faded jeans, and padded across the loft to make coffee. Six-ten. She was an early riser. One of Fred's women had left a blow dryer in the bathroom.

Jeb could hear it working. Finally she came out. Early riser. Quick dresser. One glorious woman.

"Good morning."

"Hi," she said, kissing him. "That was nice, Jeb. Very nice indeed."

"You've got sharp buttons," he said softly, shirtless, pulling her closer.

"You architects are pretty randy," she said, laughing. "I've got to going, Jeb. Where will you be in Williamsburg?"

"The Inn. For probably five days. Come down."

"Can't, dammit. I've got to get this wild-goose chase organized in record time. But I'll let you know where and when—I don't think they've got confirmed reservations yet—in Kassan that is."

"It's so dumb—schedules."

"I'm not going to forget you, Jeb, if that's what you mean."

"Nor I. I'll call as soon as I get back."

"Please do. And . . . thank you."

"I should be doing the thanking. I'll be thinking about you, Megan."

"Me too. So long, randy architect."

She kissed him again and was gone.

The water hadn't even boiled yet. Jeb waited until it did, made the coffee, and had a big scalding cupful. He slipped on an old sweatshirt and went to the window, hoping to catch a glimpse of her. Broome Street was empty and silent.

Megan stepped into the huge industrial elevator that serviced Jeb's loft. As it rumbled to the street level she realized she'd have to break off with David. And she knew that break would have come sooner or later in any event—Cleaver or no Cleaver. The elevator stopped. The door slid open. And when Megan walked out of the cavernous machine, she was smiling.

7

Kassan, A Village in the Desert.

Bandar slept by day. Agents and informers of ADDAK might be anywhere, and their eyes were sharper by day. They watched and waited, and time was on their side. Ten thousand Kassanian pounds would be a fortune to the people Bandar trusted most.

He had developed the instincts of a hunted creature, alert to any small sound, even to changes in the air itself. Bandar had no illusions about what would happen to him in the secret torture chamber of ADDAK. Now he lay on a worn blanket in a goatherd's hut, dozing. Planning the next raid and the one after that. The tradition of Arab hospitality served him well. Praise Allah. He often thought the ancient and unbreakable custom was all that had saved him. To give shelter, food, and comfort to any stranger was a tradition older than time, bred of harsh necessity in the desert.

Bandar dozed and thought what a long journey had brought him to this place. His life would have been very different had King Nayif been less fond of falconing. Bandar remembered his father, Fayed, the king's falconer. One of the king's innumerable falconers, for the king maintained several hunting camps in those days, each with its own small staff, each ready to receive King Nayif on a moment's notice. Being a royal falconer gave Fayed some stature in their little town of Dhahir. But for all that they were poor as desert

106

sand. Only when the king came were there extra comforts, scraps from the royal table, game from the royal hunt.

There was no school in Dhahir. Some of the bigger towns boasted koranic schools, and in Port Kassan, it was said, there were real schools, academies. But Port Kassan might as well have been the moon—it was that remote, a shining rumor, unreachable.

Once a month the itinerant teacher came, gathered up whatever boys weren't hunting or at work, and tried to cram their restless minds with bits of learning. For girls, the kitchen was deemed school enough, their texts the loom and pestle, kneading dough and grinding wheat. In all Dhahir there was no man, woman, or child who could read.

To Bandar the teacher was mysterious, fascinating. Imagine one who came and went in the world, who had magic in him, a man who could read! Even his name was prophetic: Muhammad.

Muhammed al-Ahred, for he was always most respectfully addressed by his full name, quickly recognized the seething unchanneled brightness in little Bandar. The boy deluged him with questions. What makes rain, and why so little of it? Who owns the wind? The other boys laughed, fidgeted, played truant. Bandar didn't care. He must know the answers, facts, the names of stars and where the moon goes when it passes through the doorway of the dawn.

In the long days between the teacher's visits Bandar practiced his Arabic script. Paper was a rare and precious thing. He wrote in the desert sand with a long sharp stick. One day the teacher left with Bandar a wondrous thing: an illustrated Arabic primer!

There was no stopping the boy now.

He learned the word for "camel," for "goat," for all the things two bright brown eyes could find in a village like Dhahir. Seeing this, Bandar's father was both puzzled and proud. A waste, most likely, he thought, but who was to say? Surely the teacher had been sent by King Nayif, and just as surely the king would be pleased to have his teacher obeyed so diligently.

One day Bandar's father summoned the boy into the little bedroom he shared with Bandar's mother. Rummaging in a big old trunk, Fayed came up with something Bandar had never seen before: an old, much-thumbed, still legible Koran. Gingerly the boy's father handed him the sacred book. Bandar knew his father couldn't read or write. He said nothing, but took the book carefully, brought it to the kitchen table, and opened it. The script was old-fashioned, but Bandar could make out certain words. And when the teacher came around again, he was astonished when the boy produced the Koran and asked for help in reading it.

Six months after that the king came hunting in Dhahir. As always on these occasions, there was a great stirring in the town, and especially in the house of Fayed Al Khadir. Bandar, lost in his studies, paid little attention. He did his regular chores, cleaning the falcon shed, shining the ancient brass pot in which his mother brewed coffee for ceremonial occasions, sharpening the kitchen knives on a whetstone.

Late one afternoon during the king's visit Bandar's father came to him. Fayed was agitated. Bandar wondered if something had gone wrong on the hunt. "Put on your good robe, boy, and wash your face: the king has asked to see you."

Bandar had seen the king many times. He seemed old and rather fierce, but many old men in the town were rather fierce. Bandar was neither awed nor frightened, for to him the Panther Throne was a glittering abstraction. He had heard the old tales spun out around campfires, of the legendary white panther of Kassan and how the throne had gotten its name.

The king's tent was specially erected for each visit. It was made the old way, of felt blacker than night, capacious, with one central pole and several lesser poles creating alcoves and nooks. Bandar knew the tent well. It was part of his father's duty to put it up and take it down. An old servant of the king's guarded the entrance. He was expecting Fayed and the boy.

The king was seated. The tent floor was layered in rich carpets, rug upon rug, a thousand colors mingling. There were big pillows for sitting on, and low brass tables laden with good things to eat, a brazier with a coffeepot. Bandar's nose twitched. The air was dense with mingled scents: sweat and cinnamon, animals and coffee roasting, smoldering acacia, honey, myrrh.

"Come in, Fayed," said the king. "And Bandar."

The king poured three cups of coffee and handed them graciously to his falconer and to the boy. There was a plate of wonderful pastries, ground pistachio nuts and honey and who could guess what else? Bandar's eyes wandered to the tray of pastry. The king laughed. "They're for you, lad, those pastries. Please help yourself."

Bandar took the smallest one and ate it.

Surprisingly, it was to Bandar that the king spoke first.

"Well, young man," he said quietly when they had taken their first ceremonial sip of the coffee, "the desert wind has brought me news of you. Of your eagerness to learn. I have heard of a boy who goes into the desert and makes strange markings with a stick. You are never alone in the great sand ocean, Bandar. Did you know that?"

The boy could only stare at his king, mystified. Had he done something wrong?

But the king was smiling. "The *jinn* bring me word of a boy who writes sayings of the Prophet in the sand. Is this true, young Al Khadir?"

A shudder went through Bandar, sudden as a sandstorm.

"Yes, sire," he said so quietly it was barely audible.

The king turned to his falconer. "Worthy Fayed Al Khadir, I must ask you to do a very difficult, perhaps impossible thing."

Fayed's silence was thicker than the rugs underfoot.

The king continued. "I ask you to lend me your son. The teacher Muhammad al-Ahred roams these villages, on my instructions, seeking out lads of exceptional promise. He has so named your son Bandar. For these boys I have made a special school in Port Kassan. A real school, with a teacher from England, with sports, a library—everything. Fifty boys study there, right on the grounds of the palace itself. These boys will be the new Kassan. They will read, write, and learn all manner of things I myself cannot pretend to know. It is even possible that some of them—the very best of them—will be sent across the ocean to study in Europe, in America." Bandar was transfixed. What was Europe? Where was America? Words he'd never heard before, nor his father either.

At Last Fayed brought himself to speak. "It is your wish, sire?"

The king smiled. "It is my hope, Fayed Al Khadir. Please

understand that I, too, have known the pain of sending a boy away to school. It is a necessary sadness, Fayed, but great things can come of it. Very great things. perhaps."

"Then my son shall go to your school, sire, and thank you."

Bandar felt dizzy. The black tent seemed to be spinning. His head was a scramble, one dream racing a hundred others. His lower lip began trembling. It seemed to have a will of its own. Then he felt a gentle hand on his shoulder. The king had risen. The hand was his.

"A great thing has happened to you tonight, Bandar," said the king. "But it is not a gift. It is a thing to be earned and cherished. You will have to work hard in my school. Are you ready for that?"

"Yes, sire. Oh, yes!"

Twenty years ago. How simple it should have been. How easy to become a minor bureaucrat like so many of the boys who had attended the King's School.

The King's School! Even now, after everything that had happened, Bandar thrilled at the thought of it. Now Bandar was the sworn enemy of King Nayif and all the El Kheybar. But he would never forget the fact that it was the old king who had opened up the world for him. Too widely, perhaps. That long-ago journey to Port Kassan had come rushing at the eight-year-old Bandar with the magical velocity of dreams come true. He saw his first automobile, rode in it on the highway. Saw his first electric lights, first tall buildings, heard a radio for the first time. The school itself was a fountain of discoveries. There he met Majid, another scholarship boy, a year older and taller then than Bandar, but a kindred spirit. Majid, who was today the second-in-command in the People's Army.

School was glorious, and a little frightening. There was so very much to learn. Bandar applied himself with all of the intensity at his command. He learned basic things like how to use a modern bathroom. He saw for the first time his own reflection in a mirror. He learned about the great inventions, old and new, how Arabic astronomers had invented the science very long ago. Bandar saw aircraft in the sky and was astonished further. Quickly he adapted to a life filled with miracles. What this taught Bandar would change the history of Kassan. Bandar learned to take the impossible for granted. He decided that anything—anything!—could happen if only you wanted it enough, worked hard and, occasionally, prayed.

Before the end of the year Bandar was first in his age group for studies. He was a wiry child and he would always be slender. Now he began growing at a phenomenal rate. In a world of compactly built men, Bandar grew to be six feet tall at age fourteen. His final growth stopped at six-three. There were many ways in which the boy excelled. No one could stop him on the soccer field. He won footraces with maddening ease. And he read, read, read. By the time Bandar was ready to graduate, he had a good working knowledge of English and some French. The king was feeling expansive. Arrangements were made for Bandar to attend the University of California at Berkeley.

On the wings of his awakening wonder, Bandar took it in stride.

Berkeley came as a shock to him. Here he was a stranger, out of his depth, drowning in a whirlpool of customs whose existence he hadn't begun to expect for all of his learning at the King's School in Port Kassan.

Bandar came to realize that Kassan, his universe, was no more than the smallest dot on the globe. No one at Berkeley had heard of Kassan, and when they did hear about it, their interest was minimal. There were other Arab students, and in their company Bandar found some comfort. But it was at Berkeley that he became a loner. Haunting the library, he read until his eyes hurt. Bandar majored in history, and this was a new source of wonderment. To discover many different ways of living, religions undreamed of, wars and revolutions and great social changes. For months Bandar moved in a kind of trance, struggling to absorb one stupefying discovery: *that things didn't necessarily have to go on being as they had been.*

Revolution was in the air at Berkeley then, and Bandar heard the familiar catchwords: Mao and Ho Chi Minh, Che, Fidel, and all the rest. He did not participate in the many student protests, but the forces behind them interested Bandar, and he expanded his reading.

He discovered that to be born in a tiny Kassanian hamlet

like Dhahir was almost like having been born hundreds of years ago. That he had leaped from the medieval past of Arabia into the jet-propelled future in just nineteen lightning-fast years. That Kassan had a long, long way to go before it caught up with even the most backward of other nations. Maybe he could help!

It was at Berkeley, too, that Bandar first discovered the sexual delights of women. In Kassan, even to walk down the street with a girl not related by blood was unthinkable. Even in the humblest villages, marriages were solemnly arranged, family to family, based on some material advantage. It might be three goats or a palace, but the bride and bridegroom had surely never been alone together before the wedding day. Or night.

Bandar had no sense of his good looks, the fact that his height and grace and romantic profile drew girls, especially American girls, like a magnet. The mere fact of sharing classrooms with girls had been an astonishment when first he arrived in California. When some other young men in his dormitory invited him to the beach, Bandar was shocked to the core. So much female flesh, so carelessly exposed! Surely it was an offense to the Prophet, who decreed extreme modesty in all things. But then Bandar was less sure that the Prophet's decrees applied in California, USA. If they did, they were roundly ignored.

Sex at Berkeley was only slightly less casual than saying hello. And while Bandar never took it for granted, he soon allowed himself to be picked up by a suntanned blonde he met in the library. Her name was Tess. They had coffee. She asked him back to her apartment for dessert. The dessert was Tess herself, free and eager and completely fascinated by this curiously innocent but smashingly attractive young man.

He stayed there three days. And by the end of it Bandar knew about many things beyond the warm magic that can happen between men and women, with or without the Prophet's permission. He discovered that, to Tess, sex wasn't a great decisive or binding thing but rather the most easygoing of pleasures. Bandar was sure she'd expect him to marry her, and he was ready to consider doing that, even though he sensed it would be impossible for a girl like Tess to live in

Port Kassan for even a few days, free as she was, with her fine rebels's disregard for the rules.

They were together almost constantly for a month, and after that Tess dropped out of school, went to San Diego with a former boyfriend to open an herb-and-tea store. Just like that. She kissed Bandar good-bye and gave him a small golden seashell on a gold chain, in memory of one long passionate day at the beach. Bandar wore the chain always. He was three years at Berkeley, working through the long summers, accumulating point after point, eager to graduate in record time.

Eager to go home again, to help build the new Kassan. There were other girls, a few casual friendships with men, but mostly Bandar kept to himself, reading, reading, reading. Although he naturally fell into discussions from time to time, and these discussions ranged from surfing to Spinoza, Bandar listened more than he spoke.

He wasn't sure of himself yet. He felt the man inside him ripening like a date in the sun, growing, threatening to burst out of his skin. He would not rush it. Bandar understood that so much had happened to him so very fast, he needed a little time to absorb it all, to digest the new learning, the many-faceted experiences that he had found on the golden shores of California.

Kassan was waiting. Bandar knew that he would go back there, that he'd have a hand in shaping Kassan's future.

Whatever that might be.

8

In a business where thirty seconds of commercial time could be sold for thousands of dollars per second, Megan had learned early on to make the best of her time.

Everything in her day's frantic schedule was compressed, distilled, analyzed, and often reorganized to make time work overtime. She gloried in it. Doing the impossible refreshed her. Now she was faced with a new and magnificent impossibility: to set up the Kassanian expedition while completeing all of her scheduled assignments.

Well, Lucas helped a lot. She'd fly to Kassan on Monday, September 15, and hope to finish shooting in about two weeks. Open return, though—you never knew. Lucas had cleared Megan's schedule from the fifteenth onward, keeping it all hush-hush as they'd agreed.

She thought of Jeb, then pushed the thought out of her mind. There'd be time enough for Jeb later on. Maybe. Being in Kassan might help, but Megan wondered how much time she'd have for him over there. It was truly impossible to tell. Whatever happened with Jeb, the pressures of her Kassanian assignment wouldn't go away. Those pressures were harder, more deeply felt because this mission was Megan's own invention. She was keenly aware of that. Her one great leap for the old brass ring, and if she fell on her face, the whole damned world would see her.

She couldn't afford to slip. Couldn't afford to come back with anything less than a sizzling, headline-making, prize-winning report. Big order. Big prize at the other end. Luckily her favorite crew was available and eager to go. Gus, the grip, had to be sweet-talked into postponing his vacation, but she'd done that before and Gus knew he wouldn't lose by it. Megan loved her crew. She'd handpicked them all and they worked together with the precision of a fine watch. Gus, who could rig any set and devise impossible camera mounts; her two brilliant cameramen, each very talented, and in ways that complemented each other. Jerry Schwartz was Megan's action cameraman, twenty-four and almost suicidally fearless. Jerry could stride into a screaming mob with cool aplomb, the portable videotape camera on his shoulder, and come back with perfectly focused footage of wrenching immediacy. One day, Megan was sure, Jerry would be shooting feature films. Until then, she cherished him. Her other cameraman was older, a perfectionist trained in Hollywood, a different breed altogether. Philo Kulukundis was an artist pure and simple. He could light like a Rembrandt: in the helter-skelter world of newscasting, his visual authority stood out dramatically. One reason Megan looked so good on camera was the fact that she often had Philo to operate the camera. Megan herself was the first to admit this, the first to appreciate his value. So it went for all her crew. She agitated for raises, spoke up for special privileges, looked after them like a mother duck in a dangerous pond. And they responded in kind. It was like a family. There was Mike Flynn, wizard electrician, and the priceless Louise, genius organizer, unruffled no matter what bombs might be bursting in air.

They had a running joke, calling themselves "The Riders of the Purple Sage." Last Christmas Megan had T-shirts made up with that printed on the front. The shirts were a big hit, a little tattered now. She'd get new ones for Kassan.

Louise poked her head in. "Can you be in Washington at three this afternoon? I've got an Undersecretary of State who'll see you about Kassan. Hardy Leighton's out of town for a week."

Megan looked at her watch. "Just barely." It might be critical, though, she told herself: better do it. The time was just before ten in the morning. Megan had been at her desk for three hours already and she'd only begun to make a dent in her schedule. "I'll try for the one-o'clock shuttle, then," she said, paused, bit her lip, and tried to remember her geography. "Louise, how do you get from Washington to Williamsburg?"

"Fly to Richmond, I think, then drive."

"See if you can route me on, say, a five-o'clock flight out of National, have a driver waiting at Richmond, Richmond to New York maybe around midnight?"

"I'll try," said Louise. "What's in Williamsburg?"

Megan smiled. "An unsuspecting gentleman who may be a source on Kassan." *Well, dammit, he might.*

Louise left. Megan went back to her files. Five minutes later the phone rang. Reception. The newest candidate for her interpreter was here. Megan had forgotten the appointment completely.

Ahmad Bin Sayed, pronounced AK-med. He was short and slender, bright-eyed with a sort of very alert chipmunk's expression that pleased Megan on sight. Graduate student at Columbia, majoring in business administration. Born and bred in Port Kassan. The Columbia translating service had sent two other candidates during the last few days. One had been shy to the point of incoherence and the other a bit arrogant. Megan knew the importance of a location crew's getting along on a personal basis. Whoever they used as interpreter would have to fit in. Ahmad, she felt, might fit in very nicely. His eyes flashed with intelligence. His skin was the color of antique ivory. He wore his dark hair short—it flowed into a well-trimmed beard that gave him the look of those old stone-relief carvings from ancient Babylon that Megan had seen in the British Museum. In fact he said he was the son of a fisherman.

She liked him at once.

They talked for nearly half an hour. For Megan this was a priceless amount of time, but she knew it wasn't wasted. To be in Kassan without the right interpreter would be hopeless.

"I have," said Ahmad, "six brothers and two sisters. They will be at your service also, should you need them." He had seen Megan on television. He was a fan, just slightly awed by meeting her in person, but clever enough to deal with the wonder. She asked about business administration.

"I will make fas-cin-ating things happen with all the oil money," he said, grinning.

"Your father is a fisherman?"

Ahmad smiled modestly. "That is, he has boats. Several fishing boats and small freighters. Coastal business, you see, in the gulf only." He paused, reflecting. "Should you want to get a thing—even a person—out of the country by unusual means, his boats might be useful."

"Unusual means? Smuggling, we call it."

"Exactly!" He beamed. "You see, Miss Megan, if you are over there investigating, you may discover things people—highly placed people—do not want to be known. It might be helpful to have an alternative means of . . . shall we say communications?"

"It might indeed. Ahmad, you've got a job if you want it."

They discussed terms. Ahmad protested. A hundred dollars a day was too much. He was, after all, only a student. His English was far from perfect. At last they agreed. It was going on to noon. Megan decided to go downstairs with Ahmad. It was time to get herself to La Guardia for the one-o'clock shuttle. As they left, Louise handed her a three-by-five file card with all the pertinent information on it: the man she was to see at the State Department, the schedule to Richmond, the flight back, even her driver's name in Richmond. It was just Louise with her typical everyday miracles of logistic planning. Megan checked her purse to see if she needed cash, decided she didn't, told Louise she'd be in at the crack of dawn tomorrow, and escorted Ahmad down the bustling corridors of Wonderland.

A few of Jeb Cleaver's tall yellow roses still remained on secretarial desks, wilting a little now.

It seemed like a year ago. It was less than a week. Jeb! Jeb Stuart Cleaver. Unlikely-sounding name. Unlikely guy.

Now, for the first time since she'd hatched the crazy project, Megan felt confident that it would really come together. That was Ahmad's doing. She'd trust herself—and all her crew—anywhere, with any assignment. Ahmad was the missing link, the single unifying force that would make it or break it.

"We leave on Monday the fifteenth. Is that all right?"

"Oh, yes, very fine," he said as the elevator slid down through the innards of Wonderland. Ahmad hesitated then, and finally brought himself to speak. "Miss Megan," he began, "I do want this job very much, but . . ."

"But what, Ahmad? Isn't the money enough?"

"Oh! Please not to think that. The money is . . . splendid. It is that . . . I do not wish to dishonor my people, but Kassan may not be safe for you."

"Not safe?"

"You will be asking questions, perhaps, that certain very powerful people do not want to be asked."

Megan felt almost maternal. How sweet he was to be concerned. How gallant. How off-base.

"That," she said breezily, "is exactly why I'm going!"

They shook hands formally on the sidewalk. Ahmad promised to call her on Wednesday, to set up a small briefing for the whole crew—about customs, what they'd need to pack, all that.

Megan hailed a taxi, and one appeared with a magical swiftness.

It was happening. Kassan was happening. Megan could feel it in her bones. Even the boy's apprehension spoke to the urgency of finding out what was really going on over there.

Megan had no doubts now. She'd find it, whatever it was. She'd be the first. On the scene in Kassan when others were barely learning what the word meant.

It was a very good feeling.

Selim El Kheybar lay naked and sweating under the fine Porthault sheet. He moaned, rolled over, and was suddenly awake in the gossamer blue light of a Kassanian dawn.

He'd had the dream again.

In his dream Selim was also alone, also naked, and riding a great silver-white panther across the dunes. He could hear the panther's deep and regular breathing, feel the touch of the cool night air rushing past. The panther's feet barely touched the sand. They rode on and on until it seemed they might go on forever. Not a bad thought. But then the dream changed. The motion continued, but something tensed and stiffened in the panther's easygoing stride. Now there was music in the dream. Music and laughter.

And Selim could see himself, naked on the white panther. But it was a carved, gilded panther on an enormous carousel, going round and round and round. He was alone on the enormous merry-go-round. And outside, in the night, pressing against the gilded fence, there were mobs of people. Observant. Amused. Howling with blood lust and laughter.

Selim got up and showered. It helped only a little. How long had he been plagued by the dream? Years, surely. Selim didn't need a psychiatrist's advice to interpret that dream. He knew all too well that it was only a weird distillation of his cardboard role as Crown Prince of Kassan.

He'd never told anyone about the dream. Surely not his father. Not Fawzia. How he wanted her back! It might take weeks to scout schools for the little panthers. Well, she'd be better at it than he: Fawzia, who had been educated in France in contradiction to Kassanian custom. Selim had many grievances against his father, but King Nayif had chosen wisely when he chose Fawzia to be Selim's wife. He'd known Selim wouldn't sit still for a traditional Muslim wife, harem-bred and scarcely educated at all.

Fawzia could and did move gracefully in both worlds: in the world of Kassanian tradition older than time, and in the fast-paced world of her husband's European and American friends. It couldn't be an easy thing to do, and Selim admired her for it. Loved her for it.

He looked in the shaving mirror and made a demon's face. The Crown Prince of Kassan grimaced back. A crown prince without power, without a crown, no more than some gaudy kite dancing at the end of an old man's string. Vulnerable to any wind.

Maybe he should have stayed in Paris.

He thought of his old house on the Ile St. Louis, where Fawzia and the boys were in residence even now. Wonderful crooked old place it was, views of the Seine on two sides, Notre Dame just across the way. Now, going on to forty years old and restless, Selim tried to remember the names of all the dozens of friends and lovers who had filled his days and nights in Paris. All those people who drank his wine and laughed at his jokes. None of the girls who had tumbled so prettily into his bed in Paris could compare to Fawzia.

No, there had been consolations in his father's summons to come back to Kassan.

Selim dressed in an immaculate white cotton Bedu robe. The headdress would come later. Today was his father's weekly majlis, and the king had requested that Selim stand at his right hand.

Justice in Kassan was the king. There were minor koranic courts to settle spiritual uncertainties, but justice in law was dispensed by the king. The king was justice, the king was diplomacy, the king was oil policy. Only the army and the police were uninteresting to Nayif, and these he gladly delegated to his son-in-law Bir-Saraband.

Well, thought Selim, *someone has to do it.*

He saw little of his brother-in-law. Heavy, coarse sort of man. Poor Tamara. Really, he saw too little of her, also. Selim could remember how it had been when he and Tamara were children—the preferred children, being the only issue of Nayif and his first and most favored wife. Of his half-brothers and sisters Selim saw little. There were twelve in all: nine boys, three girls. Much younger and dispersed throughout Kassan, playing with the enormous allowances that the king made them from the oil revenues. The oil, the dates, the pearls in the gulf—everything that grew on the land or could be dug out of it was all the king's personal property to give or withhold as he chose. Kassan was a family store, a very exclusive club.

Selim had never questioned that. It was a small-scale version of how the Saudis ran Saudi Arabia, how the emirs ran the Emirates.

So Selim resigned himself to living at his father's whim. Sometimes, impatient, he dreamed of going back to the old easy life in Europe. But Kassan was in Selim's veins, and he stayed. It was a constant source of frustration to him, but he stayed. One day, somehow, he would find a way to make himself useful in this strange land where so many things needed to be done. The schools, for example, were appalling. Sanitation in the provinces was hit-or-miss, and medical services could stand vast improvement. Yet tradition was choking the benefits that Kassan could so easily afford. Each service had its ministry: Health, Trade, Construction, Education—down the line. And each minister was some collateral relative of the king's. Selim never thought of these sticky-fingered men as his own flesh and blood, but of course they were. Partially, at least. And more than partially corrupt. This, too, was tradition. If the cost of, for example, a new chemistry laboratory tripled the original estimates because Cousin Fawd needed some new Daimlers, it must be the will of Allah. Major projects had a way of vanishing as though they had been buried in the night by sandstorms. The projects vanished into air. Their budgets usually vanished into Swiss banks. And no one seemed to care. Surely not the king.

After a while Selim stopped trying to make sense of it. He retreated into his immediate family, spent long hours with the boys, and tried energetically to father more children. So far without success.

Perhaps it was a good sign that the king had asked him to attend at the majlis today. Maybe Nayif had it in his crafty head to finally let his heir have some real say in the rule of Kassan.

It was amazing, really, a sight from biblical times.

For the king himself to sit all morning in the blazing sun while schemers and courtiers and crazy people whined and pleaded for favor: astonishing in the last quarter of the twentieth century. Nayif did this religiously every week of his life, save only the month-long feast of Ramadan. In a way if was the ultimate democracy: any man of any station could approach the king, touch him, be heard.

Selim fitted his headdress carefully, feeling the weight of it. Ordinarily he went bareheaded. With the crisp white robe, Selim donned a thousand years of tradition. He took the little private elevator down from his suite in the old palace and walked into the courtyard to join his father.

The court was a large irregular space, an unplanned interval among the forts and the mosque and stables that, collectively, made up the palace. It was paved but dusty. The dust shimmered in the heat. In Port Kassan you could no more stop the dust from blowing than the sun from rising. Thus the many walls, the slits of windows, the secret green gardens. Selim looked at the court and found it ugly. Nothing grew here. One day he'd see about new plantings, a fountain, perhaps a remodeling of all the ill-matched facades. One day. One day!

The heat was already intense. Soon it would be unbearable, but they would bear it. The king was already seated on his low bench, and beside him a scribe who would dutifully record all that transpired here. Next to the scribe stood an interpreter, for of late the numbers of foreigners at the majlis was increasing. Businessmen wanting this or that concession, frustrated by the usual channels, hoping to find a shortcut through the labyrinth of custom. Sometimes their hopes came true. More often such people were sent packing, back to the bar of the Hilton to wait, and wait, and wait. For Kassan was more than the land of Islam and oil and the El Kheybar.

Kassan was also the land of Inshallah—"if Allah wills it." The minister will see you tomorrow, Inshallah. Tomorrow came but the minister did not. There would be, in that case, another tomorrow—if Allah were willing. The days would pass. European, American, and Japanese blood pressures would soar, waiting for the will of the Prophet.

The king was a small and wiry man. His skin was tanned to almost the color of leather by incessant falconing. He sat in the sun with the patience of some ancient tortoise, viewing his suppliants with a perspective that seemed to range much further than the seventy-eight years of Nayif's age. Selim bowed to his father and got the slightest of nods in return.

There were more than fifty people in the courtyard already. More would come and go as the morning burned on. Some for amusement, some to plead, some to argue. The justice of King Nayif was often whimsical, sometimes harsh. Until recently crime had been virtually unknown in Kassan. Anything beyond the most petty thievery was considered a major incident. But the tremendous influx of foreign menial workers had created a large and unruly laboring population. Among these men there was crime: drugs and alcohol and gambling and fights over women. Just last year there had been a rape. A young Yemeni bricklayer had assaulted a girl in the old town, raped her and run away. Two weeks later, permanently disgraced, the girl had eaten rat poison and died in horrible agony. The Yemeni was hunted down. King Nayif himself pronounced the sentence: castration, to be followed by public beheading. The case caused ripples of terror up and down the gulf. Rape! Suicide! Castration! But so it was decreed, and so it was done. And the women breathed easier.

Waves of heat shimmered up from the cobbled pavement. Two old women approached the king, bowing and jabbering both at the same time. One owed the other six months' rent. Justly so, said the other, for the landlady kept the place filthy, never repaired the cookstove, and never delivered the electricity she had promised to install. Always, ranged in shadow along the back wall of the courtyard, several policemen waited to subdue any potential violence. Nayif motioned two of them to come forward. He ordered them to go with the two disputants, to inspect the apartment in question, to report back on its condition. Only then would he make up his mind as to which of the women was in the right. *Fair enough*, thought Selim, *always assuming that one or another of the women wasn't in some way related to the policemen. In Kassan, that was all too likely.*

The next suppliant was a comically fat Belgian who represented a chain of fast-food waffle restaurants. He was looking for the local concession. The king made short work of him, shunting the man to the Ministry of Agriculture, which for some reason was also charged with licensing public eating facilities.

"But," said the fat man, blustering through the interpreter, "I've been there eleven times in the past week. No one will see me."

"Then," said the king dryly, "you must go twelve times, and perhaps more." He waved the man away.

The next case was different.

A well-dressed merchant came forward dragging a young boy by the arm. The merchant owned three camera shops. He had caught the boy with a Nikon under his robe. There were two witnesses. The boy squirmed like a fish on the line. He was about nine years old, just a bit older than Selim's boys, but smaller, thinner, dirty. He wore a ragged and stained robe. His feet were bare and black with dirt. The look on the child's face was something Selim associated with small feral animals. The boy was given a chance to speak. He said nothing but only looked down, down into the hard square-cut stones of the courtyard.

"I have seen this lad before," said Nayif quietly. "In this courtyard just six or so months ago. He'd been caught stealing chickens. He swore by all that is sacred to Allah never to steal so much as a moldy fig for as long as he lived. Is this not so, lad?"

The boy said nothing.

"He is incorrigible, then. We will remove the irresistible opportunity. At this time tomorrow in the square by the street of the coppersmiths, his hands shall be cut off, and in public, so that all can witness the reward of thieves in Kassan."

The boy let out a scream that threatened every window in the palace. His shrieks seemed to cut directly into Selim's heart. Both hands! The child went limp, although the avenging merchant still held him tightly by one hand. He sagged, as though all the air had been let out of him. The screams died down and were replaced by a pathetic whimpering sound. Again, Selim was reminded of some animal.

And for the first time that morning Selim spoke up. He leaned forward and whispered into the old man's ear. "Father, please: he is a child."

The king regarded his son. "And if he had pulled the trigger of a gun and killed you, he would still be a child. And you might be as dead as if a man had done it. We punish the deed, Selim, as much as the man—or child—who does it."

"Both hands, Father?"

Selim felt a sickness rising in his gut and fought to keep it down. When his father spoke again, it was softly, to the boy: "My son intercedes for you, young man. And because he is my son I listen. My heart is moved. So I will alter my judgment on you. Tomorrow at this time in the square by the street of the coppersmiths, your right hand only shall be cut off."

The boy screamed again. Selim hardly heard it. A black rage welled up in him and threatened to drown him with the sense of his own impotence. That his father would mock him, and in public, and at the cost of a boy's hand! For a moment Selim stayed absolutely still, for if he had moved at all, there was no telling what he might do.

The king watched him, eyes half-hooded with the bright steady gaze of the hunting falcons the old man loved so well. His voice came to Selim as a whisper. "Do you think, Selim, that our God is some rubber toy to be stretched this way and that? The laws of Allah are stern laws. Our God is a stern God but a fair one. And the reason we have had so little crime—until lately—is that these laws are implacable. The time will soon come when you must enforce the laws of the Prophet. The sooner you learn their uses, my son, the happier we all shall be."

Selim was looking at his father, forming his reply, when the explosion came. With a deafening roar the first grenade went off, then the next. Then silence. The king was thrown from his bench to the cobblestones. Selim reeled, clutching his forehead. Something stung. He ran the few feet to his father, saw that he was unhurt, but lifted the old man anyway and ran to the nearest doorway. Only when he had the king safely inside did Selim turn back on the remains of the majlis.

Two of the audience were dead. Six more were injured. A siren was wailing. Someone had summoned help. The police. already in attendance, were running about in confusion. After the first two explosions there was a terrible silence as they all waited for the next—and the next. But there was nothing.

Selim walked out into the courtyard and tried to help the wounded men who lay on the rough pavement like broken toys, moaning.

Rebels, he thought. *It must be the rebels. And damned clever of them, too. They could have wiped out the king and his heir in one lucky shot. Or bomb. Or whatever it was.*

Only as the ambulance came racing through the main gate did Selim begin to feel the fear.

He turned and walked back to where he had left his father. The king was on his feet now, dusting himself off, furiously angry. Yellow fire flashed in his dark brown eyes. Again, for the second time this morning, Selim was reminded of a hunting falcon.

"These are the rebels that Ibn assures me do not exist?" Selim looked at his father for a long moment, wondering. Someone in the narrow crowded streets outside the palace wall must have tossed a bomb—a grenade, more likely—over the wall. Knowing the audience would be in progress and the king exposed and vulnerable. *Did they know I'd be there too? That they could get both of us at once?* Anyone could look into the palace courtyard. It was one of the basic gathering places of the old town.

With his arm around King Nayif, Selim helped the old man back into the palace.

Even this morning, he had worried more about some silly dream than real matters of life or death. The rebels? The rebels were a distant rumor, a few gaudy posters, an occasional small act of sabotage. Or so they had been.

Selim knew, and shuddered with the realization of it, that he and his father were terribly vulnerable in Kassan. As the rebels got bolder, better equipped, there was no telling what they might not do.

This would be the last majlis in the open air. From now on there must be doubled—redoubled—security. Arms searches, if necessary. Selim wondered if the Kassanian Army would be up to a really tight security program.

And he wondered where he could turn for help if they weren't.

Selim El Kheybar would have been more worried had he known how much thought was being given to the future of the Panther Throne in many different parts of the world at just that moment.

In a huge gray stone building in Moscow, behind a pair of double doors inscribed "KOMITET GOSUDARSTRENNOY BEZO-PASNOSTI" a senior cipher clerk for the KGB bent closely over a coded message. The message had been picked up by a Soviet fishing trawler in the Caribbean whose sensitive antennae were focused on an ordinary United States telephone satellite orbiting over the Gulf of Mexico. So sensitive was this antenna system that individual calls could be recorded, one picked out of thousands, isolated, preserved for analysis. It was a cosmic phone-tapping service, and anyone clever enough could use it. The particular message that was being received in Moscow on Friday had been phoned on Thursday morning, Texas time. From the headquarters of Revere Oil to the Secretary of State of the United States. Both Revere and the State Department were under continual surveillance by various USSR satellite-tracking devices scattered throughout the embassies and consulates in the United States and on fishing boats, freighters, and even submarines.

What Bradboy Shane had said to the Secretary was of the utmost concern to the Soviets. Bradboy was just as worried about retaining his grandfather's oil concessions in Kassan as the Soviets were about getting the Kassanian reserves for themselves. The message was terse, even brutal: Hardy Leighton was to get off his damn-fool ass and figure out what's really going on among those damn sand-nigger Arabs, or Bradboy would have his head on a hotplate. The Secretary of State's reply was quiet to the point of inaudibility, but Moscow definitely got the message.

And the message was that the stakes would soon be getting higher in Kassan. With just a little more than three weeks before the negotiations were to begin, any action that Kurakin might be contemplating had best be speeded up. Speeded up a lot. Before an hour had passed, urgent cable messages were lighting up the switchboard in the Soviet embassy in Kassan.

In Texas, Bradboy Shane fumed and blustered. If he couldn't bribe his way into a concession, he wasn't sure how to handle it. And the Panther Throne, unlike others he could mention, was definitely not for sale. That had been determined by Bradboy's own Grandpappy, the legendary Sam Revere, fifteen years ago. The new negotiations would be just that—a very sophisticated kind of auction in which all kinds of collateral considerations would come into play, aside from just money. Bradboy didn't fancy himself in some battle of wits with any greaseball A-rab who'd probably slit your throat soon as look as you, and make a side bet with the Japs how far it'd spurt. Bradboy preferred to ease his way into a situation, greasing the skids with plenty of untraceable dollars. Buy a senator here, a newspaper there, oiling this palm, polishing that apple. That was what made the world go round. His world, anyway.

Grudgingly, hating to admit it, Bradboy was deeply grateful he had a man like T. R. Kalbfleisch to be out in the field for him. T.R. knew all the smooth words, college-boy words, knew all the right moves, too. Knew his way around Washington, Paris, Kuwait, you name it. Only, he didn't seem to know shit about Kassan, and that's why Bradboy was putting on the pressure. Hard.

Bradboy clenched his fat fists as his secretary buzzed T. R. Kalbfleisch into the huge corner office.

T.R. was fifth-generation Texas, which was only a little better than having arrived in Massachusetts before the *Mayflower*. Tall and lean as a whip, T.R. looked like the cowboy he was not. Tanned and fit, his skin was smooth at fifty, his formerly blond hair going white at the temples. From his impassive face shone two eyes of a disconcerting shade of turquoise. The suit and the shirt were British and specially made, as were T.R.'s Italian shoes and German sports car. T.R. was Revere's executive vice-president in charge of international operations. That meant the whole world, from the China Sea to Finland, and T.R. roamed it like the wind. The title was deliberately vague. What T.R. was charged with was to shoot trouble dead in its tracks. If he got results, no questions would be asked about how.

Unlike his rougher-hewn ancestors, T.R.'s weapons were not bowie knives or Colt repeaters. T.R. was armed with wealth and influence and an undetectable slush fund for special operations.

His discretionary powers were immense. His track record would have astonished the industry, had it been known. Had it been known, T.R. might have been forced to take up permanent residence in Costa Rica or one of the other exile-ridden places whose main industry was maintaining flexible extradition laws.

T.R. had underwritten more than one coup. He had helped quell revolutions in certain oil-rich nations. More than once he had procured oil and gas concessions by the simple expedient of arriving at some official's hotel suite in Zurich with a large suitcase of thousand-dollar bills.

Bradboy looked at his visitor. "Kassan," he said, glowering.

"October 5—I'll be there."

"You fucked up, T.R." It gave Bradboy no pleasure to say this, although he usually enjoyed chewing out one of his vassals. "Less than three weeks till the damn negotiations, and the place is fit to blow up, crawlin' with revolutionaries, for God's sake, and what in hell are you doin' about it?"

His face made raw beets pale by comparison.

T.R. paused for a moment, wondering if it might really happen. If Bradboy Shane might not actually be giving himself the stroke he was conspicuously in line for. No such luck.

"What are you talking about, Bradboy?"

That stopped Shane for a moment. He knew how valuable T.R. was to Revere Oil, knew that there wasn't another man on the scene who could do what T.R. did so effortlessly. Bradboy knew also, if it ever came to that, that T.R. Kalbfleisch could blow a whistle on Revere Oil that would be heard around the world. Bradboy forced his beefy face into a grin.

"Shucks, T.R., I'm just teasin'. But we've got our hands full this time, see if we don't. There are funny things going on in Kassan. I hear it from our geologists, I hear it from State—though they don't seem to know damnall, either. Do you have anyone on the scene?"

"An agent in place, Bradboy? No. We have a very full dossier on Kassan. You know we can't buy the concession—that'd be easy. We have to approach the old king with our offer—and make sure it's better than anyone else's offer. The rules haven't changed since the last time. It's just that the competition's getting hungrier after Iran, Iraq, after all the other uncertainties out there."

"T.R., you listen, now: I want to know what's happening in that camel graveyard minute by minute until we negotiate. If you have to camp out underneath the goddamn Panther Throne itself, that's fine. I want to know when old King Nayif shits, and what color. And if there is anything to these stories about some kind of a Castro feller out in the boonies, let's be sure about him, too. Look what Armand Hammer pulled off with that Gaddafi. Maybe we ought to get this bandit on our side, just in case he wins. I want you to go all-out, T.R. Mount an operation that'll make that business in Caracas last year look like the goddamned Girl Scout jamboree. And let's do it pronto, hear?"

"How could we not?" said T.R. with a thin smile. "I think you're overreacting, Bradboy. All we need—to be absolutely certain—is an unlimited top line. Or the license to make our deal more flexible than anyone else'll dare make it. I think we need the Kassanian rights badly. And, what the hell, we can always sell off if we have to."

"Sold."

T.R. smiled more broadly now. It was going to be fun. "I'll be in Kassan by this time tomorrow. And we'll see."

"Bet your ass we'll see. We'll see Wadi Darr and we'll see Revere's brand on it for a long, long time."

"I'll be in touch, Bradboy."

"Do that." He paused. "Ain't no damned sand-nigger gonna get the best of old Bradboy, hear?"

T.R. walked out of the huge office without hurrying. He

wouldn't give Bradboy the pleasure. When people asked him why he put up with Bradboy, T.R. found it hard to answer. It boiled down to liking his job enough to put up with the bullying, the ignorance, the two-bit sadism that Bradboy practiced in the way of human relations. Bradboy's very insecurities meant more real power for T.R. And T.R. liked that very much, the sense of being able to make things happen.

He walked into the reception room of his office, smiled graciously at his secretary, entered the inner sanctum, and poured himself a fresh cup of coffee from the Georgian silver pot that was kept forever brimming on a discreet little hot tray on the bar.

Then T.R. picked up the phone and dialed a number in Virginia. The phone was answered on the first ring. It always was. The number T.R. had dialed was that of a relaying station of the Central Intelligence Agency. He identified himself and said the name of the man he was calling. There was a clicking and a buzzing, and then another telephone rang. And rang. It was picked up on the fourth ring.

A familiar voice repeated the number.

"Ross? T.R. here. How's Laura . . . and the kids?"

9

Jeb had been to Williamsburg several times before, but it always had a happy effect on him. The proportions of those noble old houses were so very right. It must have been an instinct, an inherent grace. A grace, God knew, that had been easily lost a hundred and some years later when the Victorians bloated, draped, and darkened their buildings out of any hope for poise or comfort.

But he'd had only a few hours to appreciate the atmosphere of the colonial capital. A message in his mailbox on arrival had informed Jeb that a Mr. Hindley would call for him at eight-thirty the next morning.

It had all seemed a little mysterious in the first place. Why Williamsburg, of all places?

The next day it became very clear.

Jeb dressed casually: an old tweed jacket, gray flannels, button-down shirt, knit Shetland tie. The young man who greeted him was even more casual. Ross Hindley might have been an undergraduate at any of the better universities. He was taller than Jeb, Lanky, sandy hair worn quite long, level gaze through hazel eyes, easy smile. He wore a down vest over a lumberman's woolen shirt and blue jeans over worn cowboy boots. A black Jeep was waiting at the door, its top down in the bright blue morning, its black roll-bar gleaming.

"Mr. Cleaver?" Ross grinned, extended his hand.

"Hindley. Good to meet you." Jeb almost added "son." In a minute they were moving past the Governor's Palace, heading out through the ripening autumn fields of northern Virginia. It was hard to talk in the open car, and Jeb didn't try. Eventually, after driving about twelve miles, mostly on back roads, they came to a long chain-link fence topped with six forbidding strands of barbed wire. It was definitely a fence to keep people out, not to contain cattle. Hindley skirted the fence for nearly a mile, then stopped and jumped down to open a padlocked gate.

Hindley drove the Jeep through the gate, stopped again, and locked it. Jeb began to get the picture. But still he was mystified. *What the hell was going on up here that they had to be so damned careful about?*

"We call it," said Hindley casually, "the farm."

Maybe it had been a farm once. Jeb couldn't begin to guess the acreage, but there must be hundreds. The drive was long, winding, and paved with blacktop. They passed a few low buildings of recent construction: cinder blocks painted pea-soup green. Camouflage? At last Hindley pulled into a compound. There were three much larger cinder-block structures, one of them three stories tall. They all had a bare, utilitarian look. Keep the rain out, and that was about it as far as style went. They might have been storage sheds, prisons, anything.

Hindley took him to the largest of the three buildings. Jeb was fingerprinted, photographed, and given a pass. The pass was laminated with the color Polaroid of Jeb's face, his right thumbprint, a serial number, and his signature.

"I feel," he said, "as though I've just enlisted in something."

Hindley laughed. "Not at all. This is a top-secret compound, that's all, and the pass and the privacy really just make the briefings easier once we start."

"I can't run away, for instance," said Jeb, wondering for the dozenth time that morning precisely what it was he'd gotten himself into.

"Long walk back to the Inn, I can tell you—I've done it."

Hindley didn't say why. They walked along a corridor now, long and narrow and punctuated by dark green steel-plated doors. The whole place had a bunker feeling to it, an institutional sort of heaviness. It seemed to have been constructed to withstand anything. Jeb wondered why. The doors, he noticed, were numbered.

When they came to number twenty-three, Hindley opened it and held the door while Jeb walked in. It was a small conference room: blackboards on two sides, a table for perhaps a dozen in the middle. There was an easel with a big pad of blank paper on it and a small Betamax with a large television set next to it. Sitting at the far end of the table was a large professorial-looking man. His name was James Gordon and Hindley introduced him as their Middle Eastern expert. Who "they" were wasn't mentioned. Jeb didn't ask.

Gordon and Hindley weren't really a team, although it appeared that the two of them would be solely responsible for Jeb's briefing. Gordon was more than a bit of a pedant, in contrast to Hindley's easygoing charm. And there was a thin knife edge of antagonism between the two. Some inter-service rivalry? Hindley had a way of poking fun at the older man that irritated Gordon. There was no way for Jeb to guess who was actually in control here, but if he'd been betting, his bet would have been on Hindley.

There was a thermos of weak coffee and plastic mugs. The briefings began right away, and for Jeb they were a revelation.

With a shuddering jolt he realized how ignorant he was of the Middle East, of Islam, of the history and politics of that part of the world.

It was so easy to have a mental picture of a dark-skinned Arab in his desert robes, mysterious and faintly sinister, probably with a hundred wives back in the harem somewhere, scheming and conniving to destroy the economy of the suddenly OPEC-dominated world. This was the Middle East of sensational headlines and political cartoonists, a place of dark superstitions and primitive fears.

Part of it had to be true. How else could you explain Iran, or the fundamentalists who killed Sadat?

Jeb learned for the first time of the differences between the orthodox Sunni Islam and the more fanatical Shia sect that had spawned Khomeini and the other fearsome ayatollahs.

Jeb's picture of the oil countries had been based on a casual acceptance of the fairy-tale riches of Kuwait, Kassan, and Saudi Arabia. It came as a shock to discover that these were among the last of the Arab monarchies, that the Arab Revolution was much more than just a catch phrase, that for a generation the old kingdoms, sheikhdoms, and emirates had been tumbling, tumbling down like so many dominoes. Iraq, Egypt, Libya, Yemen, Iran—the list went on.

"Saudia Arabia is like one of those balanced rocks," said James Gordon. "Top-heavy and trembling in every breeze. Just looking to come crashing down. It's no wonder they're nervous. They have every reason to be. As do the El Kheybar. Only, among the El Kheybar, the message doesn't seem to have sunk in yet."

This made Jeb think of Selim. He must write—no, cable!—and tonight. Tell the old Panther he was coming. Maybe he'd call Megan tonight, too.

It was just as he was thinking about her that Jeb realized he didn't even have her home phone number. Some romance.

The briefing went on. And on. Jeb's head was spinning by the time they broke for lunch. Lunch was brought to them on a wheeled tray: a surprisingly delicious assortment of delicatessen—potato salad, cucumber salad, three kinds of sandwiches—and a choice of beer or soft drinks. They ate, and when they'd finished, Hindley suggested a bit of fresh air.

It was a good idea. Jeb felt suffocated in the little room. Even though none of them smoked, it was stuffy. Hindley showed him the men's room, then they spent half an hour exploring the gently rolling landscape. Now and then, from a distance, came the sounds of gunfire.

"The rifle range," said Hindley. "In a day or so we'll fit you out with some sort of a handgun. Do you have any preferences?"

"Yes," said Jeb. "Not to have one. What makes anyone think I'll need a gun?" Jeb had shot hunting rifles, although he didn't enjoy hunting. Once, an old Army .45 handgun had practically kicked his arm out of joint. "If I had a pistol, I'd shoot myself before I got to the bad guys," he said, smiling. Smiling but apprehensive. It had all seemed so easy back among the wine and antique furniture in the Secretary of State's offices.

Hindley shrugged, as though it wasn't a subject of any great interest. "Thought you might want one. There are rebels, you know, in Kassan. It hasn't erupted yet—we hope it won't. Not like Iran or anything. But it might be handy—you never know."

Hasn't erupted, thought Jeb. *Yet.*

The air felt good in his lungs even if there were a million doubts and apprehensions floating through it. Soon enough they were back in the cinder-block building, hearing James Gordon drone on and on. At four-thirty they knocked off. Gordon provided Jeb with a small tape player and several Arabic cassettes.

"Just so you'll be a little familiar with it," he said. Jeb promised to practice that very night, and Hindley drove him back. The autumn twilight had bred a chill. The sun was just beginning to set behind the golden cornfields.

The trip back seemed quicker than it had on the way out. Hindley, as before, said very little. He stopped in front of the Inn and politely declined Jeb's offer of a drink.

"Same time tomorrow?"

"I'll be here," said Jeb, wondering just how much of this they expected him to absorb. And why.

He went upstairs, showered, phoned a reservation for one at eight o'clock in the dining room, and flicked on the little tape deck. The machine whirred softly. "Ana mistanni mukalma tilifun-i-ya," it said. Then, in English: "I am waiting for a telephone call." Then, again, the Arabic: "Ana mistanni mukalmo tilifun-i-ya."

Jeb grinned and dived into it. Made his own recording of the set phrases, played them back, erased, started again. In about ten years of day-and-night practice, he decided, he might be able to order a glass of water or ask where the exit was. After half an hour of that Jeb had just about decided to talk a walk through the village when the phone rang.

"Jeb?" Her voice was unmistakable. If he didn't have Megan's number, she sure had his.

"Megan! How are you? Where are you?"

"Downstairs. Can INTERTEL buy you a drink?"

"I'll be there in one minute."

He was. Megan looked lovely. Dark gray suit, ivory silk blouse, that hair and that smile. They kissed, lightly but not so lightly Jeb couldn't feel the electricity of it running down to his toes. They walked into the dimly lighted bar.

"I was in Washington for the afternoon," she said simply, "and there happened to be a plane to Richmond."

"Thank God."

The waiter came: Megan ordered her usual club soda. Jeb asked for sherry. Seven-thirty. Jeb was wondering about room service when her question hit him.

"You never told me your old roommate just happens to be the Crown Prince of Kassan."

He tried to pass it off lightly. "You never told me about your old roommate, either. What's that got to do with anything?"

"It's just something I happened to discover today while poking around the State Department. Someone just mentioned it. It made me wonder. In my line of work you get to do a lot of wondering, Jeb."

"And what did you wonder?"

Jeb had a feeling he wasn't going to like her answer.

"I wonder if you're leveling with me. I wonder what's really behind this embassy assignment? That's stretching coincidence pretty far, wouldn't you say?"

"I wouldn't, but I guess other people might. It's a free country. Any number can play guessing games. What does it matter who my roommate was?"

"You still see him?"

"From time to time. Maybe once in two or three years. He's busy. The crown-prince business is fairly demanding, and so is architecture. I like Selim, Megan—he's a friend."

The waiter returned with their drinks.

For the first time since he'd met her, Jeb felt uncomfortable with Megan. Some hot, probing curiosity was driving her into places that would be better left alone. Jeb liked her a lot. He wanted her. But not if she'd be forever questioning him, poking her lovely nose into every nook and cranny of his life. But Megan wouldn't let go.

"Did Leighton put it on the line for you, Jeb? Did he spell out exactly why you were chosen for this particular assignment?"

He looked at her, wondering why all that delicious beauty had to come wrapped in the barbed wire of these prickly questions.

"They had checked me out—naturally. Made sure I wouldn't steal the silver. They knew about Harvard, about Selim. Hell, they probably knew what brand of underwear I was wearing. They are nothing if not thorough."

"You're not answering me. Can't you see it's important, Jeb?"

"Can't you see it's a little bit—maybe more than a little bit—offensive to me when I get accused of . . . whatever it is you're accusing me of?"

She looked down at her drink for just a moment; then her eyes met his.

"Jeb," she said softly, "I hope you know the last thing I want is to make you angry. I mean, that really isn't why I came up here. It's just that . . . well, I am used to digging. It's in me—I can't help it. Don't want to. And when that guy spilled all this stuff on me this afternoon, I . . . well, it just seemed funny, that's all."

"Ha ha." Jeb took a decisive drink of his sherry, finishing it off. "I have an idea," he said. "Let's go eat. I am starving."

Megan had never been to Williamsburg before. He promised to take her sightseeing after supper. She mentioned that she had a car and a driver waiting. That she had to be back late tonight to be at work in the morning.

"We're leaving on the fifteenth."

"So you're determined to go through with it."

"Absolutely. Why wouldn't I?"

Jeb scanned the menu and put it aside.

"What looks good to you? I'll have its cousin, to match up with the wine."

She read: "Gooseberry fool. Just the way I feel sometimes. I'll have Thomas Jefferson's woodcock, whatever that is."

Jeb ordered duck and a California Cabernet Sauvignon.

"It might be dangerous out there, Megan."

"Is that what the CIA told you in their briefing today?"

Jeb sat back and just stared at her. He had guessed that's what the secret farm was all about, but no one had spelled it out for him.

"CIA?"

"Has to be, Jeb. Williamsburg's famous for it—that farm, as they call it, up in the hills. That's one of their main debriefing places. When someone important defects, he's whizzed up there—or to another one they have on the West Coast. There are others—I'm not sure where."

"You just don't miss a trick, do you?"

"It comes with the territory, Jeb. I've got to know these

things. Where people go. What they do. And why. Always, why."

"Why?"

"To get the facts straight. Put the puzzle together for my viewers, who may not have access—or the time or the interest—to the raw information so they could do it themselves."

"There's no such thing as raw information."

"Maybe not." She fiddled with a fork. "Jeb, why so hostile? You sound like a guy who's been—maybe—put up to doing something he really doesn't want to do."

"I want it very much. My first embassy, after all. And to see the old Panther—Selim."

"Did they lay a little something extra on you—a secondary assignment, so to speak?"

"That's really offensive, Megan. I'm amazed you don't understand that. What you're implying."

"Sorry if I touched a sore spot. Look, Jeb Stuart Cleaver. I truly didn't take the time to drag myself up here for any reason except I like you a lot. I have a hunch that forces you don't even know exist are maybe playing games with you—dangerous games at that. It's only a hunch, mind you. But my hunches have a way of coming true. Now—again with apologies—I think we'd better continue this some other time. In Kassan, maybe."

She was already out of her chair and walking across the big dining room. Jeb got up and went after her. But Megan was just a beat too fast. A big Cadillac limousine was waiting for her at the front door. She was in the back of it and locking the door by the time he caught up. The car moved smoothly away into the September night.

"Megan!" Shouting like a damn-fool schoolboy.

Jeb stood in the drive for a long time, watching the red taillights melt into the darkness. Then he turned and went into the Inn. His duck was waiting. Jeb ate it all, and one of Megan's woodcocks, and got through nearly all the wine.

And when it was all over, he still felt empty.

The next morning, after a night with very little sleep in it, Jeb asked Hindley straight out. "You guys are CIA, right?"

Hindley looked at him and grinned. "Right on. Of course, we don't exactly wear funny T-shirts that say that."

"No. You wouldn't."

"Does it matter? Has our sinister reputation gotten to you, Jeb?" It was "Jeb" and "Rose" now.

"Not at all. It's just that I wasn't sure. Nobody mentioned it, one way or the other."

"Believe it or not, we really are an information service. Thus guys like Gordon. A veritable treasurehouse of information, is our Mr. Gordon. You'll have it coming out of your ears before the week's over."

It was only too true.

Jeb was given a five-day crash course in every possible ramification of the situation swirling around the Panther Throne. Was ASSAD, Israeli intelligence a factor? Very likely—they were certainly a presence everywhere else in that part of the world, as well it behooved them to be. How likely were the Russians to intervene? Very, assuming that things got chaotic to the point where it could be made to look like they were just lending a helping hand. "And that," said Hindley, "is just when we'd jump in, too. With our boots on."

So it went. On the third day, driving back at night, Ross accepted Jeb's invitation for a drink. He ordered beer.

Their talk was easy now: the concentrated presence of three days, all day long, enforced togetherness, had formed a bond. As he drank the last of his beer and refused another, Hindley said, "By the way, Laura and I would like it if you could come up for dinner Friday. It being your last day and all."

"I'd like that very much—and thanks."

It was the first indication he'd had that Hindley was married—if the mysterious Laura was in fact Mrs. Hindley. But Jeb felt very good about the invitation all the same. As though he'd passed a test.

The next day Ross took him to the weapons room. It was impressive in its way—a very up-to-date library of sudden death. Jeb hefted several handguns, being attracted to their design without knowing a thing of their quality or performance. Finally they decided on a Walther short-barrel P38 automatic pistol in dulled black steel.

On the range itself Ross showed Jeb the stance, two hands on the grip, forget Gary Cooper, knee bent for extra bracing, squeeze it off gently, gently. Once he got used to the noise and jolt of it, Jeb managed to hit the target much more often than not. What that said about his responses in a real emergency, he wasn't sure. Still, by the end of the two-hour session he was confident that at least he wouldn't blow himself to pieces loading the thing or firing it. In a creepy way, there was something therapeutic about squeezing off all those rounds. Took his mind off Megan. More or less.

If she could see me now, he thought, *her worst suspicions would be confirmed. CIA trains yet another cold-blooded killer.*

Jeb had called INTERTEL headquarters last night on the odd chance she might be working late. He got the night receptionist, and she had no idea where Miss Mcguire might be reached, but volunteered to take a message. How many messages must someone like Megan get in a day, most of them from crackpot fans?

On Friday, after saying good-bye to James Gordon and feeling an enormous weight lifted from his psyche at the thought of never having to be briefed by that particular pedant again, Jeb was dropped off at the Inn by Hindley at five-thirty with the promise to pick him up again in an hour.

Flowers or wine? Jeb asked himself that in the shower and set off shopping soon afterward. Probably, in the country, they'd grow flowers. He opted for wine in the surprisingly well-stocked mock-eighteenth-century wineshop. Passing right by the Calon-Segur that reminded him of Megan, Jeb chose something even fancier—Cheval Blanc 1964. He had it wrapped as a gift and got back just in time to meet Hindley.

"Laura," said Ross, unprompted, as they drove through the town, "knows fundamentally what I do, and what you're going to do. I mean, unless we all marry deaf-mutes or something, there has to be a level of understanding. She might not believe me as the Good Humor Man."

"There are secrets in every business. At certain levels—designing a factory, say—even I get into areas that my clients are anxious to keep secret."

They drove in silence then, moving uphill until at last they were high enough to catch the final glimmering rays of sunset. Hindley's house was astonishing. It stood on the highest hilltop, facing west to the sunset. The house was approached by a winding drive that moved uphill through clumps of white birch and mountain laurel. It was an ancient white clapboard farmhouse that had been added to and added to again over the years until it sprawled generously across the rise, all angles, ells, juts, and corners. Somone had unified the many nooks and angles with a large terrance made from old brick. This terrace embraced the house, wrapping around it from the western facade to the barn behind the kitchen. There they parked the Jeep.

Laura Hindley was waiting, tall, slim, and lovely. Dark as Ross was fair, she looked like someone out of a legend. A very nice legend. Hindley kissed her as though they'd been parted for weeks. Flushing a little—but loving it—she turned to Jeb.

"Welcome, Jeb Cleaver," she said, smiling, extending her hand. Jeb felt like kissing it but decided that would be silly. He handed Laura the wine, for which she thanked him, putting it aside unopened.

Ross took drink orders: white wine for Laura, sherry for Jeb, club soda for himself. While he made the drinks, she took Jeb on a brief tour of the downstairs. Some of the old rooms had been opened up, tiny chambers fused into large ones. The work had been done with such care and imagination that the feeling of the original structure was retained and probably even enhanced. The floors were period, of old hand-hewn black walnut. The walls were painted a pale ivory, the ceilings white punctuated by huge chestnut beams. The windows, twelve panes over twelve, retained much of their original wavy handmade glass. The furnishings were appropriately simple: fine old country pieces mixed with comfortable overstuffed sofas and armchairs. On the floor of the living room was a spectacular old petit-point rug with a design of wildflowers. Brass gleamed from the mellow brick fireplaces. Someone had taste, and the money to exercise it.

Ross served drinks on the terrace. They spoke easily about nothing in particular as the last slivers of pink and gold vanished behind the distant Blue Ridge Mountains. Suddenly a large golden retriever came bounding from the kitchen, followed by the slamming of the screen door and small, rapid footsteps.

"Oh, God," said Hindley, "the monsters are loose."

Two identical twin boys came toddling across the terrace with cries of glee and greeting for their father. Tiny Hindleys. Hair so blond it was nearly white, eager smiles, merry laughter. They were three years old.

"Okay, monsters, meet our guest. Jeb, this is Larry Hindley and his clone, Lloyd, also Hindley. Shake hands, turkeys."

The boys marched formally up to Jeb's chair and—as one—extended their right hands with the formality of Renaissance princelings.

"They're amazing," said Jeb, meaning it, thinking of his own broken marriage, of the children he might never have.

"Mmm," said Laura, "sometimes a bit too amazing." The twins ran to the end of the terrace, where they played with the dog. The evening continued on a light, delightful plane. Nothing like business was discussed. Laura cooked superbly. Gazpacho featuring home-grown tomatoes and cucumbers, followed by native pheasant in its own juices enhanced with cream and cognac. With the bird they drank Jeb's Cheval Blanc—an ideal complement.

Kassan seemed very far away, and Megan farther.

For dessert they ate peaches from the Hindley orchard. They spoke of architecture, books, theater, music. Finally it was nearly midnight. With real reluctance, Jeb said he'd better be getting back.

"Take care," said Laura, saying good-bye on the terrace, backlit by the light from the kitchen door. "I hope we meet again."

"So do I," said Jeb, taking her hand.

The Jeep growled off into the night. Jeb looked up at the stars, American stars under an American sky. He remembered how close the stars had seemed in Kassan, twenty-one years ago. Would they have grown smaller in the meantime? Jeb wondered what his chances were of finding a woman like Laura, of having a home and kids as fine and as happy as what he'd just left.

They pulled up at the Inn. Ross declined a drink. *I wouldn't linger either*, thought Jeb, *if I had someone like Laura waiting*.

Hindley looked even more like a college boy now, his hair tousled by the Jeep ride. A slant of light from the Inn caught his smile. "Your contact over there'll be the chargé d'affaires: man named Lawrence. Take care, Jeb. We'll be in touch. And thanks. In advance."

"Thank you, and Laura," said Jeb, climbing out, then reaching back to shake hands.

Hindley was gone in a roar. Jeb turned and walked slowly into the Inn. The air was chill now, but it was nothing compared to the chill inside him.

Jeb felt about a thousand years old. Alone.

And afraid.

10

In all the world there were only three people who could summon General Bir-Saraband and be confident that he would obey. Grudgingly, counting the hours until he occupied the Panther Throne himself, Ibn still went through the necessary motions of obedience to his king, and in Nayif's absence, to Selim. The other member of this illustrious trio was the notorious prostitute Theodora.

He wondered why she'd used the secret telephone line that connected the most famous brothel in Kassan directly to his office at ADDAK just two blocks away. The phone line wasn't the only secret connection between the two buildings. ADDAK engineers had tunneled the distance to create a passage that led from the subcellar at ADDAK to the basement of Theodora's house. He was walking through that dimly lighted tunnel now, and his mind was struggling to deal with many problems.

The grenade attack on the king's majlis had startled Ibn to his shoes. They could go anywhere, these people, and do anything! And the blame, of course, had fallen on him. On ADDAK. On their failure to capture the rebel Al Khadir. Ibn still flushed with anger and embarrassment at the memory of his interview with the king. Selim, of course, had insisted on being there. The king himself was fearless, but it angered him that innocent people had died trying to seek the king's justice. From now on there would be no more majlis in the open. It would be held in the throne room instead, and every suppliant would be searched. Selim had even suggested purchasing one of the metal detectors that airports use to screen boarding passengers.

At least the attack hadn't dissuaded the king from going on his hunting trip. And, not for the first time, Nayif had brushed aside as silly his son's suggestion to bring an armed guard into the desert. He was an old man with strong convictions, and one of them seemed to be that he was immortal.

So much the better! It played perfectly into Ibn's plans. In the meantime, there were new security measures to be imposed in Port Kassan. The old palace must have its guard redoubled. No longer would the casual comings and goings be permitted. The old men of the souk would have to find someplace else to use as a club, a forum, a place to haggle and gossip.

It was ironic, for such measures were among Ibn's plans for changes to be made when he pulled off his coup. But Ibn was in no mood for irony or any other sort of analytical reflection.

The time had come to put his plan into action, and every atom of energy and craft in him was directed toward that goal. There was no time to waste. Things were moving faster than Ibn had expected. And there was a new element. The American architect Cleaver.

Only yesterday had the ambassador mentioned Cleaver. That he had been a school friend of Selim's. That he was arriving this week in Kassan to build the new American embassy. The ambassador accepted this at face value.

But Ibn sensed there must be more to it than that.

This intruder might well be bearing some secret message for the king. Something that couldn't be entrusted to normal diplomatic channels. Something dangerous for the plans of Ibn Bir-Saraband.

Because of the way he conducted his own life and political career, Ibn was deeply suspicious of everyone around him. Only Theodora could be trusted absolutely. But that was another story, a story that went back a long, long time.

Bir-Saraband had discovered her more than twenty years ago in a Beirut brothel. For a week he visited her every night. Theodora had been fourteen then, and magnificent. She had no idea who her parents were or where she came from. Racially she must be a mixture: skin the color of café au lait; enormous dark eyes with an almost Oriental slant at the corners; wide, generous, sometimes mocking lips. She seemed to have some ancestral knowledge of lovemaking, for her skills were so far beyond her years that Ibn was dazzled. He had been an irrepressible womanizer since his teens, but Theodora was a revelation. An addiction. She was the first woman he had ever met who could exhaust him in bed and be ready for more.

Typically, he looked for a way to profit from this unexpected pleasure.

Typically, he found one.

When he left Beirut, Ibn brought her with him to Port Kassan. There he installed her in one of many private apartments maintained by the secret police for assignations, inquisitions, and convenience. After a year of erotic adventures that transcended even his most lustful imaginings, Bir-Saraband had a stroke of inspiration.

He conceived the Garden of Five Thousand Delights.

It was to be a brothel on a scale that Port Kassan had never known. Luxurious, discreet, providing every illicit pleasure from girls to boys to gambling and alcohol, the Garden would be a nirvana of sensuous pleasures.

More important, it would be a source of both information and blackmail for ADDAK.

Every room would be wired for sound. Some would be equipped with hidden cameras that could be triggered discreetly by the prostitute using the room.

It worked magnificently.

Perhaps the reason Theodora's brothel worked so effectively as a catalyst for blackmail was the rigidly repressive sexual morality of Islam. In twenty years ADDAK had accumulated a file of tapes and pictures that could have toppled half the governments of Islam and generated an interesting amount of leverage in the world of international diplomacy.

Yet outside of his concern with the internal security of Kassan, Ibn had never called in even one of these markers.

He was waiting for the moment when they would do him the maximum good. That moment was coming very soon—the day he seized the Panther Throne of Kassan. Who would dare question his right to rule in Kassan when such evidence was securely stored away in vaults beneath ADDAK, in a secret closet in Ibn's own palace, and for the ultimate security, in a safe-deposit vault in Zurich?

He smiled at the thought of all that uncollected influence.

The tunnel was something more than two city blocks long. Now he was at the end of it, in the cellar under the Garden of Five Thousand Delights. Like ADDAK, this complex had been expertly cobbled together from several old houses. It faced on the Street of the Ironmongers and the main structure had indeed been the shop and residence of a prosperous hardware maker of the last century, who would spin in his grave if he could witness the scandalous goings-on today!

Ibn opened the combination lock on the heavy door, knowing as he did so that a small red light would begin flashing up in Theodora's living quarters on the top floor of the house.

Just inside the basement door was a small elevator.

Theodora might want him for any number of reasons, and busy as he was, Ibn knew her too well to refuse her call. He was surely going to benefit from this visit, although in what way, he had no idea.

Maybe she had a new girl for him. The fires of sexual passion had cooled between Ibn and Theodora, but she continued to assuage his wants with the youngest and prettiest of her discoveries. Ibn liked them young. Virgins if possible. Slender little wild things waiting to be tamed. Broken.

The orphanages of which Prince Selim was so proud served Theodora's house well. Every six months or so she would make a tour in company with the general. Heavily veiled, the perfect Muslim wife, Theodora would look at the children as they played, in their classrooms. Every once in a while she would tug at Ibn's sleeve and whisper: "That one!"

Her eye was unerring, honed as it had been in the fight for mere survival in the slums of Beirut. Almost always, her selections went on to a lucrative career at the Garden. Mostly she chose young girls, sometimes boys.

The elevator had been built with discretion in mind. It carried him silently up to the fourth floor of the Garden and there opened directly into Theodora's suite.

Theo had put on weight over the years. Still, her face had the power to bedazzle Ibn. She was waiting, as usual, with a steaming cup of her special mint tea. Ibn smiled. It was more like home to him here than in his own immense palace in the desert.

He kissed her on the cheeks.

"Well, my dear?" he asked, settling into an overstuffed armchair.

Theo sipped her tea.

"It was not an emergency, but merely a discovery that might prove useful to my general." She always called him that. My general. Theodora's voice was liquid, a curious mixture of Middle Eastern accents that was neither Lebanese nor Kassanian but a spicy blend sometimes peppered with glinting obscenities in seaman's French, U.S. Marine Corps English, or tourist German.

"I have someone you ought to see," she said gently. Her style was always deferential on the surface and irreverent below.

"How old is she?" asked Ibn, wondering if he really had the time.

Theo smiled at his assumption. "He," she said, "is perhaps thirteen. And as old as time. You will see."

Ibn frowned. She knew perfectly well his tastes did not run in that direction. But Theodora beckoned for him to follow, and follow her he did. Down the familiar deeply carpeted stairs, around a corner, and down a long hallway. This corridor was for voyeurs, for people whose pleasure came from watching others having sex. The hallway was lined with sliding panels that gave onto various of the Garden's more exotic bedrooms through two-way mirrors: from the prostitutes' point of view a mirror, from the corridor a window.

She motioned him to an upholstered bench. He sat. She slid back the panel. The room beyond had been redecorated since the last time Ibn had looked at it. It was a bedroom perhaps twenty feet square, entirely black but for mirrors on the ceiling and on the walls. There was black carpeting wall to wall, and this carpeting also upholstered a wide, low platform on which reposed a large mattress covered in dull black satin. There were hassocks in shiny black leather, and several large pillows, also covered in black. A room of darkness and mystery.

"I have," said Theodora languidly, "made a little experiment. The boy is new with us. The gifts I see in him may be illusory, although I doubt that. There is a power in him that could charm water out of the desert sand. But we shall see. I have told him he must entertain a rather special customer. Karl. You know Karl?"

The general knew Karl by reputation, for Karl had enlivened the files of ADDAK with many a remarkable photograph. Karl was an immense and muscular blond German given to administering the crueler varieties of sadism. He reveled in using whips. Chains amused him. Most of Karl's clients were English, including, on one unforgettable occasion, a former prime minister. Idly, Ibn wondered whether the boy would be able to endure such fierce caresses.

An invisible door opened into the bedroom as they watched. Karl stalked in, naked but for high black leather boots, his thickly muscled body gleaming with oil, and another sort of gleam in his cold blue-green eyes. A dangerous gleam. He carried a pair of handcuffs and a riding crop. In uniform, Karl would have done for a Third Reich recruiting poster.

He strode to the bed and dropped the accessories of his fantasy. Then he began pacing the room, working up a fine frenzy of anger. The impression was of a great jungle beast, caged, pacing, waiting to pounce. The general half-expected Karl to growl.

The door opened again. A simple thing—a door opening. Yet it was a moment Ibn would remember for a long time.

In walked a boy of almost supernatural beauty.

His skin was pale amber, his eyes big and dark, his hair black as night. Like Theo herself, he must be a mixed breed. Bir-Saraband was nothing like homosexual, yet he gasped with wonder. This was the beauty of Greek statues, the grace of legends. His looks almost transcended sex, yet there was about him something distinctly sexual. A challenge and a mystery.

He wore a simple Bedu robe of white cotton.

Karl's back was to the boy as he entered, but some small sound made the older man whirl. Karl stood, hands on hips, a snarl frozen on his arrogant mouth. It was, Ibn knew, a performance. But Karl made it seem all too convincing. To the boy it must have looked terrifyingly real. His reaction was to smile. Slowly.

Karl stood dumbfounded, his rage melting as he saw what manner of creature had come before him.

Then, slowly and with a fluidity that seemed too natural to have been planned, the boy undid the fastenings of his robe and let it fall to the black carpet. His body fulfilled the promise of his face: slender and finely muscled, it was the body of an adolescent boy, but he was genitally a man.

With a simplicity and naturalness that allowed for no fear, the boy walked the few steps that separated him from Karl. Again, he smiled. He reached up with one hand and touched the German on the cheek, lightly, reassuringly. As if to put the great hulking sadist at ease. It was astonishing.

"His name," said Theodora, "is Aziz. I found him tending a donkey in the Street of the Carpenters. He has no family."

"He does now," said Ibn quietly, unable to take his eyes off the scene that was unfolding just beyond the two-way mirror. The drama continued. The huge German was on his knees now, weeping. Pleading—but for what? Soon, the general knew, there would be sex between them. He didn't need to see it. He had seen more than enough already.

"I thought," said Theodora as she closed the panel and left Karl and the boy to their pleasures, "that Aziz might be just the thing for your American."

In the darkness of the secret corridor, Ibn smiled. Indeed the boy would do—spectacularly well. The general was glad of the darkness, of the walk that separated them from Theodora's suite. For the scene he had just witnessed had left him with an enormous, insistent erection.

The boy would be perfect for Wilfred Austin.

For years Ibn had cultivated the American ambassador. One day soon after his appointment to Kassan, the man had made the ludicrous mistake of seeking the comfort of a young boy in the Garden of Five Thousand Delights. Soon after that the general had invited Austin on a hunting trip in the desert. The houseboy serving the ambassador's tent had come from Theodora. And he had been more than compliant. Since then there had been other trips. Other boys.

Ibn had even arranged for the ambassador to happen upon a small, charming, and very low-priced apartment in the old quarter. A place, ostensibly, where the ambassador could go to get away from the rigors of his diplomatic life.

In fact it was an ideal rendezvous for the young boys whom Ibn sent there from time to time with messages. What happened after the delivery of the message depended upon the boy and on Austin. But none of these liaisons had really amounted to anything. What Ibn hoped for was a real entrapment—for the ambassador to actually keep a lover. That would make the leverage of blackmail that much more persuasive when the moment came to use it.

And that moment was approaching faster and faster.

11

Selim stood in the window of his suite in the old palace and looked out over the rooftops of Port Kassan. Usually the view pleased him—it had been his own idea to enlarge the window. But today the prospect was distressing. Every one of those roofs might be hiding a terrorist, a nest of rebels, foreign spies, and only Allah knew what else.

If the grenade that had nearly killed them all yesterday was the work of the People's Army, no one had bothered to claim the credit.

Looking directly below, Selim could see the new barriers. They were a necessary admission of weakness. For as long as anyone could remember, Kassan had been run on the basis of easy access to the king. In theory, at least, any Kassanian could simply walk into the palace, into the king's majlis, and be heard.

Now the fences were going up, the guard doubled: visitors would be searched. And still the rebels ran free. Selim had demanded to be present earlier this morning when King Nayif had asked the general why such an outrage had been possible.

Bir-Saraband had blustered, reminded Nayif how many times he'd asked for more men, a larger budget, better helicopter gunships for desert reconnaissance and combat—only to be denied. And it was true. Nayif had an almost childish disregard for his own safety.

Today, for instance, he was going out falcon hunting for

two weeks or more, unguarded, just as though nothing had happened. And there wasn't one thing Selim could do about it.

The king's word was law, and Nayif was king.

His son and heir seethed with frustration. To pin down his father was like trying to cast a fisherman's net over smoke.

He stood at the window now, overlooking all of Port Kassan, seeing it all and seeing nothing.

Selim was wondering about the rebels. What made a young man—they all must be men—turn so violently against the Panther Throne? Their propaganda was everywhere now. Posters, pamphlets, even graffiti. Especially graffiti. The royal family was corrupt, they said. Bribes and graft were rife in the land. The wealth of Kassanian oil must be equally distributed. And other such nonsense.

The custom of baksheesh was older than Islam. The extra commission that must be paid to assure the smoothness of a transaction. It was not more than tipping a restaurant waiter, yet Westerners pretended to be horrified by the practice. They classified it as bribery, and bribery was quite another matter—although it surely existed in Kassan and elsewhere in the Middle East. But the dealers' commissions were sacred, part of the deal. The fact that King Nayif had given all the most lucrative ministries and other points of contact to his relatives was no more than standard practice as well. So was it done in Saudi Arabia, so had it been done in Iran, so would it be done until the end of time. Once the revolutionaries gained power, they did it too. Quietly but inevitably the uncle of Mrs. Revolutionary's first cousin found himself in some position of unexpected influence. The old tale all over again. And what was gained but a changing of places—and definitely not always for the better?

He sighed.

There, far below, Selim could see his father's limousine pulling out of the Portal of the Dawn. King Nayif didn't know it, but Selim had arranged that a contingent of plainclothes army men would track the king's progress in an unmarked car. At least as far as the first stop, where they would all mount camels and vanish into the desert for nobody knew quite how long. Ibn had listened attentively to Selim's suggestions on this matter, and promised to follow them to the letter.

Now, watching the great black Daimler moving slowly through the newly erected barrier at the main gate, Selim wondered if he shouldn't have gone down himself. Nayif wouldn't even have a two-way radio in his hunting camp. He wanted to go back. To recede in time, to return to a simpler, better way of living.

At least King Nayif thought it was better.

Selim recalled the falcon-hunting trips of his boyhood. What adventures they had! The thrill of being allowed out with the men, learning to shoot, staying up very late to hear the tall tales by the campfire, eating with eager fingers the birds their falcons had taken that same day. How good everything tasted then.

But now it had all changed. Selim knew he could never be that boy again, nor would he try. In a way, he envied his father the ability to slip in and out of that long-lost world. Maybe old Nayif had never left it. Maybe it was the present that lacked reality for the old man. The past was safe, a comforting world with fixed rules and people who obeyed them without question.

A world with no Bandar Al Khadir in it, with no raids, grenades, posters, accusations. And no oil.

Maybe there were inequalities in Kassan. But surely there was good, too. On paper, at least, no Kassanian was without access to food, education, medicine.

Even as these thoughts gathered in his mind, Selim knew that his confidence in the progress Kassan had made was false. Yes, there were showpiece schools, hospitals, and even rural clinics. But show was the sum of it. Uncounted thousands of Kassanian children couldn't read or write. In fact, "uncounted" said it all. No one but God himself knew how many people there were in Kassan. Even in a place as advanced as Saudi Arabia there was no reliable census. In Kassan, with its shifting Bedu population, such a fixed, immutable thing was impossible.

Tell that to an American and you'd get disbelief in return. Tell it to a Briton and you'd see a patronizing smile. The smile of one who'd known all along that the bloody wogs couldn't begin to manage themselves.

And it was all crumbling, pulling apart.

At that moment the young man who served as Selim's private secretary came in with a tray of mail. Selim flipped through it almost idly. There was the expected pile of embassy invitations, solicitations from charity groups and aspiring Kassanian businessmen, a note from the Roman jeweler Bulgari about a ruby bracelet he had ordered for Fawzia as a surprise. And there, near the bottom of the heap and all the more welcome for being entirely unexpected, a note from Jeb Cleaver. It was brief, typical Cleaver:

> Dear Panther,
>
> Kassan is about to have a long-term visitor. The United States Department of State has asked me to design a new embassy for Port Kassan. I'm arriving on the fifteenth to make preliminary surveys and to work up some concepts. I hope you'll be in town, Panther. I've missed you.
>
> > Love to Fawzia and the small panthers,
>
> > Jeb

Selim was delighted. How little Jeb Cleaver could guess, with his busy, successful life, the depths of boredom and frustration to which his old friend had sunk.

Wouldn't it be fine to have Jeb right here in Kassan—in this room!—bouncing ideas back and forth again, reorganizing the world the way they had done so eagerly all those years ago in Cambridge.

The fifteenth!

It was the day after tomorrow.

The desert was absolutely still. Not a camel snorted. There was no wind at all. In an hour, dawn would begin to break over the king's hunting camp at Bidijar. There was a pale slice of moon, not quite a crescent, but the sand dunes picked up every glimmer of light and refracted it from a billion crystal grains.

The cluster of black felt tents stood out against the dull silver sand. They had the stark definition of black ink spilled on paper.

The man whom General Bir-Saraband had entrusted with this most delicate mission was a pathological cutthroat named

Hasim. Bir-Saraband had been shrewd. The man had little to lose and everything to gain by following his general's orders to the letter. If the raid were successful, Hasim could look forward to rich rewards. So had the general promised, and the general was a man of his word.

Hasim raised his black-shrouded head slowly, peering over the crest of a dune. He had left the Jeeps more than a mile behind. Every sound carried in the desert night, and they couldn't risk alerting the king and his party. Hasim squinted with eyes already well used to the darkness.

Praise Allah! No guard had been posted.

Who could believe the stupidity of the old man?

There they slept, the king and two equally feeble old friends, at the center of an empty desert crawling with rebels. And only their three servants to protect them.

The general had been right. This would be child's play. Yet a delicate consideration must be realized: the old king must be brought away unharmed.

Hasim felt a cold trickle of sweat inching down his spine. It was not from heat, for the night was cool. Hasim sweated because he could imagine what his general would do in the way of reprisals should this mission fail.

It would not fail!

With one hand, never looking back but keeping his eyes fixed on the camp, Hasim signaled the men behind him. They too were robed all in black, with black headcloths. They had been armed with special care. Each man carried a motley assortment of handguns and European rifles such as might be found in the rabble of the People's Army.

But their best weapon would be total surprise.

For weeks they drilled in the foothills, screaming the forbidden battlecry: "Fakk Raqaba!" Captured pamphlets, crudely printed and inflammatory, would be left in the ashes.

Now, in the silver-shot darkness and with his men tight around him, Hasim felt a new surge of enthusiasm. The fear was gone now, and with it the deeper shame of attacking his king. Nayif was a false king anyhow. The general had explained that, and an eerie light had gleamed in Bir-Saraband's eyes as he explained why this was so.

Hasim signaled the attack.

Swift and dark as the shadows of scudding clouds, the

raiders moved across the moonlit sand. Less than fifty yards separated them from the royal encampment. They had long since memorized the layout: the king's tent where his guests slept with him; a second tent for the three servants; and a third, kitchen and storage tent, smaller than the rest and empty at night. Six fine camels were dozing behind the servants' tent. The falcons, too, would be sleeping and hooded.

The servants died first. It was only logical—for they were younger, more likely to resist. All three died sleeping, their throats cut before they could utter a sound. Hasim saw the cook's eyes bulge open as he arched the man's head back in one swift motion and split his throat like a melon.

His men knew their work. Hasim flashed a small electric torch about the tent to make sure their job was truly complete. The three men sprawled on their straw mats, awkward in death as they had been sturdy and helpful in life. There was blood everywhere, soaking the straw matting, sopping through the faded carpet on the floor, blackening the packed sand. All was silent.

But in the king's tent it was another story. The old man had wakened. He stood uncertain in the middle of the huge tent, listening, holding an oil lamp. The attackers rushed in, Hasim leading.

He stopped at the sight of the king.

For a moment the two men stood in silence, the king wondering who these ruffians might be, Hasim gathering his courage for the attack. It was so much simpler when they were sleeping. The king saw the ruthless faces, the daggers, the blood.

"Ilhaqni-ya!" he cried. *Help!*

One cry was all Nayif had time for. Hasim knocked the lamp from his hand. One of the others snaked a black-clad arm around the king's neck and dragged him squirming from the tent.

Outside in the darkness King Nayif could hear the screams of his friends as Hasim's knife found their throats. Too quickly, the screaming stopped. And then came the rebel battle-cry: "Fakk faqaba! Free Kassan! Long live the People's Republic of Kassan! Fakk raqaba!"

The hoarse shouts burned into the old man's brain. His own people! There was a rushing of men, shouts, confusion, a light from the servants' tent, snorting of camels, a falcon's shrill cry. *Don't let them kill my falcons too*, thought the king, for somehow the birds' safety seemed more urgent to him now than his own.

Then he saw the flames.

The tents were on fire now. Nayif stopped struggling, ceased his efforts to scream: it came home to him now that he was completely alone. There was nobody to hear him. Nayif stared at the smoldering tents without really seeing them. He thought of his prized white falcon, of his friends, of the servants. They had been like friends too, well-worn companions of his hunting. *They haven't killed me and they haven't killed the camels. Why?* Nayif's mind raced over the possibilities. They were all unpleasant, not to say terrifying. The rebels, and may the Prophet curse them all, might be going to torture him, perhaps to try to force some sort of confession. Or they might be planning on ransom, or even an exchange of hostages.

He tried to think whom they might have in mind to exchange. It came to the king then that he had no idea at all what sort of prisoners Ibn Bir-Saraband might have in his jails. It had never seemed important. It was important now.

Nayif wondered when the next messenger was due from Port Kassan. A day? Three days? The last one had been . . . When? On a hunt, one day melted seamlessly into the next—it was one reason he loved the desert: time stood still here.

Time was moving very fast now.

Nayif realized that anything he might say or try to do could end with the knife.

His friends and his servants had a funeral pyre that must have been visible for miles.

If anyone thought to look.

The sky was paler now. The air stank of gasoline and charred flesh. Soon it would be dawn.

His captors lifted him roughly onto the back of a camel and deftly tied him to the saddle. As though he'd try escaping nine armed men.

How often had Selim urged him to travel on these hunts with an armed guard? Ibn might have loved the idea, a special desert guard, a new budget to play with. Where was he now, the general, with his secret police, his army, his endless pleas for more of everything? They moved out in an easterly direction, five of the rebels mounted on camelback, four others leading. Watching.

Hasim rode next to the king. Hasim was flushed with the success of his raid, so eager for his reward he could taste it.

After nearly two hours they crested a dune, and the king was baffled by the sight of three Kassanian Army Jeeps. Hasim, watching the old man closely, registered his surprise.

"We liberated your Jeeps just as easily as we captured you, old man," he said scornfully, "and before very long we will have also liberated the Panther Throne for all the people of Kassan!"

Nayif said nothing, but the words burned his soul. These men were obviously capable of anything—any treachery, any dishonor.

They lifted Nayif down from the camel and shoved him into the back seat of a Jeep. One of the rebels climbed in beside the old man. Another drove, and Hasim rode in the front passenger's seat. The three Jeeps roared off across the desert, leaving two of the rebels to lead the camels in the same direction.

From behind the highest of the nearby sand dunes a boy watched it all with astonished eyes.

Karim Shublaq was fourteen, a shepherd's third son, bred in the desert outside of Bidijar. A loner, the boy often went out by himself of an evening, sometimes camping for days in the desert. He did it because he loved the outdoors, but there was another, secret reason. A reason he dared tell no one.

Karim wanted to join the rebels. He wasn't sure where to find them, but he knew their leader's name. And one day he would seek out Bandar Al Khadir and persuade him to accept a new recruit. Karim's plans had been vague until this moment. The army Jeeps, the fire in the distance, the men in black, the old man their prisoner. Karim thought he recognized the old man. He had seen the king often enough on television at the café in Bidijar. Could it be? What did it mean? Maybe these were rebels—that would explain capturing the king. But he knew they weren't rebels. Not the kind of rebels he'd heard so many tales about. These were common thugs, hard and coarse. Karim had kept himself too far away to hear their words. Still he knew he'd seen something important. Something Bandar would want to hear about. And in that moment Karim resolved to find the rebel leader no matter how long it took or where it led him.

As the Jeep bounced over the rough desert trail, Nayif's thoughts went homing. He thought of Selim. The boy—his father always thought of Selim as a boy—might never know how much he was loved or what proud hopes his father had always cherished for him.

If I die in the next hour, Selim may remember me with hatred, thought Nayif, remembering all the times he'd challenged the boy and all the other times he'd kept Selim in the background. It had seemed so obvious—the boy must watch, wait his turn, and learn. But in the deepest corner of his heart Nayif knew that Selim saw the situation very differently. Nayif had always meant to give him more authority, some real job to do. But meaning isn't doing, and the king had held back. And now it might be too late to make amends.

His hands were tied with thick twine. He couldn't wipe away the tear that found its way from his left eye.

The Jeep roared on into the pale Kassanian dawn.

12

The flight to Kassan was more than ten hours long, no matter how you sliced it. Jeb yawned. He loved flying and hated big commercial jets. The stale air felt suffocating. It was late afternoon when the Air Saudia 747 skimmed over the boot of Italy at mid-calf. Jeb looked down, musing, wishing he'd broken the flight at Rome. Rome held happy memories for him, student memories and echoes of good times with Hillary. Better forget Rome this time. And Greece, looming up now on the far side of the Aegean. Forget Greece, too. Forget all the places he'd been happy with her.

He smiled then. That'd make the world pretty small, if he could never go back to places he'd been with Hillary. You couldn't forget. Not the places, not the woman, not the hopes or the love or the anger. All those things were buried somewhere inside, buried deep, going off like tiny poisonous time pills in your heart.

Jeb very seldom wanted a drink. He wanted one now. Closed his eyes, put the first-class seat back as far as it would go, tried to get some sleep. No use. Kassan was out there beyond the blue scimitar horizon, loaded with its own memories. Tamara memories. A girl from another time, with a Jeb so young he seemed like a stranger.

It was all mixed up with Megan.

Three times he'd tried to call her office, only to be given a grade-C-minus freeze by some impersonal secretary. Miss Mcguire is out of town for an indefinite stay. Yes, they had his last message for her. And the one before that.

Damn her, anyway! Maddening woman. It couldn't just fizzle out like this, not after she'd rekindled fires inside him that Jeb had feared were extinguished forever. Even now, thirty-six thousand feet over the ink-blue sea, his gut tightened at the memory of her. He could see the pearly softness of her skin as though it were playing on some huge cosmic movie screen about an inch from his resolutely closed eyes.

Well, he'd find her in Kassan. Port Kassan wasn't that big a town. There couldn't be more than two or three hotels that would be suitable for a television crew.

Jeb opened his eyes, raised the seat back, looked out at the spectacular panorama racing past below.

He recognized the dark finger of land that defined the Bay of Izmir in Turkey. It seemed as though the entire spellbound purple world of the *Arabian Nights* was enclosing him in its silken veil. A veil soft and voluptuous and somehow dangerous too.

The Walther .38 pistol would be waiting, Hindley said. And a man named Lawrence. Selim. Megan. Tamara. Always, Tamara. That part of his past would be waiting in ambush.

He looked down at the darkening landscape and tried to imagine his embassy. Forget the past, forget Megan, think of the work. Get the building started in your head even if you have to tear it down and redesign it a couple of dozen times. The sun had almost set as they skimmed high over the pale red-and-tan deserts of Syria. Somewhere down there was a corner of Kuwait. The dark waters of the Persian Gulf twinkled with the lights of a hundred tankers bearing oil for the insatiable engines of the free world. The present seemed suspended here in the big glossy jet. But the past and the future were rushing at him, harsh and inescapable. Now the jet was losing altitude and circling a cluster of lights that must be the bay of Port Kassan. The Corniche they called it for some zany Francophile reason. A bell sounded and the steward announced their landing in Arabic, English, German, French, and Japanese. The Tower of Babel was coming home again.

At the announcement, two elegant ladies came walking up the aisle toward the lavatories of the first-class section. Jeb had noticed them before: rich and sleek and Arabic, very chic in a mélange of European fashion: tailored suits that must be Parisian, Cartier jewels, Hermès scarves, and the inevitable Louis Vuitton purses and carry-on bags. They spoke French, easily, laughing like schoolgirls. Now the pair of them each carried a Vuitton satchel. Idly Jeb watched their progress: LV, LV, LV a thousand times over on their bags, maybe a dollar per monogram.

Ten minutes later two quite different figures emerged from the lavatories. They giggled no more. Robed from head to foot in sheer black and veiled to the eyes in the same discreet black fabric, they also wore long black head veils.

Jeb stared. The women had gone back in time, maybe a thousand years in just those few minutes. Only their perfectly made-up eyes and a certain arrogance of carriage gave them away. Otherwise, they'd blend invisibly into any group of Muslim women in any souk in Arabia.

It was a jolt. Jeb had almost forgotten about the odd situation of women under Islam. They lived a separate existence, women with women, protected by walls and tradition and the fierceness of their men.

The diamond-dust sprinkling of lights was getting bigger now. Jeb could pick out colors: the red and green lights on ships, the blue dazzle of high-intensity streetlamps, and softer, more orange lights that might well be cast by oil lamps unchanged since biblical times.

It was the new Arabia: the old slamming right into the new, a collision course of cultures, styles, and ways of living. Exciting. Maddening. Dangerous.

Jeb stared idly at the bay of Port Kassan and wondered how Selim bridged that gap. Jeb had always known the Panther in a Western connotation—first at college and then, several times, seeing Selim in Europe. At his incredibly lovely house on the Ile St. Louis in the Seine, and once again at Gstaad, Jeb and Hillary and Selim and Fawzia just after Selim's marriage. Nearly ten years ago, that'd be. Jeb thought of the presents he'd brought for Selim's twin boys. He hoped they'd all be in residence—but Selim hadn't replied to the note. With the Panther, you never knew. Still, the boys—what were their names?—would love the engines. Jeb had stopped off at F.A.O. Schwarz just before leaving and selected identical locomotives, all steel and brass and gleaming, with real engines that puffed real smoke. At least the demonstrator model did. At nearly two hundred dollars apiece, they'd better puff smoke. Jeb tried to remember if there were trains in Kassan. Even if there wasn't a Kassanian railroad, Selim's eight-year-old twins would have seen trains in Europe. Twin panthers. That must be a sight.

For Selim, Jeb decided, the transitions from Europe and American ways to Kassanian traditions were probably easy. If there had been problems, Selim had long since met them and mastered them. In Jeb's eyes Selim had always been an amazingly graceful man: even in college he moved through the world with an ease that Jeb had secretly envied. It couldn't hurt a man's poise to know that one fine day he'd be occupying the Panther Throne of Kassan.

But Tamara was something else again. The darkly veiled world of her ancestors had been reaching out for Tamara even in that long-ago summer when Jeb had first met her. Sixteen, she'd been that year. Sixteen and heart-stoppingly lovely, with eyes you could drown in and a voice like rippling water.

Jeb, at eighteen, had a good record of success with girls. He liked them as people and he liked himself enough to treat girls with a kind of playful confidence that was sometimes irresistible. But there had never been one special girl for Jeb.

Not until Tamara.

Sometimes, long afterward, he consoled himself with the thought that maybe he'd invented his love for her. Maybe the complete impossibility of it had made the girl that much more desirable. Maybe he always wanted what he couldn't have. But Jeb knew that was only a rationalization. Even now, twenty-one years later, the thought of her could cut into him with the velocity of a buzz saw.

Faced with Tamara, the first time they met, Jeb had gone tongue-tied. Weak-kneed, too: all the symptoms you never believe until they hit you. So shy he'd set her laughing. Selim had watched it all with amusement.

Jeb was dizzy with it. The month in Kassan passed in a trance of dappled courtyards, the scent of jasmine, and Tamara. Always and impossibly, Tamara. She had been be-trothed for months to the heir of the Bir-Saraband, Kassan's other leading family. It was only fitting—even Selim took the arrangement for granted. Jeb's romance never went beyond hand-holding—and one parting kiss. He wasn't going to betray Selim's friendship and hospitality by trying to add Tamara to his growing list of summer seductions. There was something so pure about her that to Jeb she seemed almost sacred. Maybe that wasn't the best way to view a possible lover, but to Jeb, that summer, it was the only way. The three of them explored the gardens of the summer palace in the hills. Behind those high white walls Tamara went unveiled, a thing she could never do in public. The days flowed by inevitably as a river. Finally, on his last night in Kassan, they walked alone in the garden after supper. She wore white, a long white cotton robe modestly buttoned to the throat. The night was cool. There was a fountain in the garden. Jeb would never forget the shape of it: like a four-leaf clover, low and tiled in blue and yellow, Arabic inscriptions on the tiles, one jet of water playing in the center.

Tamara was a little ahead of him. She turned slowly and stood on tiptoe to kiss him.

It burned.

"My beautiful American," she said softly. "Will you ever come back to me?"

Jeb held her close, fighting the words. In the end he said nothing but continued to hold her close as though the pale moonlight might freeze them that way forever.

Then Selim called his name from across the garden.

"I'll never forget you," said Jeb, and the words choked him.

She looked up at him then, a look not of love but more like terror. Then Tamara gave a small gasp and ran into the women's wing of the palace—where Jeb could never follow.

That had been his last sight of her, his last memory.

Down all the years that night lived in Jeb's heart. Through all the other women, through the joy and bitterness of his marriage to Hillary, through struggle and success, the image of Tamara endured. Sometimes it was a comfort, sometimes it brought pain.

It had been nothing and everything, as transient and lovely and unforgettable as a desert sunset.

The jet shuddered as the pilot lowered his flaps. Jeb looked down at Port Kassan. He could make out buildings now, a spaghetti tangle of highways and cloverleafs, a flash of neon.

The new Kassan.

Civilization had begun in this part of the world. If the State Department was right, it might well end here. Soon. Those lights on the far side of the gulf to the north must be Iran. Another mess. Another near-catastrophe. And they were counting on Jeb Cleaver to help avert this one.

He pushed the button that brought his seat upright, and decided not to count the odds.

13

Bandar thought it was a fine time for a funeral: late afternoon in a small village an hour's drive from Port Kassan. Blue shadows were slithering down the dunes, cutting across the unpaved streets of the town as though they wanted to track the funeral procession. There were just a dozen mourners. Slowly they walked through the gate in the town's wall and up the curving track to the cemetery on the hill.

Six men struggled with the crude wooden coffin. The others followed, including three black-robed and veiled women. They walked in silence. The scent of *caffor*, the funeral herb, lay on the hot air, heavy as grief, pungent as memory.

The battered wooden gate to the burial ground had once been painted blue. Now, scoured by windblown sand, it was bleached gray and softened, with just traces of sky-blue paint in cracks and corners. They opened the gate. The cemetery too was walled: mud-brick walls high as a man's shoulder. The grave was already dug. They lowered the coffin. The tallest of the men said a brief prayer. Two of the pallbearers picked up spades and shoveled sand on top of the heavy box. One of the women stepped to the edge of the grave and, one by one, tossed some wilting wildflowers into the hole. The men shoveled on. Soon the grave was filled, and all but three of the mourners made their way back to the village.

For a moment the three mourners stood at the graveside as though their grief was so heavy a burden they couldn't move. Then the tall man spoke. He was Bandar Al Khadir, and the coffin contained not a dead body but a selection of automatic rifles, grenades, and plastic explosives from the Russian cache.

Bandar spoke softly. You never knew who might be passing by. The man he spoke to was Majid, friend since schooldays, and now second-in-command of the People's Army. Bandar always felt better when Majid was nearby. And safer: Majid's dagger was famous—fatal and quick. The deadly blue flash of Majid's knife was the last image on the dumbstruck eyes of several ADDAK agents recently deceased. Bandar was famous, notorious. But legends were gathering around Majid too. "El Sayef," they were calling him in the souk: "the sword."

Bandar was a modest man but he knew the value of myths. A frightened enemy was an enemy half-beaten.

Sometimes they left more blood than was strictly necessary. "Was it too heavy?" Bandar asked his friend, smiling.

Majid grinned. "My heart, as Allah sees clearly, is light, old pumpkin." That was a game from the old days. Majid would invent a new and stranger way of addressing Bandar every time they spoke. Now a pumpkin; yesterday a toad; tomorrow, who knew?

"All these funerals have gone to your head."

Majid stifled a laugh. "Imagine what they're doing to the head of our revered General Bir-Saraband."

It was a fine feeling. In two weeks the People's Army had pulled off six raids, all successful. Only the grenades that had been tossed over the palace wall had gone awry, and Bandar resolved never to try such a blind attack again. To miss the king and his son and kill innocent people in the bargain was a thing he would not soon forget. Until that incident, Bandar's only victims had been military. And ADDAK men, if you could call them military.

But a few more episodes like the one at the king's majlis and the People's Army would be as much feared as ADDAK itself. Bandar had resolved not to let that happen.

Now they had friends everywhere among the common people of Kassan. This was their only wealth, their greatest strength. It gave them the power to vanish utterly into any village, or into the old section of Port Kassan itself. To some degree the ancient Arab tradition of offering hospitality to any stranger helped them too, but this was only a fringe benefit.

The three had stayed behind to plan the next attack. It must be the most carefully conceived thrust of all. And no innocent bystanders must be injured. Bandar had thought and thought. Now, encouraged by the Soviet weapons and by their own recent successes, he had conceived a plan of such boldness that it astonished even him.

Bandar wanted to attack the headquarters of ADDAK itself, to level the place and everyone in it.

Success in that would augur success in everything. It would show the people—and the king—that here was a force to be reckoned with. That the People's Army was far more than a gang of unruly schoolboys.

He turned serious now, and drew Majid and Falih close. Falih was a more recent recruit, from that time just a few years ago when Bandar, fresh back from California and college, had been a junior member of the Ministry of Education. As he spoke now, his mind ranged back to those days.

It seemed like a thousand years ago.

Bandar had found a job waiting for him, and a Kassan he hardly recognized. Partly this was due to his viewing the country with fresh eyes. Eyes that had seen wonders, miracles, and astonishments nearly every day of his four years in America. Bandar came home filled with ideas. Filled with ways to apply what he'd learned to the country he loved.

The fact that he still loved Kassan and its people, that he truly felt them as his own people, was in itself surprising. There had been temptations to simply stay in America. Some of the Kassanian boys on the king's scholarship had done that, turned their backs on Kassan, on king and family, and climbed the high towers of New York or California.

Not Bandar Al Khadir. His father had died during the four years he'd been away, and his mother remarried, and since none of them could read or write, he learned nothing of it until his return. The king's scholarship was punctual about paying tuition bills and doling out a fairly comfortable living allowance, but for news of home a boy had to rely on home itself.

Bandar had loved his father, the king's falconer. This new man was older, a heavyset man with an unsmiling face and gruff manners. Not, perhaps, a bad man, but neither was he what Bandar would have chosen. He felt badly for Leila, his little sister. Just passing ten now. Soon, by village standards, she'd be a woman. Married off, facing a life of drudgery and subservience. Bandar looked at the child, kissed her—what a pretty thing! He thought of Tess, of the other American girls he had known, some of whom he had almost loved.

There was a job waiting for him in Port Kassan. He had an office—his own office!—in the Ministry of Education. And with the office came a fine title: assistant to the Undersecretary of Rural Enlightenment. Bandar had smiled, hearing that. Surely rural Kassan could use all the enlightenment it might be given! Still, it was a chance. A chance to really do something at last.

Bandar was filled with hope.

His eyes were wide open. And what they saw distressed him. The first thing Bandar learned on his new job was that the building itself was a lie. It was huge, imposing, air-conditioned like a meatlocker, and more than half-empty.

Little Bedu boys were still drawing with sticks in the sands of remote districts. Their sisters lacked even the rudimentary learning to do that much. Infant mortality was shocking. Trachoma was taken for granted once you were ten miles out of Port Kassan, and the blindness it caused usually went unaided.

Another lesson quickly learned was that if you were the most junior of junior assistants in the ministry, it didn't do to make waves. Pointed questions were frowned on. Bandar discoved that the ministry was a jungle of nepotism.

Run by a cousin of the old king, the place was alive with even more distant cousins, nephews, and in-laws, each with his own nest to feather, each with his own schemes for self-enrichment.

In his new capacity Bandar visited his old school. The King's School had a gleaming new building now. It was the educational showpiece of the town, set in an improbably green campus at the edge of Port Kassan. King Nayif and the Education Minister both delighted in taking visitors around the place. Amply forewarned, the students would line up in ranks, well scrubbed and dazzling in their best white tunics, and sing the school's fight song.

Bandar squinted, on one such occasion, scanning the cheerful ranks of boys for the boy he had been. Gone forever, that little boy. Maybe there was a new Bandar among them, a new Majid. Maybe. He wondered what sort of Kassan they'd grow up to. If there would be a Kassan at all.

Although the ministry shuffled mountains of paper, almost nobody did any real work. Hours were kept only vaguely. People drifted in and out—mostly out—and lunches were long, followed more often than not by even longer siestas. Bandar found some kindred spirits, other young men characterized by brightness and a certain undefined discontent. These young men took to meeting in the afternoon at one coffee shop or another in the old quarter, where it was cheap and where most of them lived.

They all had similar jobs, jobs like Bandar's, minor clerical positions in one ministry or another. Instinctively, these young men avoided their opposite numbers in the army. The army, which in Kassan was voluntary, stank of ADDAK. They all knew what ADDAK was and feared the secret police profoundly and with reason.

This informal group soon discovered it possessed, and almost without trying, an extensive and very accurate intelligence-gathering system.

While Bandar and his new friends might be having coffee in the souk, the upper crust would be lunching or having tea at the new and very exclusive Jockey Club in the desert. The club's nominal purpose was to train polo ponies and to put on matches. In reality it was an elegant and very discreet place to make deals. Oil deals, construction deals, weapons deals, and various other transactions were conducted daily in low voices in the icy air-conditioned rooms. And because Majid had a cousin who had a friend who was the headwaiter at the Jockey Club, word of such deals drifted back to the young men in the souk.

To Bandar's idealistic mind it reeked of carrion and corruption. The king and his relatives were skimming the cream of Kassan's new prosperity, and what leftovers trickled down to the mass of the people were sparse and of indifferent quality.

What made all this especially infuriating to Bandar was the fact that nobody protested. Nobody demanded more. The lessons of history had not penetrated into Kassan, not even the recent and turbulent history of the Arab Revolution.

The working people of Kassan looked at this startling new world of transistors and neon with astonishment. It was as though some *jinn* had littered the desert with magical toys, toys to be viewed with wonderment. Now, in his mud-brick hut, a peasant might have a television set. And that was the Kassanian equivalent of bread and circuses. The TV-owning peasant wouldn't think to complain that, for instance, there was no school within walking distance, no hospital at all, that trachoma might blind him so that he couldn't see the flickering television screen that carried news of the great progress being made in Kassan.

The People's Army sprang to life one night in Majid's dark little room above a fruit shop in the old town. Its numbers were five, sworn to darkest secrecy. Bandar was the leader, Majid his second. Thus did the assistant to the Undersecretary of Rural Enlightenment in Kassan become General Bandar Al Khadir.

For more than a year the People's Army took no action, but merely gathered information, evidence of graft in the ministries, the depredations of ADDAK. And, very quietly, they recruited new members.

Bandar used his job to travel the length and breadth of Kassan. He stopped in villages where no government official other than the tax collector had appeared for years. Bandar asked questions, probed prople's hopes and fears. These were many. He made his interest known, his presence felt. If he could help in any small way, he did. Finally, back at the ministry, Bandar drafted a long and detailed proposal for a new system of rural education. In a single generation this plan might sweep Kassan from its medieval torpor into the present. Illiteracy could be totally eliminated. There would be education even for girls, and universities within Kassan, including a women's college!

As he wrote the plan, Bandar grew optimistic. The revolution he and his friends talked about long into the nights was a dream, and a dangerous one at that. But this—this could happen. All it would take was money, and surely there was plenty of that from the oil. Money and someone paying attention. He finished the plan, sixty-three pages long and tightly written, and presented it to his immediate superior, a fat fawning man who could only open and close his mouth like a fish in an aquarium at the sight of what he dreaded most—work.

To Bandar's astonishment, his program was greeted with both praise and approval. He detected a certain wary gleam in the small round eyes of his boss. There was no denying, of course, that the plan reflected well on all of Bandar's superiors, this one included.

The new program drifted slowly but surely up to the highest levels of the ministry, meeting with approval at every step of the way. It was revised a little, as proposals from juniors tend to be. But in essence the plan remained his, and Bandar was proud of it. The more so when he heard it was being translated into several languages and printed—on fine creamy paper, leather-bound, a book!—for display. In fact it became one of the showpieces of progress in Kassan.

But it never became more than a book.

It took quite some time before Bandar realized that no one, on any level, had the slightest intention of implementing his plan. It was to be purely ornamental, like a sculptor's drawing of a statue destined never to be cast.

This was, of course, never said outright. To say a thing directly would be the height of rudeness. Instead there were fencing, hesitation, smoke screens. And after a time Bandar stopped asking.

The desert breeds long memories.

Bandar would never forget his experience in the ministry, what it cost him emotionally, seeing the investment of his time and imagination squandered so carelessly. Maybe these people were incapable of action. Maybe it was simply a case of incompetence. That would have been the easiest explanation. But by now Bandar saw this as one more facet in a complicated and long-running scandal.

Always impatient for action, he now redoubled his impatience.

New reports flooded their little group. Someone in the Transportation Ministry told a story of German buses. Four hundred deluxe air-conditioned buses were ordered and paid for. Only one hundred were actually delivered. The Minister of Transportation soon acquired three Rolls-Royce limousines and a string of polo ponies. Nobody dared ask where the three hundred missing German buses were.

Bandar decided the time had come to act.

If they believed in a new Kassan, he said, then they must force it to happen. The ranks of the Kassanian establishment were formidable. Custom and accepted usage were backed by the muscle of General Bir-Saraband, by his army and his secret police. The king looked the other way, not partaking of the spoils but not protesting when his kinsmen did. It had to be changed. If justice were to live in Kassan, Bandar and his little group were the only ones who could make it happen. The thought was awesome. Frightening. Talking politics was one thing—a dangerous thing, if ADDAK got wind of it. But to risk your life? To chance becoming a hunted creature, forever cut off from friends, family, any kind of normal life?

It was asking a lot, and Bandar asked it.

Eyes darting fire, Bandar told his friends all he knew about the other Arab revolutions. Maybe, he thought, if they see it can happen—*has* happened—then they'll help make it happen here. Patiently, impressively, Bandar called the roll of kingdoms, emirates, and hereditary sheikhdoms that had fallen under the irresistible force of revolution—Egypt, Yemen, Libya, Iraq, and Iran: it was a long list. Now only Saudi Arabia remained, and Jordan, Kuwait, and Kassan. The emirates to the south had sufficiently democratized themselves to preclude a real revolution from happening. But the kingdoms lived in fear. Paranoia was their companion every day and every night. Repressions, political prisoners, secret police: ADDAK was bad enough but only one example. The secret police of other Arab countries were equally notorious.

At the mention of the dread word "ADDAK," the little room grew very still.

ADDAK could come in the night and take you away to a fate that would make death seem pleasant.

ADDAK was invisible, unanswerable, deadly.

Everyone knew an ADDAK story—some friend or relative run afoul of the secret police—but few were so bold as to tell about it. That was the insidious part. You never quite knew whether the person you were talking to might not be an informer.

The result was an undercurrent of fear so widespread it was taken for granted. People went about their business as best they could—praying that some stroke of bad fortune might not put them on Addak's black books.

None of the young men in that room was a trained fighter. They determined to learn, and to learn with the weapons they had—not with the ones they dreamed of. So at the beginning their training program consisted of long endurance marches in the desert—backpacking, should anyone ask. They located a young Japanese who knew about karate and took lessons in the sand. They began collecting knives and thin wires with handles at each end for garroting. They read what they could about weapons.

But the first action of the People's Army was taken using the weapon they all understood best—words.

A poster war was launched against the Kassanian establishment. Overnight, on the eve of the Tuesday Market, when Port Kassan was sure to be at its most crowded, tens of thousands of posters appeared, staunchly glued to the walls of the old town, to the ministries, to the gates of the palace itself. In bloodred ink on bright yellow paper, these posters were visible everywhere.

If a nuclear bomb had been detonated in the king's bathtub, it could hardly have caused more of a stir.

The poster was a manifesto: the philosophy of the People's Army. A list of complaints, a list of demands. And a promise to take action. It was a brave-sounding poster, and it frightened Bandar more than he was willing to admit, even to himself.

The poster demanded justice for all—jury trials by one's peers, trials with representation for accuser and accused, and in public. It demanded an immediate end to the secret police of ADDAK. It demanded the creation of a true democratic parliament on the English model, votes for everyone—even women!—and much more.

By this time they had a spy with access to ADDAK. He was only an old man whose job it was to sweep and clean the offices, but he had sharp eyes and keen hearing. He saw much and reported all of it to Bandar and Majid.

"The general," said he, smiling, "was truly jumping up and down in his fury. Not a small feat for one of his size. A demon out of hell, a walking explosion. Ordered a house-to-house search, by the way."

Bandar and Majid laughed, but not for long.

Now, years later, Bandar and Majid stood at the edge of the newly filled grave, the false grave that held a part of their precious cache of weapons.

They were as different now from the young men they had been as night is different from day. So much had happened, was happening, would happen soon.

By a miracle, they had survived. Only by a miracle.

Bandar looked at the grave and thought of his sister. Of Leila. Suddenly there was a chill in the air. It was almost as if Leila had reached out and touched him. From another grave very much like this one.

He had never stopped blaming himself for her death.

It had begun on an absolutely ordinary day at the Ministry of Education, a day soon after the posters had gone up in Port Kassan. Nothing had been said about the posters, even though a crew of Pakistani workmen was frantically scrubbing the ministry walls on the day after the attack. Bandar took a quiet pride in the fact that they had to work so hard: he'd gone to special pains in getting a very tough brand of glue.

The marble halls of the ministry were typically empty. The air was characteristically chill, with an ominous humming sound like the droning of a million bees. He had been in and out all day long, practicing keeping a straight face while inwardly gloating at the colorful results of the People's Army's first public appearance.

The red-and-yellow posters were everywhere. Knots of people gathered and read them, or listened to someone reading aloud. The very illiteracy of the people was an obstacle not to be discounted in a propaganda war.

Squads of angry soldiers were in the streets, tearing down the posters as fast as they could. Not very fast, thanks to Bandar's excellent glue.

Not wanting to appear too interested, he made his way back to the ministry. Now he sat at his desk trying to concentrate on a very interesting report on treating hyperactive children in Sweden. In the silence and chill of his office Bandar could feel small droplets of sweat breaking out on his forehead and upper lip. Maybe it was fear—and maybe he was coming down with something. Frowning at any weakness, he got up and walked down the hallway to the bathroom. He washed his face, drank some water, and immediately felt better.

Bandar left the big empty bathroom and turned, heading back to his office. But something made him pause, listening.

Something was wrong. He heard atypical noises.

From his own office he could hear voices: one angry, one placating. Fawning and protesting. His fat little boss was playing the toady again.

"I assure," said Bandar's supervisor, "that I know nothing about this Al Khadir, only the slightest—"

"Where is he, little man?" asked a rough voice. "Where do you keep the terrorist Al Khadir?"

Bandar froze, clenched his fists, and made a supreme effort not to gasp out his astonishment. How had they found him? Who could have betrayed them? In seconds he was around the corner. Bandar knew the immense building well. There was a back staircase, seldom used, and a large shipping depot in the rear. That exit might not be watched. He had to try.

He gained the stairs unseen, moving fast but not running. Not yet. A minute later he was in the basement, on his way to the shipping depot. Bandar knew old Ali Zeyd, the clerk in charge. Trucks were always coming and going here. *Maybe . . . maybe!*

The shipping bay was empty but for Ali Zeyd chatting with the driver of a truck that had just been loaded with pamphlets and textbooks.

He walked up to Ali Zeyd, grinned, clapped the older man on the shoulder. "I come seeking a favor, but in a good cause, my friend." *He should only know what cause*, thought Bandar behind the smile.

Ali smiled back.

"If Allah grants me the power, then in turn I grant it to you—and what do you ask, scoundrel?"

It was a game they had played before.

"A lift across town in this fine truck."

Ali frowned. This was part of the game: feigned reluctance. Making much of the service to build up credits against some future favor that Ali might ask in return.

"You know it's against the rules."

Somewhere far behind him Bandar heard a door open and slam shut. He felt his gut drop with a sudden involuntary jerk. The sweat came again. He forced himself to wink roguishly. "It is," he said confidentially, "a matter of some urgency . . . involving a certain lady."

Ali roared with laughter, slapped Bandar on the shoulder, and grinned like the demon of all lechery.

"I could ride in the back," said Bandar quickly. The footsteps and the voices were coming closer.

"Of course you could—get on with you, then, sinner!"

The driver raced his engine.

Bandar leaped into the van before Ali could change his mind. The driver raced off with typically Kassanian disregard of speed laws. In the darkness of the van's rear compartment Bandar leaned back against the hard metal and closed his eyes and breathed deeply.

He was safe for the moment.

How long would the moment last?

He realized now it had been madness not to have a complete escape plan, a plan with several alternates. Suppose they were hunting down Majid right now, and the rest?

Back at the depot, Ali Zeyd turned, the grin on his leathery face fading slowly. A fine-looking lad, young Al Khadir. Probably raised all kinds of havoc with the ladies. Now Ali heard the voices—angry voices—approaching. He looked up, squinting. Four men. Ali recognized one of them. The pear shaped body and whining voice could only belong to Al Khadir's boss. Damned pompous busybody, always insisting on everything in triplicate, raising riots if each invoice weren't filled out to perfection. And for what? Who cared? Did it make the paper move faster?

Ali smiled nevertheless, and bowed, and asked if he could be of service.

"Only," said Bandar's supervisor with a disdainful wrinkle of his fat nose, as though Ali smelled bad, "if you have seen the young wretch who pretends to work for me, Al Khadir."

An expression of befuddlement spread slowly across Ali Zeyd's face. "Let me see," he said slowly. "El Khazir, you say?"

"Bandar *Al Khadir*, fool!" The fat man sighed and lifted

his eyes piously toward the rough concrete ceiling of the shipping depot as though it were a golden staircase leading directly to the Prophet himself. "And may God forgive me for my kindness to the traitorous wretch."

"Ah," said Ali Zeyd. "Al Khadir. A tall young man, and quick to smile?"

"Too quick by half," said the supervisor dolefully.

"Haven't seen him," said Ali. "Not since . . . ah . . . week ago Tuesday, if memory serves me, which it often does not."

But before Ali had finished, the supervisor had turned in disgust and was halfway back down the corridor, trailed by his three grim-faced companions. Ali could sense ADDAK the way a small hunted animal senses its predators. He shivered briefly and rubbed his hands together as if to get them warm again. And the old man smiled, because—however inadvertently—he'd helped Al Khadir to escape that bunch.

The driver was a maniac, and Bandar thanked God for it. He hardly dared breathe as the truck roared out of the compound, pausing only incidentally before turning into traffic. By now Bandar knew this quarter of Port Kassan in detail. He imagined the truck's progress, although the bumping, swerving, and jolting made it harder. His eyes grew accustomed to the near-blackness. There was an interior latch on the van's rear doors. He knew Ali wouldn't have locked them. He must get to Majid and the others—warn them! If ADDAK hadn't gotten there first.

The truck lurched to a halt. Bandar could hear a distant siren, and although you could almost always hear a siren in Port Kassan day or night, it chilled him. Maybe they'd gotten the story of his escape out of Ali somehow. Maybe they were following him right this minute.

The thought galvanized Bandar into action.

Without thinking more about it, he twisted the latch and flung open the van's door. He crouched, every muscle tensed for the leap. To run, to dodge bullets, to do only heaven knew what.

He stepped down from the van and shut the door behind him as though it were the most normal thing in the world. He blinked, getting used to the glare. The van was stuck in a fine

Kassanian gridlock. So was the very familiar car a few feet behind the van.

It was the white Rolls-Royce limousine that belonged to Prince Selim.

For an instant Bandar froze in his tracks. Then he walked briskly out of the street and into the crowd. The Rolls was empty except for its driver, a study in indifference to his surroundings.

Bandar went to their meeting place, a certain café in the old quarter. Ordinarily he would have met Majid there before now: it was going on to three-thirty in the afternoon.

Majid was late coming to the Café.

It saved his life.

Bandar waited in the shadowed doorway of a tobacconist's shop nearby, his eyes unwaveringly fixed on the route he knew Majid would probably take. Majid appeared. Bandar's arm snaked out and encircled Majid's neck as he pulled his friend smoothly into the doorway, clamping a hand over Majid's mouth.

Majid's eyes bugged with surprise. Bandar could feel him tensing, ready to make a countermove. Then Majid saw Bandar, just as Bandar whispered: "ADDAK!"

The one word said it all.

Majid went limp. Quickly they made their way into an alley, where Bandar told the story as he knew it.

This was the real beginning of the rebellion in Kassan.

From now on there could be no question of keeping up a respectable front, of maintaining their official jobs while conspiring at their leisure at night or during moments stolen from the workday.

Now they were on the run, hiding, living in shadows. Now they would be hunted. They'd run the risk of being informed upon, of being recognized, caught, tortured, killed.

It had never been easy even to contemplate sedition in Kassan. Now it would become almost impossible. And they had no choice at all but to continue on the path they had chosen. To escalate the rebellion. To replace words with deeds.

ADDAK began the most intensive manhunt in its history. Bandar and Majid decided to separate, to meet again in one month's time.

For Bandar it would be a month of worry and fear, of

hope and planning, of relentless self-examination. *What was he hoping to do here, really, once all the fine rebellious words were uttered?*

Only the two of them were known: Majid and Bandar. Posters appeared, one bearing a fair likeness of Majid, the other a graduation photo from the King's School—Bandar at nineteen, skinny and frightened-looking. Now he had a beard. Soon his skin would be darkened by the sun. Bandar was not recognizable from the wanted poster. But that didn't mean he was invisible or that people might not inform against him.

He feared for his mother, for his sister Leila.

Surely ADDAK would find them and question them.

But something drew Bandar back to Dhahir. At first he thought he'd just check to see if they were all right. There were no other means of finding out, without revealing who he was and why he wanted to know.

Bandar had not forgotten the old ways. Now he sought a caravan of camels going into the back country. He signed on at a wage so small it almost made him suspicious. But the caravan's leader was a careless, greedy man and Bandar quickly lost himself among the other camel tenders, six in all for eighteen camels. The trip was slow and isolated, which suited him well. His robes grew worn and dirty and soon he fitted in perfectly with his raggle-taggle companions. The caravan was headed west and north and would eventually make its way into the back regions of Kassan, to the foothills, there to trade manufactured goods for crafts: wool and copper pots and trays. The cargo included items of lurid plastic: small pails and bowls, detergents from the supermarket to stretch the effectiveness of the hill people's infrequent laundry days, preserved sweets in jars and tubes, bolts of cotton in stripes and white for the men, in black for the women. It was not a congenial group and Bandar was pleased when their route passed within ten miles of Dhahir and he left the caravan one night, navigating by the North Star as his father had taught him to do so very long ago among these same dunes.

It seemed to Bandar as he walked tirelessly through the night that time had reversed itself. He was a little boy again, alone with the stars and the sand dunes. Alone with his thoughts, which were not the thoughts of a boy, nor would they ever be again.

Dawn came, and Bandar was not quite home.

He found a well-concealed crevice among some large rocks, dragged dry branches close across the entrance, and lay down to sleep the day away.

An hour after sunset he stood on a hill overlooking Dhahir, gazing down on the house that he had been raised in, his father's house, now occupied by his mother, Leila, and Bandar's stepfather, Hassan Fhad.

Hassan was a man to be avoided.

Bandar had never liked him, and the feeling seemed to be mutual. Bandar crept around to the kitchen door like a beggar, sure that Hassan Fhad would never deign to open this most humble of entrances.

He drew his headcloth close across his face—just in case. There were lights glowing, the occasional metallic clang of spoon on pot.

He was very hungry.

Bandar raised his hand to knock. He could hear a low droning of women's voices. It was very quiet here. Too quiet? No matter—he'd come this far. He would not turn back.

He knocked.

Leila opened the door. For a moment she didn't know him. Then her eyes seemed to widen, at first with delight and then, realizing what this meant, with fear. She gestured to him: "Stay." Hassan must be in the kitchen. Bandar vanished around the far corner of the house. She came out soon after, looked all around, then paused, knowing he'd come to her. He did, and bent to kiss her.

"How are you, little one?"

The big eyes grew larger. "Oh, Bandar. Frightened. They have come so many times, men with questions about you. Hassan says they could be from ADDAK—or connected with them. Our mother is . . . not taking it well. That's why I thought it best . . ."

"That I didn't come into Hassan's house. Of course. You are wise, Leila."

They were walking now, across the dirt road and up the hillside to the old falcon shed. Bandar remembered it well. He had spent many long hours there as a boy, helping his father tend the royal birds. It still had the musty, sour smell he

182

recalled, fainter now but distinct. The ghosts of falcons long since dead.

She opened the door.

"It is never used these days," said Leila, leading him by the hand as though he were the child. "Sometimes I come here—to be alone. To think."

"And what do you think about, Leila?"

"You, sometimes. Many times. All kinds of things. The stars, if it's night."

Bandar looked down at her, deeply touched. A lovely girl, and soon to be a young woman. Was there any hope that she'd have a life different from her mother's? Or from that of her most infinite grandmother a thousand years ago? Her life was preordained, set forth in the Koran. A life of kitchens and arranged marriage and childbearing and never, never, never to have a real choice about her own future.

The falcon shed was small and dusty. Still, it was shelter, a place Hassan never came, a place ADDAK might not know.

"You'll need a blanket," said Leila, "and something to eat."

Bandar realized he'd been afraid to ask. Afraid of drawing her into his own orbit of danger.

Her voice went on. Like the rest of Leila, it was light, graceful. "And . . . what else, Bandar?"

He smiled. "Luck, little dove. Luck."

She was gone in a second and back in a few minutes. In the meanwhile Bandar stood looking out the shed's one small window, down the hillside at the flickering lights of the little town that had bred him. There was no electricity in Dhahir.

The town might have been a million miles away.

Bandar was still at the window when she came back. She had a thin blanket over her arm and both hands filled with food. There was goat cheese and dried apricots and flatbread and a steaming cup of mint tea. Bandar thanked his sister and wolfed most of it down on the spot, standing, ravenous. He saved the apricots for the journey he knew must face him in the morning. Maybe tonight.

They talked for a while of incidental things. Leila didn't ask, and Bandar dared not tell her about the People's Army. For what she didn't know she couldn't reveal. The harshness of this astonished Bandar when he thought about it. Still, he guarded his silence as though it were some radiant treasure. Finally he sent her back. Hassan would become suspicious if Leila stayed away too long.

There was a narrow bench that must be cleaner than the floor: Bandar lay down in his clothes and wrapped himself as best he could in Leila's blanket. At last, fitfully, he slept.

In the last few months Bandar had developed a raptor's instincts, a kind of extranatural sensitivity to atmospheres, sounds, the movements of the air itself. Sometimes he thought he could even smell danger.

He smelled it now, in the last hour before dawn.

Waking, he lay still for a moment, eyes closed. Analyzing all the sounds and humors of the dawn.

It had been too long since he'd left this town. Too long to remember every sound and stirring. But he sensed something wrong. Something portentous.

He opened his eyes then. The falcon shed was just as he'd left it. There were the old falcon roosts, a dozen of them, their padded mushrooms of tops still covered in the leather, dry and cracked now, his father had fitted years ago. The brass nailheads that secured the leather were dull now. It occurred to Bandar that they'd never be polished again.

Bandar got up, stretched, yawned, and shivered. Cold. Cautiously he went to the window and peered out. His stepfather's house was still dark. Soon the women would be up: his mother and Leila and any female relatives who might be there.

He could see lights in the town. It was all so very small to him now, the town that had once seemed like the entire universe. Sixty-some houses huddled about a tumbledown mosque and a few more, like Hassan's, straggling almost out into the desert. The whitewash was fading back to mud. There seemed to be no glimmer of hope here. The wood—where there was wood—looked mummified, dry, gray.

A rooster crowed. He heard a metallic sound, a clanging. Someone had put the pot on for coffee. The town would be stirring soon. And he must leave, right now, before anyone was about to see him. The thought of leaving Leila without so much as a good-bye was painful.

So many things were painful now.

He found the remaining apricots and put them in his

pocket. Then he adjusted his headdress, folded Leila's blanket, and slipped out the door.

Bandar walked steadily up the hill. The fact that his robe was filthy would help him now. The white cotton garment had become like the dust that soiled it. Not conspicuous in this dusty place.

High on the hillside, nearly two hundred yards above Hassan's house, Bandar paused by a scrub acacia tree. He turned for one last look, down past the falcon shed, across the road and into the small windows of the house that had once been his father's. That perhaps would have come to him if the world turned in other directions.

He had left it all so far behind, it might as well never have existed. Yet he was drawn to the scene below. It had an almost hypnotic effect.

As he watched, the door of Hassan's house opened and Leila darted out, unveiled and with only a headshawl to protect her from the chill. She was carrying something. Breakfast, probably. Bandar felt a quick sharp pang of regret. He wished he could go back and thank her, say something. He could at least have left a note. Never. It might be found—and she couldn't read.

Then he heard the engine.

Leila heard it too, and hesitated. A motor was rare, a wondrous thing in Dhahir. A battered gray van roared around the curve. Bandar's heart plummeted.

"Leila" he screamed, heedless of his own safety. "Run!"

She couldn't have heard him, but turned and watched as the van slammed to a halt and four men leaped out, robed in dirty white, waving pistols. One of them went straight for Leila, grabbed her with one hand, and dragged her screaming into the back of the van.

Bandar rose up instinctively, made a move toward the van, then stopped. He was unarmed. There was no chance, not against four ADDAK agents with guns and possibly more in the van.

There was nothing he could do now but pray they wouldn't harm Leila or his mother. The other three men went into the house. Even on his hilltop Bandar could hear their clatter, their loud commands, their footsteps.

From the back of the van there came no sound at all.

Bandar watched the house, thinking what a curse he had brought down on it.

The three agents marched Bandar's mother and two other women out of the house.

Hassan followed, gesticulating like a madman. The AD-DAK squad lined all of them up against the garden wall. *They'll be shot right here and now,* thought Bandar, *and it'll be my fault. My stupidity. My shame.*

The two men who had been searching the little house came out now, empty-handed. Bandar knew there'd be nothing in the place to connect his recent activities with Hassan or the rest. There was a brief consultation between the ADDAK men. Bandar was much too far away to hear it.

Then, as suddenly as they had arrived, the ADDAK men clambered back into the van and roared off. Taking Leila. Hassan and the women stood helpless, gaping in the dust. Then, silently, they walked back into the devastated house. There was no authority they could turn to, no protest to be made. ADDAK was all-powerful. The little house sank into the profound quietude of fear.

Bandar leaned—almost collapsed—against the sheltering rock. He didn't want to acknowledge what had just happened. Or what worse things might happen still. A mixture of bitterness and fear, of outrage and impotence, swept over him like some raging fever: hot, black, and incurable. There was nothing in the world he could do to help Leila or the rest of them. Not now. Not yet.

He knew he must flee.

But something kept Bandar glued to the spot, a mixture of hope and terror. The sun was higher now. Bandar sought the rock's shadow. There were a thousand plans in his head now, and not one of them made sense.

Finally Hassan left the house. Going to his place of work—the blacksmith's shop. As usual. Praying, no doubt, that no one had witnessed the raid on his house. If that became common knowledge, Hassan would be shamed in Dhahir. To have married the mother of a known traitor!

Bandar crouched in the shadow of the rock.

It was nearly two hours before the van came back. Again, he could hear the engine's roar growing closer. Again, the gray van came speeding up to the little house, came screeching to a halt. The rear doors were opened and something was flung out. Something terrible. The van roared away.

Bandar shivered convulsively. His thin body trembled with wave after wave of uncontrollable shudders. He felt as though all of his insides had turned first to fire and then to ice. He knew what he must do now, and yet he couldn't move, any more than a stone can fly. At last he forced himself to rise.

Slowly, making no attempt to conceal himself, Bandar walked down the hill.

The house was silent.

He no longer cared if anyone saw him, if the van came back, if he lived or died.

The thing that had been flung out of the van was Leila. Naked, half-drenched in her own blood, one arm bent backward at the elbow in a manner that must mean it had been broken nearly off, she lay in the dust, twitching. Not quite dead.

He knelt beside her and cradled her head gently in his right arm and stroked her cheek. She moaned softly.

Bandar forced himself to examine her wounds. The arm was broken, dangling. Half the fingernails were ripped from her hands. Her vagina was torn, bleeding. That, too. A large bruise darkened one cheek. Blood trickled from her mouth. Bandar didn't know where to begin. But she couldn't stay like this, not there in the dirt.

Leila moaned again. There was a different timbre to it now, harsher. Her eyelids fluttered a little, then opened. Unfocused. Then she saw his face next to hers. Thought she was dreaming. Her lips tried to form a smile. Failed.

"Leila!" It was a scream of protest.

Her eyes opened fully now. Dark and lovely and shaped like almonds.

"I said . . . nothing."

She quivered, a trembling that was contagious, for her brother was shaking too. Her slim body seemed to vibrate like a lutestring. One tremor. Then she relaxed. The lovely eyes glazed.

Leila was dead.

Bandar rose then, mechanically, still looking down at that

ravaged face. Twelve years old. Her body a child's body.
That hadn't stopped the monsters of ADDAK.

The back door was not locked. Bandar pushed it open and
walked past the three silent women who waited in shadows in
the kitchen. One was his own mother.

But he was a stranger here now, an enemy.

The women saw what he was carrying and began wailing.
The shrill, chirping, high-pitched wail of mourners everywhere in Arabia. Bandar walked through the kitchen to the
hallway and down the hall to the tiny alcove that had been
Leila's room.

Gently, as though she were asleep, he laid her on the cot.
The women followed, black as shadows, wailing and whimpering. Bandar turned to them, not in anger but from a rage
beyond sorrow.

"Be quiet," he said softly. "One day God will punish the
men who did this. But before then—and before Allah—I will
do so first. This is my oath."

He turned then and walked out of the room, out of the
house, and up the hill.

This time Bandar Al Khadir did not stop, or turn, or look
back.

14

Megan liked to arrive in daylight, hit the ground running, jet lag or not. Now, from the window of her first-class seat on TWA's Flight 436 to Kassan, she could see the dawn flaming up over Iran. The Persian Gulf was flat, burnished, leaden. She ticked off the landmarks, familiar from maps.

The eagerness to begin was adrenaline in her veins.

It was always like this at the start of a project: an intensity building. There'd be problems, but they didn't know them yet. Anything was possible. Megan was doubly eager now. As far as she knew, Kassan was her secret. She almost felt as though she'd invented the place. But the slightest rumor would bring the competition homing in like smart missiles. The world of television journalism was a small world. A world in which yesterday's whisper in Tokyo can be heard, amplified, at breakfast in Moscow. Megan didn't want to take any chances. The rooms had been booked in Louise Russell's name. The Range Rovers had been rented in London by the INTERTEL office there—and under someone else's name. It was all coming together. Megan could feel the glow warming her. It was the most important assignment of her life, and she'd make it work—and spectacularly—come what may.

And to hell with Jeb Cleaver.

All seven of them rode first class. To Megan and her crew it was routine—in their contracts. For Ahmad, it was magical, a continuing delight. Megan looked at him now and smiled. *The Riders of the Purple Sage Go to Kassan*, she thought. Next episode in a serial. Fun in the desert. Into your tent I'll creep. Now she thought of Jeb once more. How good it had seemed. How quickly it flared and sputtered out. If it was out. Partly her fault, too. Hair-trigger tempers had to be watched or they might go off and wound the innocent.

Maybe Jeb would show up in Kassan.

Maybe she'd get another chance.

They touched down in Port Kassan. Nothing Megan had read or seen photographed could prepare her for the throbbing reality of the place. They walked out of the first-class section into the bustling, ice-cold limbo that was Kassan International Airport. She shivered from the excessive air conditioning. No energy shortage in good old Arabia!

Louise, with typical foresight, had all of their customs declarations and entry permits filled out and ready. They passed the visa check quickly, with Ahmad smoothing their way, spouting a stream of Arabic. Only Allah knew what the young man was saying, but Allah seemed to approve. *So far so good*, thought Megan, as Ahmad conjured up two taxis from the melee outside the airport.

The heat was startling, real blast-furnace stuff, hot and dry and utterly relentless. Megan stood on the sidewalk for less than a minute and began to understand the overkill chill of the air terminal. Ahmad made sure that the second cab knew their destination—the Hilton—and then helped Megan and Louise and Jerry Schwartz into the cab. Ahmad himself rode next to the driver.

Megan surveyed the taxi's interior with wondering eyes.

"It looks," she said softly to Louise, "like a whorehouse in Peru."

The driver had decorated the machine himself. The seats, the ceiling, and the dashboard were covered in a fuzzy synthetic material dyed bubblegum pink. In one astonishing texture it combined the fluffy length of angora with the sinister sheen of cheap satin. Cat fur gone mad. From every possible edge and border hung strips of ball fringe in bright strawberry red, hundreds and hundreds of balls bouncing merrily with every jolt and swerve. Of which there were many. The driver navigated like the bravest graduate of the kamikaze academy of Japan.

Ahmad looked back at Megan, his face half-hidden by the dancing fringe, framed entirely in punk-rock cat fur. He grinned. "Is it not festive?" Seeing Megan's reaction, he went on: "In this part of the world, Miss Megan, every man's motor is also his—as you say it—his castle. To decorate it is an expression of hospitality. He is being nice to you, do you see, by sharing these fringes and things."

Megan nodded, still a little dazed.

The cab raced toward the heart of town, cheating death so often that Megan overcame her initial terror and actually began enjoying the ride.

Back at the airport, the young man who had processed their passports excused himself from the counter. He went into the back room, picked up a phone, and dialed four digits. "She is here," he said softly. "With six helpers. En route to the Hilton."

Without waiting for a response, he hung up and went back to his post. He had been gone less than a minute.

Jeb stood impatiently in the long line of foreign arrivals at the airport. And most of the arrivals were foreign. The two chic ladies so lately enrobed in Islamic black had vanished almost immediately. Natives. Jeb's line contained a sampling of the world's human population that would have delighted Noah: there were Japanese and Americans, a pair of Catholic priests chattering in Italian, Germans, Belgians, one lone white-haired gentleman who was almost surely French, three Britishers of the hail-fellow variety, and other Americans. All men. Which made Jeb wonder where Megan was, what she'd be doing right now.

The line inched along.

At last it was Jeb's turn. A young man stamped his passport, smiled, and said, "Welcome to Kassan, Mr. Cleaver."

Good English, nearly unaccented.

"Thank you," said Jeb, smiling in return.

All of the directional signs were in five languages: Arabic, English, German, Japanese, and French. *No Russian*, thought Jeb with grim satisfaction. *Not yet.*

The baggage took its own Arabic time to appear on the gleaming stainless-steel carousel. Jeb hailed a porter, who seemed to be Indian. Pakistani, more likely, from what he'd heard about the local work force. That would be a problem for the construction foreman: dealing with workers in six languages. Poor as some of the Kassanians were, very few of them chose to dig ditches, pave roads, or do any of the thousand other hard menial jobs it took to build whole cities out of the gleaming sand. Even the sand itself was sometimes imported for construction purposes. The desert scoured the grains too well: they tended to have round edges, which wouldn't hold as cement.

While wondering if he'd be met, Jeb surveyed the airport. Another opportunity blown. It was standard air-terminal-anonymous, but with a few luxury touches: bronze, marble, and rosewood where a less wealthy client might have settled for plastic and chrome. But it was a cold and impersonal space nevertheless.

Finally the luggage appeared, including the two large boxes from F.A.O. Schwarz that Jeb had brought for Selim's kids.

The porter collected them all on a gleaming steel cart and led Jeb down a long blue-carpeted corridor to the street exit. The distance looked immense. Jeb was glad he had full use of his limbs, that he wasn't some doddering old lady.

He nearly missed the man who was waiting for him.

"Mr. Cleaver?"

Jeb looked in the direction of the voice. A tall, athletic-looking man with a mahogany suntan smiled at him.

"Wiggy Lawrence at your service," he said, shaking Jeb's hand in a grip that could crush rocks. "The ambassador asked me to settle you in. Nice digs he's snaffled for you, too."

They walked toward the big glass doors that sealed off the airport from the sizzling air outside. The doors slid open automatically as they approached.

They walked into a wall of heat so solid it might have been built in hell from bricks of molten glass. Jeb gasped. He'd forgotten that part of Kassan. Something to remember in building his embassy. Shadows and breezes, gardens and water. Reflective glass.

Wiggy Lawrence aimed the porter at a discreet black Chevrolet station wagon with the crest of the United States painted on its front doors. In two minutes Jeb's belongings were loaded, the porter tipped—by Wiggy—and they were off. The driver wore a lightweight black uniform and the conventional peaked chauffeur's cap. Jeb and Wiggy climbed into the backseat.

"Tell me," asked Jeb, "how you come to be called Wiggy."

Lawrence laughed. It was a nice laugh, easy and resonant. "Beats hell out of my real name, which is Wentworth. Can you imagine any parent calling his kid Wentworth?"

Jeb could. Wiggy was best-of-breed, but a breed nevertheless. Instantly recognizable. WASP prince. He looked and moved and sounded like the captain of some elegant sport at one of the better universities. Tennis at Princeton, for instance.

"It'd be a good idea," said Wiggy casually as the car pulled out into traffic, "if you'd fasten your seat belt, Mr. Cleaver. They drive like . . . well, you'll see."

Jeb did as he was told, trying to remember what traffic had been twenty years ago. He couldn't remember at all.

"Call me Jeb, Wiggy. I was told . . ."

"By our mutual friend Hindley?"

"Exactly."

Wiggy made a very small gesture in the direction of the driver. It was obvious he didn't want to talk about Hindley here and now.

The station wagon moved steadily, which made it unique in the flashing, darting, honking bedlam of Kassanian traffic.

Wiggy settled back, stretched out his long legs, and said, "When you see what we're operating out of now, you'll understand just how very welcome you are, Jeb. We really need a new building pathetically. I hope I'm around to see it completed."

"So do I. I've never done an embassy before. It's a great opportunity."

Neither of them noticed the red pickup truck with specially reinforced bumpers as it moved into the stream of traffic three cars behind them.

"It must be," said Lawrence, "especially in this climate. I'd kill for a swimming pool."

"You'll get it," said Jeb. "There's going to be a lot of water, whatever the place looks like."

The driver of the faded red pickup was speaking into the receiver of a CB radio set. As he spoke, he looked into his rearview mirror and flicked his left turn signal on and off. Just once. To let someone know he'd made contact.

Behind the pickup a gray Mercedes-Benz sedan cruised in the fast lane. Its driver, like most of the drivers on the crowded highway, was an Arab in Arab dress. A white head-cloth concealed most of his face. By contrast, the driver of the pickup was dressed like a workman: blue jumpsuit and a battered old red baseball cap. Mirrored sunglasses masked his eyes.

He hung up the CB and maintained his distance behind the American station wagon.

In the wagon Jeb was feeling restless. Maybe it was jet lag. Maybe it was fear. He turned to Wiggy. "How long have you been out here?"

Lawrence's reply was preceded by a laugh so sharp it was more like a snort of disgust. "Two years in earth time. In Kassanian time . . . centuries. Time is different out here, Jeb. Very slow. Very, very slow. Of course, now with the rebels and the oil and you coming out, it'll be livelier. But Kassan isn't what you'd call a fun place."

"Do you speak Arabic?"

"Only a little. Wilfred—the ambassador, Wilfred Austin—he's fluent. It's the devil to learn."

The station wagon moved onto a newly paved six-lane highway leading to Port Kassan. It was a frenzy of noise and rushing vehicles. There seemed to be no speed limits and no rules of the road. Cars swerved from lane to lane, honking furiously. A siren wailed. Brakes squealed and Arabic shouts and curses defiled the air. A small blue flatbed truck raced past them going more than eighty. In its open cargo space knelt two white camels. Nonchalant, the camels seemed to be smiling at some secret joke of their own. They regarded the maelstrom of Kassanian traffic with tolerant amusement. They knew better. They had known better for thousands of years.

"And this," said Wiggy, "is light traffic. Beware the rush hour."

Snaking in and out of traffic, the red pickup held its place, three cars behind.

They were in the heart of Port Kassan now. The superhighway seemed to bisect the place. But there were no landmarks that Jeb could remember from the old days. The city was a churning mass of cars, trucks, jitney buses, and people. Animals were everywhere. For all the noise and neon and chrome, the streets accommodated goats, camels, donkeys, and stray chickens. Jeb had only an impressionistic view as they moved along the highway. The buildings were new but already decaying. He could see cracks and gaps, and it made him wonder how best to supervise the quality of his own project. The dregs of every cheap architectural style in the world seemed to have descended on Port Kassan as if in some act of revenge. There was a stupefying hodgepodge of Las Vegas flash and neo-Bauhaus glass towers all mixed in with remnants of the old Port Kassan.

There was something very wrong here.

Too much happening too fast. And, from the look of the place, with no control at all. Jeb wondered if Selim had any say in what got built.

As they passed the center of town, the wagon turned onto a steeply banked cloverleaf leading to yet another new six-lane highway. Whoever made their concrete, Jeb thought, must be doing very well indeed.

The embassy driver approached the cloverleaf as he had the rest of their trip: steadily, not too fast, keeping on the right.

They were completely unprepared for the crash.

Jeb heard a blare of horn, a screech of brakes, and the ugly scream of tearing metal. The wagon lurched to the right, scraped the double-thick guardrail, ricocheted back into the slow lane, shuddered, and slowly righted itself.

Jeb felt the pit of his stomach falling. Sweat broke out on his forehead and ran in small rivers down his face. The accident seemed like an omen, a bad omen, and even if they weren't really hurt, it was shocking. Whatever had hit them, car, truck or tank, had simply vanished.

"You all right, Jeb?" Lawrence's voice had shifted gear from easygoing to authoritative. "That was good driving, Collins," he said to the driver. "That son of a bitch could have killed us. Crazy Arabs. They shouldn't let them drive anything faster than a lame camel."

Relief filled the car like a cool breeze.

"Thanks," said Jeb quietly, "I'm fine."

He didn't feel fine. They rode in silence for nearly ten minutes, heading from midtown Port Kassan to something like a suburb. An area of low white houses, each tucked secretively behind its garden wall. Their tiled roofs and a few green trees could be seen poking over the walls, but not much else.

The road was elevated about fifty feet above the desert. It looked as though it might still be under construction. Extruded steel guardrails continued to create a barrier between the roadway and the steep bank just beyond. Soon they came to a place where the construction hadn't been finished. There was a big cement mixer, some smaller bucket-trucks, and a stack of guardrails piled like cordwood, all abandoned by the shoulder of the road. The road surface was smooth and fresh. But there were no guardrails now.

The driver of the red pickup chose his place well. Now he tried again.

Collins must have been watching.

He gave a shout of alarm and swerved. Too late. The truck hit their left-rear fender at an angle that sent the wagon veering toward the edge. The truck held back, then floored it and struck again.

It was the second hit that sent them spinning over the edge.

Jeb tucked into crash position: knees up, arms locked in front of his head, head down. Thank God for seat belts. The wagon hung on the sandy edge of the shoulder for a long, long moment. Then it rolled over, bouncing on its roof, rolling over again.

It felt as though they'd been thrown into that cement mixer. The last thing Jeb remembered was the roof of the wagon spinning crazily, something in a funhouse. Only not funny. Not funny at all. Blackness. It was peaceful there. Nobody tried to kill you there.

Jeb woke to hear shrill voices. Arabic voices. A piercing wail. Rattling metal. Dizzy. God was he dizzy. Gut-churning, head-swimming dizzy. And something hurt, something in his chest. Then there were hands on him, dragging, carrying. Where?

He opened his eyes. Daylight.

"Wiggy," he asked. "Are you okay?"

No answer. He was on a stretcher now. Being lifted into

an ambulance. *Let them drive slowly,* he thought, then blacked out again. He woke up with the first jolt of the ambulance. Slowly, hell.

There was a light in the back of the ambulance. Jeb could see Lawrence on the rack next to him. Obviously alive. Obviously out.

It seemed to Jeb that he could see the whole accident as though watching from somewhere else: a helicopter maybe. The half-crippled wagon lurching, Collins fighting the wheel, almost saving it. Almost. In Jeb's mind the wagon moved in slow motion. Hanging on the brink, rolling, tumbling, bouncing.

What the hell is this, anyway?

The siren wailed all the way to the emergency entrance of the King Nayif El Kheybar Hospital.

Two hours later Jeb was awake and feeling better. He'd cracked a rib and it was neatly taped. Take it easy for a few days and come back for X rays in a week. Wiggy had been knocked out, but there was no other damage. He helped Jeb on with his jacket, took the elevator down from the fourth floor of the gleaming new hospital, and hailed a cab.

"Collins bought it, Jeb. Broke his neck."

Jeb looked at Wiggy Lawrence. "You know it wasn't an accident. Why?"

"I know, you know, but try proving it. The accident rate out here is crazy. The cops are a joke."

"So you jsut let things like this happen? Collins killed? Murdered. Call it what it is."

Wiggy frowned, rubbed his forehead as though that would make the pain go away. He stared at their taxi driver intently, decided he couldn't understand the conversation, then turned to Jeb.

"Being an American diplomat in this part of the world is definitely not your typical bed of roses, Jeb. This incident could be rebels, the People's Army, although they've never been hostile before—that we know of. It could be some unspecified foreign power just trying to muddy the waters. It could be someone who had a grudge against America in general. And it could be a nut who simply doesn't like black Chevy wagons. Try tracking all that down in Arabic, the way things move out here, with denials all round, needless to say, and in about ten years you'd have . . . nothing."

"And what will the widow Collins have—if there is one?"

Jeb felt the anger. Wiggy had done this speech before—it was a little too practiced, a shade too smooth.

"Jeb, please. I know what you're thinking. That we're cynical, that we don't care. Well, we do care. We care so much that we sign on in some godforsaken patch of sand like this for what we damn well know isn't going to be the Girl Scout picnic. Collins knew there was danger—just like everyone in the embassy at Tehran knew there might be. Often is. I don't want to dwell on it—because I'd go batty if I did—but do you have any idea what the mortality rate is for us?"

"No," said Cleaver quietly, "I don't."

Wiggy smiled. "Neither do I. But it has to be a lot higher than that of, say, your typical insurance salesman in Spearfish, North Dakota."

They were driving over the same stretch of road where, three hours earlier, the red pickup had tried its damnedest to become a murder weapon. Jeb thought it was a good time to change the subject.

"Tell me," he asked, "about the ambassador."

"I forgot. He wants you to lunch tomorrow. Twelve-thirty at the embassy. If the sight of the embassy doesn't give you indigestion, we've got a pretty fair cook."

Wiggy obviously knew enough Arabic to have given their taxi driver accurate directions. They pulled off the highway into a brand-new and expensive-looking suburb. Jeb had been warned that everything in Kassan would be expensive. "Expect five-dollar cups of coffee," Hindley had said, "and ten-dollar drinks—where you can find one." In real estate, Jeb knew, the inflation went up like a rocket. Leases and deeds changed hands three, four, ten times a day, sometimes doubling with every trade-off. In a residential section you measured affluence by the amount of greenery. Here, behind the inevitable garden walls, at least, there was a lot of it.

Just a few feet away from the broiling desert were acres of whitewashed walls fending off the red dust—and who knew what else? The road was blacktop here, lightly glazed with the unstoppable drifting red sand. Strange cylindrical objects of some white metal rolled across their path from time to time. The first one Jeb saw disturbed him—it looked faintly sinister, like a bomb. He asked Wiggy what it was.

"Sure sign of a greenhorn," said Lawrence, smiling. "It's just what it looks like, an aluminum Coke can, sandblasted by the wind. All the paint gone. I know a man who took a brand-new Mercedes into the desert, those damn things have six or seven coats of paint, and he got it caught in a sudden sandstorm and bang-o!—he's got an all-steel Mercedes, just like that. Actually, he was lucky to get out of it alive. People are found buried all the time. Just like the Midwest of America when there's a big blizzard."

It seemed to be a day filled with danger. The car moved on. The cans rolled and bounced as though animated from within. Finally the driver turned into a narrow blacktop road. It ended in a circular cul-de-sac backed by one low tile-roofed house whose facade was part of its garden wall. There was a two-car garage sunk into the same freshly whitewashed wall. The taxi stopped and Wiggy asked the driver to wait.

They walked up the concrete path to the front door and rang the bell. Wiggy turned rather ceremoniously to Jeb and handed him two key rings. "One for the house," he said, "and one for your car."

The door was opened by a broad-shouldered young Arab in an immaculate white robe and sandals. No headdress. He bowed first to Wiggy and then to Jeb.

"Ali," said Wiggy, "this is Mr. Jeb Stuart Cleaver, who is a most distinguished architect in America, come to build our new embassy here."

"Welcome to Kassan, Mr. Cleaver, sir."

He spoke slowly and with a lilt, but the English was perfectly understandable.

"I'm glad to be here, Ali," said Jeb, offering his hand, which the servant somewhat hesitantly took. Jeb wondered if handshaking was some sort of an insult, decided to hell with it and walked past Ali and into the house. Ali, Wiggy explained, would be cook and majordomo. There was another servant, a houseboy, and the garden was tended by a once-weekly service.

The house was simple, spacious, and cool. There were three bedrooms, a good-sized living room, and a handsome courtyard behind the house with a pretty garden and a small but inviting swimming pool. The sight of it almost made Jeb forget the throbbing in his chest. Almost, but not quite. Wiggy took Jeb through the modern kitchen and past the servants' rooms to the garage. There, to his pleasure, Jeb discovered a new Mercedes-Benz 450SLC convertible, identical but for color to the one Jeb drove in New York.

"Hindley?"

"Hindley."

Jeb wondered what else they'd checked up on. Probably everything.

Jeb invited Wiggy for a drink, suspecting, accurately, that people thoughtful enough to check up on his car and duplicate it might have a stab at copying his bar.

Wiggy showed Jeb the bar, the master bedroom, and the garden but declined the drink. Jeb's luggage and the toys were in the bedroom, looking pretty much intact. The big double bed suddenly looked inviting.

"Will I be seeing you at lunch, then?"

"No," said Wiggy, "but you'll be seeing plenty of me, fear not. Tomorrow it's just you, Wilfred, and Lulu."

"Mrs. Austin?"

A flash of mischief glimmered in Wiggy's eyes, but all he said was, "That's it, Lulu."

"Thanks, Wiggy—for everything. Is there anything I can do about the accident?"

Saying the word "accident" was already building the deception. It burned on Jeb's tongue.

"Accident be damned," said Wiggy. "I'll make the usual reports, and I'll notify our mutual friend—just in case he has any ideas. But you'll have to get used to the land of Inshallah, Jeb.

"What's Inshallah?"

"If Allah wills it. A phrase that you'll hear a hundred times a day, greasing the skids for a delay or a screw-up. The messenger will be there Inshallah. You soon get accustomed to the impossibility of fighting it. You either go with the pace or go crazy. When I say an investigation would be just about impossible, that's the literal truth. Anyone trying that kind of move—to get me, or you, or just the old symbolic US of A—has a terrific advantage here."

"I see," said Jeb, who didn't see at all. He was itching to find out what Selim would make of it. And do about it.

Wiggy went back to the cab.

Jeb turned from the door to discover Ali waiting with a tea tray. It looked very good right then. Steaming mint-flavored tea and some small almond cookies. He took a cup, thanked Ali, and walked slowly through the house, eating and sipping, getting his bearings. He walked out into the garden. It was well tended and a bit conservative for Jeb's taste, everything trimmed and manicured as though the gardener wanted to prove you were getting your money's worth. Jeb realized he'd have to find a really good gardener and discover what to put in the embassy gardens. That part would be a pleasure. He thought of Selim, wondered if you could simply pick up a phone and call the royal palace. Then Ali appeared with another, smaller tray. On it was a cream-colored envelope on which, deeply embossed, Jeb recognized a familiar crest: the rampant panther of Kassan.

Ali watched his master, duly impressed.

Selim asked him to dine at the palace tomorrow night. Informally. Jeb smiled. Thank God. He hadn't thought to pack a dinner jacket. Which, considering the embassy and the palace and all, might have been a mistake. But there must be someplace to buy one.

Jeb held the rich paper for a moment. You could feel the wealth, the power behind it. He wondered if all that had changed the Panther he remembered from long ago. Well, he'd find out, and soon.

Suddenly, there in the sunlit garden, beside the bright blue pool and next to a row of espaliered dwarf lemon trees, all the fear of this afternoon's attempt on his life—their lives—caught up with Jeb Cleaver.

Quickly he handed the paper back to Ali.

Ali turned and walked back to the house.

Jeb sat down in a white iron garden chair. For a moment he stared unseeing into the pool. Then he put his head in his hands and closed his eyes tight.

He was trembling.

Bir-Saraband didn't bother to raise his voice. The situation was beyond intimidation. The driver of the red pickup stood before him, still in the blue jumpsuit, still wearing the red baseball cap. The sunglasses were gone, though, and in the man's eyes were deep wells of pure terror.

"Twice? You hit them twice?" The general's meaning was clear. He could scarcely believe the incompetence. The man was two times an idiot. And when he had finally wrecked the embassy wagon, he failed to be sure the job was finished.

Now another attempt might be risky. Now the American architect would be watchful. Maybe the accident hadn't been such a good idea. Still, Selim must be isolated. His almost invisible position in Kassan must be preserved, intensified, if the general's plans were to proceed successfully. Any direct connection between Selim and the United States—or another major power—was risky. As he sat at his desk in ADDAK headquarters, Ibn Bir-Saraband weighed the possibilities.

A second attempt, right now, might look strange. Which amplified his fury. The accident would have been so perfect! No one could prove a thing. Now he must watch. Wait. Perhaps strike again.

He regarded the inept creature who stood trembling before him, a burly guard holding each arm.

"Take him away," said Bir-Saraband, a note of disgust mingling with the icy authority in his voice.

The man screamed.

It was a death sentence.

15

Selim had never known fear.

He heard it discussed and thought of the emotion with remote interest, the way he might have considered some very rare disease or a new species of polo pony.

Now, flying in the Kassanian Army helicopter with his brother-in-law Bir-Saraband, Selim felt a new and unwelcome sensation. It was as though someone had shot a rocket through his guts, a sudden empty feeling, falling in space, a high-flying jet when it hits a downdraft.

Fear.

They were flying low over the pinkish-brown sand. Heading to the campsite where his father's friends had been found slain. Where, very possibly, King Nayif himself lay in some shallow grave. But no. That couldn't be. Not yet.

All the abstractions of power, of occupying the Panther Throne himself, stirred in Selim and contributed to his sense of guilt, his unease. As if he'd wished the old man dead.

But if the others had been found, and no evidence of the king, then the king must live. Must be a captive, a pawn, hostage of the rebels, maybe, or God knew what else.

Ibn had brought the news just this morning.

Selim had planned to spend the day arranging a party to welcome Jeb Cleaver. All that had been brushed aside. He'd sent a note, they'd dine tomorrow, the party could come later. If the court weren't in official mourning.

The sky-blue helicopter bore the white panther of Kassan on both its flanks. It skimmed low over the desert like some immense predatory insect. Ibn thought they might see rebels. What they saw was sand, rocks, the occasional wandering Bedu with his camels and goats, once a caravan, now and then a little town.

Selim turned to his brother-in-law. "You're absolutely sure, Ibn?"

Bir-Saraband regarded the prince, taking care to conceal his pleasure in Selim's discomfiture.

"I haven't inspected the campsite myself, your Highness. But the man who came to me was quite certain. We shall see. There is another helicopter on the site now, and two of my most trusted investigators. Nothing must be said, naturally, until we know just what happened one way or the other."

"Of course not."

"All signs point to a rebel attack. Five men slain, the camp burned out, rebel literature . . ."

"Yes. You told me."

"But no sign of your father, the king. They are probably considering some sort of ransom, some exchange of prisoners, a blackmail scheme."

"Which we will of course accede to."

"Of course."

He can't be dead, thought Selim over and over. *There are too many things unsaid between us.*

There had always seemed to be an infinity of time. And now it had run out on him.

To Selim the People's Army had seemed a faint and distant rumbling, an annoyance so minor it was nothing more than an unpleasant rumor.

Until that bright fatal morning when he had stood at his father's side in the palace courtyard conducting the majlis. The grenades that came flying so casually over the palace wall had destroyed something in Selim.

Never again would he feel the unquestioning confidence that had always been as much a part of him as his smile.

He looked at Bir-Saraband and wondered at how little he knew the man who had married his favorite sister. How little he saw of Tamara these days! They had slipped into separate orbits. She went about in the world, as was her privilege. She went often to Paris, but her friends there were not his friends. Or Fawzia's. And within Kassan they met officially. And seldom.

The helicopter swooped up and to the right. Selim could see a dark smudge on the sand far ahead. Ashes. Ashes of tents, of falcons, of men.

Selim's stomach gave a sickening lurch that had nothing to do with the helicopter's final descent.

Bir-Saraband clambered down first, ducking to avoid the whirling rotors.

For a moment Selim held back, gathering his nerve. Whatever he did now, it would be closely observed and reported on. Somewhere in him was the soul of a very frightened little boy. But he must appear to be a king. And Selim wasn't sure he knew how.

He stepped down, bent and ran under the rotors then walked the fifty feet to where Ibn was conferring with a short man in Kassanian Army uniform. The hot sand burned through the soles of Selim's elegant Italian loafers. He hadn't bothered to change for the desert.

Ibn spoke. "It is as I said. The bodies—mostly bones by now, picked clean—seem to be of the servants and of your father's friends: Sheikh Abu Ben Radhawi, Ibrahim Manshim. No signs of your father. Naturally our identification is not complete. There must be a complete autopsy." he paused, frowning. "I'm not sure how long it will be before their families begin asking questions."

"The hunt was for two weeks. This is—would have been—the fourth day."

Bir-Saraband smiled. "Then we have two weeks—even three. With messages pretending to come from the camp, perhaps longer. But not forever."

"No," said Selim, astonished at the ease with which his brother-in-law contemplated deceptions, "not forever."

"It was well planned, smartly executed," said Ibn, "and I am sorry to admit these dogs are more clever than I thought. We must take every precaution, your Highness. They seem to have informers everywhere. How else would they know precisely where the king intended to camp, and that he was unarmed? These rebels may have—must have!—informers right inside the palace itself."

Ibn waited for Selim's reaction. It had been, if he did say

so himself, a striking performance, all indignation leavened with responsibility. Surely new measures of power would rain on him now!

Selim's first thought was relief that Fawzia and the boys were in Paris. His mind raced, thinking of everyone who had access to the palace. Hundred and hundreds of them, counting the servants, their wives and children, casual and official visitors. Not to mention chauffeurs, camel drivers, falconers, and the keeper of the royal Saluki coursing hounds. Most of them had been with the El Kheybar for generations.

But what did that mean, right now, standing here smelling the stench of carrion flesh, looking at these pathetic ashes?

Hadn't the father of Bandar Al Khadir been a royal servant himself? Falconer?

Who could be disloyal and yet be in the palace?

Selim forced himself to admit that the answer was: *Almost anyone!*

And he felt utterly helpless to do anything about it.

Megan was in shock. She'd just finished one of the busiest days of her career and she'd accomplished nothing. Zero. The damned phones could not be made to work, not even for Ahmad. When Jerry and Philo plugged in their videotape cameras, they'd blown every light in the Hilton. Thank God they'd thought to bring rechargeable battery packs. That was the least of it. Louise had confirmed three appointments for today—Tuesday, September 16, by international cable. Appointment number one was with the Ministry of Information, a pure courtesy thing, but you had to do it. The minister was not available. Appointment number two was with General Bir-Saraband. Not available. Maybe tomorrow, Inshallah. The third appointment had been the most promising of all: with King Nayif himself. The king was not available. All that time wasted. Just getting through Kassanian traffic alive was some sort of achievement, one that scored very low on Megan's list of priorities. Inshallah! If she heard that phrase one more time she'd scream. Yet it was everywhere.

Megan had built her life around split-second timing, precision in all things, punctuality, responsibility.

In Kassan, or so it seemed, different laws applied. *Suppose you gave a revolution and nobody came?* She paced the living room of her suite on the top floor of the Hilton, raging inside and at the same time trying to keep up the morale of her crew.

For the cameramen, Jerry and Philo, the first couple of days in a new location were always busy ones. Out they went to get as much background as they could. Not a second wasted. Even the damned interminable traffic jams were material that might be usable. That a capital city of a major OPEC nation could be brought screeching to a halt because someone's camel decided to have a nervous breakdown at the intersection was well worth shooting.

But all the same, Megan had a strong impression that nobody was minding the store. In the afternoon Ahmad asked to be excused to visit his parents. Fine, he'd earned it. Megan reviewed her notes and then decided to take a little stroll around the town.

The stroll lasted exactly one block.

She was conservatively dressed. Louis had filled her in on the whole modesty thing, so she wore a long-sleeved silk shirt, slacks, and sandals.

The street was filled with men, only men, and from their reaction you'd think she was stark naked and beckoning.

They made a strange hissing noise, the Arabian version of a wolf whistle. They also made comments that Megan had to imagine were obscene. After trying to ignore them for half a block, she began getting nervous. She knew they must be tremendously repressed, but this was ridiculous. And more than a little frightening.

She turned on her heels and got back to the Hilton as fast as she could. Never again would she go out unescorted in Kassan.

Louise greeted her with the news that women can't drive in Kassan. Megan believed it, but she was flabbergasted.

"They can't drive in Saudi Arabia, either," said Louise.

"Why, for heaven's sake?"

"Allah does not will it."

At that Megan had to laugh. But the will of God was not a laughing matter. She walked out onto the terrace. The view was amazing. Port Kassan was essentially a flat city tucked between two low hills. The port curved symmetrically from hill to hill, bordered by a highway, framed by a tacky-looking beach.

A beach with almost no one on it. Very uptight about their bodies, the Arabs. Women could never, but never swim in company with men. And even the men themselves were shy about undressing. She could see the royal palace on its hill in the old quarter. The tiled rooftops of the old town spilled down that hill, a maze of souks and craftsmen's streets that slowly melted into a forest of recent high-rises jumbled willy-nilly almost to the edge of the desert. Which was a lot closer than she'd expected.

Suddenly Megan felt tired. The jet lag catching up with her, probably, or the frustration demanding to be slept away.

She lay down on a chaise. The afternoon sun felt good on her face. Tomorrow, Inshallah, would be better. She smiled, thinking how easily she'd slipped into the fatal usage. There was a kind of music in it. Music enough to put her to sleep.

Bandar sat studying the scale drawing of ADDAK. To own such a thing was death. It had been put together over four months, bit by bit, from without and from within. The old man who scrubbed the floors and swept the hallways measured the distances with his own footsteps. Five of the old man's steps equaled one yard. Heights were reckoned in broom-handle lengths. The result might not be mathematically precise, but they'd do.

Only one oil lamp flared in the small black tent. Light was a luxury here in the foothills. A luxury and a danger, for ADDAK sent its helicopters by day and night, seeking anything out of the ordinary. Seeking and sometimes destroying.

But the camp was well hidden and protected by spotters hidden in the midst of everyday working routines for miles around. A shepherd boy with a small long-range radio in his knapsack tended sheep on the hillside across the valley, never straying far from the one narrow access road. An old woman, apparently half-blind, squatted in her doorway in the square of the nearest town, grinding wheat in a pestle. She, too, had a small radio and reported any unusual movement through the town.

The People's Army was as safe as it could be. They lived on a razor's edge of danger every minute of the day.

Bandar was used to it now. The revolution consumed him. Keenly aware of the danger and alert for the safety of his men, Bandar had long since passed beyond fear. It took a conscious effort now, to restrain himself from acts of sheer recklessness that would create their own unnecessary dangers. Now he studied the ADDAK drawings avidly, planning, planning.

He looked up in annoyance when the guards came in, scuffling and bumping, dragging a very frightened boy of perhaps fifteen. The boy was underfed, wiry, his skin burned dark by the desert sun. Pure Bedu. Pride mingled with fear in his eyes. And why not fear? Who knew what tales he had heard of the bloodthirsty Al Khadir?

"Well?"

Bandar's voice was heavy with forced patience.

The guards had strict orders never to disturb him unless it was a matter of serious urgency. This lad looked more like a trapped desert hare than an emergency.

The more senior of the guards spoke first. "He says, Comrade Bandar, that he will speak to you and only to you."

They eased their grip. The boy stood tall, struggling with fear—and winning. In a few silent seconds the boy drew around himself the last tattered rags of his pride.

Bandar smiled, sensing what this effort must cost.

"What you have to tell me is very important, I'm sure. Please forgive our rudeness. Sometimes the revolution does not allow us the leisure for fine manners."

The boy hesitated, looked down, then up, then found his tongue. It all came out in a rush. All the carefully rehearsed phrases tumbling one over the other until Karim thought it must sound like an idiot's babbling.

"The king," he said quickly, "has been taken. Away. They have burned his camp and killed his friends and taken him away."

Bandar considered this, unblinking. It seemed unlikely, after the incident at the majlis, that Nayif would go anywhere without a heavy guard. To go unprotected into the desert was madness. And yet, it was like the old fox. Bandar remembered the old hunts at Dhahir. No guards or escorts then, surely. It could be. It could also be that this lad was an ADDAK plant, a spy. Bandar watched the boy, saw the fear wrestling with pride. No. This was not a spy. But what a wild tale! *Who, other than the rebels, would want to seize King Nayif?*

He must make the boy relax, probe gently, earn his trust. "Who," asked Bandar, "told you these things?"

"General, I was there. I saw."

"When was this, lad?"

"Three days since. I have walked that long, trying to find people who would bring me to you."

Who were they? I'll slit their throats, thought Bandar, wondering which part of his carefully woven security net had frayed.

"And how did you find me?"

"A man called Majid. He believed me."

Yes, thought Bandar, *he would. And he'd be right.*

"Tell me all about it—but first, we don't know your name."

"Karim, sir. Karim Shublaq."

"Karim, then. How did you come to see these strange events?"

"I was alone in the desert near Bidijar. Practicing, you see."

Bandar smiled. "Practicing what?"

"To be a rebel. To be able to take care of myself in the desert."

"That could be a dangerous game. And you saw the king?"

The boy nodded. "I have seen him before. On television. But before the king, I saw the Jeeps. I was asleep. Their engines woke me. And there—just the other side of the dune—three Kassanian Army Jeeps. I heard voices. Slowly, quietly, I climbed the dune. There were several men, all in black, nine, ten—it was difficult to tell in the darkness. I followed them at a distance. Twice I nearly lost them. Then I heard screaming. Saw flames. It was terrible. I followed the glow to the king's hunting camp—that's what it was, I am sure. Some of the men had daggers with blood on them. I saw the king—they dragged him out of a burning tent. But no others. I think the others—however many—must be dead."

"But not the king?"

"Not the king. There were camels—the king's camels. They tied him, the king. Put him on a camel and led him away.

This time I followed more closely—they moved fast. With the camels, it was easier tracking. At last they got into their Jeeps, they and the king, and off they went, very fast, not caring how much noise they made. To the northwest. Three stayed behind with the camels. Led the camels away—also to the northwest. Finally, I slept."

"Tell me, Karim. How do you feel about the king?"

The boy looked up quickly, startled, suspecting a trap. But when Karim spoke, it was slowly and with deliberation. "An old man, in love with the old ways. I think he lives in the past. I cannot say that all the old ways are evil, but it seems to me they must change, bend, stretch. I cannot say the old man is evil, but to be inflexible is to risk snapping like a badly tempered blade."

Bandar was impressed. It would have been so much easier, possibly safer, for the boy to simply spout a few hack phrases of Che or of Mao. If indeed he'd heard of Che or Mao.

"And yet you were out in the desert practicing to join us?"

"Yes, sir."

"And if you were asked to join us, would you?"

"I would count it the greatest honor of my life."

"And your parents? Would they not hate me for taking their son, perhaps risking his young life?"

"My parents, General, would never dare to say so, but they are—I'm sure—in sympathy with your goals."

Bandar rose from his chair then and walked the few paces to where the boy stood. He extended his right hand. "Then consider this your official appointment as a soldier in the People's Army of Kassan, Karim Shublaq. We will be honored to have you join us."

For a moment Karim was overcome. Bandar could see a new dimension of sparkle in those bright eyes. Tears held back by sheer force of will.

"Thank you, General," he said at last. "You will not regret this night"

Bandar turned to the guards. "Feed the lad. Get him a place to sleep. Tomorrow will be soon enough to act on what he has told us."

They left. Bandar paced his little tent. This was a strange and unexpected development. It showed another hand in the game. *Whose?* He thought of the Soviets—surely Kurakin was capable of anything, any treachery, any degree of Byzantine scheming. But it didn't make sense. Kurakin's game was obvious: get someone else to do the dirty work. There were the Libyans—they'd approached the People's Army and had been gently rebuffed. Bandar was not available to Qadhafi, or to his emissaries. Maybe the success of the People's Army had inspired imitators. That would present problems, but maybe not insoluble ones. There was much to learn—and much to think about.

Bandar knew precisely what he'd do once he had power in Kassan. But before that day dawned, the power must be gotten, step by slippery step. To sow confusion, to strike at the Panther Throne: these were the obvious steps, and Bandar was pursuing them strenuously. The king must go. ADDAK must be crushed like the nest of scorpions it was. Corruption must be rooted out. It had all seemed very simple.

Until now. Until these other, unknown, shadowy players crept upon the stage. The game was changing, and Bandar wasn't sure he knew the rules.

It was a long time before he slept.

16

Jeb slept like a stone. He got up early and walked naked through the sleeping house and dived into the pool. His chest still hurt, but not badly. *Take it easy*, the doctor had said. He glided nearly the length of the fifty-foot pool underwater, surfaced, turned, and swam slowly back. It was silky and cool. Not a shark in sight. Nine blessed hours of sleep and he hadn't once dreamed about the accident that wasn't an accident. He climbed out, showered, shaved, dressed.

There was so much to do. Find out where Megan was staying, for starters. Check out the site. Lunch at the embassy. And—tonight—Selim.

By the time he was dressed, Ali appeared with a very American breakfast tray. Ham, eggs, grapefruit juice, and a big pot of coffee. Jeb ate, ravenously, in the garden. He checked his watch. Nine-fifteen. Time for a little exploration before lunch with Wilfred and Lulu Austin.

He went to the garage, hoping Wiggy had provided a map of Port Kassan. He had—in Arabic. Still, there was a red X to indicate Jeb's house, and other marks for the palace, the existing embassy, and the site of the new embassy. Jeb knew he'd orient himself in a few hours. He started the engine and moved out. The top was down. The day seemed cut from crystal: blue sky forever and the heat hadn't reached anything like its full intensity. The driveway was short. Before he turned out into the road, Jeb stopped the car for a moment and adjusted both sideview mirrors very carefully. *After yesterday*, he thought, *I ought to be driving a tank.*

The Mercedes was pale blue metallic with dark blue
leather. Jeb eased it into traffic and found his way into the
heart of Port Kassan with a surprising lack of difficulty. Now
he could see the old palace on its hill. Landmark. Jeb headed
that way, knowing that the old town splayed out from the
palace gates in splendid disarray. He wanted to soak himself
in old Kassan, to feel the atmosphere, smell the smells, see
the details of the ancient buildings that filled the narrow alleys
of the souk.

The shimmering convertible pushed its way into the maze
until Jeb realized he'd better park or risk wedging the car so
tightly into the tiny nameless alleys that it might never come
out.

He parked by a tobacco shop and gave the vendor's boy a
coin to watch the car. Not that Jeb feared for thievery. It was
almost unknown here. He climbed out, stretched, and walked
aimlessly into the souk.

Here in the oldest part of town the houses were like the
women: veiled and secret. Jeb knew the shuttered facades hid
courtyards, gardens, and little plazas of sometimes startling
beauty. But the faces the buildings showed the world were
like masks: stiff and unreadable. It was partly utility and
partly philosophy. The closeness of the buildings made shade
where shade was sorely needed. The tops of the houses nearly
met over the narrow streets. And even the doors and shutters
that protected the hidden world hinted at unimagined delights
within: there were arches and arabesques, doors framed in
exotically colored tiles, wood studded with ancient nailheads
and lapped with strap hinges of marvelous intricacy. Some of
the tall narrow housefronts were pierced high up with slender
grilled windows. But always the effect was veiled, secret, in-
ward-turning.

Even in the ripening day it was dark here. The tide of
neon that marked the boulevards and cafés of the new Port
Kassan hadn't penetrated the souk. Yet. Braziers glowed, a few
bare bulbs cast more shadow than they created light, and oil
lamps could be seen flickering redly in the back rooms of the
tiny shops. The air was thick with noise: greetings, transistors, vendors' cries, the urgent chatter of immemorial haggling, camels' bleats, cackles of hens, bells on a donkey, metal
hammering on metal in the Street of the Coppersmiths. Most

of the streets, Jeb knew, bore the names of the crafts that sustained them: Street of the Spice Merchants, Court of the Silversmiths, Birdsellers' Alley. The smell of the place was like a drug, essence of Arabia. Jeb's nostrils took in a heady mixture of spice and charcoal, sweat and camel dung and an undercurrent of sweet decay. It was an ancient symphony of aromas unaltered since biblical times. It was the smell of no plumbing, of animals kept at close quarters, of attar of roses, frankincense, cloves, cinnamon, and death. Heady, seductive, timeless. Moses had filled his lungs with just such scents in ancient Egypt. As had the Prophet of Islam and a hundred Roman emperors.

Jeb had some vague idea of picking up an old carpet to relieve the institutional motel-modern look of his rented house. He walked aimlessly through the ancient market quarter. By the time he'd taken three turnings he was lost completely but unconcerned: more than three hours before he was expected at the embassy. The narrow street was a babble of Arabic. People came and went, busily, languidly, but always talking. Jeb realized how very helpless he was, understanding hardly a word of it. The tapes he'd studied in Virginia seemed a joke now.

He looked into the dark little shops, trying to remember what he'd been told about haggling. The hell with haggling—first you'd have to speak the language. There was something about drinking coffee. Never refuse. Jeb walked on, enjoying the sense of travel in time. This was another world, a place with different rules, different charms. Different dangers.

The souk was a mixture of new and old, plastic and silk, chromium and antique silver. A dazzle of colors, a babble of sound.

Tower of Babel. There was a moment at the beginning of every project when Jeb acted as a sponge, soaking up every bit of information he could, be it visual, mathematical, or technical. His mind would then process all the odd fragments, arranging and rearranging them until new patterns were formed. It was a heady feeling and Jeb rode it like a wave.

When at first he heard the angry voices, they hardly penetrated his consciousness. They seemed to be nothing more than a new dimension to the jumble of noises in the souk. Then he heard the rumble of heavy footsteps running, the shouts raised by anger and fear until they soared beyond any possible limits of haggling.

Jeb turned in the direction of the clamor.

The alley was long and it curved to the left fifty-some yards from where Jeb stood. As he watched, a wave of panic-stricken Kassanians came running around the corner as if pursued by wolves. Mostly men, and two or three heavily veiled women, they ran heedless, knocking over piles of pots, trays of spices. They shouted, screaming, calling alarms in words Jeb couldn't understand and with a tone and gestures that were unmistakable. From somewhere behind this surge of terrified humanity came a loud explosion, more shouts, more thundering footsteps.

Jeb quickly looked around. The mob would engulf him in seconds if he didn't get moving. The alley wound on into darkness, and it might just be a trap.

The next shop was a cooperage. Heaps of kegs, a few larger barrels stacked almost at random. The cooper and his helpers were busily rolling their merchandise back into the dark recesses of the shop. The house above the shop seemed vacant. At the second-story level there was a small balcony overhanging the street, no more than two feet deep and framed by a sturdy-looking wooden trellis. Jeb didn't have time to think twice.

He hopped up onto the nearest big barrel and from there he jumped, praying in midair the damned railing would bear his weight. He caught on with one hand, faltered, and grabbed it with the other. The rest was easy. Now he was half-standing, half-clinging to the ancient wooden balcony. It was solid, dusty, the most beautiful refuge Jeb could imagine. His injured chest throbbed now: a painful warning.

In the street the panic was worsening. A solid mass of terrified people was streaming by, going Jeb knew not where, or why. He clung to his perch like a barnacle on a rock in a typhoon. Another explosion. But now Jeb could see what had caused the alarm.

Around the bend in the alley came soldiers, four abreast, blocking the street from side to side, rifles poised, bayonets fixed, not marching exactly, but stalking. Behind the front rank came others, searching every shop, every house. Jeb wondered what they'd make of him. Their progress was steady, nothing like as fast as the crowd they'd driven before them. *House-to-house search*, thought Jeb. *Why by the army and not the police?* The explosions were warning shots, as though the file of soldiers wasn't frightening enough.

He crouched low, making himself small and ignoring the pain in his chest. *Take it easy, the doctor had said. Lots of luck.*

The soldiers looked determined. They were only three houses away when the grenade went off. It must have been thrown from a rooftop. The detonation rocked the balcony. Dust and debris fell like rain. Jeb closed his eyes at the moment of impact.

The explosion raged and echoed in the tight little alley until it seemed as though a whole army was shelling the place with cannon. But it was just the one grenade, and bad enough.

The roaring died down, and now Jeb could hear the screams. He opened his eyes. Maybe ten seconds had passed, but to Jeb it was a lifetime. The street was almost empty now.

One of the Kassanian soldiers lay sprawled in the dust. His severed head regarded its body from a bale of old rags ten feet away. The other soldiers had retreated around the curve. They were huddling, confused, without leaders. Maybe the dead man was their leader. Jeb realized he had to get out of there, fast.

He might be a suspect in the bombing. If the soldiers attacked again, he'd be in their path.

Jeb lowered himself to the ground and ran, crouching, keeping the barrels between himself and the sightlines of the soldiers down at the other end of the alley. He could still hear the blast reverberating in his ears. The sound of his own feet in the dusty alley echoed like a herd of maddened elephants.

But the street was strangely silent now.

As though all those people were cowering inside somewhere, holding their breath. He came to a corner and turned, straightened up, slowed to a brisk walk, and kept walking. Now there were people. Two more turnings and he was in another part of the souk. It was crowded and busy, and except for his pounding heart and the sweat on his face and the pain in his chest, the attack on the soldiers might never have happened.

Jeb paused in a deep, shadowed doorway for a moment and tried to think. He was completely lost. He looked down at the pale tan poplin suit: it was smudged with dirt, and one of the knees was torn a little. He'd have to get home and change before lunch.

If someone didn't take him in for questioning first. Jeb reached for his handkerchief, mopped off his face as best he could, straightened his tie, and kept walking. Act normal, that was the thing. Never saw a soldier. Never heard an explosion. He walked for five minutes, stalked by fear, expecting at any second to hear the harsh command to halt, to feel the rough hand on his shoulder.

Nothing.

He walked deliberately, hoping nobody would notice his high-wire act. He made his way down the narrow street, a street without signs, maybe a street with no name. It was an eerie and unsettling feeling. Somewhere in Kassan. He should have taken Ali, hired a guide, something. It was crazy to venture into a place like this not speaking the language. Kassan was turning into a minefield. Jeb looked at the street in front of him, half-expecting something else to explode. Finally he came to a cluster of shops selling carpets. He paused outside one of them, a dusty little canyon of a place. Jeb peered inside and saw only a jumble of colors, a blur of dark shapes, bales of tied carpets. Some of them looked as though they might be beautiful. He wondered how he'd get a shopkeeper to unroll one. Would that constitute a commitment? He paused, silent, interested. Suddenly a boy jostled him, murmured something unintelligible in Arabic, and passed on, a bale of cinnamon on his head. Jeb, with his New Yorker's reflexes, instantly felt for his wallet. It was there. He smiled, briefly, at his paranoia. This was Arabia. They might toss a grenade in your direction, no hard feelings, but they'd be very unlikely to make off with your wallet.

He stood near the entrance of the carpet shop, undecided, wondering how to even begin haggling. Then Jeb felt a hand on his shoulder.

"Perhaps," said an unfamiliar voice, "I can be of some assistance, Mr. Cleaver."

Jeb whirled in the direction of the voice.

This was just one little surprise too many. If Wiggy—or anybody else—was having him trailed, he might at least mention it.

What Jeb saw when he turned was an apparition.

There stood the wreck of an English gentleman. Tall, taller even than Jeb, his posture had that languid droop to it that hinted of Cambridge during the 1930's. The stranger's skin was sallow for such a sunny climate, ivory tinged with yellow. There were two unhealthy-looking red spots on the man's cheeks. They gave him an almost clownish appearance. His long bloodhound's face had a puckered, creased, deflated-balloon look to it. Eyes rimmed with crimson presided dejectedly over watery bags. Jeb wondered how many shiploads of gin it had taken to achieve this gothic ruination.

"William Earnshaw at your service, sir."

The apparition extended his hand, slender and damp in its frayed sleeve. The suit, Jeb decided, had been good once. It had also been white once, but that time had long passed. The color had evolved into something between ivory and dun.

Jeb shook the man's hand, wondering if he had anything contagious.

"You'll be wondering how I know you, sir," said Earnshaw, cocking an eyebrow upward at a quizzical angle. "Well, there're no mysteries about old Billy Earnshaw, just ask anyone at the club. At your service is Earnshaw of the Port Kassan *Gazette*, sir, correspondent upon matters British and other matters as well, paid by the line, and little enough, I assure you, what with inflation. Now, then, you'll be wanting a rug?"

Jeb smiled. The waves of whiskey that floated at him with Earnshaw's words confirmed his guess. Entire fields of malt and hops had perished to create that breath, those eyes.

"That's what I had in mind."

The red-rimmed eyes blinked. Earnshaw's eyes had a birdlike quality, flanking as they did his emaciated, beaked, red-tipped nose. A degenerate owl, thought Jeb. A degenerate owl seeking a bit of a commission on a carpet, maybe. Or a drink, or only a word with someone from the English-speaking world.

How did he know my name?

"You are in luck, then, if I do say so myself," said Earnshaw. "I know these fellers, Mr. Cleaver, and I know a bit about their merchandise, too. For instance . . ." He drew very close to Jeb and whispered theatrically in his ear. "For instance, stay bloody away from old Hakim over there, he'd sell his mother for a tealeaf. But here"—and he pointed at the shop nearest where Jeb stood—"here they are honest as the day is long *and* afflicted by a tragedy from which you might conceivably profit."

"Tragedy?"

Earnshaw's eyes looked heavenward.

"Three daughters!" he whispered, as if pronouncing some dreaded curse. "An Arabian catastrophe. Three dowries, don't you know? Two this year alone. So they are most eager to, ah, negotiate. Come with me."

He took Jeb by the elbow. Soon they were in the shop sipping tiny cups of thick, sweet coffee and watching as two strong men unfolded carpet after dazzling carpet from what appeared to be an endless supply. One in particular appealed to Jeb. It was a simple, bold tribal design in faded sapphire blue and rust with accents of darker blue and ivory. The design was almost reminiscent of certain American Indian carpets Jeb had seen in the Southwest. He mentioned this to Earnshaw.

"Good show!" Earnshaw winked broadly. "Naturally a trained eye like yours would separate the wheat from the chaff. Hamadan, I make it, and definitely not new—say, turn-of-century. Shall I have a snicker at it?"

Jeb nodded, and Earnshaw began negotiations in what sounded like fluent Arabic. His gestures were all fustian melodrama: mock horror, disdain, outrage. Earnshaw became a road-company Iago delighting in the game, the scheming. On any other morning it might have seemed funny.

Jeb looked at his watch. Eleven-fifteen. He'd better get moving if he was going to go home and change. Earnshaw took the hint, and in five minutes they were walking down the alley—Jeb with the carpet rolled up under his arm and three hundred dollars poorer.

"A decent value, I make it," said Earnshaw. "Not a complete steal, of course, that would take more time. Do consult me if you want another."

Jeb was pleased with the carpet. Compared to New York prices, it was practically free. Not large, measuring perhaps four feet by six, it would nevertheless add texture and richness to his austere living room. He made up his mind to come back.

"I'd like to buy you a drink, Mr. Earnshaw, but I have an appointment and I'm afraid I'll have to change my clothes first."

Earnshaw was walking at Jeb's side. Now he leaned forward a bit to look Jeb in the eye.

"Bit of a hugger-mugger in the old souk, eh? Heard the bomb—or whatever it was. Was it a bomb, Mr. Cleaver?"

"I don't know. But it was an explosion, sure enough, and I nearly got caught in it."

"Yes," said Earnshaw a bit vaguely, as though his interest wasn't entirely engaged. "There's a lot of it going round these days. The rebels, don't you know. Ruthless buggers, they are. But enough of those fellers. Can't be late for your luncheon with Twinkletoes, now, can you?"

"Twinkletoes?" Jeb looked at his companion.

"His Excellency the ambassador from the old U.S. of A! No harm meant, mind you, he's a splendid fellow, really. A bit, ah, pedantic at times, is all."

"You know him?"

"Mr. Cleaver, you'll soon discover what a very small town is Port Kassan. Everyone knows everything. Everyone who cares to, that is. As for that drink—I accept rain checks!"

"I'll issue one. I have another problem—I've completely forgotten where I left my car. It is a blue Mercedes convertible and I left it in front of a tobacco shop that has a blue sign with gold letters."

"Cuban Charlie's!"

Earnshaw's delight in producing this gem of intelligence was both childlike and infectious. "You see," said Earnshaw, "that's about where every newcomer gives up hope. Well, Cuban Charlie's an honest man, and you'll find your car as you left it. We are getting new elements—undesirables, really— these days, you know, Pakis and Turks and what-all. But the locals are reliable. For the most part."

"I'm glad to hear it."

They rounded a corner that Jeb didn't remember turning before, and there, gleaming, was the blue Mercedes.

"I'm grateful for your help, Mr. Earnshaw. Can I drop you someplace?"

"Thanks all the same," said Billy Earnshaw, "but I've got a spot of business just down the street." He reached into his baggy old jacket and produced a slender and surprisingly elegant leather wallet. From this he extracted a crisp white business card which he presented to Cleaver with a slight self-mocking bow.

"You can always reach me at the *Gazette*, Mr. Cleaver, or at any rate I check in there from time to time. Meanwhile, enjoy your carpet. And your séance with the prince this evening. Charming fellow, old Selim. Send regards."

Jeb simply gaped.

"Who are you?" he asked in a low and urgent tone, "and how in hell do you know these things?"

Earnshaw grinned the quick and mischievous grin of the Kipling schoolboy he must once have been. "Temper, temper, Mr. Cleaver! No tricks, mystery, or magic—any child can do it. Any child, that is, who's been embedded in this evil furnace of a town for thirty-some years. I am what I am, Mr. Cleaver. Billy Earnshaw of the Port Kassan *Gazette*. It is a very small town, Mr. Cleaver. A very small town indeed."

With this he bowed, turned on his heels, and vanished into the souk.

Jeb stood quite still for a moment, then tossed the rug on the passenger seat and climbed into the car.

Ten minutes later he was driving fast as any Kassanian on the highway toward home.

17

Bir-Saraband smiled. At least one thing was going well.

The tape had come through the usual channels, but it was definitely not the usual tape. Three times every week the tape recorders that monitored the American ambassador's little apartment in the old quarter were cleared and sent directly to the general.

There were four voice-activated microphones in the flat. One at the front door, another on the telephone, one more in the front parlor, and another just over the bed. The apartment had been Bir-Saraband's idea and Theodora had helped him find it. Austin had been grateful. A place, he said, to slip away from the cares of the embassy. To work on his book, a study of Arabian mythology. A place, although this was never discussed, for Wilfred Austin to meet the young boys for whose bodies he seemed to have an unquenchable desire.

The apartment was on the second floor of an ancient house in the Street of the Spice Merchants. Now, as Ibn played the tape, he could envision the place. Wilfred at the front door. The boy Aziz acting his role to perfection.

"Mr. Ambassador, sir?" All this in Arabic.

Bir-Saraband laughed aloud, imagining the effect that the sight of the lad would have on Austin. The ambassador's reply was tentative, struggling for the authority that never quite came naturally to him.

"Do you come from the general?"

"Yes, sir, your Excellency."

"Come in, please."

How very simple it was, thought Bir-Saraband as the tape reeled out to its expected conclusion. In Aziz, the general was confident he'd created the perfect trap. For two weeks now Theodora had coached the boy. Aziz was a born actor, a natural manipulator. Gifted as he was with beauty, he had the morals of a viper and no nerves at all. The infinite uses of sexuality seemed to have been born in him fully formed. Women were drawn to him as helplessly as men, and Aziz used them all. One day, Theo had warned, he might grow dangerous.

Ibn gave it not a second thought. One day the moon might fall into the gulf. In the meanwhile, the Panther Throne was waiting, and Aziz would help Ibn Bir-Saraband secure it.

He listened and smiled. As he'd hoped, the boy was asked to stay—indefinitely. Now was the time to activate the camera, a tiny movie system equipped with the latest Japanese film, a film capable of delivering a clear image in almost total darkness.

The moment was coming; Bir-Saraband could feel it. His moment in Kassan, his time of power, of recovering for the Bir-Saraband all that they had been cheated of so very long ago.

And the American ambassador was going to help him achieve that glittering seat of power. Voluntarily or not.

Megan looked at the man she was about to interview and tried to find some sympathy for him. The Minister of Information was a large man in a large office in a large ministry. His role in life seemed to be driving Megan Mcguire crazy. First he'd delayed, simply failed to keep appointment after appointment. Now that she'd cornered the old fool, he was even more obfuscatory.

Of course, he must be disconcerted by the fact of having a woman in his office. She knew, from Ahmad, that no Kassanian women were permitted in any office building.

Only the worldwide reputation of INTERTEL had secured this appointment. The minister cleared his throat for the third time. He was fat, olive-skinned, bearded, wearing thick-lensed eyeglasses in black plastic rims. He had a richly developed line of banalities. All government officials were paragons of wisdom, justice, and foresight. All new Kassanian projects were to be the best, the biggest, the most advanced of their kind in Arabia and, very possibly, in all the world.

The minister was speaking now, slowly, as Ahmad did a thankless job of simultaneous translation. The subject was rebels.

"This so-called People's Army, Miss Mcguire, is as nothing. A small group of degenerates. It is—forgive me—the corrupting Western influence on our youth. Music . . . blue jeans . . . unruly hairstyles. Decadent. But they are, thanking Allah, of no consequence."

The minister's plump fingers played with a pen that looked like solid gold.

"And what," Megan asked patiently, "about the bombing in the souk this morning?"

His eyes went blank. "Bombing? Here in Port Kassan? Surely, madam, you are misinformed. There was no such incident."

Megan raged, and her anger was doubled because she could see the hopelessness of challenging him. She hadn't been in the souk, but she trusted Ahmad utterly, and Ahmad had reported the house-to-house search and the grenade-tossing episode in some detail.

She forced herself to smile.

"I think we have imposed upon your valuable time too much already, sir," she said, all but choking on the words. "Thank you for your help. This has been a highly educational meeting. It gives me a very clear picture of the state of public information in Kassan."

He regarded her dully, perhaps not daring to question the mockery of her words.

Megan rose, gathered her notes, and walked out of the enormous office, followed by a rather bemused Ahmad.

The Minister of Information waited until the door had closed after them. Then he picked up the telephone.

Jeb felt better behind the wheel of the Mercedes. Here, at least, he was in control of something, even if it was only a car.

Ever since he'd landed yesterday, Jeb had experienced a sense of disorientation that had nothing to do with jet lag.

Too much was happening to him and with too little explanation. The bombing incident this morning was exactly the kind of thing Hindley would want to know. Jeb made a mental note to look up Wiggy Lawrence at the embassy before lunch. Some sight he must have been, dragging back to the house this morning, dirty and in tatters, carrying the carpet! Ali had viewed him with a calm that had to be Islamic, offered to mend the suit and have it cleaned, admired the carpet. Which did look fine in the living room. Jeb had showered and changed and was en route to the embassy now.

The embassy stood at the edge of the city on the site of a decayed date plantation. Only the main house remained, built extravagantly at the turn of the century in a style that was really a collection of styles: British Victorian with Arabic touches, a hint of the Gothic. It loomed up from behind its garden walls, forlorn and haunted. A Marine Corps guard manned the gate. He waved Jeb in, saluting smartly. *How many of them,* Jeb wondered, *are there now, and how many will I have to house in the new compound?*

Those were details that State had yet to provide him.

He parked the car at the front door of the house and stood for a moment regarding it with a mixture of awe and horror. It was every bit as ugly as Wiggy had said. The house was stucco with wooden trim, painted a deep and depressing shade of mustard with pale yellow accents. The front door was open. A receptionist's desk had been placed, awkwardly, in the cavernous front hall. Behind it sat a woman of indeterminate age who looked strikingly like a toad. Jeb gave his name and half-expected her to croak.

Instead she smiled and in a voice of uncommon warmth said, "Welcome to Kassan, Mr. Cleaver. I'm Florence Moon." She extended a plump white hand. "The ambassador will be right down."

She buzzed him from a tiny device on her desk. Jeb made a brief circuit of the entrance hall while he waited. It was an object lesson in what not to build in a hot country. Everything was dark, heavy, encrusted with varnish. *Paint the whole place white,* Jeb thought, and *bring in some greenery, some bright colors.* It was an occupational hazard for him—he automatically began redesigning rooms, buildings, entire cities, whether asked to or not.

"Ah, Mr. Cleaver," said a voice at his elbow, "how good of you to come."

Jeb turned to face the ambassador.

On little cat feet, he thought, considering how closely Austin had approached him without making a sound. Wilfred Austin was tall and very thin, scholarly-looking and pale, his gray eyes watchful behind rimless glasses. *Nervous,* Jeb decided. *Well, I'd be nervous too, if I lived in this mausoleum.*

"I am," he said as they climbed the wide oaken stairs, "very sorry about your accident yesterday. These people are children, in many ways. Unused to things mechanical."

He looked at Jeb, twinkling, as if sharing a joke.

"He tried to kill us, Mr. Austin. It was murder. I was shocked when Lawrence said there's no point in pursuing an investigation."

"Well, of course, Wiggy's right. There simply isn't. But ... murder? You're quite sure?"

"Murder." Jeb decided to let it drop—for the moment. Hindley—hell, the Secretary of State himself—ought to know how very lightly his people in Kassan took a little thing like premeditated bloodshed.

They reached the second-floor landing. Austin turned confidentially to his guest. "Is the little house to your liking?"

Jeb managed to smile. There was a Victorian cadence in the man's voice. Twinkletoes indeed.

It strangely matched the embassy, and that might be the problem. Strangeness.

"Very much so," said Jeb. "I like it a lot, and the car. One of the bedrooms will make a decent studio."

Now they were climbing a third flight of stairs.

"We live on the top two floors," said Austin. "Lulu will be waiting."

She was waiting in her private domain, a large Edwardian glass-and-wrought-iron conservatory at the back of the house. Seen from the dark hallway, the room was a green explosion. Someone had taken great care to bring it alive with plants and flowers. There were miniature orchids, begonias, jasmine, and other flowers Jeb couldn't identify. The moist air was thick with their mingled perfumes. It was a moment before Jeb saw his hostess.

Lulu Austin was standing on an iron bench wielding pruning shears with some abandon.

"Mealybugs," she said, stepping down. "Give those little bastards an inch and they'll eat the whole shooting match. You must be Cleaver. Welcome to Kassan."

She extended a hand. Jeb smiled, wondering if she knew the sort of welcome he'd had so far.

It was a few minutes before Jeb realized she was quite drunk. Not falling-down drunk, but more than tipsy. They sat in an alcove formed by palm trees in tubs. The furniture was comfortable: green wrought-iron armchairs fitted with green-and-white chintz cushions. On a side table were bottles of liquor and mixers, a pitcher of water, an ice bucket, and glasses.

"What will be your pleasure, my dear?" Austin played the gracious host a shade too brightly.

Lulu smiled, and Jeb got an inkling of what she must have been like, once, long ago. Radiant. She must be about the same age as her husband—late fifties—but she looked far older. Her features were those of a classic WASP beauty: regular and finely boned. But a puffiness had set in, a softening and sagging that were not relieved by a style of makeup that might be more appropriate for a night at the opera than luncheon in Port Kassan."

"Just a little sherry, please, darling," she said. "Mr. Cleaver, what can we get for you?"

"Lillet with soda, please, and a slice of lime."

Austin made the drinks and poured himself some ice water. *Got it in his veins, too,* thought Jeb, enjoying the pale orange refreshment fizzing in his own tall glass.

Lulu regarded him as though he might be a new botanical specimen of some interest.

"Your coming here is a great event for us in our little backwater, Mr. Cleaver. We hope to see much of you."

Why did it sound threatening? Jeb decided it was just the day, only his mood. He smiled.

"Somebody's decided Kassan isn't going to be a backwater anymore, Mrs. Austin. It's a great honor for me—I hope I'm up to it.

"I'm sure you will be."

Lulu Austin didn't touch the sherry her husband had

poured for her. There was a dish of roasted cashew nuts. Jeb ate a few and realized he was hungry. There was a pause.

"If I can," said Jeb, "I'd like to study the routine here at the embassy—the flow of work, how many people you see, the styles in entertaining. All that'll help me plan better."

Austin cleared his throat. "Absolutely. Lawrence is the man for all that. We'll set it up directly after lunch."

Jeb could only guess, but he had an impression that what diplomacy was done here was done by Wiggy Lawrence.

"As for entertaining, we've been blessedly quiet lately," Austin continued, taking occasional small sips of his water. "It is difficult, the mixtures of Arabs, the whole religious question, it seems we're always at the point of offending someone."

"Always," said Lulu dully, an echo of some deeper hurt or buried resentment. "Kassan is a little more liberal than, say, the Saudis. The Wahhabis will throw you in the slammer for so much as taking a drink."

"Which," said Austin, "doesn't prevent the desert from being littered with empty J&B Scotch bottles. Don't know why it's always J&B, but there you have it. They drive out in their cars, you see, and carry on like naughty children."

A servant appeared to announce lunch.

They all rose and followed Lulu to the dining room. She walked slowly, too steadily, measuring every step.

The dining room was predictably dark and pretentious. But the food was a refreshing surprise: a delicious cold soup of the gazpacho family followed by a grilled white fish with spinach puree and flaky almond-and-date-filled Arabic pastries for dessert. One glass of wine was served. Jeb noticed that Lulu hardly touched hers. Maybe he was wrong about her being drunk. Maybe she was being kept afloat by some other chemical. All through lunch Jeb found himself struggling to keep the conversation going. There seemed to be a distance between the two Austins that could be bridged only with great effort. He could easily imagine growing tired of that exertion. And he had another and even stranger feeling. A feeling that Lulu Austin was trying to warn him of something—some danger.

"This part of the world," she said after he'd described the

incident in the souk, "can be very dangerous if you don't know your way."

"Really, Lulu," said her husband testily, "you believe all the servants' gossip."

"People disappear," she went on as though he hadn't said a word. "ADDAK gets them."

Austin's laugh came quick as a whiplash. It was not a merry sound. "Of course, nobody ever disappeared in America, darling," he said with mockery that was anything but gentle. "These tales are greatly overstated here. It's because Port Kassan is such an inbred, gossipy sort of place."

"Tell me about the rebels," said Jeb as the servant came round with tiny cups of the thick, inevitable Arabic coffee.

"There really isn't much to tell. Fact is, nobody knows how many there are, or how big a threat they might be. The palace—understandably—plays it down. It's to their interest to keep up a good front, the assurance of stability, all that. The oil concessions are up for renegotiation in just a few weeks. But of course you know that."

"It must have been rebels this morning, in the souk." Jeb was watching his host with fascination. The question of rebels seemed distasteful to Wilfred Austin, the sort of thing that well-bred people simply don't bring up in polite conversation, like sex or money.

"Do you really think so?"

"Who else would it be?" Jeb kept the anger out of his voice. *I am paying this creep's salary out of my own tax dollars and he can't bring himself to see what's right before his eyes.*

Lulu interrupted then. "Sometimes," she said gently, "it's hard for Wilfred to imagine how very cheap life is here, Mr. Cleaver. You see, he's an idealist. He loves the Arabs."

Austin made a small choking sound and took a final sip of his coffee. "They are a noble people," he said quietly. "And a vanishing one."

"And they hold human life very cheaply," said Lulu, smiling brightly as she rose to indicate lunch was over. "Do take care, Mr. Cleaver."

"I'll do that," he said. "And thank you for lunch. It was delicious."

She said nothing, just smiled. At that moment Jeb remembered something he'd heard in Virginia. "*It's her money, you know*," James Gordon had said in one of his interminable briefings, as though that explained everything. If Wilfred and Wilfred's career were an investment of Lulu's she had been defrauded, Jeb thought.

They shook hands at the dining-room door. Jeb and the ambassador walked together down the echoing uncarpeted stairs. Wiggy, it developed, was having lunch with the French. Jeb decided the report on this morning's incident could keep a day. He'd have more to tell Wiggy after seeing Selim tonight. Or would he?

Jeb followed the embassy limousine in his convertible. The drive to the land that had been acquired for the new embassy took fifteen minutes, heading north and east to the low range of hills that framed the bay, echoing the palace's hilltop at the other end of the Corniche.

Jeb had been dreaming of this plot of sand for over a month now. It didn't disappoint him. The site was spectacular. A high point in a flat country, it commanded sweeping views in three directions: over the city, out across the bay to the gulf, and, to the west, the beginnings of the great Kassanian desert. There were slightly less than fifteen acres: not huge, but ample. They walked the dusty perimeter for nearly half an hour before Austin began to make polite sounds about leaving. Jeb said good-bye, and Austin said something inconclusive about getting together again soon. Jeb nodded, smiled, and began walking the site again before the limousine had driven off. He was lost in possibilities. The potential was wonderful, awesome. Better than he'd dared to hope.

From the look of the land it might never have been built on or even farmed. It was a roughly shaped hilltop, mostly red sand with a few outcroppings of reddish-tan rock. The site would have to be terraced and walled: this was a given.

But Jeb didn't want a conventional, imposing embassy sulking haughtily behind forbidding walls. It must be more open, more inviting than that. Defensibility, security, were considerations that could not be neglected, either. After Iran, no embassy would be built without its possible defense in mind. Which didn't mean it'd have to look like the Bastille. Jeb stood there in a trance of possibilities. Terraces, gardens, falling water. Especially water. The desert's great luxury could actually be put to work here, cooling the buildings as it delighted the eye. And the ear. He thought of the great anthropological museum in Mexico City that seemed to be floating on a sheer column of falling water.

The Arab architects of ancient times had known how to work miracles with the tiny amounts of water at their command. Now, standing in the baking heat of the Kassanian afternoon, Jeb decided that whatever its final form, his embassy here would pay homage to that tradition.

It was very quiet on this hilltop.

Jeb knew he'd come back, that he'd check the angles of the sun from dawn until sunset, watching the shadows move, calculating views, discovering where shade could be achieved most usefully, mentally grading slopes, designing entrances and exits, judging the complex's visual impact as seen from without, from within, from every angle.

It was a fine moment. The embassy could be anything. Jeb knew from years of experience that a time would come when various realities would impose themselves, that problems undreamed-of would arise and demand solution. But now everything was possible, every beauty, every daring concept, every glittering reward.

"Hey, Jeb!"

He almost jumped. So deep was Jeb's involvement with the dreams in his head that he hadn't heard the car drive up. Wiggy Lawrence strode across the sand, dressed in immaculate tennis whites.

"I heard," he said, "you had a rough time in the souk this morning."

Jeb told him all about it. Wiggy listened carefully, nodding from time to time. Jeb kept it brief, concise, ending with his strange encounter, meeting Earnshaw at the rug merchant's.

At the mention of his name, Wiggy grinned. "Good old Earnshaw creeps around Port Kassan waiting for his Somerset Maugham. He's a sad case. A ruined . . . I don't know what. Some sort of a remittance man, I guess, with not much being remitted these days. Queer, of course. A drunk in the bargain. He may be harmless. But then again . . ."

"I guess places like this attract that kind of wreck," said Jeb. "I have to tell you he gave me the willies. I mean, he actually knew I was having lunch with Austin and supper with Selim."

"That's his party trick, Jeb. He's a gossip writer. Writes a sort of society column for the *Gazette*. If Port Kassan can be said to have such a thing as society. Comings and goings at the embassies, that sort of thing. Nothing to do with real scandal, of course. That wouldn't be allowed in print." Lawrence looked toward the open desert. "I came up here for a couple of reasons, Jeb," he said. "One is, it's a good place to talk business. No way they can overhear us."

"Should I be worrying about that?"

"It can't hurt to watch what you say on the phone. I've had your place checked—for listening devices—and I'll do it regularly as time goes on."

"I have to tell you I find Austin's attitude a little weird. I mean, he just doesn't want to know what's happening. He kids himself that our little encounter with that truck yesterday was an accident."

"Thus Hindley," said Lawrence succinctly. "And thus Cleaver."

"I thought you'd want to know how I feel."

"I appreciate it. As you may have guessed, Jeb, it's a very tricky situation out here. On all fronts."

"Got it." Wiggy wasn't getting into personalities, but it was impossible to misunderstand his meaning. Jeb thought of the problems he must have, living at close quarters with the Austins, threading his treacherous way between reality and Wilfred's rose-colored perceptions of it.

Wiggy looked at his watch. "Gawd, the French will declare war if I'm not on their tennis court in ten minutes. I brought you a little greeting from Hindley, Jeb. That's why I really came."

Jeb looked at him.

"I left it in your glove compartment. It's a thirty-eight-caliber pistol Hindley said you might like."

Jeb smiled. He'd wanted that gun this morning, foolish as it seemed.

"Thanks, Wiggy. Let's have lunch one of these days, or supper if you're free."

"I am very free," he said ruefully. "My wife's in Nebraska for a whole damned month—her mother's terminal, poor lady."

"Sorry to hear that. Wiggy . . . where in town would an American television crew be likely to put up?"

"Do you mean the INTERTEL bunch? Megan What's-her-name? They're all at the Hilton—can't miss it, it's the tallest building in the middle of King Nayif Chaussée."

He climbed into his car, a small dark green BMW sports coupé, and drove off very fast. A rooster tail of fine red dust hung in the air behind him. It was a very small town, then, just as old Earnshaw had said.

Jeb opened the glove compartment of the Mercedes and saw the neat, plastic-wrapped package Wiggy had left there.

A small town, Lulu had said, where life is very cheap.

Not mine, Jeb thought as he climbed into the car and switched on its engine. *Not mine.*

18

Late morning in Port Kassan. The loudest noises Kurakin could hear came from the garden outside his open window. Clip, clip, clip. Someone was trimming the already precise boxwood hedges. He got up from his desk and looked out the window. The garden seemed empty. Clip, clip, clip. His buzzer sounded then, low and insistent. He picked up the receiver and grunted agreement. Then he smiled.

The film was ready.

The Soviet embassy's screening room was small but luxurious, fitted with overstuffed armchairs. Here, sometimes, Kurakin showed Hollywood films to dinner guests or propaganda films to the embassy staff. Here, too, he sometimes viewed film sent from Moscow for his eyes only. But what he would see this morning was different. Although the Kassanian general didn't know it yet, the film was a gift from him, from Ibn Bir-Saraband.

It had been nearly a month ago when Bir-Saraband, ever boastful, had let something slip. Something about an arrangement he'd made for the American ambassador. How Bir-Saraband had laughed, a man among men, mocking the American's weakness, bragging of how he'd pimped for the fellow, how he'd set up a little apartment in the old quarter.

The next day a team of Soviet electronic experts visited the apartment. Their routine was magnificently simple: on the day before Bir-Saraband's ADDAK people went to extract the tapes, the Soviet technicians copied the material and left the originals in place. When ADDAK installed cameras, the same routine applied.

An old, old story. Spies spying on each other.

Now Kurakin sat back in his easy chair as the lights dimmed. It was much as he'd expected. The KGB called such places of assignation "swallow's nests." *The swallow is enjoying herself,* an encoded message might read. Or, heaven forfend: *The swallow has flown.* This particular swallow was as remarkable as Bir-Saraband had claimed, thought Kurakin as he watched the boy enslave poor old Wilfred Austin. This film would be useful. More useful than the stupid general could realize. The point was to use it quickly. Very quickly. Kurakin was pleased, for he knew precisely what this sad little bit of pornography would buy for him.

Late at night, in a small locked room in an abandoned fort in the foothills of the Burujurdi Mountains of Kassan, an old man prayed to his god. The room was so dark that he had to guess at the five daily prayer times prescribed by the Koran. He also had to guess at the direction of Mecca, but King Nayif knew the Prophet wouldn't mind about that. Yet the old man was troubled. His heart burned for vengeance. It was eating him like some incurable ulcer. *Who were these people, these rebels, and what did they want with him?*

Four days and four nights had passed since the raid.

How long would his absence go unremarked in Kassan? Nayif was sick with regret for his friends and doubly sick because Selim had urged—all but demanded—he take an armed escort on the hunt. And he, Nayif, had dismissed the suggestion as a weakling's fears. Now he saw his own foolish arrogance for what it was. For what it must seem to Selim.

Painfully he got up from his knees.

These monsters must have some purpose in keeping him alive. Or else, why hadn't they made short work of him as they had the others?

Nayif El Kheybar, sheikh of sheikhs, King of Kassan, ruler of the Panther Throne, master of all he could see from this tiny window high overhead—assuming he could reach it, which he could not—shivered in the darkness. Only partly from cold.

The chill in his old bones extended to the deepest and most closely guarded recesses of his soul.

It was almost as though he had died already and was looking down upon Kassan from some high cool place. From the top of a cloud. Where had the rebellion come from? Had he helped cause it by some foolishness of his own?

Nayif tossed on the hard cot. He thought of the desert viper, mottled and dry as the sand it lived on. The serpent had a trick of covering itself with sand until only the two beady eyes protruded. Then it would wait, with awesome patience, until some foolish small desert mouse or other creature should venture near. But when it struck, the desert adder moved faster than the eye could see. That fast. That deadly. *And the rebellion is that viper,* he thought, *and I the foolish victim who trod carelessly in his ignorance. I walked up to death and danger because in my pride and in my utter blindness I could not believe it was real.*

He believed it now. Now that it might be too late.

Sleep would not come.

Somewhere outside, a jackal screamed. It was almost human, almost like the screams of his murdered servants in the hunting camp. Nayif squeezed his eyes shut and thought of all the things he'd do differently if ever he lived through this horror. It was a long, long list. But it began and always ended with his son.

With Selim.

Megan would not admit defeat.

She sat with her secretary, Louise, and Ahmad Bin Sayed in the living room of her suite in the Port Kassan Hilton. Ahmad manned the phone.

"It must have windows that open," Megan said. "No windows, no deal."

Ahmed smiled, nodded, and continued speaking in rapid-fire Arabic. A great adventure was beginning, and he would be a part of it! Finally he grinned and hung up the receiver.

"Done," he said triumphantly. "At two this afternoon, weather permitting, but in Kassan it is always permitting."

"About the only thing that is, dearie," said Megan, smiling. It was a wild chance, but she was more than ready to take it. Four days in Kassan, and not one inch of the sort of footage she needed for her feature. Not a rebel in sight. Nothing but a stonewall treatment from the establishment that'd have the Nixon/Watergate crew shredding their vested suits in envy.

"Now," she said, "let's get a bit of lunch. Everything else is ready."

It was.

The Range Rovers had arrived in good condition, and local English-speaking drivers had been hired for all of them. And a new gimmick had arisen out of the need for secrecy in shooting videotape. Both cameramen, Jerry and Philo too, had found that people's reactions to their equipment varied from horror to shyness to aggression. Real candid shots were just about impossible. So they had bought, used, a laundry company's van, drilled several nearly undetectable holes to shoot through, and cruised the streets, filming at will. Megan had seen the results and they were impressive. Official permission had been granted to shoot, formally, in the palace, at the King's School, and in other predictable places. The shots of the Panther Throne itself were compelling—as how could they not be, considering the riveting magnificence of that multimillion-dollar bit of furniture. It was all excellent background, but up till now it was background for a void. Center stage was empty, and Megan knew in her heart it'd stay empty unless she did something quickly.

At ten minutes before two a black Range Rover drove up to a side entrance of the Port Kassan airport. Ahmad explained to a disinterested guard that they were charter customers of Gulf Aero. The gate swung open. Ten minutes later they were airborne in a brand-new Cessna: Megan, Ahmad, Jerry Schwartz with his portable Minicam videotape machine, and two good-sized suitcases. It was a six-passenger plane and they all fitted in comfortably.

Two-fifteen. Cleared for takeoff.

Ahmed was bursting with excitement. He'd never been in a small plane before. Now, high in the sapphire-blue sky over Port Kassan, he sat just behind the pilot, next to Megan, feeling like he owned the world. Below him lay all the familiar scenes of his boyhood, suddenly, magically, transformed into one enormous toy. He pointed out the street where he lived, the old palace, some of his father's fishing boats, a soccer field he'd played on as a child.

The Cessna circled.

"About fifteen hundred feet, would you say, Jerry?" Jerry nodded his agreement, and Megan reached back for one of the two suitcases.

She was determined to make the first toss herself.

"Ahmad, dear," she said cheerfully, "would you please tell the nice pilot to keep on making wider and wider circles, but at just this height?"

Ahmad did that. Megan opened the window, then lifted the lid of the suitcase.

"Geronimo!"

Fistfuls of bright yellow leaflets trailed out behind the aircraft and fluttered to earth. Hundreds and hundreds, thousands and thousands. Ahmad opened the window on his side and helped. Gleeful as children, he and Megan showered Port Kassan with the bright single-page messages. After she'd emptied one suitcase, the pilot was instructed to fly out over the desert to five smaller towns. Each in its turn was showered with the yellow papers.

Kassan, Megan had observed, wasn't particularly tidy in any event. Abandoned cars lined the highways, and various kinds of debris could be seen, casually uncollected, almost everywhere. The Kassanians seemed not to notice, and for this Megan was grateful, because in a place like Switzerland they'd throw her in jail and toss away the key—just for littering.

What they might do when they read these leaflets was an open question. Megan relied on INTERTEL and the United States of America to act as a buffer against anything severe. She knew any country had the power to expel journalists. She also knew how such an action would look to the world when she made it public, which she most surely would do if they tried anything funny.

Jeb Cleaver found three of Megan's leaflets in his garden when he got back from the embassy site. Ali translated. Jeb grinned. It was an invitation to Bandar Al Khadir to contact Megan at the Hilton. Simple as that. How else, bright yellow-paper asked, could the real story of the rebels be known? Jeb called the Hilton. The switchboard was jammed.

General Bir-Saraband was shown one of the leaflets minutes after they began falling.

"She must be stopped! At once!"

"But, General, sir," said the lieutenant who had brought the offending paper, "they have already been dropped all over Kassan. And—I have checked, sir—there is no law against it."

"There is now!"

"She is an American citizen, sir, and a famous journalist to boot. I think we cannot touch her."

The general's heavy fist pounded on his desktop. Paper weights jumped. "I want her followed every minute. I want her progress impeded any way we can. I want accidents to happen."

"Yes, sir."

Bir-Saraband held up the yellow paper.

"AMERICAN REPORTER DESIRES MEETING WITH BANDAR AL KHADIR," it began, and continued in flawless Arabic to spell out exactly why Megan wanted to meet the rebel leader, what her credentials were, and where he might make contact. "How else will the truth be known?" was the closing, followed by Megan's scrawl of a signature.

The general read it slowly, containing his fury.

This was what came from allowing females to meddle in the world of men's business! He stormed out of his office in the Army Headquarters Building, knowing as he walked that his lieutenant was right. He couldn't do anything overt. He could not afford an incident, not now. Not with the Panther Throne almost in his grasp.

But this didn't mean he'd lack vengeance.

His mind leaped quickly and with relish over the possibilities of what he would do to this Megan Mcguire once he got his hands on her.

And he would get his hands on her.

19

Jeb remembered the white Rolls-Royce. It was an enormous relic of the 1930's, a long rakish limousine all Art Deco curves and swirls, knife-edged hood with nickel-silver piano hinges and free-floating headlamps big as rain barrels. The car gleamed pale ivory in the Kassanian twilight. On the side door of the passenger compartment was painted, discreetly, in 24-karat gold and blue enamel the rampant panther of Kassan. The driver was a tall angular Bedu in robes of pure white. He helped Jeb load the two crates from F.A.O. Schwarz, then bowed and opened the door.

Jeb climbed in and abandoned himself to the fantasy. He tried to recapture that day twenty years ago when he'd first stepped into this car. Into the magical, dangerous dream world it would take him to. Was Selim using the white Rolls to bring Jeb a special message? Maybe he was saying that nothing had changed, really, that things would be the same between them. But of course nothing was the same. Only the car had endured.

The big car seemed to float, completely insulated from the world outside. It moved in a cool, unruffled atmosphere all its own. Easy to see how people who rode such machines habitually could get a very distorted view of the real world. Once the car had been fitted with ordinary clear glass windows. That was one change. Now the windows were one-way mirrors and the view from inside was muted. The car was well known, and traffic seemed to melt before it. No one honked or tried to cut off the white limousine. The road through the old town was barely wide enough for the car. People scattered in amiable confusion. Goats, chickens, cats, and the occasional camel gave way too, a sea of life forever parting in front of the car's Doric prow and reforming in its wake.

Jeb felt small in the vast interior. Rosewood gleamed. The deeply tufted seats were upholstered in a shade of gray that belonged to the dawn; it seemed to shimmer softly with an opalescent hint of warmth. It was silk, densely woven. The floor was carpeted in wool of the same subtle color, and over that a small and exquisite silken Persian carpet had been laid, ivory with arabesques of the deepest claret red and cobalt blue. Jeb delighted in the unabashed luxury of the car. But he found himself wondering what a poor Kassanian might think of Selim's improbably costly chariot.

He thought, too, what a very conspicuous target it must make.

Now they drove slowly by a small, seedy café. A few mismatched chairs and tables encroached on the narrow sidewalk. At one of these tables sat a disturbing vision: Billy Earnshaw holding a tiny coffee cup in both hands as if to steady it. Sitting next to him was a Kassanian woman, heavily veiled, talking with animation, pleading. Earnshaw seemed indifferent to what she said. Jeb remembered his performance haggling for the carpet. Maybe this was more haggling. Maybe. As the white car slid past his table, Earnshaw raised his right hand in a kind of mocking salute, never taking his eyes off his companion's veiled face.

Jeb shivered. He knew Earnshaw couldn't actually see through the mirrored windows. He also knew as surely as he knew anything that Billy was well aware who the car's passenger was, and where he was going.

He looked in the other direction and tried to concentrate on the architecture. It was so much more interesting here than in the newer parts of town. Now they were following a tall mud-brick wall. The palace wall. Jeb's memories of the car were more vivid than his recollection of the palace. Actually, they'd spent most of that long ago month in the white summer palace high in the foothills of the western mountains. Jeb's memory was a hazy collage: gardens, fountains, long horseback rides in the desert with Selim. And Tamara.

There were several gates in the big wall, and Jeb was interested to find them all barred. All but the biggest. This was manned by six armed guards in the palace livery: a dazzle of gold braid, blue-and-white headcloths fastened by twin ropes of blue and gold, naked scimitars, bandoliers, and pistols. They were fierce and operatic-looking at the same time. Jeb wondered exactly how useful they'd be in a real emergency.

Now he remembered the name of this gate: the Portal of the Dawn. It faced east. Thirty feet wide and twice as high, it terminated in a pointed arch of fine proportions. Once this arch had been framed with colored tiles. Jeb could see a few broken ones as they passed through. Why didn't the El Kheybar fix the thing up? So much of Port Kassan was a pure mess: abandoned cars by the roadside, heaps of rubble everywhere, the highways dancing with tin cans and other litter. There seemed to be a prevailing belief that Allah would straighten up the town. Well, that could wait. Jeb had no intention of beginning his reunion with the Panther with a criticism of local garbage collecting.

The courtyard inside the Portal of the Dawn was large and irregular and busy even at this hour. Men—and only men— came in and out of the palace and stood in little groups talking animatedly. There were dozens of guards posted about, guards in military uniform rather than the theatrical costumes worn by the men at the gate. The Rolls moved slowly across the darkening courtyard and stopped before a small door that Jeb didn't remember at all.

The driver got out, opened Jeb's door, picked up both of the rather heavy packages, and followed him in.

Someone had been watching. Waiting. The old wooden door swung open as they approached it, silent as the electric-eye doors in supermarkets. But it hadn't been electronic courtesy. A neatly dressed young Arab in a dark blue suit bowed.

"Mr. Cleaver?"

"That's me."

"Please come with me, sir."

Jeb followed him, and the driver followed Jeb. They crossed a large, empty, dimly lighted hallway. On the far side was another door. It was thickly built of old wood and so strongly reinforced with great iron strap hinges that Jeb wondered if it might have once been an outside door. It looked stout enough to fend off charging elephants. It opened to a gleaming steel-and-brass elevator.

There was room for just the three of them. The tiny discotheque of an elevator rose silently. It was impossible to tell how far. It stopped and the door automatically slid open. The first thing Jeb saw of Selim's private apartments was himself, reflected darkly in a wall of mirrors dead ahead. Once again he had the unsettling feeling of having walked into a dream, a place where nothing was quite what it seemed. Where all the rules were different. The young man took the lead now, and Jeb and the driver followed him down the corridor. The mirrored wall seemed to go on forever. It had a trick of eliminating perspective. The right-hand wall was painted dark blue, as was the ceiling overhead. The ceiling had been pierced for baby spotlights that shone down on a magnificent old runner of a carpet.

But the room at the end of the hallway was even more fantastic. A cave for the space age, it was part primitive, mostly day-after-tomorrow modern 21st century Arabian baroque. The back wall, pierced by the hallway that led from the elevator, was of the roughest stone, very old. Jeb recalled that some parts of the palace had been built before the First Crusade. This wall looked like one of them.

But the rest of the enormous room was science fiction. The floor, to begin with, was lacquered to a mirror finish in the darkest shade of blue. It was a color so intense that to walk on it was like stepping out onto the face of night itself. The left wall and the right wall curved. They were covered in suede to match the rock-faced rear wall. Against one of these walls was the room's only artwork: a golden Japanese screen in six panels depicting a stand of deep blue iris. Like the room itself, the screen seemed both ancient and modern. Jeb guessed it must be five hundred years old.

The fourth wall was entirely glass.

The view over Port Kassan was amazing, breathtaking. The window must be forty feet wide and at least fifteen feet high. And it must have been specially cut into the palace. Each panel of glass was set into a thin chromed-steel frame whose polish matched that of the glass itself so completely as to seem invisible.

Jeb turned to the young man. He noticed that the chauffeur had gone, leaving the two boxes on the floor.

"Prince Selim will be slightly delayed, Mr. Cleaver. He asks your forgiveness and that you please make yourself at home. Here is the bar, and here, should you need it, is the W.C."

Jeb smiled at the British usage and thought the young man must be a product of the King's School. As he spoke, the secretary—he must be Selim's private secretary, Jeb decided—opened a large console cabinet lacquered the same deep blue as the floor. In it was a most un-Islamic bar setup. Ice in a crystal bucket, five kinds of wine, uncountable aperitifs, and one example each of the world's choicest vodka, Scotch, gin, bourbon, rye, and aquavit. The bathroom was artfully hidden behind a panel in one of the suede-covered walls.

"Thank you," said Jeb. "I'll be fine."

"May you enjoy your stay in Kassan, sir."

"Thank you. I will."

Jeb felt the smile tightening on his lips and thought: *At least I'll try.* Enjoyment hadn't exactly been a feature of his stay so far. And only tonight would he face one of the two things he feared most in Kassan. That was the possibility of betraying his friendship for Selim. The other was raking over the smoldering coals of his feelings for Tamara.

He stood in the huge window and took a deep breath. It had to be faced.

What had Selim become in these twenty years?

Jeb didn't know. Maybe he didn't want to find out. There had been too much magic in the old days to risk tarnishing it now. In Jeb's eighteen-year-old eyes Selim had been an almost legendary creature, all poise and fire and ease, moving through college with a panther's grace and cutting a radiant swath through the romantic daydreams of a hundred debutantes, laughing, the dauntless companion of Jeb's happiest days. And at the end of the ride for Selim, glittering and inevitable, was the Panther Throne. Waiting.

It had all seemed so very easy then.

Now, standing high in Selim's ancient palace looking out over the city, Jeb tried to remember the dreams they'd dreamed. He looked down on the millions of lights of the city and found himself wondering which one of them shone on the copper hair of Megan Mcguire.

He'd left a message at the Hilton switchboard.

Maybe that was all over too. Maybe it had just been another kind of dream, born of desperation. He stepped closer to the glass, as though it might bring him closer to Megan. To any reality.

"Don't jump, Jeb Stuart. Everything will be all right."

Jeb whirled and saw his old friend and knew at once that everything was definitely not all right. Selim's face was smooth and as handsome as ever. But it was drawn into a mask of tension that even the real warmth of his greeting couldn't erase. Jeb grinned and went to him. For a moment they were laughing, talking at the same time, embracing. Kids again.

But only for a moment.

"Well," said Selim, plucking a catch phrase out of their college days, "I'll drink to that."

Jeb had once introduced Selim to the hearty joys of bourbon whiskey. Now, without asking, Selim reached into the console bar and deftly poured Wild Turkey into a pair of crystal cognac snifters and handed one to Jeb.

"It is very good to have you here, Jeb Stuart."

"What's wrong, Panther?"

Selim tried for a smile, but it eluded him. "That obvious? You've got me at a very tough time, Jeb, and maybe that's why I'm even happier to see you than I might be if everything was hunky-what?"

"Dory. Hunky-dory." That had been one of their games, teaching Selim gangster's tough talk from old movies.

Now he did smile.

"We will talk seriously later, Jeb Stuart. Right now I just want to enjoy you. Fawzia and the boys send their love—but from Paris, alas. But you'll see them soon—I expect building an entire embassy isn't exactly a weekend's work?"

"You're right. I brought your identical little panthers two identical gifts," said Jeb, gesturing to the two sturdily wrapped boxes.

In minutes the two of them were on their knees on the polished floor, laughing as they tried to assemble the complicated locomotives from an all-too-precise instruction sheet.

"Kerosene," said Jeb. "The damn things run on kerosene."

Selim got up and picked up a phone and spoke a few words of Arabic. In five minutes the elevator door opened and a servant appeared with a can of kerosene and a small tool kit. Jeb read and Selim assembled. In half an hour one of the engines was all together. The little steam engine had only to be filled with fuel and ignited. There was a small brass funnel provided for this task. Carefully, working with precision that would have done credit to a surgeon, the Crown Prince of Kassan filled the little steel tank and screwed on the stopper.

"Now," he said, "a great moment in engineering is about to happen!" Selim found a slender gold cigarette lighter and flicked it on.

The results were astonishing.

There was a flash of fire and a loud roar. Smoke billowed up from the little engine. Instantly an alarm went off nearby. Selim and Jeb flung themselves back, Selim's arm covering his face, which had been very close to the engine when it went up. There was an instant of silence in which only the alarm could be heard. Then came a thudding of footsteps, and suddenly four guards were in the big room, rifles drawn. Aimed at Jeb Cleaver.

Jeb froze and his heart seemed to stop in his chest. If one of these soldiers was a little trigger-happy, anything might happen.

It seemed like a year before he heard Selim's laughter. There were hasty words in loud Arabic, and the rifles were lowered.

"Jeb, are you all right?"

Jeb turned away from the guards and looked at his friend. There was a big black smudge on Selim's cheek, but he was still laughing.

"I'm just fine. You can call off your hounds now."

Selim was quiet for just long enough that Jeb regretted saying those words.

"Ah, Jeb, I am sorry. Only lately have such measures been necessary. And not, I assure you, on your account."

He stood up, taking his whiskey glass with him.

"Come," he said, "your glass is empty." Then Selim pointed at the ruined locomotive. "Some damned engineers we are! They're lovely trains, Jeb. I apologize for wrecking this one. Tomorrow I'll have more flown over—assembled, you can be sure."

He poured more drinks, and now they were both at ease again. Or almost at ease.

"Go look in a mirror, Panther," said Jeb. "You're about ready for a minstrel show."

Selim retreated to the bathroom, and Jeb reread the instructions.

"The petcock," he said when Selim returned. "We didn't open the damned petcock. It's a pressure valve. That's why it went up."

"And to think my people imagined I was entertaining a delegation of rebels. They must be very disappointed."

"It's that bad?"

Selim sat down on one of the dark blue banquettes. "It's even worse than anyone knows." He sipped the bourbon. "All my life, Jeb, I have known that one day I must rule. Today I discovered that this 'one day' may well be tomorrow, or the day after that. And the idea scares me."

Jeb looked at him. "Your father . . ."

"The official story is, he's out in the desert hunting. As indeed he was. But they raided his camp. Rebels. Killed two very dear friends—harmless old men—and three servants. And apparently made off with the king."

This hit Jeb with the force of a mule kick. "Is there anything I can do?"

Selim smiled, a thin weary smile. "That's the real horror of it. There's nothing anyone can do, but perhaps to wait, and that's the most painful thing of all."

"But surely you can search?"

"Oh, of course. And so we are, quietly, house to house, village by village. But there are simply too many places, if a clever group wanted to hide my father. And they are clever."

"No ransom demands?"

"Not yet. It has been suggested they might want an exchange of prisoners."

"Panther, if you'd like me to go . . ."

Selim looked up and smiled. "No, Jeb. Stay. It does help to have you here. It may seem unbelievable, but in all of Kassan there's really no one I can talk to as a friend."

"It goes with the territory, Selim. Prince Charming was always a prince. You never heard much about how charming he was once he climbed onto that throne."

"Perhaps. You see, I have been kept very much in the dark about these rebels, and about other things. Perhaps I've created the situation myself. I don't know."

"I've heard," said Jeb carefully, "rumors of these rebels."

"Until a week ago they were just rumors. Then one day—broad daylight, mind you—at my father's majlis, the public audience in the courtyard, a grenade . . . two grenades . . . were thrown into the crowd. Trying for the king . . . and me. Well, they got four people. Luckily, we escaped. But it was only luck, Jeb."

"Thus the guards?"

"Exactly. It is a tense time for us, Jeb. You know the oil concession will be renegotiated soon?"

"So I've heard."

"Kassan needs the money, Jeb. We aren't like the Saudis. We aren't rolling in it. I have great plans for Kassan, once . . . Well, you know. But the oil companies must be assured that the Panther Throne will endure, that the oil will flow uninterruptedly. That's why the rebellion is particularly unpleasant just now."

"More than unpleasant, it sounds like."

"And this American—forgive me—the lady reporter with her leaflets! Inflammatory!"

"I know the lady, Selim. She's okay. Believe me."

"Okay in New York, maybe. Port Kassan is . . . another part of the forest, as your poet said."

It sure is, thought Jeb, wondering how to change the subject.

There was a small commotion in the hallway. Voices, one soft and admonitory, the other loud, imperious, angry. Speaking Arabic. Footsteps sounded decisively on the carpeted hallway.

Both men turned toward the sound.

A tall barrel-shaped man strode in, speaking as he moved. He wore some sort of uniform, dark blue and festooned with braid and gold buttons and medals in many colors. His face wore a scowl. He carried with him a brutal aura, part anger and part something less definable, a sense of imminent violence. At this person's side, obviously cowed, was the young man who had escorted Jeb into the palace.

Selim spoke sharply.

There was an immediate silence as the intruder noticed Jeb.

"I think," said Selim with an edge on his voice that could have sliced meat, "that you haven't met my brother-in-law, Jeb."

Selim introduced them.

The general shook Jeb's hand forcefully, not smiling. *A bear in the desert,* Jeb thought, *and an angry one at that. Poor Tamara!* Bir-Saraband didn't even try to be sociable. He nodded briskly at Jeb and then resumed his rapid-fire Arabic. Two minutes later Selim escorted his obviously uninvited visitor to the elevator, said a few words softly, still speaking Arabic, and returned.

When Selim came back, there was an infinite weariness in his eyes. "All that," he said, "was about very little. He doesn't trust telephones, you see. Has to say it in person."

"He's Tamara's husband?"

"Yes. And what he had to say is that there's no news at all."

"It's a strange kidnapping that has no ransom demands."

"Yes. Do you think you can eat, Jeb? I'm not sure I can, but let's try."

A round table for two had been set in an alcove. Its cloth was the same dark blue as the floor. The crystal and silver gave an eerie impression of floating in air. Or maybe it was the unaccustomed amount of bourbon Jeb had drunk.

"Well," said Selim as they sat, "tell me about Jeb Cleaver. How's Hillary, for instance?"

"Not good, Selim. We've divorced."

"I am sorry to hear that. She's a lovely girl."

Was, Jeb thought. *Was lovely, Was fun. Was mine.* "Yes," he said softly, "she is."

The food was superb, French rather than Arabic, and two wines came with it. Neither men could really eat. They sipped the wine, toyed with the perfect croissants, tasted the filet of beef.

Coffee came, and Selim suggested they take it in the other

part of the room. Where their bourbon glasses were waiting. Selim, unasked, refilled them.

He handed Jeb a glass.

"Well, Jeb, it isn't the welcome I'd hoped to give you."

"It does me good to see you. I just wish I could help." Jeb sipped the whiskey, not caring now that he'd had too much of it. "It's as though a few weeks had passed, not all those years."

"Twenty-one years," said Selim thoughtfully. "We were both younger than that, weren't we, when we first met? Freshman year. It's half our lives, Jeb."

"Half our lives so far, you turkey. I'm planning on at least twenty more."

"I pray you do."

"I know you've had a rough day, Selim, but look: if you prepare for the worst, it probably won't happen. When I design a building, it's got to be built to withstand, say, an earthquake such as the world has never known. Or I wouldn't feel comfortable about it."

"Kassan is due for its earthquake. The season, I fear, is just beginning."

"You really believe that?"

"I didn't yesterday. Today I'm not sure. Tomorrow . . . Who can say? We have had a very smooth ride so far, too smooth, maybe." Selim drank. "This alleged Arab Revolution has been with us all for a long time. The big fat kingdoms and sheikhdoms are ripe to tumble—if they haven't gone over already. Ask the Shah next time you see him."

"If you were king in Kassan, what would you change?"

"If! Corny old poem by . . . who? No matter. I could use the Panther Throne, Jeb. There is much to be done here." He walked to the window and gestured with his left hand. "There it is. Kassan. As the world sees it, a sea of gushing black oil. Oil that will one day run dry. And then where is my poor little country? Fifty years ago we were nomads starving in black goat hair tents in the desert. We can be nomads again, quicker than you think. Or exiles, some of us, warming greedy hands over fat Swiss bank accounts. In either case, there would be no Kassan as we know it. You see, Jeb, the oil is there, a gift from God. We did nothing to earn it. We don't even have the technology to pump it out of the ground and refine it ourselves. We make **nothing here.** Think about your own situation. In all of **Kassan, there** isn't even one native-born architect. Not one. **We import** them, too. From Lebanon, mostly. And it isn't only **the architects.** It's everything—all is imported—the engineers, **the skills,** most of the raw materials, all the cars, planes, televisions. All. Even the workers who build our roads. Roads going nowhere, often as not. And for all of it, Kassan is still a primitive country.

Jeb was silent for a moment, letting it all come out.

"I think you'll be fine on the Panther Throne, Selim."

Selim grinned. "If and when. If my father lives . . . well, he keeps things—as you Yankees say—close to his chest. But thank you, Jeb."

Again Jeb drank. His glass was nearly full, but it was the third glass.

"Remember the bourbon tree?"

Selim roared. Happily. "Do I remember my name? The bourbon tree!"

It had been in their freshman year at Harvard. On a warm May weekend on Cape Cod. A friend's house, a big old Victorian summerhouse all shingles and gables, with a huge pine tree in its backyard, high on a bluff overlooking Buzzard's Bay. One lazy afternoon Jeb and Selim had climbed that tree and perched high up, clutching large tumblers of bourbon. Nothing their girlfriends could say would entice them down, not until the sun had been well launched on its journey to the other side of the world with many a comical toast and Selim and Jeb were well launched too, on an epic binge.

Every springtime after that they made a ritual of it. Luckily the house belonged to a close and tolerant friend. On the first really warm weekend in May, Selim's white Jaguar convertible could be found racing down Route 128 to the cape, Jeb in the passenger seat and a few bottles of aged bourbon wrapped in towels in the trunk. Soon after that they'd be up in the bourbon tree toasting the sunset once again. The seasons changed and the girls changed, but the glow of that memory hadn't dimmed. Not by a watt.

"To the Knights of the Bourbon Tree!" Selim raised his glass, laughing.

Their glasses clinked.

"I wonder," said Jeb pensively, "if it's still there. The tree."

Selim frowned. "Larry wouldn't sell that place."

"No. He wouldn't. You know, Panther, I haven't thought of him for years. I've lost touch with so many people from those days."

"Yes, one does. I am very grateful, Jeb, that it didn't happen with us. The losing touch."

"It never will, Panther. Not if I have anything to say about it."

Selim paused, blinked, perhaps searching for the right words. "Nor I," he said at last, very simply.

Jeb looked at his watch. It was past midnight.

"I've got to be going, Selim. Thanks for everything. I'm sorry about the fire."

Selim smiled. "Don't be. My fault entirely, thinking how clever I am with tools. Tomorrow we will replace the trains. And the little panthers will love them, I promise."

"I'll be in touch, Selim. And you will let me know if there's anything . . ."

"Be sure of it." He picked up the phone and spoke a few words of Arabic into it. "There may be. Right now, it's just too mysterious. I'm afraid Kassan isn't as well equipped—or as practiced—as your country when it comes to dealing with criminals."

"I'll call tomorrow. And you can reach me anytime at the house or through the embassy. Man called Lawrence."

"Oh, Wiggy," said Selim. "I know him. Good at tennis."

The elevator door slid open and Jeb rode down in silence. The white Rolls-Royce was waiting.

The car was just as he remembered it: confident, silent, invulnerable. It drove silently out of the courtyard, empty now but for the guards, and passed through the Portal of the Dawn.

Like the car, the palace itself seemed eternal, beyond the reach of time or fate.

But that, too, was an illusion.

In the silence of the night Jeb could feel the old sureties crumbling around him. Like temples falling at the end of some old biblical movie.

Tomorrow he'd have to decide whether to tell Wiggy Lawrence about the king's disappearance.

Jeb shivered. He'd never felt so entirely alone in his life.

20

Megan didn't dare ignore the summons to the American embassy. Wilfred Austin was on her list of people to interview, but this was obviously no interview. It would undoubtedly be a grade-A chewing-out. Maybe an attempt to revoke her passport. Let 'em try! The important thing was, it had worked.

Just thinking of the sensation she'd caused made her smile. All those smug Kassanian bigwigs behind their fat desks, patronizing her. Denying that Al Khadir even existed. They'd played their silly game with the wrong girl this time.

It was going to be a busy day. First the ambassador. Then Jeb. And tomorrow—if his message was real—tomorrow she'd actuallly meet with Al Khadir! There had been dozens of phone messages when she'd returned to the Hilton yesterday evening. One from Jeb. Another from Wilfred Austin's secretary. The others were being answered by Ahmad and Louise, together or separately. She'd called Jeb right away, got the word he was out, left a message she'd drop in late in the morning. This morning.

Now her Range Rover pulled into the gate of the American embassy. So far the Kassanian drivers had proved more than adequate. Considering the traffic, Megan was almost pleased that women were forbidden to drive in Kassan. That had come as a shock to her until she began learning how much else was forbidden to them too.

What a dump, Megan thought, walking into the gloomy reception area of the embassy. Thinking that made her think about Jeb. About all that had gone wrong between them, and could it be too late to make it go right again. Later. Think about that later.

"Welcome to Kassan, Miss Mcguire," said Florence Moon, whose career had kept her out of the States for so long she had no idea who Megan was. "The ambassador is waiting for you upstairs."

Megan went right up. The gloomy, darkly varnished oak and the idea that a lecture was about to be delivered brought back her Roman Catholic grammar school in a quick unwelcome rush. Monsignor will see you in his office. The knell of doom.

She found his office door. Closed, naturally. She knocked. "Come in," a voice said faintly.

Austin was sitting at his desk looking like the mummy of Woodrow Wilson. He stood up, smiled a little flicker of a smile, and walked around the desk to greet her.

"Thank you for coming, Miss Mcguire. It's a bit awkward. Would you like some coffee?"

"Thanks, yes."

He indicated a chair and Megan sat in it. A stiff-backed, narrow-seated, uncomfortable chair. Naturally.

"Well," he said after pouring two tiny cups of black, black coffee and handing her one. "You certainly made an impression, Miss Mcguire."

"A bad one, no doubt. I really didn't mean to antagonize anyone, Mr. Austin. But after being given runaround after runaround, being here several days and getting no real information at all out of the establishment, I simply decided to take matters into my own hands. To do anything else would mean wasting more of INTERTEL's money."

"Just what information are you seeking?"

Megan needed practice at controlling her Irish temper. This seemed a good time to start. The man had the voice of a raisin. "Seeking," for God's sake.

"Believe it or not, I'm seeking the truth. About Kassan. I'm sure you've heard the rumors—of a rebellion, of corruption in palace circles, of a growing Soviet presence here. Well, those rumors got themselves all the way back to New York—and to Washington—and I want to get to the bottom of them. Find out what's really happening over here. I want to know what makes Kassan tick. Everything, from the Panther Throne to the gutter. Kassan's getting hot. I think it could get hotter. I think Kassan's going to be the next Iran—or another Cuba. And I think the citizens of America have a right to know that, and to know what their government intends to do about it."

"My, my. You are very forceful, if I may say so, for one so young."

Megan simply looked at him, not believing her ears.

He continued. "Surely you can understand that the palace—the establishment, as you call them—is very sensitive to any implication there may be instability in Kassan."

"That's their problem, isn't it? It won't make the instability go away, just by denying it."

"You must try to see their point of view. This adventure of yours with the leaflets made them very, very angry."

"I do understand," said Megan, smiling with a warmth she definitely didn't feel, "that the establishment is used to total control of all media. One look at that joke of a newspaper—"

"The *Gazette?*"

"The *Gazette*. Stalin would have blushed at putting out such shameless propaganda."

Austin managed to smile. "Perhaps. They are, of course, very primitive in many ways."

He said that, Megan thought, *as though being primitive were a virtue*. "I'm sure you can help me, then, Mr. Austin—I understand you're an accomplished Arabist."

He actually flinched. Megan was puzzled. She'd only intended to flatter him a little. Maybe the old trout really could be persuaded to help.

"Of course, that's why we're here. To help."

"I didn't break any laws. We did check that out before taking off."

"You can be sure there'll be new laws on that subject very soon. The palace, you see, thinks you are encouraging a rebellion."

"The palace doesn't know its elbow from . . . an oil well. They keep telling me there isn't any rebellion. So why are they this uptight?"

He's afraid of something, Megan thought. *What?*

"I really don't mean Kassan any harm, Mr. Austin. I didn't

come here with any preconceptions—other than it's a volatile situation. I think even you'd agree with that."

"Oh, indeed. No doubt about it."

"They can do themselves a lot of real damage by trying to bury reality. That never works. Someone just happens along and digs it up again, stinking all the harder."

His coffee cup rattled as he set it down on its saucer. "You know, of course, that the Revere Oil concession expires in two weeks?"

"Yes."

"And you understand that renewing it is very important to us—to the United States—just now?"

God help me, he's going to make a speech. It's Flag Day.

"There may be considerations here that you aren't aware of, Miss Mcguire."

"Then you can bet I'll be aware of them before I'm through." She was getting angrier. This man was as bad as the Minister of Information.

"Yes, I see. And of course it is my duty to look out for your safety while you are in Kassan."

"Thank you."

"It seems to me your actions are not in the best interests of the United States."

"Don't you mean they may not be in the best interests of Revere Oil?"

"Often these things coincide, Miss Mcguire."

"Look," she said evenly, knowing that her own private boiling point had just about been reached, "you have a job to do. So do I. As an American, don't you believe that freedom of the press is one of our most sacred assets? Maybe even more sacred than some Arab's oil? Of course I know how vital the oil looks—to the Russians, say. Of course I know how very frightened the royal family must be—"

"Frightened?"

"Frightened. Just as the Saudis are frightened. That they'll be the next domino to tumble down. Their fear—and their resentment of me publicizing that fear—is a measure of how very insecure they must feel. Three ministries swore to me there are no rebels. So why are they all put out when I pulled my little airplane stunt? The real threat is their own refusal to call a spade a spade. Or a rebel a rebel."

"Flirting with rebellion is dangerous anywhere, Miss Mcguire. It is my duty to warn you of that. If you persist, I really can't be responsible for your safety here."

Nor can I be responsible for the safety of your little reputation when I begin writing about you, thought Megan. But she said nothing along those lines. *Don't make it any worse than it is, dummy. You might need him yet.*

She smiled and rose. "I can look after myself, Mr. Austin. I've been under combat fire in Vietnam and Cambodia. I've interviewed Fidel and Mao, and nobody ever accused me of being biased. I think Americans have the right to the truth of what's happening over here, and I intend to find out. Government denials and obfuscations just won't cut it. Not with me."

She put out her hand. He took it. Austin's hand was as dry as some creature who lived in the desert. Under a rock.

"Please be careful, Miss Mcguire."

"I only take necessary risks. Thank you."

"Good day, then."

Megan walked out and down the gloomy stairs. *Necessary risks,* she thought, smiling to herself. Austin was a creep, a toady. But the interview hadn't gone all that badly, considering. Considering that it was well within his power to kick her out of the country.

Now came the morning's next challenge. Jeb Cleaver.

Ahmad had written down Jeb's address in Arabic. Now, leaving the embassy, Megan trusted to her driver and to Allah. By venturing even a block into Kassanian traffic you were casting your lot with the gods of chance in any event. Now, sitting up front next to her driver, Megan took in the view and reflected that the gods of chance might just have begun smiling on her Kassanian expedition.

At least they weren't actively frowning anymore. Not after the note that had appeared magically on her breakfast tray in the Hilton.

At first she thought it must be some sort of invitation from the hotel's management. There had been two such since her arrival: to receptions of one sort or other. Her name was written on the rich cream-colored envelope in a bold but entirely legible hand.

First she had coffee. Then she opened it. And then she gasped audibly. It read:

Dear Miss Megan Mcguire:

If you will come to me alone and unarmed, at a place in the desert known only to me, I will be pleased to see you. You may reply simply by leaving an envelope on your breakfast tray when you have finished eating. If you order lunch in your room, my response will be brought to you then. I am sure you will understand my necessity to take precautions.

> Sincerely yours,
> Bandar Al Khadir,
> General,
> The People's Army of Kassan

Delight had to compete with astonishment in Megan's reaction. Doubt came later, but she buried the doubt. Of course it could be some kind of a hoax. It could be ADDAK, or CIA, or anyone who might want to lure her out of town. Except that she wouldn't be alone. And she might not be unarmed. She wouldn't be alone for the excellent reason that she wasn't allowed to drive in Kassan. Megan was very careful in framing her reply:

Dear General Al Khadir:

Thank you for agreeing to meet with me. Naturally I am very pleased. I must beg you to allow me to bring one driver, who will be an American man, not Kassanian. This is because, as you must know, I would be arrested on the spot were I to attempt driving alone. We will be unarmed. I would like to videotape our meeting because I think it is important that the world should see you and hear what you have to say in your own words. If this is agreeable to you, I will be available anytime that is convenient.

> Yours truly, ...
> Megan Mcguire
> INTERTEL News

It had been left on the breakfast tray, and Megan was counting the seconds until his reply came.

While Megan was with the ambassador, Jeb was meeting Austin's chargé d'affaires at the site of the new embassy.

That had been Wiggy's idea when Jeb phoned first thing in the morning. And a good idea, Jeb thought, urging the Mercedes quickly along the now-familiar route. Logical for both of them to be there. Very tough for anyone to overhear.

Jeb had come to his decision quickly. Before Selim's car had dropped him at his house, he'd decided there was no point in not telling Lawrence about the king's disappearance.

It'd be known very soon in any event. The sooner the better, probably. Wiggy was waiting. They walked to the middle of the well-cleared site, just on the off chance that someone might be hidden in the bushes by the road or behind a rock. Jeb told his story concisely.

"God," said Wiggy, "it's true, then."

"You suspected something like this?"

Wiggy shrugged. "This town's like all company towns, Jeb. Crawling with rumors. Scratch a mosquito bite and by lunch tomorrow the gossips'll have you in a leper colony. Everyone knew the king was away hunting. He often is. But there have been other rumors—that Nayif is ill, for instance, that he'd been flown to New York for surgery. But this is very weird, Jeb. Very weird. If it were the rebels, Selim would have heard by now. After all, it's . . . how many days?"

"No one knows exactly. The corpses were stripped to the bone by predators, but Selim says that could happen overnight. Maximum five days, minimum two."

"One of the mysteries is, nobody knows Al Khadir. His best pals are all with him—fighting. He was quiet, perfectly behaved, way above average, much admired at his job in the Education Ministry—until all this blew up, and of course ever since then he's been labeled every kind of criminal degenerate. All the usual antirevolutionary crap. My guess is, he's smart enough that if he did manage to snatch the king, he'd quickly find a way to make use of the old man."

"Wiggy, could it be the Russians?"

"Sure. Anything from nuclear war to constipation could be the Russians. But why?"

"These oil concessions. Nayif's pretty well known to be on our side there—if he's on any side. Maybe the Russians, or even someone else, might just think their chances would be better with Selim."

"Possibly. Doubtful. They wouldn't risk holding him if that were the case. They'd arrange an accident, and let me assure you they know how. They've had plenty of practice."

"They profit by confusion, right?"

"They sure try to." Wiggy laughed, a short harsh laugh. "And where there doesn't happen to be any confusion, they aren't averse to helping it along a little. Did Selim mention the negotiations?"

"Not at all. His head's spinning. Suddenly it dawns on him he might wake up tomorrow morning on the Panther Throne. I guess that scares him a little."

"You think he's not ready?"

"He'll grow into it. Selim's not dumb and he's not a coward. But he might just be suffering a little from culture conflict. I think he's let himself drift out of the mainstream here. He doesn't seem to have a real base of power—or even any close friends."

"That's not his fault. Old Nayif runs the place as though it's a Bedu camp. Makes every decision himself. All but the military and the police, they don't interest him, so he leaves them to Ibn Bir-Saraband. Who just laps it up."

Jeb looked at his watch. Ten-thirty. Megan had left a message saying she'd be at his place around eleven.

"I've got a date, Wiggy," he said. "If anything more comes up, I'll call."

"Thanks. We appreciate it."

Jeb climbed back into the convertible, wondering just who was included in Wiggy's "we." Hindley, surely. And maybe the whole shooting match. He drove off fast. There was a lingering feeling of having betrayed Selim's confidence, but there was another feeling too: that Selim needed all the help Jeb or anyone else could bring him.

Megan hadn't arrived when Jeb got home.

He went into the small bedroom he'd set up as a studio, sat down at his drawing table, and began sketching. These were quick random drawings, conceptual things, here a detail, there a bold sweep of massive shape. And none of it seemed to make sense.

When Ali announced Miss Mcguire, it was a double relief.

First that she'd come to him, second that she'd freed him from the frustration of ideas that wouldn't jell.

She stood in the living room looking gorgeous in a white slack-suit and a deep blue silk scarf at her throat.

He kissed her. It was quick and it was casual, but at least she didn't hit him.

"Hi," he said. "Welcome to Kassan."

"Jeb . . ."

"I want to apologize. I was terrible in Williamsburg."

"I wasn't exactly Little Mary Sunshine."

"Forgive and forget?"

"It's a deal." Now she kissed him back. Truly.

He led her to the garden.

"How's it going?"

"Until yesterday, when I dropped those leaflets, terribly. Now, the joint's jumping, so to speak."

"Three of them landed right here."

"Jeb, I need your help. Are you free tomorrow?"

"I can be. What's up? She looked cautiously around the garden, expecting to see a spy behind each espaliered lemon tree.

'Total, hundred-percent secrecy?"

"Scout's honor."

"I want you to drive me somewhere."

"Not to buy a hat, I'm assuming."

"You got it. I was going to take my cameraman, but I have a hunch it ought to be you. It's a chance to use both of your connections. With Washington. And with Selim."

"I'll do it. What is it?"

"If it's on for sure, I'll tell you then. I'll know by early afternoon. Will you be here?"

"On pins and needles."

She got up then. Jeb realized he'd been dreaming about this meeting for weeks, and now it was going to be over in about five minutes. And pretty damned businesslike she was, too.

"Jeb, I may sound a little goofy, but believe me, I'm not being coy. This is the kind of thing lives might depend on, so there's no point in . . . well, jumping the gun."

"I understand. I think. Anyway, I'll be here."

"Thanks a lot. And, Jeb . . . I'm really glad you're here."

"Me too. That you're here."

She kissed him on the cheek and was gone.

Jeb stood in the garden for a moment, hardly believing she'd been there. Then, slowly, he made his way back to his studio, glanced at the sketches he'd made, and ripped the sheet off his drawing pad.

Clean start. Just what the doctor ordered.

Damn, but she could be maddening. What was it tomorrow? Well, at least she'd asked him and not someone else. That was a start, maybe. Jeb picked up the soft pencil and forced himself to do a detailed overhead projection of the site from memory.

An hour later he was only halfway through. But the lines on the pad were making sense at last. At least something was making sense in this land of hidden meanings and shifting realities.

Jeb asked for a quick salad luncheon and ate it by the pool. At half-past one the phone rang. Megan.

'We're on." There was an edge to her voice that Jeb had never heard before, an excitement, an urgency. He wondered what he'd have to do to get her to sound that way about him. "I can't go into details now, Jeb, not on the phone, but if you'll show up here at the Hilton, 1626P, that's the penthouse, at nine, we'll have breakfast and I'll tell you all about it, okay?"

"Absolutely. Can I bring anything special?"

"Dress for the desert. I'll bring a picnic, and the cars have ice-water holders built in. We should be back by evening."

"I look forward to it. I guess."

"So do I—in spades. See you at nine?"

"So long, Megan."

Click, gone. He walked back out into the garden and ate a peach. It was a very good peach, but Jeb hardly tasted it. Ali came for the tray, asked if Jeb wanted anything more.

Jeb just shook his head in reply.

He sat for several minutes in a kind of daze, idly watching a lizard on the garden wall. The lizard was small, mottled brown, and very quick. He was stalking some local version of a dragonfly. The lizard would freeze against the bright white surface of the wall, waiting. The dragonfly darted here and there, occasionally lighting on the wall just out of lizard range. Or so the insect thought. Then the little hunter would creep forward slowly, slowly, slowly. Once . . . then twice, the insect escaped in a blur of opalescent wings just as the lizard lunged.

On his third try the lizard won.

The dragonfly hesitated just a heartbeat too long. The lizard attacked and caught the glittering insect with its tongue. Quivering and buzzing and half the lizard's size, the dragonfly was dragged inexorably to sticky death. Jeb found himself mentally cheering the lizard. Patience rewarded. The little lizard was of Kassan and like Kassan. Where, it seemed, someone was always waiting and watching, calculating the right moment for attack. Jeb turned, about to call Ali, to order more coffee.

That was unnecessary. Ali stood silent, a few feet away, watching, hesitant. How long had he been there?

"Sir," said Ali, "there is a lady."

She gave Ali no chance to say anything more.

From the shadows of the house behind Jeb's servant swept another kind of shadow. A dark slim figure, heavily veiled in the traditional manner, robed from head to foot in Muslim black, veiled to the eyes. And what eyes.

They stared at Jeb from out of the past.

She approached gracefully and quite fast. She walked past Ali as though he weren't there. Jeb watched, speechless. She came quite close and then paused by an ornamental table of white wrought iron.

"Well, Jeb," she said in a low husky voice that was not at all the voice he remembered, "can't I have a kiss for old times' sake?"

Tamara Bir-Saraband, Princess of Kassan, walked the few feet that separated them. As she moved, she reached up and detached the veil and headdress. They fell rippling to the tiled terrace. On her gaunt and elegant face was a strange and almost trancelike smile.

Jeb felt as though he had fallen off the face of the planet. Then he was kissing her full on the lips. He felt the hunger in her and kissed her again.

"I can't believe it," he said quietly.

Tamara freed herself with a little laugh then, stepped back, and regarded him curiously, holding both of Jeb's hands in hers. She was very thin. For a moment neither of them could say anything. Then they embraced again, clinging, prisoners of time, trapped by a magical summer long ago and by everything that had happened since then.

"So," she said finally, "my beautiful American has come back at last. Not back to his Tamara, of course. That would be too much to hope for. But in any event back—back to this place." She looked away for an instant, then back. "If only we could go back in time."

"I've often wished that."

"Have you, Jeb?"

"Tell me," he said. "Everything."

She sat down on the white iron bench. He took a chair close by. "Everything," said Tamara with a small and rueful smile, "would take a very long time. And be very boring besides. In the meantime, do you suppose this good Muslim wife could have a glass of wine?"

Jeb rose to get it, and wondered how much bitterness there must be stored up in her for it to come out so soon. He came back with a tray, two wineglasses, and an ice bucket holding a bottle of chilled Muscadet.

"I shall drink to you, Jeb Stuart Cleaver, if I may."

"Twenty-one years," he said. "Longer than I had years to my age when I first met you. You've grown up, Tamara."

"One does." She sipped. "Delicious. I have heard great things of you, Jeb, from my wandering brother, over the years."

"He flatters me. I work at being an architect. I love it. I try."

"How remarkable to love what one does. I wish I could say as much."

"What do you do?"

"Ah. Good question. I am my father's daughter, my husband's wife, my children's mother. And I am nothing. I seldom see my husband. Do you know him? The great general?"

"We've met."

"He is a beast among beasts. Am I shocking you, Jeb?"

"You're making me sad. I was in love with you that summer. At least it seemed like love."

She twirled the pale wine in its tall-stemmed glass.

"Yes, it did rather, didn't it?"

Finally she stood up and came to him and took his hand. "Now," was all she said or had to say.

They walked into the house and to his bedroom, a processional through time. The fine sheer black robe that she was wearing slid to the floor in a ripple of gossamer silk. The black slip underneath it was French and trimmed with handmade lace. She shed it with a quick gesture and stood before him radiant in her golden skin. Jeb paused in his own undressing and thought: *There are female panthers too.*

Their lovemaking was an explosion. She was hungry, searching, restless, consuming him with her eyes, her hands, her tongue. Jeb abandoned himself eagerly and entirely, gave himself to the lovely game. Afterward Tamara stretched lazily and entwined her slender arms around Jeb's neck. He was glistening with sweat in the artificially chilled room.

"My beautiful American boy has come back to me," she murmured softly, dangerously. "You will never know, Jeb Cleaver, how much I have wanted you . . . needed you. All these years."

He could say nothing, and so he kissed her.

"How I have searched for you—for someone like you—in unimaginable places." Her hand was stroking his chest slowly, slowly, lower, then lower. He moved in response. "In Paris," she went on as though the searching, caressing hand belonged to someone else, "there has been many a fine young American boy who somehow reminded me of you, Jeb, strong like you or with your curly brown hair, tall quick young men who ended up with something nice from Cartier's and a wild memory. But they were not you. They were never you."

Jeb felt a pang as though she had stabbed him in the heart. He closed his eyes for a moment and woke sometime later to find her dressing. Her smile when she saw him was lovely, softer now, but with something wild behind it.

"You are," she said simply, "even more delicious than in my dreams. Thank you, Jeb. Whatever happens now."

Jeb didn't know why, exactly, but there was danger in her voice.

"I thank you."

He got up and slipped into some old blue jeans and an alligator shirt. She was all ready to go. He kissed her lightly on the forehead.

"Jeb," she whispered, "take care. Realize that your servants are almost certainly my husband's people—ADDAK."

"But why?"

She laughed harshly, bitterly. "Because that's the kind of swine he is, dear Ibn. I am in no danger—I think. The king's daughter is still useful to him, whatever I do—as long as I do it discreetly. But he is a beast—an animal. When I say that, I do animals an injustice. So . . . take care, Jeb."

"Can I help?"

She smiled a smile of infinite sadness. "You can pretend to love me a little from time to time. That helps."

"I wasn't pretending."

She smiled again, a cold perfect scimitar of a smile. And he knew then it was no good even trying. That she was far beyond self-deception. There was something truly reckless in Tamara. In her eyes, in her smile. In her lovemaking. Something untamed and dangerous. A panther born and bred.

Why hadn't she stayed a dream, a golden memory?

"I must go now, Jeb."

He saw her to the door. An enormous Mercedes limousine was waiting.

"Thank you, Mr. Architect, for a most educational afternoon."

And she was gone in a ripple of black silk chiffon.

Jeb stood in the glaring Kassanian sunlight watching her go, and he stayed there for a moment even after the great hulking car had pulled away.

Then, slowly, he turned and went back into the house. He sat down heavily in the living room and rubbed his eyes.

And he wondered where in the souk you went to buy back your dreams.

21

Jeb pushed the Mercedes through the seething traffic of eight A.M., allowing more time than he really needed to get to Megan's hotel. He was more eager than he'd expected to be when she asked him to drive her——where?

Maybe it was just being with her again, being on good terms again. Good terms that Jeb intended to make better. Now that he knew how volatile she could be, he'd watch it. Tread softly, take care. Except for the maddening way she had of getting right under his skin, be it with pleasure or with anger. He smiled, thinking of how she'd looked in his house yesterday.

And then Jeb stopped smiling.

He thought of Tamara, too. Tamara, in her own solid-gold do-it-yourself hell. He'd have to do something about Tamara, and soon, and Jeb didn't have even the beginning of an idea as to what it would be.

He tried to figure the odds of Tamara meeting Megan. Some scene that would be. There was a ramp leading from King Nayif Chaussée into the Hilton's basement parking garage. Jeb pulled into it and accepted a ticket from the attendant and took the elevator right up to Penthouse 1626.

"We look like a team," he said when she opened the door. Dress for the desert, she'd said, and Jeb was wearing cowboy boots, lightweight but tightly woven tan poplin trousers, and a matching windbreaker over a white alligator shirt. Megan wore a safari suit in the same color, and a white silk blouse.

She kissed him. "Wait'll they see us sing and dance," she said. "Thanks for coming early. I have breakfast all set up."

She led him through the living room to the big terrace beyond. A serving cart was there, napped in white, with orange juice, coffee, and a variety of croissants, brioche, toast, jams, and butter.

"Very nice," he said, taking in the 180-degree view of Port Kassan.

"Yes, it's the only place in town from which you can't see the Hilton."

Megan poured juice and coffee. Jeb helped himself to a pair of croissants and sat down in a nearby deck chair.

"Tell me about it," he said. "You're being very mysterious, for someone in the broadcasting business."

"If I let the wrong people know where we're going today, they'd probably hand me my head on a platter."

She came very close, leaned even closer, and whispered, "Jeb, we're going to meet him—Al Khadir!"

For a moment Jeb just sat there. *So the damned yellow leaflets had done their job.*

"You're sure—I mean, are you really sure it's him?"

"Who else would it be?"

Her voice and her manner were confident, but Jeb wondered how much of that confidence was really bravado.

"I'm not sure—just a hoax, maybe?"

"It could be, but I don't think so. Anyway, we have to find out. Jeb, it could be the scoop of a lifetime. Like interviewing Fidel before he ousted Batista."

Jeb could see the excitement shimmering in her eyes. He could hear the eagerness vibrating in her voice. And he remembered Williamsburg very clearly. He wasn't going to ruin his second—maybe his last—chance with Megan, not if it meant driving to the moon for no reason at all. He looked at her and smiled. "I think it's fabulous, and I'm glad you asked me."

She smiled and drank her orange juice to the last drop.

"Stay here, Jeb. I just want to check the cameras and things one more time."

She did that and was back in ten minutes.

"All systems go. Are you ready?"

'Ready. What can I carry?"

Jeb was amazed at the compactness of the videotaping equipment. Only the two battery packs had any real weight at all. He carried the Minicam and its portable battery packs, and Megan lugged a large wicker picnic basket.

"We have three thermos jugs of lemonade," she said, "and one of iced tea, and fruit and sandwiches—he may not give us lunch."

He may give us a bullet in the gut, thought Jeb, saying nothing. He took a few minutes to make himself familiar with the Range Rover. Some machine. It appeared to be ready for just about anything: there were extra water tanks, a reserve fuel supply, and special insulation and sealing for the engine, doors, and windows. The idea was to resist blowing sand and dust. It had the capability to convert to four-wheel drive if they had to get off the road.

"Do you have maps and a compass?"

"Check." She said it so briskly Jeb had to look to see the impish grin before he knew she was laughing at him. Still, he was relieved. Once they were out of sight of Port Kassan, getting lost would be easy.

He started the engine and pulled slowly out onto the street. Megan was navigating. "Straight down Nayif Chaussée," she said, "until we hit the six-lane highway that goes past the airport."

Jeb drove cautiously. There'd be time enough for speed when they got out of town, and he wanted to get the feel of the Range Rover. Compared to his little Mercedes, it was about like driving a small truck. It was three blocks before Jeb noticed the gray sedan.

The car was a four-door Mercedes-Benz painted battleship gray. The shine had worn off and there was a dent on the left-front fender. Two men in Western-style business suits were in the front seat. They both wore sunglasses. And they seemed to be following the Range Rover too attentively.

"Don't look back, Megan, but I have a funny feeling we've got company."

He turned left at the next corner. The Mercedes turned too. This side street was much narrower than Nayif Chaussée. There was barely room for two cars to pass. *Good,* thought Cleaver; *no chance of their overtaking me here.* The gray sedan was right behind him now. The slow pace of traffic enabled Jeb to watch the Mercedes carefully. His hands tightened a little on the Rover's big steering wheel. He studied the road ahead.

On the left corner of the intersection he was approaching, a building had been torn down. In its rubble there had sprung up a makeshift open-air market. A few tattered cloth umbrellas shaded fruit and melons. Old men squatted in the dust with odd bits and pieces for sale, a motley assortment of hardware, used pots, plastic sandals, lurid artificial flowers, all arrayed on worn blankets. Veiled, black-robed women browsed and haggled. Little boys darted here and there, laughing, making mischief like small boys everywhere.

Jeb had an idea. He slowed the Rover to a crawl.

A big truck was lumbering toward the intersection, pulling slowly in from the left. It was a water wagon, really a huge wooden barrel lashed to the rusting truckbed, a locked spigot on its side. Jeb had noticed such trucks before in Kassan—the well that came to its customers.

The water truck showed no signs of stopping. Jeb waited until it was almost halfway across the intersection. Then he floored the accelerator and the horn button at the same time.

"Hang on, Megan!" he said quietly as the Rover shot ahead and around the truck's front bumper, grazing it a little as they passed. Jeb got a glimpse of the truck driver's astonished face, surprise quickly changing to outrage.

They were already halfway down the next block when they heard the crash. Jeb smiled but didn't even turn his head. He doubled back to Nayif Chaussée and made it to the six-lane highway with no other incidents.

"Do you think it was ADDAK?" Megan's voice was level, but Jeb could detect an edge of fear in it.

"It was someone trying to tail us—not very cleverly. Which sounds like ADDAK. Could be anyone. Let's hope they were dumb enough to use just one pair of bloodhounds."

Jeb kept an eye on the rearview mirror, but for the next ten miles he saw nothing suspicious. Megan pulled a paper out of her pocket. "After we pass the airport, it's six miles to the turning," she said, "then eleven miles to the ruined mosque—that'll be on our right."

In twenty minutes they were in the middle of a desert so barren Port Kassan might never have existed. All the crowding and clamorous traffic of the capital city vanished here, replaced by low rolling dunes of red-beige sand. The sky was enormous here, a fat blue bowl.

They said very little. Jeb had been more shaken by the trailing incident than he wanted to admit. It meant someone was watching the Hilton garage. These Range Rovers were conspicuous, and Megan had three of them in her entourage. Of course, that could be made to work for her—with decoys.

"Here's the turning, I think," she said.

They drove on a narrow two-lane road until the old mosque appeared on their right, just where Megan had said it would be. It must have been a lovely thing once. Now it stood lonely and forlorn with the roof of its main chamber caved in, the blue-and-yellow tiles cracked and broken, its garden already invaded by the hungry sand.

Jeb stopped the car and they both climbed out, eager for a chance to stretch a little, even if it did mean abandoning the well-chilled air inside the Rover.

"Now we look for the next part of our instructions: he says they'll be in a crack in this wall."

Megan indicated the ruined garden wall. There were hundreds of cracks, and the wall had once been whitewashed. It took ten minutes with both of them looking.

Jeb found the thing. *Clever,* he thought. *If you didn't know what you were looking for, you'd never dream of looking at all.* And for the first time on this crazy expedition Jeb began to feel a little optimism creeping into his very apprehensive attitude.

They climbed back into the car and drove off.

"Proceed on this road for twenty miles," Megan read. " 'Turn right at the first village, drive precisely nine miles into the hills, and look for a round stone which will appear to have rolled into the middle of the road. When you see the stone, park the car—off the road on the left shoulder. Walk up the path that winds up the hill to the right. Al Khadir will await you there.' "

Jeb looked at her. Cops and robbers. Counterspies. His brain was a jumble of all the adventure movies he'd ever seen. The brutal reality of the gray Mercedes hitting the water wagon was only the first reminder that he was getting in deep. Very deep. Into someone else's war, maybe.

Time seemed arrested here in the desrt. The sameness of the landscape, the vast dry emptiness, the enormous sky, all conspired to give another dimension of unreality to the experience. Jeb found himself stealing glances at his watch as though he were afraid Megan would imagine he was bored. Hardly bored.

They had been driving more than two hours when they got to the little mud-brick village that marked their turning.

The land had changed subtly the last few miles. The flat horizon grew bumps, and now, approaching them directly, Jeb discovered that the bumps were sizable hills. Jeb's sense of danger made all his instincts doubly alert. He tried to memorize every turning in the road, imagining some high-speed escape. Could he find his way back here at night? Probably. Thinking that made him wonder if this rebel Al Khadir would ever let them go. The most hunted man in Kassan might feel just a little nervous about receiving two strangers into his hiding place and letting them go away freely. Perhaps to return with an army.

No traffic sought out this lonely road. The blacktop turned to dirt at the far side of the little village. Jeb studied the buildings as best he could: "undistinguished" was hardly the word for it. Here was a small poor village that had always been small and poor. No house more than one story, no mosque, nothing but low mud-brick walls, here and there a small window or a characterless doorway.

No craftsman had ever plied his trade here. There was none of the fantasy that enlivened the tall houses in the old quarter: no grilles or iron intricacies, no balconies or arches.

There was something sad about the place, sad and almost empty. It was hard for Jeb to imagine living there.

Outside the town they began climbing above the desert floor.

"The Burujurdi," said Megan.

"The what?"

"The Burujurdi Mountains—we're in the foothills. At least I think we are." She pulled out the map. "Yes. Almost." Jeb remembered the western mountains, a low rocky range that made a natural border between Kassan and the enormity of Saudi Arabia to the west. The hills seemed to go on forever,

273

and Jeb realized what a fine hiding place they must make for anyone who could live off the land.

"Take a look off to the left," Jeb said, "and you're suddenly in the year one."

Then on a hillside was a young boy tending a flock of sheep. He might have been ten years old and wore a tattered robe of white-and-blue-striped cotton and carried a long staff. His sheep were happily grazing on what appeared to be barren sand and rock. There must be some vegetation up there.

"I wish," said Megan, "that we could get him on tape, but I guess there isn't time."

"David," said Jeb, "waiting for his Goliath."

"I bet that's how Al Khadir feels," she said, "all the odds against him."

"Are they?"

"I wish I knew. Maybe we'll find out today."

And maybe we'll die doing it, thought Jeb.

The round stone was almost precisely in the center of the road, three miles past the young shepherd.

Jeb pulled off the road onto a shoulder that was a little wider than what he'd been seeing. "Half-past eleven," he said. "When are we expected?"

"Noon. You hungry?"

Jeb realized he was famished. "I shouldn't be, but I think our pals in the gray car might have set the old adrenaline flowing."

She touched his arm, just lightly.

"I was terrified, Jeb. You did that well. Ducking around them as though it was the most natural thing in the world."

"I wouldn't call it natural. And I hope those bastards drowned after they hit the barrel."

The sat in the car for a few minutes, ate sandwiches, and drank lemonade.

"Maybe we'd better be going," Megan said after a while. "We don't know how far it is."

"It sounds dumb to ask, but should we lock the car?"

She grinned. "Sure. These cameras are pretty valuable, after all. And . . . well, it looks empty out here, but who knows?"

They locked all their equipment into the Rover and walked briskly up the path.

THE PANTHER THRONE

Ever since they'd parked, Jeb had had a prickling feeling at the back of his neck. The feeling of being watched. He blinked in the sunlight and told himself he was being stupid. Stupid and paranoid.

The track was barely visible. It wound around the hill and up, always upward. Eventually, after two turnings, they came to a level place, a wide shoulder of the hill. It might have been a little longer than a football field, strewn with big rocks and here and there a scraggly bush of some sort.

About halfway down the length of the little plateau there was a sort of fissure in the slope to the left.

It might have been made by a seasonal stream, or even carved by the wind. Jeb looked at it and knew, suddenly, that Al Khadir would be hidden in that narrow crevasse.

Whatever instinct told him that, he decided to keep the possibly false information to himself. This was Megan's game. Let her play it the way she wanted to. The path was played out now. They walked up the wide and nearly level space toward the shadowy cut in the hillside. To their right the naked hills tumbled down to the desert floor. Red sand, beige dust, the occasional outcropping of stone. In a painting it might look picturesque. In reality it was the color scheme of desolation.

The silence was absolute. Nothing moved. There was no stirring of the air.

Then they heard a shrill unmusical cry, a bird's call. Or so it seemed. They kept on walking.

They were at the mouth of the ravine now.

"I'd guess," said Jeb, "that he'll be up there. It's the best hiding place around."

It was.

For a moment they stood in the sunlight, saying nothing, staring up into the shadowed ravine as though it might speak to them.

Then they saw him.

A tall dark figure of a man in the classic white Arabian robe and headcloth. He had stepped out from behind a huge rock. The tall Arab stood there, and a shaft of sunlight caught him, the dazzling white of his robe against the deep shade behind. He made one gesture, beckoning. There was a silent majesty in it.

Jeb felt as though he was walking into a dream. The tall dark man might have come out of a Gypsy's prediction.

The man said nothing until they were very close.

Then Bandar Al Khadir walked toward them, extended his hand, and said in excellent English, "Welcome, Miss Mcguire. You are just on time, and I appreciate this. I do not know your friend."

"General Al Khadir," said Megan conventionally, trying to repress the excitement in her voice, "this is Jeb Stuart Cleaver. He is an American architect, and he will be designing the new American embassy for Kassan."

Bandar looked at Jeb. It was not an unfriendly stare, merely speculative.

"Yes," he said at last. "We have heard of you."

They shook hands.

"Come," said Al Khadir, and led them farther up the narrow valley.

There was a small encampment at the head of the ravine. Six black goathair tents were grouped close together. A small cooking fire was well-isolated by rocks and set into a pit.

"We live, as you see, very simply," said Al Khadir, gesturing for them to sit on some boulders of a convenient size. "It is necessary to be portable. To be able to move on a moment's notice."

"I wonder, General," asked Megan, "if it might be possible for you to send someone for my cameras. We left them in the car."

Bandar spoke rapidly and loudly in Arabic.

Two young men appeared from behind one of the tents. They were thin as rapiers and there was something edgy—something a little frightening—in their glance. They looked like hunted things. Or like hunters. Jeb decided they were probably both.

He handed Al Khadir the car keys and Megan described what she needed.

"You were observed, you see," said Al Khadir, "so I am confident that you have not brought . . . uninvited guests."

"Tell, me, General—" Megan began, only to be interrupted by a hearty laugh from Al Khadir.

"Please, I am no more a general than you are, kind lady. It is useful in our movement—to keep a tight organization, there must be rankings, discipline, but it is not a thing that I, as the head of the movement, take very seriously."

He paused, looked up, and waved an arm.

Jeb and Megan followed his gesture with their eyes. The top of the ravine was perhaps a hundred feet overhead, a steep and jagged rim of stone and underbrush. There, just visible, was a man armed with an automatic rifle. Jeb wondered how many others there might be up there. The ravine would be a classic trap if anyone tried to force his way up here unwanted.

"Not," Al Khadir continued, "Like Bir-Saraband, who gets himself up like something from a comic opera, all draped in gold and shining with medals. I take the revolution very seriously, Miss Mcguire, but such ornamentations seem to me . . . well, silly."

Megan listened carefully, planning her interview. The man had a vibrant magnetism about him. Charismatic, to be sure. And very sexy too. She almost blushed at the thought, but there it was. Al Khadir was handsome in a rangy desert-bred way. The hawk's nose, the huge deep brown eyes, the neatly trimmed beard and proud yet easy carriage all added up to something very impressive. She knew he'd look wonderful on camera, and Megan was grateful that Al Khadir had consented to be taped. There was something indefinable but most striking about him. In ten minutes the young men reappeared with the Minicam and its battery packs and Megan began calculating angles, light and shadow. The Minicam had a tiny square monitor built into it. She could frame her subject, zoom in and zoom out, stop the thing and start it all at the touch of a button. Once she got the basic tape, editing could be done back at the hotel or even in New York. Assuming that the tape got out of Kassan. That was another worry, another bridge to be crossed when she came to it.

"What I'd like, General, is for you to tell us, in your own words, just what you're hoping to accomplish here in Kassan."

He nodded. She positioned him sitting, about ten feet from the camera. It wouldn't be as sophisticated as if Jerry or Philo shot it, but Megan was confident that she could do a good basic job of framing and composition. She'd often worked the Minicam, both on location and in the studio, just to learn how various effects were achieved. Now she was glad of the practice.

Camera rolling, she told herself. *Take one, and may it find its way back to Wonderland!*

She made a mark in the sand and asked Jeb to stand there, focused on him, then set the camera running and stepped into the same spot. "This is Megan Mcguire," she said, "INTER-TEL News. I am in a secret rebel hideout somewhere in Kassan. And what you are about to see is the first interview ever with the leader of the People's Army of Kassan—General Bandar Al Khadir."

Having spoken her piece, Megan went back behind the little camera and focused on Bandar.

"General Al Khadir," she said, hoping the recording equipment would keep functioning, "would you please tell us about the Kassanian revolution in your own words?"

Bandar nodded gravely. "In order to understand Kassan," he said quietly, "you must know about my sister Leila, and what happened to her, and why."

For more than twenty minutes Bandar went on. He told his sister's sad story simply, without histrionics. But before he had finished, Megan felt herself blinking away tears. Then he went on. Leila was but one of thousands. Bandar outlined the essential corruption of the government, the laziness of various ministries, instances of graft and inadequacy. He named names and cited instances. Now all those years of Bandar and Majid and their friends monitoring the ineptitude of the various ministries and the army and the health-care establishment paid off. He spoke with absolute assurance. And while Megan realized she'd have to do some frantic fact-checking back in Port Kassan, she found herself believing every word. Megan always tried to maintain a certain professional distance from whatever she was investigating. As Al Khadir spoke on and on, she felt that cool analytical distance lessening. She was hanging on his next word, thoroughly caught up in what he was saying. In the facts and hopes and horrors that gave weight and force to his words. Megan looked at Jeb from time to time. He was reacting the same way. The rebel leader was more eloquent than he knew.

It was going to be an incredibly powerful piece of video-tape. Megan felt a tingling, a building excitement. This was the real stuff. This was what she'd gone out on a very long limb hoping to bring back from Kassan. It was happening!

Bandar was working to a conclusion now.

". . . and," he said, after describing the latest injustice involving the distribution of medical aid to the provinces, "there is no one who listens, no one who really sees these things. There is no justice. This is why the People's Army has come into existence. This is why we will succeed. I speak to the people of America—of free lands everywhere. America, you who once struggled to remove the oppressive laws of a king who ruled your land but would not listen. Our struggle is your struggle, two hundred years later and in another land. But it is the same struggle, and against the same sort of injustices. Our battle cry is 'Fakk raqaba!' It means to lift off the yoke. And though many of us may die in doing it, the yoke will be thrown off. This is my pledge—on the word of the People's Army of Kassan!"

He paused, waiting for her reaction.

For a long moment Megan couldn't say one word. She was that deeply moved by what he had just said.

"Was it all right?" There was a note of worry in his voice. "Should I do it over again, Miss Mcguire?"

She regained control of herself. It wasn't easy.

"You were wonderful. Truly wonderful. When this tape gets on the air, General, you'll see some changes in Kassan. I think that's a safe promise."

The smile that broke out on Al Khadir's face was a beautiful thing to see. It was an awakening, a sunrise, a silent explosion of happiness.

"Thank you," he said, "very much." He rose and walked close to them. All during his speech and afterward, Jeb had said nothing at all. Partly because he was profoundly impressed by the man's words and partly because Al Khadir was so completely the born ruler. Jeb couldn't help making the comparison, the fatal and inevitable comparison, between Selim and this fellow.

It was not a contest that Selim could hope to win.

Al Khadir walked with them down to the car. The two young men followed with the equipment. Megan and the Arab leader walked ahead, deep in conversation. Jeb followed them, and the boys brought up the rear.

Now Jeb understood why Megan had asked him to come. Risking only Allah knew what. Once again, Jeb recalled their argument in Williamsburg. How very right she'd been.

And how tough it was going to be for him to admit it. They reached the Range Rover and loaded the equipment.

Megan and Al Khadir shook hands. Jeb hadn't heard their conversation on the trail. She'd tell him later. Maybe.

He turned to the general. "Good luck, General," Jeb said, extending his hand.

"Thank you," said Al Khadir with a gracious smile, more like the host at an elegant picnic than the most wanted political criminal in Arabia. "And thank you for escorting Miss Mcguire. Take good care of her—she is a valuable person."

"I will," said Jeb, and he climbed into the Rover and drove off.

"Well," said Megan as they did a U-turn and drove down the winding road to the village, "how about that?"

"I liked him, even though I kind of hate admitting it."

"So did I. But why hate to admit it?"

"Selim."

"Selim. Selim has his work cut out for him, wouldn't you say, if this guy is his main competition?"

"Yes. That's just what I'd say. Poor old Panther."

"Would Selim agree to be interviewed, Jeb? I've been getting a runaround from the palace like you wouldn't believe."

Jeb took a deep breath. "He really has been busy—there's a lot of stuff going on right now that—"

"—that nosy reporters shouldn't be asking about?"

He looked at her, feeling her temper rising.

"I'll talk to him, Megan. But I can't answer for what he'll say. He is under a lot of pressure."

She laughed. "If he thinks he's under a lot of pressure now, wait'll my interview airs. He's under pressure, Jeb, because he's had his head buried in the sand—he or his father."

"You're probably right. But he's still my friend, and you can't just walk up to the guy and say, oh, by the way, how about handing over your kingdom to this charming rebel I know?" And he thought: *she doesn't know about Nayif's kidnapping. And I can't tell her.*

They passed through the village. It was every bit as

deserted-looking as before. And again Jeb had the feeling that unseen eyes were watching them.

"You have a way of getting the tape back?"

"I think so—pray so. First we'll make several copies, check the quality, all that. Not that we really have the luxury of a reshoot. But I'm taking no chances. I'm going to try several ways—all of them a little clandestine. You know what would happen if ADDAK got wind of this."

"I wonder," Jeb said evenly, "what will happen when it airs."

She laughed. There was a fine defiance in it.

"A lot, my dear," she said. "More than we can imagine."

22

T. R. Kalbfleisch had been a member of the Port Kassan Jockey Club for five years, but this was only the second time he'd set foot in the place. The air was chilled, the silence was almost like that of some great empty cathedral. Here in the main lounge there were islands of deeply tufted red brocade armchairs in little groupings on a sea of red wall-to-wall carpeting. The idea was to isolate groups of businessmen so that the most secret discussions could be conducted without the necessity of whispering. In the dining room, too, the tables were widely separated.

T. R. had come early for his appointment with Wiggy Lawrence. It was Friday, September 19. The Sabbath in Kassan. The Jockey Club was open all week long, but today there was just a skeleton crew of servants, for it was sure that none of the Kassanian Arabs who formed half the club's very exclusive membership would be present. There was a total of three hundred members, strictly limited. The non-Kassanian members represented a pantheon of the world's most powerful businessmen and political leaders. As the ambassador-at-large of Revere Oil, T. R. was inevitably a part of this group.

The initiation fee was one hundred thousand dollars. Annual dues were twenty-five thousand. And there was a waiting list for new memberships that stretched from Texas to Tokyo. Opulent meals could be ordered here, but no wine. There was an immense swimming pool in which no swimmer had ever been seen. Women, of course, were strictly prohibited.

The club was thriving. This pleased its manager, a plump

Kassanian named Kalid. Kalid was the nephew of a distant cousin of King Nayif's. Kalid's round face was almost always smiling. He had a lot to smile about. The club was making its manager very rich. Not a tin of caviar nor a pound of sugar was ordered by the Jockey Club without Kalid's taking a handsome commission. Under certain circumstances, Kalid found it possible to speed up a membership application. Then, too, he was in an ideal position to introduce—for instance—a German manufacturer of expensive halogen street-lamps to the Kassanian Minister of Highways. Such social niceties were yet another lucrative hobby for the cheerful, rotund man.

Today Kalid himself had greeted T. R. Kalbfleisch, Sabbath or no Sabbath. T. R. wondered why, but only briefly. T. R. had far more important things on his mind than the comings and goings of club managers, however royal their connections.

He sipped mint tea and looked at his watch. It wasn't necessary. Wiggy, as usual, was precisely on time. T. R. rose, smiling with a cheer he didn't feel inside.

"Howdy," said T. R., mocking.

"Good to see you, T. R.," said Wiggy, not missing a beat. "How's everything in Texas?"

"If you mean Bradboy, he sends his regards. But a cat on a hot tin roof is relaxed by comparison to our Bradboy. Very uptight about the fifth of October."

"It's in the air," said Wiggy, "like a virus."

"Here, too?"

"Here especially." Wiggy, from long habit, glanced casually around the room before he spoke. There was not another soul to be seen in the enormous room. He touched T. R.'s arm lightly. "To say that the natives are restless would be underestimating it.

One of T. R.'s silver-fox eyebrows rose just a little. He hated having to admit that Bradboy Shane might have guessed right for once. He hated even more the thought that his own confident appraisal of the Kassanian negotiations might have been wrong.

"And the king?"

Wiggy frowned. "That's part of the, shall we say, confusion. King Nayif hasn't been seen for more than a week. The official story is that he's out in the desert falconing with some old buddies. That's the official story. The rumors that contradict it—well, if you had a dollar for every one of 'em, you could forget about the damned negotiations."

T. R. cleared his throat. The sound echoed in the enormous lounge. "How about a bite of lunch, Wiggy?"

They got up and walked to the dining room. This was a large glassed-in terrace green with palms, giant ferns, and orchids. The floor was of white marble and white pedestal tables sprouted like the most elegant of mushrooms at very discreet intervals. Although it was early for luncheon in Kassan, there were three occupied tables. At one a pair of Japanese dined alone. At another five overweight Germans laughed heartily. Such were the acoustics of the Jockey Club that their laughter seemed to vanish into the thin air like smoke. From across the room it was an eerie sensation, the feeling of watching fishes in an aquarium, or of seeing television with the sound off. The headwaiter showed T. R. and Wiggy to a table in a niche formed by large white marble planters overflowing with greenery.

The menu, like everything else about the club, was opulent to the point of fantasy. Maine lobsters were available at fifty dollars the pound. Caviar was a bargain at twenty dollars the ounce. Prices were listed in Kassanian pounds, British pounds, U.S. dollars, Swiss francs, and deutsche marks. T. R. wondered how the Japanese felt about the omission of the yen. Maybe it was an official reprimand of some sort.

Wiggy ordered caviar followed by pheasant in a lingonberry sauce. T. R., typically fastidious, had a clear consommé and broiled Dover sole.

"What would you not give," asked Wiggy wistfully as he tasted the fresh Caspian caviar, "for a glass of Montrachet?"

"I'd give a lot more," said T. R., "to know just what's up in the palace. That's why I'm here, Wiggy. We thought it'd all go pretty smoothly—the negotiations—because we had no reason not to. But everything looks different now. Those rumors you mentioned have been heard even in Texas. And that means they've been heard in a lot of other places as well. Are they rumors? Does anyone know for sure?"

"Nobody who's talking to me about it knows. The big news, of course, is the rebels. And we hear all kinds of dumb stuff about them, too. The army—Bir-Saraband—claims they hardly exist. Hotheaded kids. Students. Other people aren't so sure. And they've made a few serious raids. Including tossing a few grenades over the palace wall last week. Right into the king's majlis. It was a miracle that they didn't get old Nayif and Selim too. Both of them were within a few yards of the hit. Four people were killed, actually, and a few more were injured."

"And who's doing what about it?"

Wiggy looked up at his host. He didn't know T. R. well, but he knew all about Revere Oil. T. R. represented one of the world's six major oil companies, and that distinction alone gave him more power and prestige than most governments. Wiggy could feel the force of that power now, understated because that was the Kalbfleisch style of doing business. But Wiggy knew very well that unless he delivered whatever it was T. R. wanted, and delivered it fast and neatly wrapped, pressures could be brought to bear on him that would effectively destroy his career in the State Department.

It wasn't a good feeling. It wasn't a good feeling at all, and the ominous implications of it were compounded by the simple fact that Wentworth Lawrence III didn't have one idea in the world what to do about it.

They were drinking Perrier water with lime.

Wiggy took a long sip. "I'll do whatever I can, naturally, T. R.," he said. "There are a few unofficial sources you ought to talk to. And of course we'll get to the palace immediately. To Selim if not to his father—"

The sentence was broken off halfway by a roar and a crash so loud they were unreal, beyond thunder. Wiggy saw the huge plate-glass window rippling like silk in the instant before it shattered. The first detonation was ringing in their ears as both men dived to the floor. They crouched low, hugging close to the marble planters, putting the planters between themselves and the exploding windows, protecting their faces with upflung arms. There was a second explosion, then a third. Then silence. The silence was almost more frightening than the blast, because it was a pregnant, threatening pause. They stayed curled up behind the planters, waiting for whatever hell might break loose now.

It seemed as though hours had passed before the screaming

began. Slowly T. R. got up, still crouching, ready to hit the floor again. The dining room was empty.

Wiggy was on his feet now too. They tried to remember where the other diners had been. Only a big table lying on its side bore messy witness to the party of Germans. The dining terrace was at the rear of the club, and the first explosion seemed to have hit it directly. All the big windows were shattered. It was a miracle, T.R. decided, that somebody hadn't been beheaded by flying glass.

They walked back through the lounge. It too was deserted. The screaming had stopped now. From the lounge, which looked completely untouched, they made their way down the central hall to the foyer. The front doors had been blown off their hinges and the white marble of the foyer was open to the hot afternoon.

Sprawled on his back just inside the blasted-out doors was Kalid, the manager. His immaculate white robe was in bloody shreds. There was blood, a lot of blood, in a big pool spreading across the polished white stone. T.R. went up to the fat man and picked up his wrist. "Wiggy," he said, "could you please check the kitchen—see if any of the help is still around?" But Kalid was beyond helping.

Wiggy went off searching and T.R. stayed beside the lifeless Kalid. Just then the doors to the men's room opened and one of the Germans appeared, pasty-white and still trembling. *He's been sick,* thought T.R., feeling no pity whatever.

Wiggy came back, shrugging. Now they could hear sirens. In a few minutes a police car came screaming up to the front door. The officer in charge knew little English, but Wiggy spoke a few words to him in Arabic, gave his card, and signaled T.R. that they could leave.

T.R. had come in a taxi. Wiggy drove him back to the Hilton. He threaded the green BMW expertly through the traffic.

"People's Army, do you think?" asked T.R. after a silence that seemed to last hours.

Wiggy shrugged. "They'll be blamed for it, certainly. And probably they did it. The club is an ideal target for them—very symbolic. And something about the Sabbath—less chance of hurting anyone. Too bad about Kalid. He was a cheery sort."

"Smarmy, but you wouldn't wish him dead."

"I've got a few names, T.R., if you can spare a minute at the hotel. People you might want to talk to—unofficially, of course. In the meantime, we'll be doing everything we can to find out what the score is."

T.R. smiled. It was a thin knife-edge of a smile. "Good," was all he said.

Ten minutes later they were in T.R.'s suite at the Hilton. Kalbfleisch poured them each a stiff cognac.

"I'm afraid," said Wiggy gratefully, "that I need it."

"We both do. I didn't realize, Wiggy, and I should have, that things were this precarious over here."

"They weren't—until very recently. A matter of weeks, really. My guess—and it's only a guess—is that the situation has changed in some important way. For instance, just suppose that Gadaffi or one of his kindred spirits decided to underwrite the Kassanian rebels all of a sudden. That'd explain the escalation."

"It is an escalation, then?"

"Absolutely. You won't get any government confirmation on that, but it's a fact. And we haven't seen the end of it."

"It sounds a lot like Nayif El Kheybar is besieged in his own country."

"It does. He is. He may not know it yet, but that's exactly what's happening. Faster every day. And we—officially, that is—can't do one thing about it."

T.R. sipped the cognac. "How about unofficially?"

"That's not my department, as you know. But we are trying, and from several angles. I'm not sure, T.R. It's too soon to know, really."

"I see," said Kalbfleisch. "Well, then. About those names."

Wiggy stood up and went to the writing table and began writing. It didn't take long. Then he handed the paper to Kalbfleisch.

"Folker Stutz," said Wiggy, "is the representative of several German manufacturers here: Siemens, Mercedes-Benz, Braun. But aside from that, he keeps an ear to the ground. Buy him a good dinner and you may hear some interesting things. He's reliable, too. Not in anyone's pocket, but interested in possibly expanding his present connections."

"I'll call him." T.R. had a sense of wasting time, of an invisible stopwatch ticking off the seconds until the negotiations. Maybe these names from Lawrence would amount to something. And maybe they were some kind of a smoke screen.

"Earnshaw," Wiggy went on, "is one of our local characters—and don't let his scruffy appearance put you off. He goes everywhere and he sees things and hears things that you or I might not have access to. I'd start with him, frankly, and do the German later."

"Thanks, Wiggy," said T.R. smoothly. "You've been very kind."

Wiggy left with the uneasy feeling that T.R. might feel he hadn't been quite kind enough.

Wiggy drove straight to the embassy, left his car in the driveway, and ran up the stairs to his office. He hated to be late for an appointment, bombs or no bombs.

In fact, he was just on time.

Wiggy's visitor had made himself at home.

Ross Hindley was stretched out in the biggest chair, leafing through magazines. A fresh cup of coffee was steaming at the edge of Wiggy's desk.

"Hi," said Wiggy. Hindley looked up, smiled, got half out of the chair, and shook hands.

"Hello. You look like a man in a hurry."

Lawrence looked at his guest. He'd met Hindley only once before, briefly. But there had been some correspondence and quite a few cables on the scrambled diplomatic line. Hindley had arrived with only a few hours' warning. CIA style, Lawrence guessed. Or maybe some emergency he didn't know about.

"There was a little excitement at the Jockey Club," said Wiggy, trying to keep his voice casual. "The rebels bombed the place."

"For sure?" Hindley's eyes sparkled. "You're positive it's Al Khadir?"

"Not positive. I didn't see them. But that was what people were staying. I was with Kalbfleisch—Revere Oil . . ."

"I know the gentleman. Interesting."

Wiggy just looked at him, not daring to ask the obvious question.

"What can I do for you, Ross?"

"I'm not using that name this trip. William G. Hyde, it

says on my passport. Civilian passport. Only you know who I am. Your boss knows me as Hyde. I have a letter of introduction. Haven't used it yet. I'm just doing a little quiet checking up, Wiggy. With the emphasis on quiet. Cleaver, for instance, isn't to know I'm here. How is Cleaver, by the way?"

"Seems fine. There have been a couple of funny incidents." Wiggy told him about the car crash, about the incident in the souk.

Hindley frowned. "But nothing conclusive. You don't really know who's behind it?"

"No. The easy answer is rebels."

"There are no easy answers, Wiggy. Not in Kassan."

"You've heard the rumors about King Nayif vanishing?"

"Yes. Rumors. He's a cagey old guy. Has Cleaver made contact with the prince?"

"That's what I wanted to tell you. He sure as hell has. And the rumors are true." Wiggy filled him in on what Jeb had reported.

"Why didn't you cable that?"

"I only heard it yesterday. When you said you'd be over . . . well, why trust the cables?"

"Right. Keep close to it, Wiggy. I'm staying someplace where no one is likely to know me. Repeat, Cleaver is not to know I'm here. I'll be around for a few days. And I'll check in by phone, set up a meeting or two. Probably not for a day or so."

"Fine." Wiggy liked Jeb Cleaver. He wondered why Hindley didn't want Jeb to know he was in town. Another question it wouldn't pay to ask. With these damned spooks, you never knew which end was up.

"Right now," said Hindley, rising, "I've got a date with a man with a parrot." He left, smiling, enjoying Wiggy's puzzlement.

23

The palace of Ibn Bir-Saraband gleamed whitely from its emerald-green gardens. It was late morning. Inside the palace, Tamara lay in her bath thinking of Jeb Cleaver. Of yesterday.

How much of her life had she invested in that moment? Years of longing had all come together in one electric afternoon.

It hadn't, of course, been the way she'd hoped. It couldn't have been. But still and all, it was Jeb. She smiled. Her beautiful American.

Tamara tried to recall the exact moment when she realized how deeply she loathed her husband. There hadn't been an incident, no one particular act that had turned love to hate. There was a reason for this, she realized. Love had never been part of the equation between her and the man her father, the king, had selected as her husband so long ago. Tamara had been no more than an aristocratic Arab wife. Obedient to his every wish, in bed and out of it.

She thought of herself as Jeb had first known her. Sixteen and a virgin, and virgin when she went to Ibn's bed. He had been brutal that night, and he was brutal now. The difference was that now Tamara could distinguish between love-making and lust, between tenderness and the bestial ruttings of her husband. She shuddered even now, thinking of her wedding night, how she'd imagined that maybe it was always like this, for all women. Stained with her own maiden blood and shrinking from his next onslaught.

The bathtub was wrought of pure silver, sunken into the plant-filled conservatory that was part of her bedroom suite. Four hundred pounds of sterling silver had been melted to make this tub. The faucet handles were carved from Persian turquoise, and small mosaic chips of the same rare gemstone had been inlaid into the silver of the tub itself in a rippling pattern. The water was perfumed with essence of jasmine, and fresh jasmine petals were scattered on the water each morning before she bathed. Tamara liked the tub. There was little enough else to like in this gilded prison.

Now she heard a pattering of sandaled feet. A maidservant appeared with a note on a silver tray. Languidly Tamara dried her hands and reached for the note. Whatever it was, it might be a diversion.

She recognized her husband's handwriting, a scrawl as forceful and as arrogant as his body. For a moment Tamara paused, considering. It was rare enough that he visited her these days, much less sent notes. How often had she considered divorcing him? On the surface it was easy: you only had to say the words. But for an Arab woman, divorce was an enormous step. Her children would be raised by her husband's family. She would have no place in the world other than as a dependent on the charity of her own family. Tamara knew there'd be no shortage of that, but still, she wasn't prepared to leave Kassan entirely, nor to take up a life as a hanger-on at the court of her brother Selim. Whose own wife, charming as she was, would forever take precedence over the suddenly déclassé sister-in-law.

She opened the note. *The princess*, it declared, an announcement rather than an invitation, *will be pleased to accompany her husband upon a most urgent visit this afternoon. The general's car will call for the princess at two p.m. Please be formally veiled. By His Excellency General Ibn Bir-Saraband.*

Tamara dropped the note onto the silver tray and nodded affirmatively at her servant. Her appearance was calm, but Tamara was anything but calm inside.

Her first reaction was anger. How dare he summon her thus, so suddenly, without proper warning. She'd had other plans for this afternoon. She wanted to go into Port Kassan, to shop. At present for Jeb's little house. A wall hanging, perhaps, or a carpet. The place looked like a hotel, and not the Plaza Athenée, either. But there was no question of not complying.

Ibn probably had some foreign bigwig in tow, and the bigwig had a wife, and it would all be consummately boring. Tamara often had to entertain such women while the men were off doing whatever men did on such occasions. Telling each other lies, pulling off deals to make each other richer. Tamara thought carefully about what to wear. She chose a simple slack suit of black crepe de chine, fresh from Dior and never worn. Then the sheerest of black robes, a black veil and headcloth and dark sunglasses. No jewelry other than the Florentine gold panther earrings Selim had given her long ago. The panthers of El Kheybar. If her guest were sophisticated, she would understand and appreciate the elegance. If, on the other hand, she were the wife of some provincial arriviste all clinking with a shepherd's dower in heavy gold, too bad for her. She might learn something.

But what did Ibn want, really? Was he putting on some show of marital happiness, perhaps for her father? Tamara walked through the women's wing of the palace, across the great central courtyard with its six fountains, its avenues of flowering almond and lemon trees, its peacocks and parakeets and songbirds.

The general's limousine was waiting.

Tamara slid into the wide seat and arranged herself as far distant from the bulk of her husband as she conveniently could. As always when she met him after some time, a little ripple of fear went through her. Ibn had that power—had always possessed it, really.

A slight nod was his only greeting.

The limousine sped out of the palace gates and into the desert. So they weren't heading into Port Kassan after all. Tamara wondered what was up, but she wouldn't give her husband the satisfaction of asking him.

The armor-plated Mercedes rolled across the desert with the velocity of a tank. In the cool, dark interior, shielded by her veil and her dark glasses, Tamara reflected: *My Arab blood has done this much to me. I am still enough of the well-bred Muslim wife that never for an instant did I really consider not coming with him today. How easy it would have*

*been for any other woman, almost anyplace else in the world,
simply to have a headache. Or to refuse point-blank.*

In the silence the car moved across the red-beige landscape. Tamara could have drawn from memory detailed maps of the Place Vendôme in Paris or Jermyn Street in London. Yet here, not twenty miles from her father's old palace, she was as lost as if Ibn had whisked her to some polar icecap.

For some time she contented herself with surveying the landscape, tedious as it was. The car had mirrored windows to deflect the curiosity of pedestrians in the city. From the inside everything appeared as if seen through a gray fog. It amazed Tamara that this bleak, interminable desert could inspire some men—her own father!—to a strange and addictive love. That they could be entranced by these shifting sands, by the implacable heat and the unreachable horizon. She smiled then, behind her veil. Of course! It was always the men who were so captivated. Never their women. Never the females, who were the grinders of wheat, haulers of water, bearers of children.

The limousine sped through a small town, its horn blaring. There were no crowds to scatter, but the few pedestrians gaped at the speeding plum-colored apparition as though Allah himself had landed in a golden chariot.

Tamara turned and caught her husband staring at her with an intensity he usually reserved for the sales films of American and French weapons manufacturers.

As though he might look into her very soul. She turned her head and pretended to be interested in the barren desert outside. The car felt like an expensive rolling prison. She knew about its armor, the bulletproof glass, the virtually indestructible tires. All to preserve the monster riding next to her.

The road ran straight as a spear. Occasionally they raced past an astonished camel driver, and once they nearly ran a bright green pickup truck right off the road. Ibn liked fast driving, but Tamara sensed a special urgency in this trip, and she wondered why.

They had driven for nearly an hour when the Mercedes slowed down at the outskirts of a fair-sized provincial town. Tamara couldn't guess its name: there were no signs, and Ibn said nothing. The car edged its way into the central square.

The square had a certain faded dignity, although four tennis courts would have crowded the space. One end of the plaza was occupied by the town's principal mosque. It was old, built of whitewashed brick, its arched door and windows framed in blue tiles, a tall minaret picturesquely topped by a bulbous onion-shaped dome tiled in designs of stars, moons, and arabesques in three shades of blue. From the very top of the dome rose a gilt-bronze hand, reaching up as if to touch the hand of Allah. The lonely minaret stood sentinel over the dusty tile roofs of the town. *Jeb*, she thought, *would like this place*.

There was obviously going to be a ceremony. Already people had begun to gather in the square.

The chauffeur maneuvered the enormous car into a point of vantage at the opposite end of the square from the mosque. He parked so that Tamara's side of the car had the better view. *Prearranged*, she thought. *And why?* It was unlike Ibn to show her any but the most necessary of formal courtesies.

She distracted herself by examining the square in some detail. There was an interesting old wellhead near the mosque, old and octagonal and made of stone deeply carved in some sort of floral pattern. There was so little of the old Kassan left. It seemed a pity not to preserve places like this. Tamara decided to speak to Selim about it. Kassanian peasants, like peasants anywhere, would cheerfully tear down their priceless old buildings, only to replace them with plastic and neon. It had already happened, and with obscene speed, in Port Kassan.

Tamara was seized with an urge to leave the car and examine the square more closely. Anything to escape from Ibn.

Then it began.

From a side street came two tall young men, one behind the other. They carried between them a sort of stretcher suspended between two long poles, the poles carried on their shoulders. It was a heavy burden and they moved slowly to the edge of the square. Then they knelt, slowly and in tandem, and unburdened themselves. At the same time, three other pairs of young men entered the square from three other directions, bearing similar loads. Small rocks, gathered from the desert.

Tamara took a very deep breath, for now she knew what was going to happen here.

She clenched her fists underneath the sheer fabric of her robe. For one shuddering instant Tamara thought it might all be meant for her, that Ibn was leading her to an adulteress's death by stoning. A wave of nausea rose in her. She closed her eyes and then opened them again. He wouldn't dare! *Or would he?*

Paralyzed, she waited.

Could he see her eyes behind the dark lenses? She looked at the door nearest her. All of these cars had automatic central door locks, but perhaps the driver had forgotten. She could run! But where? *I am the king's daughter, Tamara of the El Kheybar. Princess of Kassan.* Still, it wasn't impossible that Ibn would be vengeful enough to disregard the disgrace such an accusation would bring to him. Hadn't the Al Sa'ud executed one of their own princesses just a few years ago? Trembling, she forced herself to look.

All of the stones had been unloaded now. The young men who had borne them were lost in the growing crowd. It was an orderly group, but even here, insulated in the back of the Mercedes, Tamara could sense their excitement building. There were women in the crowd, and even children. Like a fair day. The vendors of coffee and lemonade were doing a lively business. She heard a small metallic noise and turned to Ibn. He was fumbling with the catch on his attaché case.

It was very quiet inside the limousine. Tamara watched the scene outside with growing fascination. She had never seen a public punishment: not even a whipping or a chopping off of hands.

Now the crowd on the left side of the square parted. A phalanx of men walked into the square with almost military precision. Twelve men in all, in two columns of six. They marched to the very center of the square, turned, and faced the mosque. Only then did Tamara see the small black figure who walked with them, between the two columns of men and in the center of the line.

The victim. The adulteress.

She was a short and slender creature, more the size of a child than of a woman. Robed entirely in black, just like all the other women in the square. Just like Tamara.

The men stepped away, melting to the sides of the square, but not joining the crowd. These would be the men of the woman's own family. Guardians of her virtue. Shamed by her betrayal of it—of them.

She was quite alone now.

Tamara felt just as lonely. She felt her own heart falling down and down into some dark and bottomless pit.

Now a man stepped out of the mosque. He was short and solidly built, all in white and wearing a white headcloth. Only his beard really distinguished him from other men in the square: this was long and white, untrimmed. A mark, perhaps, of his age and wisdom. For he must be the town's main holy man. The man who would have heard the evidence against the woman and then pronounced her sentence.

The silence outside was deep, penetrating, heavy.

One of the men who had marched with the woman into the square now bent awkwardly and picked up a stone. Tamara could see it clearly: about the size of a hen's egg. He hefted the stone in his right hand, bouncing it a little. As though he were considering a purchase.

He can't! thought Tamara, trying to imagine Selim in the same position, or her father.

But he could.

A sigh rippled through the square, soft and mournful as the desert wind in the evening. He lifted his hand awkwardly, a man unaccustomed to throwing.

But the stone found its mark all the same.

It caught the woman on the shoulder and sent her staggering a few steps backward. Now the others of her kinsmen found stones. Threw them. It was their privilege and their responsibility. At first their aim was bad. Only one or two stones out of dozens hit the woman. Then their aim got better. Others joined in. Tamara tried not to look. But she couldn't keep her eyes off the woman in the square. The worst part was the women. The townswomen. One of them picked up a stone and hurled it at the adulteress, catching her in the right temple. It drew blood. The woman who had thrown the stone gave a yelp of pure glee. She picked up another and threw it harder. Laughed again. A sport. Others joined in. It was more than a ritual for them. It was a kind of release. Bringing down the one who had dared to betray the ancient code.

Their vengeance had a repellent fascination for Tamara. In a town like this, these women must have known their victim by name.

The adulteress was on her knees now, her head bowed. But she uttered not a sound. Blood poured freely from several wounds. The hail of stones increased. Even in the well-insulated car, Tamara could hear the soft, deadly thudding as they hit. Even the little children were playing at it now. Tamara found her eyes brimming with tears. That her own people—that anyone!—could behave like this. She stole a glance at her husband.

Ibn was smiling. As she watched, his tongue flicked out. As though he were tasting the blood. Tamara began to feel queasy. The scene in the square seemed to ripple and fade.

Then she heard it. At first Tamara thought the low moanings, the small cries of pleasure, were coming from the crowd outside. Then Tamara heard her own voice: "Jeb . . . oh, Jeb! My beautiful American." There was more. Much more. She closed her eyes and thought of yesterday afternoon. How beautiful it had been. Of how Ibn had wrecked it for her now and forever. He said nothing. Tamara forced herself to open her eyes again and look at the spectacle Ibn had so much wanted her to see.

The woman was motionless now, sprawled in the accumulating rubble of stones, covered in blood, and utterly silent.

Tamara wondered whether anyone else was being forced to witness the horror. Inside the big car, Ibn's tape played itself out. It seemed to take hours.

Eventually the stoning ceased. There was no fun in it anymore. The woman was dead or soon would be. The spectators began drifting away. It was a mark of how provincial a town this was that some of them dared to look closely into the mirrored windows of the car. In Port Kassan it would have been known. Feared. The curious faces bobbed and floated past, eyes bulging, fishes in an aquarium. In the cool twilight of the limousine's interior Tamara was glad for her dark glasses. Glad that Ibn couldn't see her eyes. And still she waited for him to speak.

The car began moving slowly through the dispersing

crowd. He said nothing. Only when they were well out of the town did Tamara regain her composure enough to speak.

"Ibn Bir-Saraband, I divorce you." She repeated this three times, which made it a legal act sanctioned by koranic law. Tamara expected to feel a sense of relief at saying the words she had wanted to say for years. But all she felt was a dull pain. Too much had happened, and for too long a time, for the weight to lift off that easily.

Ibn turned as she spoke, and regarded her. "You will never see your children again," he said. "Nor should you, considering your morals. That village whore was pure as the moon by comparison."

At any other time she might have laughed. For Ibn to comment on anyone's morals, man, woman, or beast, was absurd. But Tamara was too exhausted to laugh. And she was frightened, too. Ibn wouldn't have expected this reaction. The tape recording must be a part of some plan, a plan that would be sidetracked now. She sighed.

"Since we are divorced, Ibn, you never need worry about my morals again."

He had no reply for this. In silence they sped back to the palace. Slowly, slowly, the sense of release flowed warmly through Tamara's veins. Selim would understand. She could live abroad—in Paris, perhaps. Depending on what might happen with Jeb, even in America!

They pulled in through the palace gates and up to the main entrance. The driver got out and opened Tamara's door.

Ibn turned to her. "You will live to regret this day."

She laughed. He never could stand being laughed at. "I regret the day I first saw you, Ibn. My regrets on our marriage are more numerous than the stones we saw thrown this afternoon. A few more will go unnoticed."

"Don't say I didn't warn you!"

Tamara stepped out of the car without deigning to reply. She walked up the marble path, trembling from head to foot.

Half in ecstasy. Half in fear.

24

Jeb stayed home on Friday. Megan had said she'd be busy arranging for the videotape to get out of the country. He tried phoning Selim and got the secretary. Jeb wasn't sure just what he'd say to his old friend when next they met, but there had to be something. But in spite of all the complications, he looked forward to a whole day at his drawing board.

It suddenly came back to him why he was supposed to be in Kassan after all. The embassy needed building, that was for sure.

He rejected eleven of his own conceptual drawings before the real problem became clear. All of his early sketches involved one structure: sometimes it was big and imposing, the embassy as mosque or mausoleum. Sometimes it sprawled. Now, looking on these drawings as though they'd been done by some not very competent stranger, he realized that it shouldn't be one building at all. There was the answer! It should be an assembly of buildings, linked pavilions, all different sizes, different shapes, united by water gardens and built all of the same materials for harmony. Harmony but not symmetry.

And he knew just what material he'd use: the lovely old faded-rose brick you sometimes saw in the old town. There must be a way of duplicating that soft, sensuous color, even if it proved impossible to use authentically old materials. Bricks, an ivory-colored limestone for contrast, lots of water, arcades, gardens!

Jeb stood up, grinning to the empty studio.

This was the moment, he knew it well. There was always such a coming together of scattered bits of ideas, a fusion.

Now it would all focus in a great flow of creativity. Jeb recognized all the happy symptoms. He picked up a new, freshly sharpened pencil, ripped the last of his rejected drawings off the pad, sat down, and began sketching fast. His pencil seemed to dance over the paper, to take on a life of its own. He saw the compound grow like some magical flower.

First, seen from below and outside, an imposing wall. Cut into it and parallel with the upward-sloping hill was a long, wide, walled driveway: elegant. Easy to defend. The parking facilities would be underground. In fact half the compound would be underground. Above, low, graceful pavilions linked by gardens, by water, by tradition. It would be new and old at the same time: both conservative and daring. A truly separate residence for the ambassador and his family, and another, smaller pair of houses for the chargé d'affaires and for the use of important guests.

Jeb drew steadily for three hours, got up, stretched, walked in the garden, and drew for an hour more.

Now he had three sheets of conceptual drawings, related but different in some important respect. Now it was a question of balances, of making a scale model of the site and toy buildings, playing with the groupings, rigging up an artificial sun in order to design the patterns of light and shade.

When Ali came to tell him lunch was ready, Jeb almost resented the intrusion. Then he saw the beautiful salads that Ali had prepared and realized he was hungry. But before Jeb ate, he called Megan at the Hilton and asked her to come for dinner that night. He felt an almost boyish pride in his drawings. He wanted her to see them.

"Oh, damn!" she said. "Jeb, I'd love to, but something's come up. Business. Could we do it tomorrow?"

Jeb hid his disappointment. What would a few lousy drawings mean to her anyway?

"Sure," he said. "About seven? By the way, did you send that birthday present to your grandmother?"

Megan laughed. They hadn't arranged a code. But it wasn't a bad idea, from what she'd heard about ADDAK.

"You know how Granny Mcguire loves brass trays. Yes, Jeb. It went out this morning."

"See you tomorrow, then."

"So long, Jeb."

He hung up. Living with Megan would be like living with a fireman on twenty-four-hour call. Except that for Megan the fire might be halfway around the world.

The boy Karim was as proud as he'd ever been since the day Al Khadir accepted him into the People's Army. His first mission! And he was carrying it out alone.

Karim had been stalking the king's kidnappers for four days now. He rode one camel and led another. And he had supplies enough for a month. The camel he led carried dried fruit, goat cheese, and flatbread. And the beast herself was a walking reservoir of milk.

His cover story, should he be questioned, was that he was delivering the camels to an uncle who was trekking a caravan into Kuwait.

He'd begun near the site of the king's burned-out camp. Retracing his steps had been easy for about two hours. He located the place where the Jeeps had been parked. And he followed the narrow track they'd taken: north by northwest.

Now he wasn't so sure. The track had run out, and he was somewhere deep in the foothills of the Burujurdi. Two nights he had slept alone, hobbling the camels and wondering: *Where would he have hidden the king if the king had been his to hide?* The desert was vast. The foothills were too numerous to scour one by one. There were no easy answers. On the third night Karim had come upon a five-camel caravan of goatherds moving from one pasture to the next.

True Bedu, they had welcomed him and fed him and not asked too many questions. The rule of hospitality in the desert was that it could last three days. Karim did not test its duration, but thanked his hosts the next morning and moved on.

Tonight he would sleep alone with the camels here on this desolate hilltop. It was good. It was part of being a man. The wind had carved a sort of niche out of the hillside. It would give shelter from the scouring sand, if the sand were to blow. He dug his fire pit deeply. The fire he made to brew his tea was a small and nearly smokeless one. The tea was welcome in the fast-cooling night. Karim attended to the camels, hob-

bling them deftly near some scrub where they might graze.
Then he said his evening prayers and made a simple meal. By
the time he had finished, slowly chewing the last dried date
and washing it down with more tea, it was completely dark.
He unrolled his blankets on a place where the sand seemed
free of pebbles. Then he made a final check of the camels, of
the perimeter of his little camp. There was just a sliver of a
moon. He stood for a moment staring out into the deep
purple night.

Then he saw the light. Just a speck of light, tiny and brilliant as a star. But it was no star. In the crystal desert air it
was hard to gauge the distance. Quickly, lest the light vanish
forever, Karim checked for landmarks. Here was a curiously
shaped rock. There, an old dried-out acacia stump. And between them, somewhere out ahead, the light. He smiled. The
light could belong to anyone. To the herders he'd slept with
the night before, even. But perhaps not. Karim took the light
for an omen. It would guide him.

And tomorrow, early on, he would discover its source.

Megan put down the phone with an unfamiliar feeling of
guilt. Maybe she should have told Jeb about Al Khadir's
message. But why? He couldn't come with them tonight, good
as he'd been yesterday. There simply wouldn't be room in the
van. And besides that, she didn't want to expose him to any
unnecessary risks.

That tonight would be risky, she had no doubt at all.

The note had appeared on her breakfast tray, just like the
first one. It was short and to the point. They were to set up
their cameras facing a certain cluster of buildings in the old
town, just before midnight tonight. If they did this, their efforts would be rewarded. No further information—just the
now-familiar signature of Bandar Al Khadir.

Megan was thrilled. He trusted her! The videotapes from
yesterday were already en route out of Kassan to Kuwait,
thanks to Ahmad's father. One of his fishing boats would run
it up the coast, and the captain had promised to deliver the
bundle personally to the INTERTEL stringer there.

Now Jerry was out in the Rover scouting the location.

Megan, Louise, and Ahmad were checking up on several
questions that had been raised yesterday. Particularly about

ADDAK. Because Ahmad had needed only the briefest glance at the hand-drawn map to recognize the location.

"Oh, Miss Megan," he said, his eyes growing bigger, "this, please, is a dangerous place. This is the headquarters of AD-DAK in Port Kassan. Not a nice place. Not for Kassanians, anyway."

She smiled. The boy had shown no signs of cowardice before this, and Megan couldn't believe it of him now. It wasn't cowardice. It was plain undiluted fear, and in Ahmad's voice there was all the confirmation Megan needed about the terrible stories Bandar had told on the videotape.

"It's all right, Ahmad," she said gently. "You don't have to come."

His manners were almost good enough to mask his relief.

Instantly Megan had organized the shot. One camera could be trained on the old town from her terrace here at the hotel. The other—containing Megan and Jerry Schwartz and Gus, the grip—would be hidden in the laundry van they'd bought. Megan was sure no one had tumbled onto that ruse as yet. The Riders of the Purple Sage were about to ride out on a dangerous adventure.

She showered and changed into a slack suit similar to the one she'd worn yesterday, but in blue denim. And her running shoes, just in case. Then Megan ordered a light supper for all of them to be served in her rooms. Jerry calculated they'd better pull out at ten-thirty. Philo would man the terrace with his longest lens trained on the old quarter. If anything flared, he'd get it for sure.

While they waited for supper, Megan got up and turned on the immense television set that stood in a corner of the suite's living room. A fat Arabic lady was wiggling as if in agony, singing mournfully, a dirgelike tune punctuated by wails that sounded as though her heart would break—and maybe the television set too. This particular lady was the biggest pop singer in Arabia. She wailed from tinny speakers in taxis, whined from a million televisions, and appeared in large posters advertising everything from laundry soap to health insurance.

Megan flipped the dial. An elegant male voice in clipped BBC accents was discussing the threatened ecology of Uganda. Flip again. Roy Rogers and Dale Evans were singing together in what appeared to be a snowstorm. Flip again. Here was the Arab lady, in a different spangled costume and on a different channel, still wailing about the cruelties that fate and her impetuous heart had gathered unto her all-too-ample bosom. Megan joined in the laughter and turned the thing off.

Supper came—and no message from Al Khadir. None was needed. They ate, checked all their gear, and left just before ten-thirty.

Jerry drove with truly Kassanian abandon. They took not the Rover, but a small Fiat sedan that Louise had rented this morning. Megan intended to change cars every day, if that was what it took to elude whoever had been following her and Jeb yesterday. There wasn't time for more adventures with water wagons. They took the Fiat to an old warehouse they'd rented near the docks. In it was the laundry van. Their Trojan horse. They'd rented the warehouse from a friend of Ahmad's father's. Its sole purpose was to hide the van from anyone who might be watching the hotel, and to set up an easy distribution point where videotapes could be duplicated and sent on their way without undue comings and goings at the Hilton.

To cover herself, Megan had many local-color tapes in her suite. As far as she knew, the place had never been searched. But there wasn't any point in taking chances. Not in Kassan.

Port Kassan was jumping tonight, Sabbath or not. Lights blazed, music racketed and echoed in the crazy narrow streets, the Arabic lady wailed of love's labor's lost, vendors cried their cries, camels snorted, and everywhere resounded echoes of a thousand blaring car and truck horns.

But on this empty street in the shadow of fear, just up the hill from ADDAK headquarters, it was completely silent. Spooky. No pedestrian walked the street. The van was rigged so that Jerry could shoot from three positions, all hidden. His preferred angle now was to shoot over the front passenger's seat and through the windshield. For running shots in traffic, several inconspicuous peepholes had been drilled in the van's sides, and fitted, seamlessly, with nonreflective glass that was a fine match for the van's slightly faded paint.

Ten to twelve.

Jerry checked his camera for the third time, scanning the

tiny red and green monitor lights, checking the image in the little monitor screen. He'd been kind about Megan's own performance with the minicam yesterday. Gus stayed behind the wheel, just in case. Megan was crouched next to Jerry in the rear of the van, on the driver's side. They spoke rarely, and in whispers.

Five to twelve.

Now Jerry started his camera in earnest, framing the five dark houses that were ADDAK. The disguise of those houses had been carried out expertly. Only the multiple clusters of antennae on the roof gave a hint that these were anything different from the houses on either side.

Jerry kept his eye to the viewfinder.

Megan and Gus were breathing so quietly that the only sound in the dark interior of the van was the faint electronic humming of the tape machine and its battery pack.

Then hell broke loose, right on schedule. Midnight.

A great flare of orange light as the nearest corner of the ADDAK complex blossomed into an enormous chrysanthemum of flame. Half a second later they heard the roaring. The van shook like a kid's plastic toy, quivered once, and settled down.

Megan stared at the conflagration, fascinated and repelled.

There was another blast, louder than the first. Part of the wall facing the street crumbled, and they could see more flames running along the rooftop. The many antennae were starkly silhouetted by the flames. The street was beginning to be clogged with burning rubble now. Megan wondered exactly how they'd get out of here.

Then she heard the screams. Megan had seen combat fire in Cambodia and any number of local disasters at home. But never had she heard sounds like these: damned souls tormented in a very real hell. Jerry's voice was flat, unemotional: "Gus, take this amplifier and ease it out the window, can you? Gotta get it all." Megan knew the long-range pencil mike could pick up a whisper at two hundred yards.

By the time the third explosion went off, people were trying to grope their way out of the burning buildings. Some ran, trailing flame. At least one man jumped. They were all men, of course. One man burst like a gunshot from the main door, his Arab robe on fire. He was halfway across the street when an unheard gunshot picked him off. "Of course," said Jerry almost to himself. "They've got snipers on the rooftops." He took a deep breath. "Look up, Megan."

Megan looked up, following the direction of his camera. On the third floor of ADDAK, someone was pounding away at one of the heavily boarded-up windows with a big chair. Finally half the window was open. They could see flames inside. Silhouetted against them was the shape of a young man. He hesitated not a second, but climbed out on the window ledge and lowered himself by his arms and jumped.

Three stories onto cobblestones.

But he wasn't dead. Both legs must have splintered, Megan guessed, because he couldn't use them. He crawled, dragging himself across the street. Away from the horror. Inch by bloodstained inch, dragging his shattered legs like dirty laundry, he oozed across the street. The once-white robe was torn entirely off his chest now. He moved with a weird crablike motion. But he moved. Megan half-rose from where she was crouching. She had to go to the man, help him, do something! She was reaching for the door handle when Gus's big hand clamped gently over hers. "I know how you feel, Megan. But there's nothing we can do. Nothing."

She blinked, awakening from the trance that horror had driven her into. In that moment Megan thought of Al Khadir, standing tall and proud in his hideout. Glistening with idealism. She could almost see his eyes now, penetrating in their intensity and yet thoughtful too. Eyes that could see the whole future of Kassan. Where was he now? Was it his finger on one of those rifles up on the rooftops? Were those fine brown eyes dancing at the sight of all this blood and destruction?

Suddenly all of the adventure drained out of the night. Megan felt plain sick. There was a quiver in her belly, and for an instant she felt like throwing up.

Dully she turned her gaze back to the young man in the street. Almost as she looked, a sniper found his mark.

A round black hole appeared in the boy's forehead. He arched his back and fell forward with all the life gone out of him.

Now, beyond the roaring flames and the occasional crack of a sniper's rifle, they could hear another sound. Sirens. For a moment nobody said a word. Then Megan spoke. Flatly. "Gus," she said, "let's get out of here."

Ten minutes later they were back at the warehouse. The trip had been made in utter silence.

Now Jerry took command. "Megan," he said, "why don't you go back with Gus. I can handle everything here, and you can do your introduction. If the fire's still going, maybe Philo can shoot you on the terrace, with that in the background."

She looked at him gratefully.

"Good thinking," she said, feeling the effort it cost her to smile. "If I can do it."

"You can do anything."

She rode back with Gus, thinking about that. About the feeling, until lately shared even by herself, that she, Megan Mcguire, media whiz, could do anything.

They rode up Nayif Chaussée in silence. The street glittered, apparently unaware of the chaos at ADDAK. As she stepped into the elevator a few minutes later, Megan wondered how long it would be before she forgot that boy on the cobblestones, writhing, and his last silent scream. She thought of the fine speeches she'd made to Jeb, all about what a great noble duty it was to get to the bottom of things.

Some bottoms were deeper than others.

The elevator doors opened and she walked down the thickly carpeted hall to Penthouse 1626.

25

General Ibn Bir-Saraband had passed beyond outrage into a dark and vengeful hell of his own creation. He sat alone in his big office in the Army Headquarters Building, the door locked and bolted. Only ten minutes ago he had returned from surveying the damage the rebels had wrought on AD-DAK. To call it damage was understatement. The place was a ruin, and everything in it.

And to think that but for Theodora he might have been trapped there like all the rest! Ibn had been invulnerable for so long that the realization he'd had a very close call shocked him all the more profoundly.

Theo had called. He had gone to her. And there in her drawing room at the Garden of Five Thousand Delights she had played the Mcguire woman's interview with Al Khadir. Shame upon shame! They were watching it with a grim intensity when the first explosion went off. Hearing the unspeakable words. Seeing the serpent Al Khadir face to face for the first time. And the woman's voice, so calm, feeding him questions. All the lies about ADDAK had been broadcast. Theo's copy of the tape had been recorded off Rome television earlier in the day. How much of Arabia had picked it up would be impossible to know. But there it was, an accusation. America, Europe—the entire world would know his shame. His incompetence at not being able to repress a motley band of desert rats. The People's Army, indeed.

Outrage dimmed his hearing. It was only when the second explosion went off that Theo suggested they venture out onto her roof garden. And there, together, they had seen the flames engulfing ADDAK just three blocks away. The screams of those trapped inside were very audible over that distance. And the crack-crack of rifle fire. Ibn could imagine it all. He wanted to go to his men, but she restrained him. "You must save yourself, my general, for more significant things."

As ever, Theodora saw the whole picture.

He stayed on the roof until the sirens announced that help was coming. Ibn watched the flames engulfing his masterpiece of creation: ADDAK. But his mind was busily planning his revenge.

The Mcguire woman would pay dearly for insulting him. To kill her would be a kindness. She must suffer even as he was suffering. Humiliation.

All of his frustrations devolved on the Mcguire woman. Tamara's surprising rebellion was somehow caught up in it too. But for the Mcguire woman the rebels might have gone unnoticed until he crushed them. Now they had achieved celebrity—more fame in an hour's television broadcast than Ibn Bir-Saraband had ever known.

Well, she would pay. It was only a question of how, and how soon.

Ibn and Theodora climbed down from the roof garden. He hardly remembered taking leave of her. His mind was a jumble, a confusion of plans. But one thing emerged very clearly: it was time to act. He must implement his plan, right now, without wasting a moment.

In fact, he could achieve several of his goals and wrap them up together in one bold stroke. He sat at his enormous desk and pondered his next moves. And it came clear to him. And it would all begin with the red-haired monster of a female on television.

Now, for the first time today, he smiled. He pushed a button that would summon an aide, stood up, and walked briskly to unlock the door. Now he would give life to the plan that was forming in his head. Now he would partake of the vengeance that was rightly his.

Now he would take those final steps that would lead him to the Panther Throne itself.

* * *

Selim stood in the great cavern that was his drawing room overlooking the city. Slowly, like a man dreaming, he hung up the phone. He had just spent an hour talking to his wife and twin sons in Paris. How he wished he were with them! They might as well have been on the moon. And it was a hard thing he had asked Fawzia to do. To extend her visit a few weeks. Selim couldn't be specific on the phone. But it was safer for them there. Too much was happening in Kassan just now for him to have the added burden of a wife and sons to worry about.

Tomorrow he'd ask Ibn Bir-Saraband to double the body-guard on his family in Paris. Fawzia would hate that, but it would be done.

He was looking out at the view when Tamara walked in. He hadn't heard the elevator. She spoke his name, came to him, kissed him on the cheek. Selim smiled. He saw too little of his sister these days.

"I've left him," she said, as ever coming right to the point.

"Ibn?"

"I divorced him at three-fifteen this afternoon, for the record."

Selim reached out with both hands and held her thin shoulders. How beautiful she was. And how unhappy.

"Tell me about it," he said, leading her to one of the dark blue banquettes.

Her smile was etched by acid. "You wouldn't want the details, dear Selim," she said. "After all, you're the guardian of morals for all your people—or will be. He is a beast, leave it at that, and today he did something so very beastly that I simply decided I had done my duty as his obedient Muslim wife for too long to put up with any more of it."

Selim frowned. He had never really questioned the human aspects of his sister's marriage. These things were arranged: it was the tradition. If she obeyed all the rules, happiness would follow. That was the theory, and the theory was Islamic law. He poured them both a cognac.

"Tamara, Tamara," he said, "if it is too painful for you to talk about it . . ."

She laughed then. A harsh sound that reminded him, bru-tally, of what her laughter had been. A lovely rippling thing, carefree as the wind. That alone told Selim more than he wanted to know. He reached out for her hand and took it in his. All the years and distances that had come between them since the closeness of their childhood seemed to melt away.

"Whatever I can do, my dear sister, will be done."

Her smile was more than grateful. "I throw myself on your mercy, Selim," she said gently. "Ibn said he'll keep the children from me. Not that I see all that much of them as it is."

"You'll see them as often as you like," he said quickly, thinking what it would be like if he were somehow deprived of his sons. "For the moment, Tamara, stay here with me. When you've rested, go to Fawzia's palace—she'll be in France for a month at least. Or go abroad. Or we'll build a place specially for you. The thing is, don't worry."

"Dear Selim," she said, rising, pacing the floor, "how very lucky I am to have you as a brother. Not everyone would be so understanding."

The explosion rattled the glass in the big window. Selim was on his feet in a second. They stood together at the window. From this height it was almost like looking down on a map of the city. The whole corner of an intersection in the old town was on fire. Flames shot up fifty feet into the deep blue night. The second explosion came fast on the heels of the first. There was a pause, then a third blast.

"ADDAK," said Tamara flatly. "And if Allah is kind, he'll be there."

Selim looked at her. "You're sure?"

"Beyond doubt."

Selim picked up the phone, spoke urgently in Arabic, identifying himself, cutting through the tangle of calls that jammed the police emergency switchboard. Then he spoke again and listened.

"You're right. I must go there."

"Don't be ridiculous, Selim. Why? To defend one band of criminals from another? Save yourself for a real fight—for a cause worthy of you."

Her words cut into his heart. As he stood here, safe in his father's palace, Selim realized that he had never questioned ADDAK. Not its existence, nor its practices, nor the results of those practices. Oh, surely, he'd heard rumors. Dark rumors. But he'd brushed those aside. As had his father. This was Ibn's territory, Ibn's game. Ibn loved to play soldier, enforcer, all of those boring things.

Now, burning wildly far below him, Selim saw the bright scorched harvest of his brother-in-law's activities.

Selim clenched his fists. From somewhere far below, deep inside the palace, he could feel the Panther Throne, glowing in its eternal shadows, the gilded panthers writhing. It seemed as though the ancient throne was mocking him. Challenging him. *What will you do,* it seemed to ask, *to prove yourself worthy of me? Your land is in flames, your father is a prisoner, and where are you, Selim of the El Kheybar?*

He turned toward his sister without really seeing her. Tomorrow he must do something. It was with a growing sense of horror that Selim realized he had no idea in the world what he would do, or how.

He was entirely alone in his own country. There weren't five army officers he knew by name. That, too, was Ibn's territory. The police—poor fellows, they tried, but all of them put together couldn't organize traffic on even one block of downtown Port Kassan.

"Don't worry, Tamara," he said with a confidence that had no foundation in his heart. "It's going to be all right."

Bandar crouched next to Majid on the rooftop directly across the street from ADDAK. They were both firing the sniper rifles Kurakin had given them. Three of the false graves had been exhumed in preparation for this night.

Too much was happening for Bandar to really enjoy his success. That it was a success, there could be no doubt. It was lucky, he thought, that no Kassanian in his right mind wanted to share a street with ADDAK. These old buildings were almost entirely empty, used as warehouses for shops nearby.

He stared into the flames and wondered how hot the fire must be that would burn away the memory of Leila. It was possible, perhaps, that some of the ADDAK scum escaped through the back of the complex. But surely no one who tried this exit would survive. Bandar was less interested in body counts than the symbolism of striking directly at the heart of the most feared secret police in the Middle East.

He could see Megan's van parked up the hill. They'd have

a fine show, something to match the interview. Bandar hadn't seen that interview as yet, but word of its broadcast had reached him. How fast Megan Mcguire acted! And how very effectively.

At the sound of sirens, he gave the signal to disband. There were just a dozen handpicked rebels on the rooftops. Now they would disperse separately, each going to some pre-selected bolt-hole.

Tomorrow evening, they'd regroup. Each new rendezvous was chosen by Bandar or by Majid, and only at the last possible moment. If a man carried no secrets, his secrets could never be revealed. And none of them was under any illusions about the lengths ADDAK would go to in order to get those secrets.

There was a café in the old town, popular with students, which boasted a large and colorful bulletin board. Anyone could leave a message there. There you could find signs for rooms to let, objects for sale, the enticements of low-class prostitutes, job offers, and the like. But the bulletin board was especially well-liked by lovers. It was a means by which they could rendezvous. "Beloved," one of their messages might read, "meet me by the light of the moon, in the alley next to the Inn of the Camel Drovers, next Tuesday no later than eleven." Romantic nonsense, but a perfect formula for disguising more serious invitations to a meeting. These notes were never signed, except by fanciful love names. The People's Army used the names of birds. Bandar was the nightingale, Majid the dove. Selim was the falcon and Bir-Saraband the vulture. King Nayif was the albatross.

Tomorrow they must plan their next action. And soon after that he must see Megan Mcguire again, perhaps get a new message, through her, to America.

Tonight's action was a declaration of war, more than the attack on the Jockey Club, more than his other, minor raids. He thought of Kurakin, and of the Russian's eagerness to give more help—in exchange, probably, for the future freedom of Kassan.

Suddenly, climbing down a dark interior stairway of a house half a block from the still-blazing ADDAK complex, Bandar realized how very tired he was. Planning his raid, he'd hardly slept for days. He gained the street without incident, walked calmly around a corner, down an alley, and then turned another corner. Luckily, his hiding place was close by. He'd used it before. It was an ancient mosque, very small and half in ruins, kept up only for the sake of the well-loved holy man who lived there. Bandar knocked softly at the side door, a heavy wooden affair much worn by time and usage. Eventually he heard the shuffling of feet. The old man himself opened the door, bowed in silence, and beckoned Bandar to come in. It had been arranged. The holy man was a boyhood friend of Majid's uncle. There would be bread and cheese and water, Bandar knew. There would be clean straw on the floor of the little storeroom where he'd sleep, and one rough blanket.

He said good night to his protector, quickly ate the food, drank the water, splashing a little of it on his sweaty, dusty face. Then he lay down. Far away, he could hear a siren wailing. It sounded no more threatening than the desert wind.

Bandar closed his eyes. He was too tired to sleep immediately. He wondered if by some magnificent stroke of luck Bir-Saraband himself had been trapped in the burning buildings. *Don't count on it*, said the voice of caution. Tomorrow would tell, one way or the other. And all the other tomorrows. Sleepily Bandar wondered how many more Kassanian dawns Allah would allow him to see.

The last image in his mind before he slept was of his sister. Leila. Not as he'd last seen her, for that was unbearable. Instead, Bandar imagined the girl as she must be now, at ease and in no pain, walking in the cool green garden that is the Muslim heaven: *Al-gammah* being the garden, and *Al-ferdons* paradise itself. Cool and green it would be, with rippling water and birdsong. And Leila, whole again and freer than she had ever been on earth, walked slowly in a meadow, singing softly, gathering wildflowers.

Then Bandar slept.

Megan sat on her terrace enjoying a late breakfast and thinking about the king. She was scoring beautifully on the rebel side of her story. Between the interview with Al Khadir and last night's raid, it made a powerful view. But it was a one-sided view.

To round out her picture of Kassan, Megan needed to get

closer to the Panther Throne. She knew Jeb might be able to help her—if he would. Well. Tonight she'd have dinner with him. Tonight, maybe, she'd convince him. That was why, really, she'd asked Jeb to take her into the desert to meet Al Khadir. She lay back on the chaise, enjoying the brilliant sunshine and the well-earned leisure. From far below, the street sounds of Port Kassan drifted up to her, pleasantly distant: brakes screeching, horns wailing, camel bells, shouts of joy and anger. If she sat up, she could see the harbor. One of Ahmad's father's boats was already en route with last night's videotape.

Louise had called the palace: Prince Selim was not available. Prince Selim had yet to be available, or his father, either.

Well. A lot had been done. More would be done. Starting tonight.

Karim smiled. It had been wise to leave the camels hobbled at his campsite. They would have been a drawback in this rocky terrain. He had risen with the sun, said prayers, washed with a miser's portion of water, milked the she-camel for breakfast, packed his pouch with dates and cheese, filled the waterskin, and set off.

The acacia stump became Karim's beacon, looming as it did above the rise. He walked steadily, marking his direction by the angle of the sun. He walked three hours before he found what he was looking for. Up and down and up again he climbed, cresting every rise and looking back, checking that his acacia stump was still in view. Now he was thirsty. Here was a great boulder that cast a most welcome patch of shade. Karim squatted there and drank a quenching sip from his waterskin.

Then he heard them and made himself very small in the dark shadow of the rock. The two brigands passed not five feet away, talking freely, imagining themselves to be entirely alone. Their words made Karim's blood curdle.

"Kill the old bastard and be done with it, I say!" The speaker's voice was a peasant growl, heavy with menace.

His companion was more reserved. "You are truly willing to stand before Allah and slay the rightful King of Kassan? You are braver than I, Hassim."

Karim held his breath. This was incredible. *Where had these men come from? Where were they going?* The rougher of the two voices spoke again, almost in Karim's ear: "How long must we rot in this dump?"

"The radio says nothing. For two days he has not been in touch."

"Kill the old man and vanish, then, how about it?"

"He'd find us—you know that—even at the ends of the earth. And you know what he'd do when he did find us."

There was a silence after that. *Who were they talking about—this dreaded person who would find them wherever they fled?* The men passed on. As distance softened their voices, Karim peeked out from behind his boulder. Now he could detect a faint trail. Slowly, keeping low and in shadow, he followed. There was a gentle rise, the crest of this hill. More big rocks to hide him. And from behind one of them he could see it all. A ruined fort. How it came to be in this desolate spot, he had no idea. The two men wore dirty old robes. They walked up to the fort and into it. Karim waited for an hour, but there was no sign of Nayif. Still, their words were assurance enough. This must be the place. They'd come here from the raid. Karim thought he could remember that coarse voice—the voice of the man who would kill the king.

Finally he decided that it was more important to get the news to Al Khadir than to wait hoping for a glimpse of the old man who might never be allowed out in daylight anyhow.

Karim turned and walked back to camp as fast as he could. He was smiling from ear to ear. *Mission accomplished!*

Megan looked at Jeb Cleaver, and thought, simply: *I want him. I want it to be the way it was. The way it could be again. Maybe. Why are there always complications? Why is it always so tough?*

Until she'd met Jeb, Megan's job had been enough. IN-TERTEL had become family, lover, faith.

Now she looked at him as he stood just inside his front door, holding it open.

"You can even come in," he said, kissing her lightly. Megan came in. She hadn't really noticed his house on her last brief visit. Nice. Nothing spectacular, but nice. It could have been in Palm Springs or a dozen other recent, expensive tropical resorts. She'd had an indulgent afternoon at the Hilton, featuring a long-overdue visit to the hairdresser and a luxurious, perfumed bath. Now Megan was dressed in a simple shirtwaist of celadon-green silk. One very thin gold chain set with a single tiny diamond was at her throat. On her wrist, an old gold bangle she'd picked up at the King's Road antique market in London last year. For the first time since she'd landed in Kassan, Megan felt truly feminine. And she could tell it wasn't lost on Jeb.

Jeb led her into the garden. They sat in the white chairs by the pool and sipped white wine. It was quiet, cool, peaceful. Last night might never have happened.

"Did you catch the interview with Al Khadir?"

"No, sorry, I didn't. That's fast work, Megan. When was it on?"

She laughed. "Don't hold your breath till it airs in Kassan. But INTERTEL broadcast it from Rome by satellite. Some people apparently got it here—with not very good reception. In both senses of the word."

"I've been holed up here all day, working."

"Then you don't know about the raid last night?"

He poured some more wine into his own glass. Megan had barely touched hers. "I must sound pretty stupid. What raid?"

"Bandar raided ADDAK. Very successfully. In fact, he wiped them out. Three bombs, a lot of fire, snipers to pick off the stragglers. Your friends in the palace have a war on their hands, Jeb. It could escalate. It's been escalating day by day since we've landed. If it goes on at this rate for another few weeks, the whole place could be in flames."

Jeb tried to smile. Unsuccessfully. "And Selim doesn't return my phone calls," he said. "I've tried him a couple of times. Either he's out of town or he's very busy. I can't believe he'd give me the runaround."

"You think I'm meddling?"

"No. Believe me, I don't. I think you're great, and I take back anything I said in Williamsburg. From what Al Khadir says—and I believe him, Megan—a poor person here has no more rights than a French peasant under Louis XVI. And that stinks, even if Selim is an old pal."

"The question is, what to do about it."

Ali appeared then, to announce dinner.

They went inside. In a corner of the living room was a low tray, a circle of hammered brass, its surface intricately engraved with fine Arabic calligraphy. Big pillows were scattered on the floor.

"I ordered an Arabian meal," said Jeb. "We'll sit on the floor, if that's okay with you. In a Bedu tent it'd be a carpet on the sand."

It was very okay with Megan.

They sat comfortably on the floor, propped up by the fat pillows. Ali came out with two dinner plates. Centered on each plate was a large white onion stuffed with a fragrant mixture of ground lamb and pine nuts. On the table was a tall glass pitcher filled with something that looked like rosé wine. It was a mixture of rosewater, fruit juices, and water, garnished with fresh mint. A bit on the sweet side, but refreshing.

"It's fabulous, Jeb," she said after the first bite.

Yes, thought Jeb. *For an ADDAK spy, Ali cooks very well.* He lifted his glass. "To your grandmother's present."

Megan laughed. "That was a very good touch. I think we'll hang on to Granny for a while. What's happening with your embassy?"

"It's beginning to take shape. Later on I'll show you a few sketches if you like."

"I like."

They ate hungrily. Ali took their plates and came back with others, then with the main dish. It was a sort of chicken stew featuring olives, tomatoes, and saffron rice. It had a pungent, almost currylike flavor that Jeb couldn't identify.

"Cardamom," said Megan when he asked. "It's one of the oldest spices in this part of the world."

"I think," said Jeb, rising from the comfort of his pillow, "that it might be time to switch back to wine." He quickly returned with a fresh bottle of California Chardonnay—a gift from Wiggy. CIA wine, he thought, tasting it. Wherever it came from, the wine was ideal with the entrée—crisp and flowery.

"Best meal I've had in Kassan," said Megan as Ali came back with dessert: melon spiked with lime and garnished with mint. There was Arabic coffee too, thick and sweet. The feeling in Jeb's living room was a good one: comfortable.

They were at ease with each other again. Jeb counted that a major achievement. For a while they sipped the coffee in silence. Then she spoke.

"About those sketches . . ."

They got up. The studio was only a few steps away. Jeb flicked on the angle-armed architect's lamp that was clamped to the drawing board.

For a long moment she simply stared at the drawing.

"It's going to be wonderful, Jeb. I've never seen anything like it."

He laughed, more pleased by her praise than she could possibly know. "Sure you have—in some of the little old villages in the desert, clusters of buildings, all similar, all different. Of course, this will be a little more stylized, a little more grand. But it's the village feeling I'm after. And with plenty of water. Pavilions in a water garden, water flowing all over the place. Even into the main reception room here . . ."

"I see. It'll be delightful."

He had come up close behind her, to her left. Now Jeb reached out, pointing to a detail of the main reflecting pool. Her hand touched his arm. It was a gentle touch. A gentle touch with about a million volts of electricity in it.

He turned. She was looking at him, not the drawing.

Jeb said nothing, but drew his arm around her, pulling her close. Her glance never wavered. Slowly, like a big wave rolling in to shore, a smile curved its way along her lips.

"And that," said Jeb softly, "is how it's going to be."

They kissed.

Suddenly there was no Kassan, no Panther Throne, no sweet long-ago memories turned sour. Just Megan and Jeb in a fierce gentle world of their own devising. The bedroom was only a few steps away.

How they got there, neither Jeb nor Megan would have been able to say. The room was filled with the soft blue shadows of Kassanian twilight. The sheets were cool. Everything else was a delicious inferno, and Megan approached it smiling, because she had thought this might never happen again. For Jeb their reunion was a celebration, all the Fourths of July in the world in one glorious fusion, a mingling of flesh and fantasy, the sense of drifting off together into an endless purple night filled with love and shooting stars. They gave themselves to the magical dark journey and wished it would never end.

Much later Megan woke, gloriously exhausted and yet replenished too. She looked at Cleaver. He was sleeping. But as Megan watched, he stirred, muttering something unintelligible. He reached for her without opening his eyes. Megan caught his hand and kissed it. Then his eyes opened, blinked. He smiled at the sight of her. And kept right on reaching.

The luncheon had been excellent, but Wilfred Austin still had no idea why the Soviet ambassador had invited him, and him alone. Now Kurakin was insisting they go down to the damned screening room. Well, it wouldn't do to be outright rude to the fellow. He was obviously very pleased with whatever it was they were going to see. Practically bubbling over.

It was an attractive little room, all gray, a regular miniature theater seating perhaps two dozen. All the other chairs were empty now. The lights dimmed.

"I must apologize for the quality of some of this," said Kurakin regretfully, "but you'll understand that the conditions were not the best for proper lighting."

The leader portion of the film unreeled, a blur of patterns and meaningless Cyrillic characters. Then Wilfred Austin gasped. There he was, in a white suit, opening the street-floor door of his house in the old town. He looked at his host. Kurakin was intent upon the screen. Austin felt his stomach churning, nausea rising.

Cut. Now he was looking at the face of the boy Aziz. The face and the body, to be exact. Aziz lay on the bed, on his back, smiling. Waiting. He didn't wait long.

Austin closed his eyes, then opened them. The image was still there. And sounds. Love words in Arabic. Panting. At one point the boy laughed. It was like a knife going into Wilfred Austin.

The film ran for nearly ten minutes, then stopped as abruptly as it had started.

The lights came up again. Wilfred Austin buried his face in his hands, leaned forward, and tried hard not to vomit.

"There is, of course, much more," said Kurakin softly, "but what you have just seen is, I think, sufficient."

"Don't!" It was a cry of pure torment.

"Don't what, dear Wilfred?"

"Don't go on about it, dammit!"

Austin looked up then, his eyes suddenly red. The eyes of a trapped rabbit, thought Kurakin from behind a sympathetic glance.

"Please, Wilfred, pull yourself together. We are men of the world. If you choose to find your pleasures in avenues that might seem curious to the narrow-minded, well . . ."

"What do you want of me?"

The words came out in a rush. He was almost panting. Kurakin had a moment's worry. The last thing he wanted was for the American ambassador to have a stroke on the premises of the Soviet embassy. That would be tragic, whatever the cause. That wouldn't do at all.

"You are always so straightforward, Wilfred. I like that in a man. There happens to be a small favor you could do for me. Nothing that would be in any way compromising."

Kurakin spread his words like butter. The smoothness of them was lost on Austin. All Austin could see was the crevasse that had suddenly opened up beneath him, deep and beckoning.

"Go on."

"These bothersome negotiations. They're still set for the fifth. The king's . . . ah, indisposition seems not to have altered that at all. What I'd like to find out, Wilfred, is the bidding limit of your American friends at Revere Oil. Kalbfleisch is already here, I am told."

"But they'd never tell me that—if there is a limit."

"Come, now, Wilfred. There are always limits."

Wilfred Austin stared dully at the empty screen that had so recently and completely altered the course of his existence.

"I'll see what I can do," he said so quietly it was no more than a whisper.

"You sound less than enthusiastic, Wilfred. For an assignment of this delicacy, I think great enthusiasm is required. I need that figure, Wilfred, very soon. Let us say, within three days."

It was Sunday, the twenty-first of September. Just two weeks until the negotiations.

"I can't promise you I'll get them."

"I'm sure you'll try," said Kurakin, smiling as he rose from the overstuffed gray chair. The Russian led the way out. Austin's mind raced like some laboratory animal in an impossible maze. He wondered who else had seen that film. With a sickening lurch he imagined the ambassador showing it at parties, even to Lulu.

Now they were in the embassy's imposing foyer.

Kurakin beamed, shaking hands, although there was no one about to see the charade.

"I have every confidence in you, dear Wilfred," he said, all joviality. "A man of your skills can surely do . . . everything."

The twinkle of irony was unmistakable, even to Wilfred, who was still reeling from shock.

By some miracle of will the American ambassador kept himself upright. He walked down the embassy steps and into the waiting limousine.

In the cool silence of the car's rear compartment the tormented man rested his head on the soft woolen upholstery, closed his eyes, and tried to think.

The car pulled out into the demented traffic of the steel-blue Kassanian afternoon.

26

Billy Earnshaw smiled through his wonderment. This was the stuff of fantasy. To be courted—there was no other word— by a rich American oilman. T. R. Kalbfleisch had bought him drink upon drink, bent over backward to be charming, flattering. It had been a very long time since anyone like T.R. had voluntarily spent time with Billy. And Billy savored it.

The man wanted information. He'd come to the right source. Billy was well practiced in teasing, lacing his small talk with hints and innuendos leading up to the inescapable conclusion that Billy was a true insider. That he could tell a great deal if it pleased him.

They were sitting in a discreet corner of the Hilton's penthouse restaurant. It had been a long, winy luncheon, and now each of them held a giant balloon glass with a double shot of vintage cognac. Billy had to struggle to restrain himself from tossing it off at a gulp and asking for more. Instead he merely swirled the glass, sniffed appreciatively, and set it down. Big things were in the air. Billy could sense it the way a vulture senses a fresh kill. And he wanted to be something like clearheaded when the decisive moment came.

Millions—maybe billions!—of dollars were shimmering and dancing in the atmosphere about them, chimerical, seductive, and just beyond the grasp of Billy Earnshaw. As so many things had been just beyond him, all through his long lifetime. Still, he smiled confidently. Dame Opportunity hadn't quite forsaken him yet, fickle whoring bitch that she was.

Tom Murphy

Billy weighed his words as though each one was a rare emerald. This Texan was nobody's fool.

"You've heard, of course, that she's left him?" Billy arched a knowing eyebrow, sure that T.R. had no idea what he was talking about.

Kalbfleisch smiled politely. "Who left whom?" Kalbfleisch carried off the "whom" without choking on it. This impressed Earnshaw more than T.R. could know. Billy laughed, the soft conspiratorial sort of laughter that might be shared by two very old friends.

"You must forgive me, Mr. Kalbfleisch: one gets so very provincial out here—I just assume the world shares my deep abiding interest in gossip. But this little adventure might be pertinent to your problem. She—the Princess Tamara, Selim's sister by the first and most favored wife of King Nayif—has just divorced her husband. And he is none other than the general of the army—Bir-Saraband."

"I see," said T.R., who didn't.

"The general is usually considered the second most powerful man in Kassan, after only the King himself."

T.R. resisted the strong temptation to look at his watch, to end this silly interview. Yet, there was undeniably something to what Lawrence had said: this old ruin of an Earnshaw did obviously have access to both the palace and the gutter as sources of information. How could it hurt to have him on retainer?"

"Suppose, Mr. Earnshaw," said T.R. impulsively, "that we come to an agreement. You seem conversant with everything that's going on here—and that is just what I'm looking for. A sort of listening post, both reliable and confidential. To keep on top of things in a way official channels just don't allow."

Earnshaw had played poker with experts. Now he was astute enough to say nothing at all. He just twirled the glass and looked at his host inquiringly.

"I'm not talking about anything, er, underhanded, you understand. You'd have some sort of a title, all the health benefits of a regular Revere Oil employee, and your duties would be extremely flexible. No need for regular office hours or anything like that."

Billy Earnshaw made himself hesitate. He had come to the

luncheon thinking this unknown American might possibly be good for a quick hundred Kassanian pounds.

"I would," he said at last, "require a contract."

"Of course. That's understood. Would a flat fee of fifty thousand American dollars per annum be satisfactory for the first three years? That's what my employers authorized."

Now Billy drank. Just a taste. It went down like melted satin. Fifty thousand! He would have sold his mother for five hundred.

"Well," he said, "I'd be a damned liar if I said it wasn't interesting, sir. It is very interesting indeed. You'd want some sort of regular report ... what? Weekly? Monthly?"

T.R. smiled. "Maybe both. Basically we'd be in touch by phone—you'd have an office for phone calls and such things in our headquarters on Nayif Chaussée." Now T.R., too, tasted the cognac. "Let's drink to it."

They raised their glasses. The fine thin crystal made a pleasantly musical note in the silence of the after-luncheon hour in the restaurant. T.R. reached into his pocket and produced a sealed envelope, handed it to Earnshaw, and nodded. "This is a small bonus, Mr. Earnshaw, for signing on. If you'll come to our office tomorrow at, say, eleven in the morning, I'll see to it that all the other paperwork is ready for you."

Earnshaw grinned. If you were living in some blasted fairy tale, the enchantment might as well go on and on. Gracefully, as though this sort of thing happened to him all the time, he pocketed the envelope without opening it.

"You are most considerate," said Billy, extending a withered, nicotine-stained hand from its yellowing cuff. Kalbfleisch overcame a deep reluctance to touch the man and shook his hand warmly.

"I hope," said T.R. "that this is the beginning of a long and fruitful relationship."

"I am sure it will be," said Earnshaw as the Texan signed the check and they rose to leave the restaurant.

It was nearly four in the afternoon. The big, glamorous penthouse room was almost deserted. At a corner table on the far side of the room, two middle-aged businessmen in Western-style but obviously off-the-rack business suits watched the departure of T.R. and Earnshaw with undisguised interest. Five minutes later they left too. In the lobby, one of them went to a pay telephone and quickly placed a call.

Megan looked at Jeb in the darkened bedroom. Once again, he seemed to be sleeping. He had amazing capacities for sleep. For other things, too. *Don't lose your cool, Megan,* she told herself. Then she grinned in the darkness. Whatever cool she'd come into this room with had gone, maybe forever.

The goddamned phone rang, shattering the moment. Jeb sat up as if shot from a cannon, blinked, and reached out for it.

"Hello?"

"Mr. Cleaver?" A woman's voice. But what woman's?

"Speaking."

"I am sorry to bother you. This is Louise Russell. Megan Mcguire's secretary. Is she still there?"

Jeb grinned. "She sure is."

He handed the phone to Megan, got out of bed, and took a quick shower. Then he slipped into a pair of old Lee jeans, an alligator shirt, and running shoes. And all the while Jeb was thinking how magical it had been, this time, with Megan. He could hear her talking in the other room. There was a dark side to the magic. Her damned job. Calls at one A.M., for God's sake.

When he walked back into the room, he couldn't help overhearing the conversation. "Well, darling," Megan said, "open it. But . . . ah, don't be too specific about what it might say, if you take my meaning."

There was a pause, while Louise obeyed.

"God in heaven!"

Another pause, very brief this time.

"Don't move an inch, Louise. I'll be there in fifteen minutes."

Megan hung up the phone then and looked at Jeb.

"Can you drive me, Jeb? I came in a cab. Plus . . . well, it's very important and we shouldn't talk here."

Five minutes later they were in Jeb's Mercedes convertible speeding through the night.

As soon as they were well out of the driveway, she turned to him. "Jeb, Bandar's found the king."

The car swerved, recovered, sped on.

Jeb bit his lip. "How long have you known that?"

Megan looked at him. He was staring intently into the traffic ahead, driving faster now. "I didn't really know. And you obviously weren't about to say anything about it. But we heard the rumors, how Nayif hasn't actually been seen in public for a few weeks."

"I'm glad you didn't ask. I would have lied."

"I know. And I understand, Jeb, really I do."

"Then let's go right to Selim."

"Don't you think we'd better see exactly what he says in his note? Louise couldn't go into details, naturally."

Jeb only nodded, thinking of Selim.

Louise was watching. She shook hands with Jeb and handed the note to Megan.

Megan read it aloud:

Dear Miss Megan Mcguire:

I must ask your help. Through means which I cannot at present reveal, we have located the place where a certain very valuable recent kidnapping victim is being held prisoner. This kidnapping, let me emphasize, was not done by us. But we do intend to use it for our advantage if possible. We plan to rescue this person and to use him as the basis for certain negotiations with the present government. In order to establish that we are fair and honest people, I would very much like it if you were able to record our activities for television. If this is agreeable, reply through the usual means tomorrow morning.

Most urgently yours,
Bandar Al Khadir.

Megan looked at Jeb, questioning.

"We've got to get to Selim with this. Do you have a copy of your videotape—the Al Khadir interview?"

She nodded.

"Bring it, and let's get going. Right now."

"Jeb, it's late—"

"You bet it's late. It may be too late for Selim. Look. You wanted an interview, right? Well, here it is. We'll get to him if we have to slide down the chimney!"

Megan gathered the video cassette and the note and they were off in five minutes.

Jeb expected to be stopped at the Portal of the Dawn, but Selim must have given orders to admit him at any time. He pulled the little sports car up to the private door to Selim's apartments. As before, it opened magically before him. *They must man it round the clock,* he thought, wondering if that were standard or because of the present state of emergency.

The same blue-suited young man stood holding the door, as though it were the most normal thing in the world. "Mr. Cleaver," he said, "welcome. The prince, alas, is in conference."

For one crazy moment Jeb wondered if that was Selim's code for being engaged with a lady. No matter. He'd want to hear the news.

"It can't be as important as what we have to tell him. Please interrupt—I'll take the responsibility for it. Tell him that we bring news of someone . . . someone he most urgently wants to hear about."

The young man nodded and opened the door wider. Megan and Jeb followed him to the elevator.

"Wow," said Megan when she saw the main drawing room of Selim's suite.

"Please," said the young man, "make yourselves at home, madam and sir. I shall tell His Highness what you said." He left the room silently, as if on noiseless tracks. Something about the smoothness of him gave Jeb the willies.

"How," he asked Megan, "would you like a nice stiff un-Muslim drink?"

She smiled. "Right here in headquarters? Maybe if he has any wine. White, please, with soda."

Jeb opened the hidden bar and made a spritzer for Megan and a large uniced bourbon for himself.

He led her to the window. "In the excitement," he began, "I didn't have a chance to say—"

She took his hand. "I know. It was wonderful. And—I hope—it'll just get better and better."

"If you look at the Corniche," he said, pointing at the nearly perfect half-circle that bordered the bay, "you'll see a dark patch off to the left at the far end. That's the hill that'll be the embassy site."

"I'd like to see it by daylight."

"You will."

At that moment Selim walked in. "Jeb! I am so sorry—I got your message . . ."

Jeb turned to him. "Selim, meet Megan Mcguire."

She smiled. "How do you do?"

He bowed. "Alas, miserably. But, welcome."

Jeb was about to speak. Then something occurred to him. "Selim, could you turn on the radio—loudly?"

Selim looked puzzled, but obeyed. The Arabian lady wailed her sad song incongruously into the sophisticated room. Only then did Jeb speak, and very softly.

"Selim, your father has been found—alive."

For a moment Selim just looked at Jeb, then at Megan. Dazed. "This is not a joke—not a trick of some kind?"

"We have the best reasons to believe it. A message from Al Khadir himself. Mind you, it was not Al Khadir who did that raid. But he has located the king nevertheless."

"Jeb, the man is a criminal. He is not to be believed!"

Then Megan spoke up for the first time. "How can you say that? Do you know him? Have you ever heard him speak?"

At first Selim's eyes radiated anger. For a woman, and a stranger, to address him thus was outrageous. Then he remembered that she had been brought here by Jeb. He calmed down before he replied. "No, madam, I have not."

"Your Highness," said Megan quietly, "I understand why you must think as you do. This man has sworn to topple the Panther Throne. He has killed people in Kassan. He was behind the raid on ADDAK last night, and the raid on the Jockey Club—and other things. But I have met him. I have heard his side of the story. And I think before we talk any more, you should too."

Jeb cut in before Selim could reply. "Selim, do you have a videotape player?"

In silence Selim went to the wall that contained his audio/video equipment. He pulled open a panel to reveal the newest of Japanese videotape cassette players. Megan fitted her cassette into the machine. She started it playing.

While Jeb and the prince watched her interview, Megan watched Selim. At first he seemed unreadable, frozen in his anger, trapped in his unwillingness to see the other side.

Slowly, as though being drawn by some irresistible force, Selim hunched closer and closer to the screen. *Poor bastard*, Megan thought. *If it were possible to crawl right into the picture, he'd do that, too.* Twice during the narration of Bandar's principles and hopes for Kassan Selim closed his eyes tightly as if to shut out the image of his sworn enemy.

When Bandar finished the story of his sister and what Bir-Saraband's goons had done to her, Selim stood up suddenly, electrified. Then he seemed to collapse back into the over-stuffed banquette, his eyes glistening with something that might have been anger. Or even tears.

Finally it was over. The screen glowed blue. Moving stiffly, like a very old man, Selim stood and flicked the switch to rewind it.

"Well, Selim," Jeb said quietly, "there's your criminal."

For a moment there was no sound at all other than the whir and click of the machine as Selim rewound the tape and removed the cassette. Then he turned to Jeb and Megan. His face was pale, the face of a man who has seen a ghost.

"It was one of your poets who said: 'I have lived too long in foreign lands.' I am sorry, Miss Mcguire, for being angry at you. I am a stranger in my own land. That alone—for he who shall be king here—is a crime. I have seen only what I chose to see, done what I chose to do. I have lived here for years. But I might as well be . . . a Martian."

Megan spoke gently. "The message I just received is very clear. I can't say what he intends to do, but this I believe: Al Khadir is a man of honor. If he says he didn't take your father, then he didn't."

"You are right, madam. He is Bedu. No Bedu would speak as he speaks unless it were the truth. Still, he is an enemy of the state. He may kill my father."

"Would you talk to him, Panther, if it could be arranged?" This idea had come to Jeb as he spoke it. A long shot—very long. But maybe the only way in the world to save the situation. "On some neutral ground . . ."

"Yes. Yes, I would. If he gave his word, I would give mine. For whatever it might achieve. But, Jeb . . . there is something very wrong here. Who, then, did take my father? And why?"

Jeb had an idea about that, but he wasn't ready to state it.

"We'll find out for sure when we find the king," he said. "And in the meantime, I think the best thing we can do is to ask Megan to set up that meeting, Selim. The sooner the better."

Selim stood up. "Do what you must, Miss Mcguire," he said. "I will meet him anywhere—under any reasonable circumstances." He took a deep breath. "And in the meantime, I'll summon the general—"

Before Jeb could speak, Megan interrupted. "Don't do that, please. Al Khadir hates that man deeply—you heard the tape. I think we'll be a lot closer to success if he's kept out of it—at least for the moment."

There was a pause. Jeb realized how much they were throwing at Selim, and how fast. He prayed the Panther was up to handling it.

"As you say," was his only reply.

Jeb said, "Selim, it's getting pretty late. Let's get together tomorrow. Megan will make her arrangement—if she can—and then we'll plan."

Selim laughed. There was a bitter edge to it. "So the Crown Prince of Kassan enlists in the People's Army?"

"If it gets your father back, why not?" Jeb put his hand on Selim's shoulder. "And if it stops the killing?"

"You think it will, Jeb Stuart, Knight of the Bourbon Tree?"

Jeb smiled. "I think it's your only chance."

"Well, good night, then, and thank you for coming. For bringing me this strange but, believe me, very welcome news."

"I'll call you midmorning, Selim. Make sure you're available, okay?"

"I'll be the most available person in Kassan."

The Mercedes was waiting, looking sporty and incongruous in the empty, moonlit courtyard of the old palace.

On the way back, Jeb asked her, "How do you get in touch with Al Khadir?"

She smiled. "It's almost ridiculously simple, but it works." Megan explained the room-service courier system. "I'll leave a message on my breakfast tray, Jeb, setting up a meeting in the afternoon. He should reply at noon. The reply—bet on it—will be positive. Then it's just a question of where and when."

"There's another element. I think someone's going to try to throw a wrench in it."

"Any particular someone?"

"General someone. Think about it, Megan. Who's the one real rat in this situation? Not Selim. Not Al Khadir. We know this Bir-Saraband's a bad guy—Al Khadir knows it, and . . . well, I guess you haven't met him, but there is something very rough about him. The kind who'd truly stop at nothing. And everything we know about ADDAK certainly bears that out. I don't want to make accusations like that to Selim, but suppose—just suppose—the old general wanted the throne for himself. It wouldn't be the first time something like that's happened in this part of the world. Think about Nasser . . . Gadaffi . . . what's-his-name in Iraq. All military men, overthrowing kings."

"It's a thought. It's a good thought, Jeb. But we don't really know, do we? I mean, pulling a stunt like this—kidnapping the king—wouldn't be at all past the Russians. Or the Libyans."

"Well. Time will tell, to coin a phrase."

Jeb dropped her at the front door, kissed her lightly on the cheek, and said, "I'll call you tomorrow . . . when?"

"Don't. I'll call you when I've got something firmed up."

"Good night, then. It's been a long, long day."

Her smile said it all. "Hasn't it? Good night, Jeb."

It was nearly three in the morning when he pulled into his own garage. Yawning, he let himself in. The house was dark but for one small light Ali liked to keep on in the main hallway. Jeb walked into his bedroom, remembering the Walther .38. It was in the top drawer of his bureau. He flicked the light on in the bedroom. Smiled as he saw the rumpled sheets.

His hand was on the drawer pull when the drawer moved. For a minute he just stared at the thing, wondering if it was his imagination. Then, just slightly, it moved again. Something was inside. A sort of soft rustling. Definitely not a mouse. Very quietly, Jeb backed away, his mind flipping quickly over a dozen alternatives. He went into his studio and picked up the steel T square from his drawing board. A long strip of tempered stainless steel three inches wide capped by a heavier crosspiece at the top. Not the best weapon, but better than nothing.

The only other weapon in the place was in that drawer. Someone must know that. Or have found it out by searching.

He got a thick Turkish towel from the bathroom and wrapped it around his left fist. He gripped the T square in his right hand. Then he worked the crosspiece of the T square into the handle of the drawer. Paused briefly, the adrenaline building.

Then he jerked the drawer open and ducked away from it. The snake moved so fast that at first Jeb hardly knew what it was: one fat streak of reddish-tan death, mottled with chevrons in ivory and black. It was out of the drawer in an instant, striking with a force that carried it through the air and three feet onto the thick wall-to-wall carpeting. For a second the creature seemed to be stunned. Jeb struck with the heavy crosspiece. Glancing blow. The snake twisted on itself, spotted Jeb, reared back. He threw the towel over its ugly, blunted-heart-shaped head. The snake was surprised. It thrashed wildly. Jeb struck it again and again. Still the beast flailed about, never quite throwing off the towel. Jeb hit harder. He heard something snap. But still it moved. The fifth blow did it. The snake quivered like a harpstring, gave one last flip of its thick body, and lay still.

Gingerly, not trusting his luck, Jeb used the crosspiece of the T square to lift off the towel. There lay his uninvited guest.

The snake was dead, its back deeply gashed in three places, part of its evil-looking head sheared off. A pinkish-yellow ooze seeped from the cuts. His jaw quivering from both outrage and fear, Jeb poked the thing. No reaction. Still clutching the T square, Jeb stood warily in place for a moment, breathing hard, listening, wondering if the snake had friends. He wasn't left wondering for long.

"*Bitis perenguei,*" said a familiar voice. "The Arabian sidewinder viper. Pity. It could have been made to look like an accident. Little pal wandered into your garden—they sometimes do, Jeb."

Slowly, not wanting to believe his ears, Jeb turned.

There stood Ross Hindley, smiling, pointing a large pistol directly at Jeb's heart.

"By the way, Jeb: do put that thing down. You're a little too quick with it tonight."

Cleaver looked across the sudden silence. *Hindley?* He looked the same. Same boyish grin. Same alert eyes. Only the pistol in his hand was different, but that made all the difference in the world. Jeb thought about the beautiful house in the hills, about the little boys, about Laura.

"Tell me about it, Ross."

The gun moved not a millimeter.

"It's simple, Jeb. You're getting too close to Al Khadir. It's beginning to look as though the People's Army might really pull off their revolution, and we can't have that. We absolutely can't afford to have another Iran, much less another Gadaffi.

"What does that have to do with me? Why does State care who's running Kassan, so long as we get our oil?"

Hindley just laughed as though that was the best joke he'd ever heard. But the laugh was sliding a little. Sliding right off the far edge of control.

"Who," asked Hindley quietly, in another tone of voice altogether, "said anything about State?"

"Then . . . what?"

"The operative word, Jeb, is oil. Specifically, Revere Oil. Let's just say I'm protecting their interests. A little more thoroughly than official channels might allow."

"Against Al Khadir?"

"He's off the wall, Jeb. We need tame rulers in this part of the world—and the supply's running short. Look at Iran. Look what happened to Sadat when the fanatics got feeling feisty. Bang-o! Al Khadir has a real chance at the Panther Throne, thanks to you and your pal Mcguire. That could bring in the Soviets and who knows what-all. We're just reducing his chances, Jeb. And you happen to represent his main chance right now. You and the lady."

"And you'll kill me to prevent it."

"An operational necessity. It's nothing personal, Jeb. Believe me."

Nothing personal. Jeb looked into Hindley's eyes and tried to guess what lay behind them. What complications, what fears, what dreams. But they just remained Hindley's eyes, alert and sparkling. Eyes that could smile or kill with equal facility.

Jeb had never faced death directly before. Not like this. Not staring right into it. He knew he should be playing for time, talking fast, maybe, trying to talk Hindley out of it. But he couldn't think of one more thing to say.

"Nothing personal, you say. Just like that."

Jeb was looking over Hindley's right shoulder now. Then he looked back. There was a flicker of—what?—in Hindley's expression, a small quiver. Jeb could see the trigger finger tensing.

"You'll never believe this, Jeb," he said, "but I'm really sorry." Then he pulled the trigger.

The shot rang out, and Jeb instinctively dived aside. But that wasn't what saved him. Ali's foot came out of the shadows behind Ross Hindley and knocked the gun from his hand while at the same time Ali scored a direct hit, a lashing karate slice of his left hand to Hindley's throat.

Hindley's eyes glazed as he fell.

For a moment Jeb just stood there staring at the crumpled form of Hindley. Then he turned to Ali.

"To say 'thank you' isn't really up to it, Ali, but thanks all the same."

Ali bowed and smiled. The perfect servant.

"He isn't dead, Mr. Cleaver. And maybe it's time I introduced myself. Charlie Richmond, United States Central Intelligence Agency, Division C."

Jeb found himself grinning foolishly as he took the man's hand. He looked so absolutely authentic, not to mention the perfect Arabic—and the cooking.

"What's Division C?"

"Counterintelligence of a rather special brand. Internal, as it were. And as for the rest of it, well, my dad Anglicized our name, because it's unpronounceable. But we're Lebanese. From Atlantic Avenue, in Brooklyn." Charlie Richmond paused, then went on. "I owe you an explanation. An apology, really. This was risky. Letting him come into the house like that. We were tracking him, of course. When I got the report he was headed over here, carrying this satchel, I figured it was the best chance we'd get to catch Mr. Hindley red-handed. Give him enough rope, and so forth. I didn't know about the snake."

Jeb was too relieved simply to be alive to analyze the situation. He grinned weakly.

As he spoke, Charlie/Ali was trussing up the still-unconscious Hindley. With mountain climber's rope, thin but very businesslike. "I know it's late, but you'll understand if I ask for a lift to the embassy. It's the only safe place for our pal here. We can get him out of the country in the diplomatic pouch, so to speak."

Five minutes later they were speeding toward the embassy. Hindley, still limp, was in Charlie Richmond's lap in the Mercedes. "He knew so much about me," Jeb said absently, still not quite believing what had happened. "Even the model car I drive—this one."

"Well," said Richmond, grinning, "it's our business to know stuff. Lately we've had a few cases of people using their knowledge to pursue extracurricular activities . . . like Wilson and Terpil and their cute little peddling of weapons systems to guys like Gaddafi. In the case of Hindley, he was taking on assignments for Revere Oil. My division was set up a few years ago to watch out for such things."

"And thank God for that," said Jeb as he pulled into the embassy drive.

Late as it was, the place was blazing with lights.

Austin's giving a party, thought Jeb, glad that he hadn't been invited. Richmond asked Jeb to stay with Hindley while he scouted out the security officer. Jeb could see shadows moving behind the windows, and he heard murmuring voices. He was nearly numb with fatigue. He'd been tired enough before the episode with the snake. Jeb wondered if he could ever again open a bureau drawer and be at ease doing it. All he wanted now was sleep. If he could sleep in that room again.

Charlie came back with Rogers, the marine lieutenant who acted as the embassy's security officer.

"What's wrong, Charlie?" Jeb had only to look at their faces to see that something was very wrong here.

"The ambassador," Charlie said quietly, "just blew his brains out."

Jeb tried to feel something for Austin, but all he felt was drained of emotion and very, very tired.

They drove back then. As they let themselves into the silent house, Jeb asked, "What now?"

"Sleep. For you, that is. I have a few phone calls to make—it's okay, I've got a scrambler. And they'll be very long distance. Tomorrow, you go right on calling me Ali. And you keep your date with Al Khadir if you can."

Jeb didn't even bother asking how Charlie/Ali knew about that. He said good night and showered and walked right past the damp spot on the carpet where the snake had died. He felt alone, entirely and completely alone. The last image to cross his mind before sleep finally rescued him was of Hindley's eyes, smiling, in the distant blue twilight high in the hills of Virginia.

27

Selim woke at dawn. He'd slept only a few hours, but, waking, he felt changed and revitalized in a way that had nothing to do with mere rest. There had been a fragment of a dream. Or maybe it was a long-buried childhood memory bubbling up to the surface. He was in the mountains with his father. They were snaring birds to help train some new falcons. The old man knew all about snares: snares for hares, for birds, even for larger beasts. The snare must be invisible to its victim, light but strong, and above all, quick. It must tighten in an instant when the bird least suspects it.

At six A.M. he summoned his private secretary, the quiet young man who had twice escorted Cleaver into the palace. "Abdul," said Selim, "something has come up, silly perhaps, but confidential too. Only you can be trusted to carry it out." And Selim invented a reason for Abdul to drive out to Tamara's palace and retrieve some golden knick-knack she wanted. The trip would take no less than two hours.

When the young man had gone, Selim went directly to Abdul's rooms, a small apartment on the floor above. What Selim found there made him both sad and very angry, for he had taken the boy out of the King's school and given many advantages. Judging by the bankbook he found hidden in Abdul's Koran, someone else had given him greater and more material advantages than a good job in the palace.

Selim had an excellent idea who.

His next action, and it was still before seven in the morning, was to call his brother-in-law on the general's own hot line. How proud Ibn had been, having this special device that could reach his palace, either of his offices, or his car. Selim got him in the car, which was interesting in itself. Ibn to be up and about so early!

"Ibn, it's Selim here," he said cheerfully. "I'm so sorry to trouble you—by the way, is there any news?"

"None, your Highness, alas: we are searching everywhere."

"I'm sure you are. Ibn, something tedious has come up— the Minister of Religion insists that I go to open the new mosque at Sana'a. Well, it's to be this afternoon. I'm leaving in the white Rolls at one—be there by three, I hope, Allah willing. But in view of all our little difficulties, I wonder if you could arrange a bit of an escort for me—not too much, but better they be armed, don't you think?"

In the backseat of his limousine Bir-Saraband smiled. Fate was turning his way at last! What more perfect opportunity could there be? "Consider it done, your Highness. From the time you come out of the Portal of the Dawn, my people will be with you."

"Thank you, Ibn. Sorry to be a bother."

"It's nothing. Nothing. Have a good trip."

And may it be your last, he thought, settling back into the seat. A few seconds later Ibn picked up the phone again. It was going to be a very eventful day in Kassan.

Megan asked Ahmad to come early for breakfast. They were eating and talking at eight-fifteen. Megan had already written her note to Bandar, telling him that Selim was willing to meet, and to help in any way possible, and to reply by noon at the latest. She smiled when she thought how enormous her room-service bill was going to be, and what a cheap investment at that.

They were having a second cup of coffee when the knocking began. It was polite knocking, but somehow different from the typical Hilton room-service knock. It was more confident. She opened the door.

There stood two tall young men in glittering uniforms. Kassanian Army. Megan smiled. "Yes?"

"Miss Megan Mcguire?"

His English was good, but with a strange sort of hesitation between the words. *Beats hell out of my Arabic,* she thought.

"I am Megan Mcguire."

"I present the compliments of my general, Miss Mcguire, and he wishes an interview with you."

Megan looked at him, testing the waters: was there a hint of intimidation here? "Which general?" she asked, knowing there was really only one.

"The Commanding General of the Armies of Kassan, Ibn Bir-Saraband, madam."

"Oh, yes," she said, "that general. Is there a time for this appointment?"

Maybe I can squeeze it in, she thought, *quick, before noon, kill all the birds with one stone.* There ought to be time. Army headquarters wasn't far away. She'd passed it many times.

"As soon as it may be convenient, madam."

"We'll do it right away, then," she said, smiling her brightest smile. "Won't you come in? I'll be with you in a moment." Megan was already dressed for the expedition: a safari suit, Frye boots, and, for color, a deep blue silk scarf around her neck. It would have to do for the general. In her bedroom she dashed off a note for Jeb, saying where she'd be and why, and telling him to come to the hotel and wait if he hadn't heard from her by ten-thirty. Then she called Louise Russell, repeated all of this to her, and asked her to call Jeb if the interview lasted longer than ten-thirty.

"Got it," said Louise briskly. "Have fun."

Then Megan introduced Ahmad as her interpreter and announced that, as usual, he would be coming along. The soldiers—they must be officers, but Megan couldn't tell of what rank—stiffened a bit, then bowed with an almost Oriental politeness and waited by the door. Megan picked up her purse, her notebook, a small tape recorder, and they all left Penthouse 1626.

She shuddered when she saw the car that was waiting: it was a gray four-door Mercedes sedan just like the one that had tailed her and Jeb that day. Only last Thursday! Today was Monday, the twenty-second. Everything was so weird in Kassan that Megan found herself forgetting the numbers of the days. The car pulled out onto Nayif Chaussée. Megan and Ahmad shared the rear seat. One of the soldiers drove, and the other rode with him. Nothing was said during the short journey.

Headquarters was only twelve blocks away, a vast and monolithic building that obviously wanted desperately to be impressive but couldn't make up its mind as to how. It was set far back from the road, a great U-shaped structure of gray stone that seemed ready to swallow its own entrance driveway. It had all the grace of an Art Deco tomb. Megan had seen buildings quite like it in Italy: Fascist-era railroad stations, more often than not.

Megan was pleased. Whatever had prompted the general to see her at last, after dodging several appointments, this would help fill in the last remaining blank area of her Kassanian tapestry. She remembered what Jeb had said late last night, driving back from the palace. And even more vivid was her memory of Bandar's view of the man. *Well,* she thought, *I've met many a monster before, and tamed more than one of them.* As they pulled up to the enormous front door of the headquarters building, Megan was amused to see some Pakistani workmen furiously scrubbing away at a huge rebel slogan: *"Fakk raqaba!"* done in yellow spray paint on the wall.

The English-speaking soldier escorted them in while his companion waited behind the wheel. The entrance was flanked by an honor guard, two soldiers on either side, dressed in uniforms even gaudier than those of Megan's escorts. These guards sported automatic pistols in burnished leather holsters and also long, decorative, and dangerous-looking ceremonial swords. The effect was both operatic and sinister. Probably just what the general had in mind, from what Megan had heard of him.

They walked down a very long central corridor built in the same depressing gray granite as the exterior of the building. It was absolutely empty. There was a haunted feeling here, more like a crypt than a busy office complex. The building, she knew was less than five years old, but there were cracks in the plaster ceilings and here and there a broken window. The attitude toward maintenance seemed to be "Let it fall apart, it's so easy to build another." They weren't used to owning things, these Arabs, nor to preserving them. She wondered how Jeb would deal with this prevalent attitude in building his embassy.

Three-quarters of the way down the vast central hallway they turned left. Facing them was a pair of enormous double doors. The soldier opened one of them, waited for them to pass through, then closed it. Firmly. Now they were in an anteroom. More double doors. Again, the opening, passing through, closing. Megan felt a little tremor of nervousness. Like being led into a nest of Chinese boxes, one within the other. Very tight boxes, made of impenetrable stone.

In the third antechamber, before the third set of very imposing double doors, the soldier turned to Megan. "The general will be pleased to see you alone, Miss Mcguire."

Then he turned to Ahmad and whispered something in rapid-fire Arabic. It was not a friendly whisper. Megan watched, with growing apprehension, as the boy's eyes grew round with fright. His fists clenched. But before he could speak, the soldier spoke again. A threat had obviously been made. Ahmad looked at her, a quick, fleeting, pleading glance. Then he looked down, ashamed. *He is asking for-* *giveness*, Megan thought. *But for what?*

The soldier opened one of the double doors and ushered Megan in. She stood there for a moment, taking in the enormous office. When the door clicked shut behind her, Megan turned. No sign of Ahmad or the soldier. She was alone now.

The room was very large. Tall windows heavily curtained in dark red velvet. Dazzling Persian carpets on the floor. Gilded bronze was splashed over heavy Louis Napoleon chairs, cabinets, and a massive desk. Behind the huge desk sat a huge man. Bir-Saraband.

More massive than fat, he was nevertheless monolithic. He looked like a bull. A not very friendly bull. In fact, he glowered.

"Come in, Megan Mcguire. Please to come in." His English was thick as his neck, and halting.

As Megan stepped forward, she heard a decisive metallic click from the door latch behind her.

Someone had locked it.

The general rose slowly, growing like some thick gnarled tree. Under an ape's thrust-forward brows his small dark eyes glowed meanly. He wore a simple uniform today. Tan jacket over tan jodhpurs, immaculate English riding boots. All he lacked was a whip. Megan had an uneasy feeling that there probably was one, and not far away. Whenever she felt threatened, Megan's gut instinct was to strike first, try to ride it out on a wave of bravado.

"What does this mean?" she asked indignantly, the color rising in her cheeks. "Where is my interpreter?" She took a deep breath. "I demand to see him!"

Slowly a smile spread across the heavy face of her captor. And he was her captor, no doubt about it. The smile oozed, like a ripple sliding across a pool of oil.

"You demand." He said it slowly, and paused as though he were chewing on the words, sucking all the flavor out of them. "You demand. Interesting. You are an enemy of Kassan, woman. Bitch. Whore!"

Megan opened her mouth to scream, and as she did, a very large and very strong hand was clapped over her mouth. Too strong, too tough even to bite—and she tried. Other hands grabbed her arms. *Where had they been hiding?* She struggled like a fish in a net, turning her head this way and that. There were four of them. Not soldiers. Thugs. Dressed in ragtag desert clothes, a mixture of dirty Bedu robes and castoff Western trousers, boots, and shirts, they had one thing in common. A look of desperation, the look of men who would do anything. Megan's heart took a plunge that sent it falling nonstop to the farthest reaches of despair. A gag of rough cotton was forced into her mouth and tied tightly. Choking. They dragged her to a far corner of the room. Ropes were produced, and Megan found herself being lashed, spread-eagled, to the four wooden legs of a low black leather ottoman. The men worked so quickly, she knew they must have had practice. A lot of practice. She closed her eyes. *The worst that can happen is, I die,* she told herself. She was wrong.

Megan never knew which one of them hit her. It was a sharp slap on her left cheek, and it stunned her. For a moment she stopped struggling. For just an instant she blacked out. When she forced herself to open her eyes again, she was trussed like a calf ready for branding, arms and legs straddled. Now someone was tearing at her clothes.

Of course.

This isn't happening, she thought. *It's a nightmare.*

But it was happening. She looked up. There stood Bir-Saraband. He was laughing now, smirking as he unzipped his trousers, yanked out the dark, thickening penis, and came closer. Closer.

Then Megan shut her eyes very tightly. Maybe if she couldn't see him . . .

And then he was in her, rutting like a pig, thrusting, tearing, hurting. If he could push her through the stone floor, he'd do it laughing. Finally, after an eternity of pain, he was finished. But Megan's ordeal was just beginning. They were going to take turns. For a moment she blinked her eyes open. The tallest of the four thugs was there, rubbing himself, waiting his turn. It came, and the others'. Sometime before they were finished with her Megan lost consciousness. Completely. Mercifully.

When she came to, she thought she had died and gone to hell. Her body was one throbbing ache. As though she'd been dipped in boiling water and then flogged. She was still trussed tight, but differently, arms bound behind her, legs lashed together. *And she was moving.* Bouncing on hard steel in total darkness. Darkness and heat.

Why, please god, didn't they just kill me?

Megan drifted in and out of consciousness. There was no way to measure passing time. She opened her eyes. She was lying on her back in the back of a van. A very little light came in through cracks at the back—where the doors must be. The van was moving fast. And, blessedly, she was alone back here. That must mean the doors were locked, that whoever was driving knew she couldn't escape. And he was right, she thought, twisting her tightly bound wrists.

The truck rattled on. *They have something even worse in mind for me now,* she thought, and the horror was multiplied by the realization that she was almost beyond caring.

Megan wondered if there was enough water in all the oceans of the earth to wash her clean again. Then she closed her eyes and drifted off to merciful sleep.

Jeb slammed down the phone. It had taken him twenty minutes even to reach army headquarters, and then he got a royal runaround. Nobody had seen or heard of Megan Mcguire. The general was unavailable. Could he call back tomorrow, Inshallah?

It was eleven-thirty, and Jeb was in Megan's suite with Louise Russell. They had ordered an early lunch, not to eat but to keep open their line of communication with Al Khadir. Bandar's answer appeared on it. *Acceptance!* Instructions, how to get to the rendezvous, down to probable driving times. Jeb was burning to go. To get to Selim. And now, damn-fool Megan . . . It was too much. She was probably caught in one of these infamous traffic jams.

"Louise," he said at last, "I'm going to the palace, to Selim. Here's the number—his private number. Call me the minute you hear anything . . . Wait, let's copy these directions in case she has to come in a separate car." They did that, and Jeb was in Selim's apartment by noon.

Selim's spaceship of a living room looked vastly different by day. It bounced with light. Port Kassan seemed like a bleached-out color photograph in the distance, punctuated by the occasional spark of glitter as the sun glanced off a windshield.

Selim was waiting.

Jeb noticed something different but indefinable about his old friend as they shook hands rather formally. Something had come alive in Selim this morning. There was a brightness, an energy, that hadn't been in him even late last night.

Very briefly Jeb filled him in on Megan's disappearance. It was beginning to look like that now. Selim frowned. "Jeb, that was a very foolhardy thing for your lady friend to do, if you will forgive me." Immediately he went to the phone, dialed a number. "Ibn's hot line," Selim explained with his hand over the speaker. Then Selim made contact, spoke briefly in Arabic with his brother-in-law, and hung up. "He says they had a charming talk for perhaps twenty minutes and that she was then driven back to the hotel. I don't believe it."

"What can we do?" At that moment Jeb felt he could go straight to army headquarters and take the place apart stone by stone.

"At the moment, Jeb, nothing. I can't prove that what Ibn has said isn't true. But I have laid a snare for my dear brother-in-law. We shall know before very long what his word is worth."

Jeb showed Selim the letter from Al Khadir.

"Good," said Selim. "I know this place. We should leave here at precisely one-fifteen. By the side gate."

"Why so precise?"

Selim only smiled. "Have you had lunch yet, Jeb?"

While they were eating a variety of excellent salads washed down with iced mint tea, the private secretary came in. Abdul was transformed: he wore full Bedu regalia, white robes and headcloth, the deep blue head ropes with gold cinches that signified the royal household. And dark sunglasses.

"Excellent, Abdul, excellent," said Selim with a smile. "Now, when you get to the mosque, present these to the holy man with my compliments." Selim rose and produced two wrapped packages. "Quickly, now, the car is waiting."

Abdul bowed and left carrying the boxes.

When he had gone down in the little elevator, Selim stood up, clapping his hands together in almost childish glee. "Now," he said. "Now we will see what my brother-in-law is made of. Come, Jeb."

They went to the window. Immediately below, they could see the far interior corner of the courtyard, the Portal of the Dawn, and about a hundred yards of the street beyond.

As they watched, Selim's old white Rolls-Royce limousine poured itself through the big gate. "What Abdul's costume is really all about," said Selim happily, "is to make anyone who is watching think he's me. He is about the same size, don't you think, and with the robes, the glasses, the car—" Selim was interrupted by the explosion.

The Rolls-Royce was about a block past the gate, just entering the old quarter. The blast was enormous even from high up in the palace. The rear section of the car disintegrated. There was a great orange flare as the gas tanks caught fire.

Selim turned to Jeb. "My dear brother-in-law has just murdered me, Jeb. I am a dead man."

"But how . . . what about Abdul?"

"Abdul was his agent. As I should have guessed before last night. As for my driver, I pray he escaped. He is a good man. But, it was a necessary sacrifice, if it proves to be one. I had to know for sure, Jeb, before . . . before I do the things I am probably going to do today."

There were a dozen things Jeb might have said, but he didn't say anything. He was proud of Selim. Selim was taking the situation into his own hands at last. Jeb only hoped it wasn't too late.

"I'm going to call Megan's secretary. If she hasn't turned up, let's get going." Jeb did that. Louise had heard nothing. Jeb heard that news with a sinking heart. He asked Louise to call Wiggy Lawrence at the embassy, tell him the whole story, call out the marines, the police, whatever. Then he hung up.

"Okay, Panther, you're on."

They left in one of the INTERTEL Range Rovers. Selim drove. They went out of the side gate unchallenged: the pandemonium at the main gate would tie up Kassan for hours. As they drove, a thought occurred to Jeb.

"Selim, when I spoke to Louise—Megan's secretary—I forgot to tell her to tell the embassy you're really alive. Shouldn't we stop and do that?"

Selim never took his eyes off the crowded road. "No, Jeb Stuart," he said quietly. "Let's first wait and see if I am alive by this time tomorrow."

Bandar's instructions this time were more complicated than they had been when Jeb and Megan went to meet him. After two hours of fast driving on ever-narrowing roads, they found themselves on a goat track heading up a steep hill. They were beyond the little town where Jeb and Megan had turned off before. Jeb was glad he'd decided to take the Rover. No conventional suspension could have tolerated the path they were on now. Bandar's instructions told them to look for a fallen tree blocking the trail. Park there and walk on. Here it was. And here they parked. They walked for fifteen minutes, the trail narrowing until at last it came to a clearing. A herding place for someone's goats, Jeb thought. The sparse grass had been entirely eaten away. The bare ground shimmered with late afternoon's last heat waves. Then, at the far side of the clearing, Bandar stepped out of cover and stood foursquare in the middle of the far end of the clearing, his long arms crossed over his chest. Bandar wore a belt that had a small dagger in it, but he was otherwise unarmed.

"Let me face him alone, Jeb. It is better." Before Jeb had a chance to reply, Selim was walking slowly, deliberately, and with a full measure of pride in his bearing. It took less than a minute, but for Jeb it was the longest, slowest walk he'd ever seen.

Selim stopped precisely in the middle of the clearing.

Silence raged and thundered.

Selim bent with fluid grace and scooped up a handful of red sand. Then he straightened and threw the sand straight up into the air. The red grains seemed almost to float, shimmering, back to earth. And still the silence thickened the air between the two men.

Astonishingly, Bandar repeated the gesture. Just as slowly, just as elegantly. Two grown men, Jeb thought, each sworn to kill the other, playing in the sand. But it was obvious they weren't playing. Now they began walking slowly, each to meet the other.

And for a long time they stood together in the midst of the clearing, speaking in low voices. Jeb couldn't hear a word of it.

Selim looked into the eyes of the man he had considered his most mortal enemy. The eyes of a saint and of a murderer. But eyes that would not lie.

Making the ancient Bedu sign—the peace gesture from one stranger to another—was a treaty more binding than all the fine words scrawled on paper in palaces by liars.

Selim spoke first. "General Al Khadir," he said quietly, weighing each word, "I come from Megan Mcguire—with her friend the architect Jeb Cleaver. She has been detained— possibly by Bir-Saraband. Without my knowledge or permission. If you have my father, I will do anything I can to get him back in good health."

Well spoken, thought Bandar. *But can he mean it?*

Then Bandar spoke. "It is luck sent by Allah that we have discovered where your father is being held. We know not by whom. But the raid was not our raid, and your father is not our captive. Someone chose to make it look thus. But we do not attack unarmed old men, even if they are of the El Kheybar."

"I believe you, General. And I have reason now to think Bir-Saraband may be behind all of it." Briefly Selim explained the events of last night and this afternoon.

"I see," said Bandar, both surprised and impressed. "We shall attack the fort where your father is imprisoned. There may be much bloodshed. If we succeed, let us then talk afterward about the future of Kassan. If we fail, then we fail together."

Selim hadn't known what to expect, but surely it was nothing like this. "Thank you," he said. "It is nobly spoken."

Bandar smiled then, for the first time. " 'Nobly,' Prince Selim, is not a word we often use in the People's Army. But we count it an honor if you will join us. And Cleaver, whom I know."

Selim turned and waved to Jeb. Jeb came forward and shook hands with Bandar. Now, from unsuspected hiding places all around the perimeter of the clearing, came armed men. All but a few were young. They had a special look about them, hard to describe but distinctive. An eagerness, an enthusiasm, a reckless bravery. They were lean and quick. Their eyes flashed with hope and intelligence. And they were dangerous, thought Jeb, for these were young men with nothing to lose.

"We must march," said Bandar, "and quickly. It is a whole day's journey, but we shall have to do it in two days' time, for we march by night. There is already another small group of our people at the fort, watching. We march tonight, rest tomorrow, march tomorrow night—Tuesday—and, depending on what we find, attack Wednesday night." He paused. "If all is well."

"If all is well," Selim echoed. "Good. Let's get on with it."

28

From a corner window on the top floor of the Garden of Five Thousand Delights Ibn had a clear view of the main palace gate. He sat in that window at one o'clock, sipping tea and watching the Portal of the Dawn with an intensity that surprised even Theodora.

The stately prow of Selim's white Rolls-Royce seemed to ooze through the gate: it was that long and moved that slowly. Now it came down the main street leading to the old quarter. Ibn held his breath. Suppose the charge didn't take!

The roar was more musical to his ears than all the lutes in heaven. It was a pressure mine. Three pressure mines, to be exact. Any one of them would have done the job. He saw the flare and the smoke and the flames, although the car itself was out of sight.

Impulsively he leaped up and ran from the room.

Ten minutes later he was directing the cleanup. The entire rear compartment of the Rolls was shattered, its roof and windows gone, the corpse inside unrecognizable. The driver, oddly, had escaped with only a broken arm and facial burns.

Ibn was back in his office at army headquarters when the phone call from Kurakin came through. Had he heard about Austin? the Soviet ambassador wanted to know. Ibn listened in disbelief, as Kurakin fairly crowed with triumph. *One less card to be played,* thought Ibn through a dull red rage. For he knew what must have happened. The treacherous Russian had somehow gotten to Austin first. Now there could be no counting on the Americans for extra support in his coup.

Now his plan would have to change, and if he wanted help, he'd just have to come begging for it—to Kurakin! That was the subtext of Kurakin's message, and Ibn heard it all too clearly.

He decided not to tell Kurakin about the death of Selim El Kheybar. Let him find that out for himself.

When the conversation was finished, with all due formalities and promises to get together soon, Ibn hung up in a dark and angry mood. His double triumphs of earlier in the day were fading, and so was the euphoria that went with them.

Now he must stage a dramatic rescue of King Nayif. Now he must wipe out all of the handpicked ADDAK agents who were holding the old man, for if even one of them talked, everything would be over for the Bir-Saraband dynasty in Kassan. It should be easy. They suspected nothing. Hassim and his six companions would be a pushover. If Ibn rescued the king, he was a hero—and maybe Nayif could be persuaded to abdicate in his favor. If Nayif died—and that could be arranged after a quick conversation about the abdication—then there was only one strongman left in Kassan. Ibn would be the only logical choice.

Yes. It made sense. He reached for the phone. The raid must be organized with the greatest secrecy. He wished now that he'd simply had the Mcguire woman taken out into the desert and buried. Preferably alive. Instead, thinking to use her as a pawn, as a hostage, he'd sent her up to the old fort in the hills to his henchmen and the king. Well, she could easily be silenced in the raid. The thing now was to plan that raid, plan it to the last detail.

Tomorrow? Too soon. Day after. At night. A dozen men would do it, twice outnumbering Hassim's little gang.

Three Jeeps. Automatic rifles with those new Belgian silencers. Pick off the ADDAK men one by one, sniping, silence them all. It would work! He could taste victory. Selim's death was a good omen. The Panther Throne would not be vacant for long.

Megan lay in the steamy darkness trying not to think about what Bir-Saraband had done to her. It was no use. The scene played itself out in her head again and again, until it took on the nightmare aspect of some sickening pornographic loop of film running over and over. Then, slowly, the first tears came. Her shuddering panic turned to sobbing. It helped. Only a very little, but it helped.

She dozed for a while. Then the truck gave a hideous jolt. Her head banged against the steel floor of the van. Then everything was suddenly very quiet. It took Megan a moment to realize they'd stopped. She heard men climbing down from the front of the van. Loud talk in Arabic. *They're arguing about whether to rape me one more time before they kill me,* she thought.

Then the back door opened and someone dragged her out. Very roughly. She was flung over a man's shoulder like a sack. Now the man was walking. *They can rape you to death,* she thought. *They break things inside you.* Megan had heard such tales in the INTERTEL newsroom. The details never made it on the air, but they were real enough all the same. The man carrying her stopped. More conversation in Arabic.

A door opened. Footsteps echoing on wood. They were inside a building, then. Where? Now someone lowered her down onto a cot. Not quite as roughly as before. Megan kept her eyes closed. Now—miracle!—the footsteps seemed to be going away. The door closed. A bolt was shot home. She was alone. And once again the tears came.

Sometime later—how long she couldn't guess—Megan was awakened by more voices. The bolt slid open, the door opened. She turned her head and opened her eyes. An old man, very old, with rather a kind expression on his face, was coming into the little cell. He was carrying an old pottery bowl. A clean cloth. He knelt, gracefully for so elderly a man, beside her cot.

And then he pulled out a knife.

She watched it, hypnotized, unable to think or scream. He must have seen the terror in her eyes. He spoke.

"Please . . . not be afraid," he said haltingly. To Megan it was the sound of all heaven's trumpets echoing through the dark vault of her fear. Then, quickly and gently, he cut the ropes that bound her hands and feet.

There were just eighteen men with Bandar Al Khadir. The discipline among them was astonishing to Jeb. How Selim felt, it was impossible to tell, for they marched in utter silence through the night.

At first the hike was rough on Jeb. All the tennis in the world wouldn't get you ready for the pace these folks set. But eventually he developed a rhythm. They walked in the middle of the long single-file column, Selim first and then Jeb. Jeb was very conscious of the fact that he and Selim were the only members of the group not heavily armed. All the rest were equipped with—at the least—rifles. Often they had pistols as well, and every one of them had his own Bedu dagger, eight curved inches of blue-steel danger.

Maybe fear would come later. What Jeb felt now was a sense of wonder. *What was he doing here, after all?* From time to time he thought of Megan, but not knowing where she was or what might have happened to her was so totally painful that he fought it the way he'd fought that snake last night. This was only partly successful.

The desert at night was anything but black, and Jeb forced himself to concentrate of the raw, unspoiled beauty of it. The range of purples and intense sapphire blues that marked the sky was both subtle and dazzling. And the desert hills were a gold mine of color day and night. They marched. Jeb lost track of time. For a moment he felt hunger, and that passed.

The stars were clear to the point of astonishment. It was easy to understand why people in this part of the world had invented celestial navigation.

The cool pure beauty of the night seemed to bring his fears about Megan back more quickly than the afternoon had done. Where was she right now? Alive? Imprisoned? Comfortable but furious in her suite at the hotel?

How many men—besides Bir-Saraband—would dance on Megan's grave for filming the interview with Al Khadir?

Jeb thought of all the names Bandar had named. Dozens? At least. He shuddered, and not from the cold.

They walked on in darkness.

Billy Earnshaw was perfectly serious. "Well, old friend, and haven't we been through the wars together you and I, and haven't I stood by you and you by me all these years?"

The mangy parrot squawked agreement.

Billy swirled the amber whiskey in an old tooth glass he'd

liberated from Shepheard's Hotel in Cairo a very long time ago. *Got to get some new glasses. New place to live, for all that. With real plumbing, air cooling, clean walls. Place that doesn't smell like steerage on the Ark. And clothes. Oh, the silk shirts without end, the linen crackling, calfskin glowing, handkerchiefs, too, Dionysus, bales of 'em, and for you, dear old companion of my evil days now past, a grand new cage, something on the order of the one like a miniature Taj Mahal that the old Queen had, all brass and gleaming, my dear. Yes!*

Earnshaw reached for the bottle—and so what if it was just past eleven in the morning? Good old Johnnie Walker Black Label. Only about an inch left in the bottle. Can't let it evaporate, now, can we, that'd be wasteful. Waste not, want not. How long had it been since he'd had an entire bottle of good whiskey? Never mind, those days were gone forever now. Temporary reversal. Forty bloody years of temporary. All behind him now.

Kalbfleish's advance had been five thousand American dollars. Dear Kalbfleisch. A man of perception and insight. A man with the ability to recognize such qualities in others.

Billy emptied the glass. Nearly noon. Better get dressed. You're a man of affairs now, a man with a certain position in the world. Shaving was, as ever, an effort. The water less than fresh. Too much trouble to go down four flights to fetch more. Temporary inconvenience. At least there was one clean shirt.

He was knotting a brand-new cravat when the knocking came. Odd, that. He had so few callers these days. Well, the word of his good fortune would get around. Such news always did in this part of town. Probably someone wanting to touch him for a few quid. No problem, he'd say, smiling graciously. After all, it wasn't as though he couldn't afford to. Billy walked to the door, stumbling over a pile of dirty linen. Must see about a proper laundress.

The two men were strangers. But he knew at once they must be Russkies. The cut of their suits said that more clearly than any mutterings in their awkward language could. Suits built like boxcars, they wore! Billy mourned for the elegance that had perished with dear Nicky the czar. Wouldn't do to throw that in their faces, though. He managed, just barely, a welcoming smile.

"Mr. William Earnshaw?"

"At your service."

"I present the regards of His Excellency the Soviet ambassador Nikolai Kurakin, and can you have luncheon today?"

My, my, thought Billy, *word most certainly did get around.*

"As it happens, I am free. It would be a pleasure."

"Very good. Please to come with us, then?"

Billy hesitated. Oh, why not? They've probably come in one of those amusing Soviet limousines.

"Of course. In a jiffy."

The larger of the two Soviets looked the other in the eye. His companion nodded, once, curtly.

Earnshaw slipped on his sadly wrinkled jacket and turned to face them.

"Now, you be a good boy, Dionysus, and Billy will bring you a lovely croissant from the ambassador's."

The parrot shrieked his farewell.

The Russian gentlemen stood aside as Billy closed the door and locked it.

Then, not very steadily, he walked down the crumbling stucco stairway, the two Soviets close behind him.

There came a moment when Jeb thought the march would go on forever. And the time came when he didn't care, when he stopped thinking about the blister that had long since burst on his left foot, the throbbing in his chest from the cracked rib, or the dull ache of suppressed hunger. Hell of a way to spend maybe your last night on earth. He thought of Megan, of Selim, of the Panther Throne. Was any of it worth the risk? Megan was, surely, but this might or might not have anything to do with her. And Selim. How far do you walk for a friend? Jeb fought ghosts in the darkness. Tamara. Dark thoughts walked with him in the rocky hills. Thoughts like: *I might die and never know what happened to Megan.* Epitaph? All He Wanted Was to Build Good Buildings."

Finally, after hours that Jeb had stopped counting, Bandar called a halt.

Selim turned to him and grinned. "Welcome to Kassan, where all is luxury."

He's actually enjoying himself, thought Jeb, and immediately felt better. Jeb considered what it must have cost Selim, in sheer bravado, to set up the destruction of his limousine. Maybe to sacrifice the driver, injure innocent people. Selim went up to Al Khadir and spoke to him in low tones. He came back with a goatskin. The water in it tasted of goat, but it was more refreshing just then than the most delicate spring water in the Alps.

"Very slowly," said Selim, as if to a child. "If you gulp it, you might get sick."

Thanks, doc. How are you feeling?"

Selim smiled. "Better than I have for a long time, Jeb Stuart. I feel that, maybe, there's hope now."

They rested for half an hour, marched three hours more, then camped in a cleft between two hills just as the sun was rising. Jeb fell asleep seconds after he closed his eyes, and slept right through until late afternoon. It was a thick sleep, necessary and dreamless.

Selim woke him, gave him some food and more goat-flavored drinking water just as the sun was setting. They moved out before dark. The second night's march was a repeat of the first. But now Jeb was more ready for it. He ached less. He worried more. Bandar had a little CB-type radio, and it had brought no news of Megan.

Jeb found that it was no good telling himself they'd done what they could, that she'd asked for it—whatever "it" might be—that he'd make it all up to her one day.

He knew with a cold stab of pain in his heart that "one day" might not come. For him. For her. Again, they took a short break sometime after midnight, then resumed the march.

The hills were quiet as the moon. Maybe once in an hour they'd hear a jackal's screech far away or, closer at hand, a scurrying of some small desert mouse stalking a meal or fleeing to avoid becoming one.

The moon was about a quarter full, but that was light enough. The air had a clarity that seemed to magnify distant objects, be they the next hill in the range or the most infinite star. Jeb had to keep reminding himself that there was magic in the night, because the brooding doubts and fears threatened to overwhelm him.

With the steady pace of their marching, with his own internal turmoil, Jeb hardly noticed the slow and subtle change in the light as night's deep purple eased into sapphire blue, then a pearly sort of gray.

Suddenly Bandar called a halt, raising his right hand like a traffic cop, a gesture that was repeated by every man in the line. The rule of silence held firm: not a word was spoken.

Then they heard three shrill cries: a bird's call.

The cry was answered by Bandar, who cupped his hands and mimicked the sound with astonishing skill. Then Jeb remembered what Megan had told him about Al Khadir's childhood. Son of the royal falconer. He had learned his father's lessons well.

Selim came close. "The Arabian bustard calling to its mate," he said softly. "It is a sound every Bedu knows from birth."

Four men appeared from behind a rock.

They huddled with Al Khadir and the boy Karim. After a few minutes of intense, guarded talk, Bandar detached himself from the huddle and approached Selim. More Arabic. Jeb saw his friend's face change from inquisitiveness to something very like awe. Al Khadir permitted himself the smallest trace of a smile, nodded, then went back to his men.

Selim paused for a moment. He seemed to be catching his breath. "It's true!" he said at last, as much to himself as to Jeb. "They've seen him—my father."

Now they were guided to the hiding place that had been chosen, and well chosen, by the advance guard. A small bowl, a declivity in the hillside directly above the old fort, but well concealed by the curvature of the land and by several large boulders that had the appearance of having been flung down by some angry god.

Again they rested. Again Jeb slept for nearly six blessed, healing hours. He woke blinking. The desert sun had made a furnace of their hiding place. Jeb stood up, stretched, yawned, felt the scratchy stubble of beard growing on his chin. No wonder so many of the Bedu wore beards. The water it'd take to keep a man clean-shaven could keep a caravan alive for days. He walked around the campsite. Bandar's men were cleaning their weapons, sharpening daggers, loading rifles, distributing grenades.

Jeb felt isolated, out of it—unarmed. He and Selim were there on sufferance, barely tolerated. He wondered if Bandar would trust them to join in the attack.

And he wondered whether he would join in, if asked. Something made Jeb recall Selim's words to Megan: "I have lived too long in foreign lands." Selim's father was inside that fort. And Jeb knew in that instant that there could be no question of not helping. If his help was needed. Wanted.

Nikolai Kurakin looked through the little window and frowned. Such scenes gave him no pleasure. He always recoiled from Ibn Bir-Saraband's tales of torture, told as they were with an enthusiasm that amounted to lust. Still, it was necessary. The information must be extracted, and if subtle persuasion didn't work, harsher methods were the only alternative.

If only this wretched Earnshaw had the grace not to scream. The interrogation team had been flown in from Moscow. They had worked on Earnshaw for three hours now. What remained of him was not pretty to look at. Nor were the sounds he made attractive to hear: mostly whimpers now, occasionally a moan. And Kurakin had learned nothing he didn't already know. Earnshaw had admitted, right off, his association with the man Kalbfleisch from Revere Oil. But he refused to admit knowing anything about Revere's strategy for the forthcoming negotiations.

Kurakin watched for perhaps ten minutes, then turned away. Disgusted. The man would, of course, have to be disposed of now. His body would be found in the harbor—or perhaps not found at all, if the voracious gulf crabs had their way with him.

Who would mourn Billy Earnshaw?

Inquiries might be made, but they would never lead to the massive doors of the Soviet embassy.

Kurakin felt defeated, and this was not a customary sensation. First Austin—the coward! Then this.

Kurakin stepped into the small stainless-steel elevator and took it up from the basement to the main floor of the embassy.

He walked out a side door into the garden and took a deep, refreshing breath of the cool perfumed air. A relief.

Most welcome after the depressing scene he had forced himself to witness down below.

Poor, poor Billy Earnshaw.

Bandar looked down at the ruined fort.

All of his men were deployed on the hillside, crouching behind rocks, lying flat on the ground behind scraggly bushes, still and silent as the rocks themselves. He could feel the magnetism of imminent action. It drew him toward the fort. He had been too controlled for too long on this march, weighing the potential danger—or, possibly, help—of Selim.

The fort was a puny thing. There were, seemingly, only six or perhaps seven men guarding the king. How easy it would be to kill them all—and Nayif El Kheybar too. But Bandar had given his word, and nothing in the world would make him go back on that. He looked at Selim and the American architect now. They were close together, talking earnestly. The irony was not lost on Bandar that he might well be killed trying to rescue the King of Kassan, the very man whose throne he had sworn to topple.

Well. If Allah willed it, it would be.

Now he went to Selim and the American, at the same time summoning Majid and the boy Karim. With a certain ceremony, he handed Selim first a rifle, then a pistol, then a dagger. He repeated the gesture with Cleaver. "Thank you," was all Cleaver said. Selim said not a word, but in his eyes there was a world of gratitude and . . . Something else. A wary respect, perhaps. Bandar smiled.

"Now," he said, clearing the air of much accumulated tension, "let us plan our action."

Everyone had an idea, and everyone, each in his turn, was allowed to speak. The consensus was that the most effective attack would somehow lure the defenders out of the fort, where they could be picked off by sniper fire, reducing their numbers until resistance was minimal.

"A fire," said Jeb quickly. "Let's burn the stables."

Karim spoke up. "Four camels in the stables, and a Jeep."

"All the better," said Al Khadir. "It'll bring them out. The more they have to save, the more anxious they will be to save it."

It was agreed. Night was falling quickly. Soon only the ruined watchtower of the ancient fort caught the last yellow rays of the sun. Only when the entire valley was deep in shadow would they dare to move out. The night sky was clear to infinity, but they all felt the tension in the air, thick as thunderheads. There was a weight to it, a density. And it was charged to the crackling point with hopes and fears.

A young man came running up to Bandar and said something urgently, in low tones. Jeb watched this: some treachery?

Bandar turned to Selim. His face was unreadable.

"It seems," he said quietly, "that we are about to have visitors. Bir-Saraband is headed this way, very fast, in three Jeeps and with a dozen armed men. Now why, Prince Selim, do you suppose the general would do a thing like that?" There was an unmistakable tinge of irony in Bandar's voice. Jeb felt a quick icy jab of fear.

Selim looked at the rebel leader with a calm and unwavering gaze. "Because he thinks I am dead—as I told you, General. Because he wants to kill my father too, and seize the Panther Throne for the Bir-Saraband. Or so it seems. If he knows of this place, it is almost certain that he put my father here. The raiders of the hunting camp used army Jeeps, remember? How very easy it must have been—a few bits of your propaganda, a few trusted men trained in rebel language, your famous battle cry, how simple. And what a fool I've been not to have suspected him. Until last night, I had no doubts of his loyalty to the Panther Throne."

Bandar looked at the Crown Prince of Kassan.

"I believe you, Selim," he said, and turned away to talk to his men.

Silence grew on the hillside like some voracious tropical plant. There were lights in the fort now. Smoke curled up from some unseen chimney at the back. Whoever was inside feared no surprises. Ten minutes dragged by like hours. The man called Majid was on Jeb's left. Now he strained forward, listening. Softly Majid gave the now-familiar bird call. Only a minute later did Jeb hear what Majid's desert-keen ears must have detected earlier on: the low distant thrumming of engines. The engine noise came closer; then it stopped. If these were Bir-Saraband's Jeeps, then he must be planning his own surprise raid on the fort.

Jeb looked at Al Khadir. But Bandar was staring into the night with a hawk's intensity.

Bandar had honed his night vision until he could see things that were invisible to Cleaver or Selim. *How very stupid,* he thought, *that the men in the fort hadn't posted at least one guard. Overconfidence.* A guard would have seen what Bandar saw now: a file of uniformed Kassanian Army men creeping along the side of the dirt track that led up to the fort. The general was identifiable by his size alone. There were an even dozen of them. Each with an automatic rifle. Bandar went to Majid. He said nothing, but made a gesture. Bandar drew one finger across his throat in the immemorial sign of throat-cutting. Majid smiled and unsheathed his dagger. Then he went and chose three of the rebels: they put down their rifles, drew their daggers, and melted into the darkness.

The rest of Bandar's men took up positions that he had previously assigned to them, encircling the fort but distant enough to eatch the general's actions without being detected at it.

It looked as though the general had figured out a scheme similar to their own. Bandar watched with interest as one of the Kassanian Army men crept around by the stables that were at the rear of the fort and to its left. Three minutes later a fire announced itself with a soft roaring and an orange flare. A camel screamed. Two men ran from the fort. Two muted shots were just audible: silencers. One of the men fell, struggling, clutching his leg. The other fell dead. The rifle shots were muted. Silencers, Bandar guessed. Now there was return fire from the fort: sharp crackling reports. No silencers there. Shouts. Confusion. Two down. Maybe five others inside. Bandar peered intently into the darkness, wondering how Majid and his team were faring with their knifework. Soon it would be time to act. Very soon.

Tamara borrowed her sister-in-law's limousine for her last visit to the Bir-Saraband palace in the desert. Although it was an open secret in the court of Kassan that she had divorced Ibn, Tamara herself had been silent on the subject. She was still, officially, the general's wife, and this had its uses. For only when his office assured her that the general would be away for at least two days and nights did she presume to go back to the palace with two maids in order to pack. No force on earth would have persuaded her to meet him again.

But the carefully designed wardrobe, her jewels, her photos of the children, paintings, a collection of Roman glassware, all these must go. They were hers. She wanted them. And, above all, Tamara couldn't bear the thought of one of Ibn's whores touching her things.

It would all go to her father's palace in Port Kassan while she decided what to do with the rest of her life. And that depended on Jeb Cleaver.

She had tried three times to work up the courage to call Jeb, burning with desire and scorched by indignation that he hadn't cared enough to contact her. Maybe he was simply afraid, and if he was, then Jeb was less of a man than Tamara knew him to be.

Maybe there was someone else. But still, how could he not want her? Tamara roamed the palace like a caged panther, making lists, picking up and rejecting small objects, discovering things she'd forgotten. Her maids were already at work on the clothes closets. There the task was simpler: Tamara wanted it all. Soon, as the afternoon wore on and the job wasn't even fractionally done, it became obvious that she'd have to come back another day—or stay over and work through the night. The idea of coming back, ever, to this place was repugnant to Tamara. She instructed her maids to prepare for a light supper and sleeping here rather than in Nayif's palace.

Opening and shutting drawers in her own bedroom, Tamara came upon the little revolver. Selim had given it to her once a few years ago when there had been a rash of burglaries in Kassan. It was an elegant thing, Italian, all chased steel and with an ivory handle set with rubies in a design that made the Arabic letter T. She smiled, seeing it, remembering happier days. Selim had taken her out into the desert and taught her to use the little weapon. Now it lay in its silk-lined case, loaded, gleaming. She put it into her purse.

She thought of the coming night. The palace, as always, was filled with servants. It did not please her to stay, but the alternative pleased her even less.

Tamara resigned herself. She opened another closet, looked

at the thirty-eight ball gowns inside, and thought of Jeb Cleaver.

The Kassanian Army soldier was very close now, kneeling behind a rock and firing his rifle at the fort. Majid was on him in a second. Jeb saw a flash of steel as Majid's left arm whipped around the man's jaw, pulling it back and tightening his throat. In the same instant, Majid's right hand swept across with a swiftness and economy of motion that was almost balletic: he sliced the soldier's throat from ear to ear.

The man made a sickening, gurgling sound and fell limp. Majid wiped his blade on the man's sleeve, grinned at Jeb, and moved on. Selim was with Bandar—as an honor, Jeb wondered, or for security? And he, Cleaver, had been assigned to the second-in-command. Fine distinction. Jeb had never killed a man, never thought of himself as being violent in any way.

The sight of Majid casually slicing a man's throat was more than shocking. It stirred some dark primitive urge in him that he had never suspected was there.

Majid struck three more men, just as quickly, just as effectively. Only the last of the four heard Majid's approach, turned, and tried to fire. But even then Majid was too quick for him: stunned him with a jab to the jaw and sliced his throat as efficiently as he had the others.

They were close to the fort now. A bullet hissed overhead. There was no way to tell how many of the fort's defenders were still alive. Majid gestured to Jeb to crouch down. There was a peculiar stench in the air. It came from the stables. *Burnt camel,* Jeb guessed. The windows at the back of the fort gaped blackly. They could hear voices now, from the front of the fort. *The general, maybe, rallying his forces. However many of them might be left by now.*

Bir-Saraband pressed his attack. It had gone well from the first. The stables fired, two rash defenders picked off with ease. Tougher now, of course. Now that the ADDAK men inside the fort realized what was in store for them. There was a chance they might take out their wrath on the king. So be it. A head appeared at a window. Ibn took aim and fired. Fired again. The head disappeared. How wonderful to see

real action at last! These shots, these fallen bodies, were the
first open signs of the Bir-Saraband coup. Ibn already thought
of it in those words, the way it would be written in the histo-
ries. Selim's death would be put down to the rebels. He
looked at the orange flames shooting up from the stables. It
was almost as though he could see the Panther Throne itself
glittering in the firelight. Beckoning. Waiting.

Now Ibn paused, changed his position a little, seeking better cover. No need to take unnecessary risks, not when everything was going so well. He settled in the lee of a boulder
and watched the firefight. But—over there!—to the left,
something was wrong. There had been four of his men there,
keeping up a barrage of rifle fire. Now there was nothing.
The aim of the men in the fort couldn't have been that good.
Had his men turned coward and fled? Never. Ibn could not
accept that possibility. He'd trained them himself, handpicked
them for this mission. *Must find out.* He edged to the left,
moving slowly, silent for all his bulk, staying behind whatever
cover there was.

Something squished underfoot. Like stepping on a toad.
Recoiling, he bent to see if it was—yes!—one of his own
men, and wounded. The soldier had fallen facedown. Ibn
rolled him over, feeling for a pulse.

What he felt was the gaping slit in the man's throat.

Ibn drew back his hand as though he'd touched fire.

Still warm. *Something was out here!*

He looked quickly all around. As though he could quell
the fear that suddenly ballooned inside him, pressing on his
lungs, making him gasp for breath. *Something was out here,
and he was out here with it. Them.* Fighting nausea, he wiped
his hand on the dead soldier's shirt. Then, more softly than
before, he crept along, left, left. There was an ominous pause
in the firefight. Maybe whoever was stalking the night had
gotten them all, all his men! All but himself!

Bir-Saraband felt more alone than he ever had. And more
vulnerable. He crept back, using the high ground, heading
away from the fort now, back toward the Jeeps. It had been
folly to come with so small a force. He had trained his AD-
DAK men too well. He paused for an instant, breathing hard.
Sweating. Unused to fear.

Something shifted in the air just behind him.

Ibn whirled. He was facing a man with a knife. A stranger. A very deadly stranger. Instinctively Ibn feinted to his left, at the same time bringing up his foot straight into the attacker's groin. The knife slashed Ibn's arm, but his foot found its target. The young man fell to the ground, rolling as he hit. Ibn raised the automatic rifle, dripping blood on the grip. He couldn't see his target anymore, but he squeezed off eighteen rounds into the darkness.

From the darkness came one hideous screech. Then silence. The knife had been very sharp. Ibn didn't feel the cut as yet. But there was blood everywhere. He slung the rifle over his shoulder, grabbed the wound with his good hand to stanch the bleeding. And he ran.

No one tried to stop him. Maybe nobody else was left. He gained the Jeep, found its first-aid kit, and improvised a rough bandage. Still the wound bled. He climbed in and started the engine. No thought now for anything but escape. Safety. Come back with the whole Kassanian Army! Blast them with mortars! The Jeep's engine coughed twice and roared to life. Ibn sped away from the fort, flicked on the lights and floored the accelerator. He might make army headquarters in three hours. No. His own palace was an hour closer. There'd be servants there, phones, help. He'd go to the palace. Much better. More private than headquarters. Safer. Much safer. And safety was the only thing on Ibn's mind right now.

The Jeep roared into the darkness.

Jeb had his eyes fixed on the black unglazed rear windows of the fort when Majid nudged him, making a gesture to move out. They circled the stables, moving cautiously. Two bodies were visible. Men from the fort. Here was the burned-out shell of the stable. There, a Jeep, miraculously untouched.

They crouched behind it. Majid leveled his rifle, aiming at the rear window. A head appeared. Glint of moonlight on a rifle barrel. Majid fired. The head disappeared. No way to tell if the sniper had been hit.

Again the signal: "Follow me!"

Christ, thought Cleaver, *he wants me to go in there*. Then they were running. Majid went in first, vaulting over the windowsill into . . . what? Not thinking anymore, not wanting to think, Jeb vaulted after him. Pitch darkness. Jeb landed with a horrible squishy softness on the body of the man Majid had shot. Stumbling, he regained his footing and drew his pistol. At first he could see nothing but the shape of the window, orange with firelight, and blackness inside. It took a minute or two for the lenses of Jeb's eyes to adjust. He crouched silent a foot from where he'd landed, tense, waiting. For what?

The blackness evolved slowly into shapes he could deal with. Majid was at the far end of the room, his back against the wall, edging toward an open door. It led into more blackness. They were in some sort of pantry. Jeb could smell dry grain. There were half-empty flour sacks on the floor. Dusty shelves. Majid was moving a little more deliberately now. Jeb decided to keep close behind.

They could hear the firefight from the front of the building, but it was impossible to tell from exactly where.

Now Jeb had a terrifying vision. Shooting the king by mistake. It had been twenty-one years. What would Nayif look like now? He touched the pistol as though it might give him some reassurance. The steel was warm in his hand, the safety was off. And it wasn't reassuring at all.

Now Majid was through the door. A burst of automatic rifle fire from up front. Chattering. Crazed woodpecker spitting lead. Jeb slid through the door after his companion. Majid inched along. They were in a narrow hallway now. Jeb about six feet behind. A turning. Majid vanished around it. There was a second of silence.

Then a hideous scream. Jeb froze, and it seemed that his blood froze in him. The cry had been Majid's. Now Jeb rounded the corner. There was no place else to go but onward. He could just make out Majid's body. Throat slit. A big man bending over him, searching. Jeb didn't take time to think. The pistol was up, braced by his left hand, squeezing. The big man crumpled over Majid's compact body. Half his head had been blown away.

Jeb moved on. Not stopping. Couldn't stop. There was shouting from up front now, shrill cries in Arabic. Victory? Terror? Maybe both. Jeb kept moving, held the pistol high. Fear had a language all its own.

Megan crouched by the door of her cell, straining to listen. It had begun with explosions. Gunfire? Screams from outside. Smoke. *They were trying to attack the fort.* Whoever they were.

Megan had thought she was beyond fear. Wrong.

To have survived so much and be wiped out in some bandit raid. Bandits raiding bandits. She remembered, too vividly, the raid on ADDAK. The boy writhing in the street. Now she'd die the same way. Or worse: roasted alive in this damned little cell. Bandar, Jeb—none of them had any way of telling she was in here. If it was Bandar attacking. And, it suddenly dawned on her, it might be. Or Bir-Saraband's thugs. But why? He'd sent her here. It was all crazy and frightening, and the more she thought about it, the sicker she felt. Sick with fear.

Such a stupid way to die.

Slowly anger replaced her fear. Megan began pounding on the door. "Help! Help!" What was the word in Arabic? There were footsteps outside. Megan immediately began to regret her impulsive screams. They were probably the wrong footsteps. A grating sound. Megan knew it well by now. Bolt being withdrawn. Instinctively she flattened herself against the wall. This would be ADDAK, to shut her up forever. She darted across the tiny room and snatched up her one rough blanket. Maybe she could throw it over his head. Kick him. Disarm him. Anything. Something. The door opened slowly.

"Lady?" The old man. The dear, kind old man. She put down the blanket and went to him. He was smiling. And in his hand was a long, curved Bedu dagger. With blood on it. He bowed a little and handed her the dagger. Handle-first. He had charming manners, this one. It would have been funny if death hadn't been a few feet away.

She took the knife, holding it clumsily, hefting it until she got a feel for the thing. But she never took her eyes off the old man. At last he spoke. As always, his English was halting.

"I . . . Nayif. King." Megan gasped. He motioned for her to follow.

Jeb was in a long, narrow corridor. At the end of it, light, gunfire, screams. The core of the battle. All the light flickered. There was a lot of smoke, woodsmoke and gunsmoke. His eyes burned.

Suddenly there was a roar, a big blast, and the building trembled. A chunk of mud brick and stucco crashed down from the ceiling. Missed Jeb by about a foot. Dust rose, mixing with the smoke. He coughed, gasped, kept moving. There was a hazy, unreal quality to the air now. Smells of powder, smoke, sweat, fear. He tried to remember the exact configuration of the fort: central door, two windows on either side of it . . . What else? He kept moving. Kept the pistol high.

Now he was at the entrance to the big central room. Jeb edged half his head around the doorframe, alert to duck back. There were four men in the room. Two were alive. They paid no attention to Jeb. They darted from window to window, firing at random, trying to give the impression their numbers were greater. They were Arabs, but not in any uniform. Scraps and rags. Frightened, desperate men. They were much too young to be the king.

One of them paused at a window, knelt, raised his rifle to fire. Jeb took careful aim and squeezed off a shot. The man screamed, arched upward, fell back. He wasn't dead. But Jeb's bullet had done something permanent to his spine. He lay there twitching, unable to move his legs. Jeb slid into the big room just as the other man whirled, saw him, and got off a rifle shot.

At first Jeb didn't feel it at all. Maybe a little burning in his right thigh. He raised his pistol again, but his attacker had ducked behind an overturned table. More gunfire from outside. It had no effect in the big room. There was a kerosene lantern on a bench near Jeb. Impulsively he snatched it up and threw it hard, across the room. It smashed against the wall behind his adversary. Instantly a sheet of flame spread across the floor. A scream. The man behind the table darted to the far corner of the room, bobbing and weaving. Jeb fired again, and again. Missed both times. A click. The man was reloading.

Jeb edged toward the overturned table, keeping a corner of it between him and the other man. The table itself was beginning to burn now. Soon the whole damned place would be in flames. Jeb realized he couldn't show himself at a window or one of Bandar's men would surely get him. Swell. But there was no room in his brain for fear. Just a crazy urge to survive a few more seconds. Get off one more good shot. Jeb crouched, raised the pistol again, bracing it, waiting for the other man to make a move. Nothing. The seconds dragged. The oily stench of kerosene burning filled Jeb's lungs. A movement behind him. *Behind him?* He'd forgotten the first man. Instinctively, Jeb turned. Which was just what the second Arab had been waiting for. A shot rang out. Jeb fell forward, clutching his chest.

As he fell, cursing his own stupidity, Jeb could hear a sound like laughter from the far corner. The pistol clattered to the floor. He tried to get up. But the tide of unconsciousness beat him to it.

Megan followed the king out into the smoky hallway. She clutched the Bedu dagger as though it were the key to life itself. *King Nayif?* In a crazy way, it made sense. Bir-Saraband must have been behind his disappearance, too. But there wasn't time to think about the king now, or about anything else except getting out of here in one piece. The cell was in a wing of the fort. Megan had no sense of the layout. The gunfire and the shouts and screams were a little muffled. The king was ahead of her, walking softly. *He must be armed himself,* she thought, *if he can spare me a knife.* One corridor led to another. The king vanished around the next turning. When Megan got there, he was gone. She didn't dare call his name.

This hallway was the long stem of a T. She could turn left or right. She paused, gripping the dagger more tightly, listening. The most noise seemed to come from the right. She went left. Inching along. Wondering if, after all, she might not have been safer back in the cell. No. Not locked in. More gunfire. Jeb must be out there somewhere—if this was Bandar attacking. *Please let him be safe.*

Megan's foot stepped on something soft. Warm and soft. A body. She moved on, faster now, stomach churning. This hallway ended in a rectangle of light. Flickering light. Smoke and gunfire. Megan hesitated. There was a lull in the firing. She moved forward.

The door. Gritting her teeth as she poked her head around it, half-expecting to be shot for her trouble. The room was a shambles. On fire. A man, a Bedu in rags, standing, his back to her. Aiming a rifle very carefully. She looked down at his target.

Jeb Cleaver lay on the floor, bleeding from the chest.

Then Megan was moving, fast but silently, not thinking at all. The Arab standing over Jeb didn't hear her. Megan paused for half a second, trying to think where she could do the most damage. The knife slashed down. It was very sharp and it went in fast and smoothly, angling down between two ribs.

At first there was no blood at all. The man didn't scream, didn't turn, didn't seem to feel it. In her frenzy Megan had no time to consider these things. She yanked the knife out, raised it high, and struck again and again. He turned now and saw her, but too late. His eyes were already glazing as he fell.

Megan stood there, numb with horror, looking down at the man she had just killed. At his blood spreading across the rough brick floor. Mingling with Jeb's blood.

She knelt in blood to help Jeb. Only then did the tears come.

Jeb's eyes were shut, and he hurt all over. There must be daylight in the room, a red haze beyond his closed eyelids. Noises, voices. Arabic voices. Someone placed a cool damp cloth on his forehead. Gently. Gentle hands. He opened his eyes and looked up.

Megan was bending over him.

Her hair was a mess, she had a black eye, and there was a streak of grime on her forehead. She was the most beautiful sight Jeb Cleaver could remember seeing in all his life.

"I died," he said slowly, slurring the words, "and went to heaven."

She managed a smile. He tried to sit up. A racking pain in his chest instantly sent him back down. "What happened?" he asked.

"Later, darling. Not yet. We're all right—I think. The king's alive—we're all alive except Majid." She gestured as she spoke, and across the big soot-blackened room Jeb could see Selim deep in conversation with his father.

"We'll be evacuating soon, Jeb," she went on. "There's a

Jeep, thank God, and some camels. You've got to get to the hospital. Several of us do. I won't feel safe till I'm back in Port Kassan—someplace where that bastard can't get me."

"Bir-Saraband?"

"The beast."

Al Khadir came in before Megan could elaborate on that. He came to Jeb. "How are you, Mr. Cleaver?"

Jeb smiled. "Being alive makes all the difference."

"You did well in the action. I thank you."

"I was with your friend Majid when they got him. I killed the man who did it."

Bandar paused. "He was a fine man. Majid. You did right. Other than Majid, only one other was killed. Cuts, one minor bullet wound—nothing, really. You are the worst."

"I'll be fine," said Jeb, wishing he were more convinced of it.

"Yes," said Bandar, "you'll be in the hospital soon." Bandar turned away then. He knew he'd mourn Majid for as long as he lived. But that would come later. Bandar asked two of his men to help carry Majid's body out of the fort to a clearing on the hillside. He dug the grave himself, dug it deep in the dry sand. They wrapped Majid in a clean sheet from the fort and lowered him into the grave. Then Bandar filled it, turning aside the offers of help. Shovel by shovel, even as he had dug the pit, he filled it. A thing he must do himself. Bandar thought of two boys in the king's school, kicking a soccer ball back and forth on the dusty field after everyone else had left. He thought of Majid's ready grin, of the crazy names he made up to tease his friend.

When the grave was filled Bandar rolled four small boulders on top of it. Discourage the jackals. He stood for a moment looking at what he had done. His men had gone back down the hillside to the fort. They clustered, silent, watching him. Waiting.

There were prayers to be said, but Bandar did not say them. He raised his right arm in a kind of salute. A breeze sprang up, blowing the sand a little. In a few days there would be no trace of Majid at all, but for the memory. Finally, Bandar turned from the grave site and walked back to his men.

They left by Jeep ten minutes later, crowded in but almost

giddy with relief that the night's toll hadn't been worse. Jeb rode in the front seat, where he could stretch out a little. Selim drove. Megan, Al Khadir, and the king squeezed into the little shelf of a backseat.

"Now," said Bandar, "we must be very careful. The general is still at large—we assume—and he has friends, weapons, and vehicles. He must not find us."

Selim smiled a bitter smile. "We have just been on a bit of a hunting expedition—should anyone attempt to stop us."

There was only light traffic until they got close to Port Kassan. No opposition of any kind. This was a little disconcerting.

It made them wonder if Bir-Saraband was entrenched somewhere—in the palace, even—planning some sort of counterattack.

They went straight to the American embassy. This had been Jeb's suggestion. The safest place in Port Kassan until all the facts about Bir-Saraband were known.

Wiggy was tired but coping. And absolutely astonished when they presented themselves. King, crown prince, leading rebel, Jeb, and Megan. Looking like the wrath of several gods. On top of all that, Lulu was in hysterics, Hindley was locked in the guardhouse, and reporters were besieging the place.

Wiggy found them all rooms and arranged for Jeb and Megan to be taken under guard to the hospital. After her examination and treatment, Megan phoned Louise and asked that she bring some clothes and makeup to the hospital. Selim had ordered a police search for Bir-Saraband, but as yet there was no word of him.

It was late in the evening when Megan came into Jeb's room at the hospital. The black eye was fading, more yellow now than purple. Makeup helped some. Other than that, she looked fine.

Wiggy was with Jeb. Megan hesitated, then decided she'd have to make a statement for the embassy too.

"I only want to say this once," she said quietly, "and I'll make it simple. Bir-Saraband invited me for an interview. He knew I'd come—it was the one missing piece. I went with Ahmad, my Kassanian interpreter. They took him—let's find out about that, if we can, Mr. Lawrence. Suddenly I was alone with the general. But I wasn't alone. The general had invited four of his thugs. And they tied me up and raped me." She shuddered. "All of them. Why they didn't kill me too. I'll never know. I guess I should be grateful. I must have fainted, because when I came to I was tied up and in a van. They took me to the fort. Put me in a cell. The king got to me somehow. He helped. In fact, it was he who set me free last night. Nice old man. You know the rest."

There was a stunned silence. Jeb reached out for her hand and took it, just holding it tight, saying nothing. Then there was a knock on the door and Selim came in.

"He is dead," said Selim in a flat and exhausted tone of voice. Nobody in the hospital room had to ask who "he" might be.

Tamara had always been a light sleeper. Now, on the last night she would ever spend in her husband's palace, she could hardly sleep at all. Hours passed. She dozed, woke, and dozed again. She lay looking up at shadows on the ceiling. They had stayed up late finishing the packing. It was all done now. They'd leave early in the morning. It was past two.

She closed her eyes and tried to will herself into sleep. Useless. There were too many ghosts, too many dreams, too many unanswered questions.

What was that noise?

Someone clumsy was stumbling around . . . where?

Suddenly Tamara was wide-awake. She had never known fear, not until the day Ibn had taken her to see the stoning. But there were such things as burglars these days. The foreign workers, people said. But things happened. Not to mention rebel attacks. It would be more than ironic if the woman who hated General Bir-Saraband more than anyone else in Kassan were slain for being his wife! The gun Selim had given her was still in her purse on the night table. She slid out of bed, a slender shape in her nightgown of pale ivory satin. Tamara got the pistol out of her purse. Kind of Selim to have shown her how to use it. She clicked off the safety catch, pulled on the long, flowing negligee that matched her nightgown, and picked up the pistol. It might not be much good if there were several of them, but it was surely better than nothing.

Who would dare to invade the palace of Bir-Saraband?

She went to the door of her bedroom and paused, listening. No point in wakening her maids—good girls, but silly; they'd just scream and add to the confusion.

Now someone, whoever it was, bumped into a piece of furniture. Something crashed. Glass breaking, or porcelain. Suddenly aware of her bare feet, Tamara paused and found her slippers.

Then, taking a deep breath, she opened the door and walked cautiously down the hallway that led to the central portion of the palace, where the noise was coming from. The pistol was in her hand, close by her side, concealed in the folds of her robe.

Better not to appear waving it around. This might be nothing more than some drunken underling of Ibn's.

The hallway turned a corner, and suddenly he was there, lurching toward her.

Ibn.

There was only a dim light coming from one of the side chambers, but it was light enough. She could see the blood. She could smell the fear. He was clutching his left arm with his right. There was dried blood on the left arm, a crude bandage. And now, more blood, the wound open again. He must have lost quite a lot of blood, Tamara thought rather clinically.

Ibn staggered toward her, his face a mixture of emotions. The face she had promised herself she'd never see again. There was fear on his face. That was a novelty: Ibn afraid. What demons must be after him to create fear in this nerveless, arrogant brute? She didn't care enough to find out. He came forward slowly. She thought of him, complacent in his limousine, watching the stoning.

"Tamara . . ." he said.

Her name sounded filthy on his lips.

"Help me."

It was the only plea she had ever heard from her husband. Impossible not to comply.

Tamara raised the little pistol and fired it until the chamber was empty.

Jeb sat at his drawing board. There were more stitches in

his chest and his leg than he wanted to think about, but he could still draw. The new embassy had come to life on the paper.

He'd drawn it from several perspectives, dead-on, overhead, sideways. He had sketched out the details, the pools and gardens, the long driveway. It was almost presentable now. In a few days he'd fly to Washington, get his approvals—Allah willing—and come back to start construction.

Megan walked in behind him.

She'd moved to his house from the Hilton when her crew went back. Megan had the third bedroom. She wanted company but not sex. She had a mortal fear of being alone, no matter how dead Bir-Saraband might be. For the first two days she'd let him kiss her, nothing more. Today was the third day. And today she was going home.

The cable had come yesterday: "FREDDIE'S SPOT YOURS IF YOU WANT IT. COME HOME QUICK. WE LOVE YOU. LUCAS B. LUCAS."

She held it gingerly, as though it might be contaminated. "Well," she said, "poor girl's dream comes true."

He kissed her cheek. Goddamned brotherly, it felt like. "Congratulations! It's just what you wanted, isn't it?"

"I wanted it too much. Sure. And I'll take it, too. I just wish I felt more . . . well, more up about it."

He stood up and put his arm around her. "You will. Once all this fades a little in your memory. There'll be no stopping you now. But then, there never was."

Now, a day later, she was all packed. Selim had insisted on sending a car for her. It was due in a few minutes.

She came to the drawing board.

"Not bad, for an amateur guerrilla."

He laughed. "Let's hope State agrees. I like it, though."

"So do I, and so will they. Jeb?"

"What?"

"There was one good thing about this damned sandlot."

He stood up and went to her and put his arm around her. "It doesn't have to end here, Megan. I live in New York too, you know."

She reached up and touched his cheek. "I remember."

Charlie Richmond appeared. He'd dropped the alias, but he was still ensconced. "You car's here, Megan."

It was another Rolls-Royce, brand-new, white but nowhere near as elegant as the old one. She didn't want him to come to the airport. The driver took her luggage.

Now Jeb put both arms around her. That felt good to him. He wondered how it felt to her. "I'll be back next week. Will you be there?"

Megan kissed him, blinking fast to keep the tears back. "You can bet your lucky T square I'll be there."

Then she ran down the path to the enormous white Rolls with the panther crest on its door.

Epilogue

The dedication of the new United States embassy at Port Kassan took place on a bright May afternoon three years after the aborted Bir-Sarabrand coup.

Megan had wangled permission to cover it for INTER-TEL, even though her new job kept her out of the field more often than she was in it these days. But Megan would have come anyway, in her other role: Mrs. Jeb Stuart Cleaver.

Jeb had been out to Kassan and back so often these last few years it was a miracle he'd found the time to get her pregnant. But pregnant she was, and delighted about it. They'd decided to have either three or four kids, depending on how she felt after number three. Right now, standing in the sunlight between Jeb and the new ambassador, Wiggy Lawrence, Megan felt just fine.

There were still bad moments. She had had a bad moment just this afternoon, driving from the palace to the embassy. Past the Army Headquarters Building.

Selim insisted they stay with him. He met them himself, waiting at the airport, an unheard-of honor. King Selim. His father had abdicated soon after the incidents of three years ago. Nayif lived in his summer palace in the hills now, happier than he had ever been, falconing whenever he wanted to.

The ceremony was mercifully brief, followed by a reception in Jeb's wonderful gardens. The trees weren't fully grown yet, but already it was a magical place. Water rippling everywhere.

That night Selim and Queen Fawzia gave a big dinner with

a small guest list: Jeb, Megan, Wiggy and his wife, and General Al Khadir. Still a general, but in Kassanian Army uniform now. He had become Selim's principal adviser. "I still fell peculiar," said Bandar to Megan, "walking in the front door of the palace—or any official building!"

They could laugh about the old days now.

Dinner was long and luxurious, with wine and many toasts. And after it was over, Selim handed Megan a box. "From my father, Megan, who sends his regrets for not being here. He feels he must hunt, you know, and at the crack of dawn. First things first."

It was a Cartier box in deep red leather. Megan's hand trembled as she opened it. There, against deep blue velvet, lay an amazing brooch: a panther rampant, carved from yellow gold and entirely covered by pavé diamonds, with a single ruby eye.

"Oh, Selim . . . it's incredible. Thank you . . . and your father."

"I must tell you," said Selim, "it isn't unique. We had them made for Fawzia, for Tamara, and for our little girl, Leila, born in January. It is to remind you of a special time in Kassan."

As if I'd forget, she thought, reaching for Jeb's hand. As usual, it was right there.

They talked long into the night, looking out over Port Kassan from Selim's huge window. At one point Jeb took Bandar aside. "Tell me, General: what became of the boy who found where the king was hidden?"

"Karim?" Al Khadir smiled. "Rising fast, as well he ought to. In the dear old Ministry of Education. Where I've had the great revolutionary pleasure of sacking just about everyone. He will go far, Karim."

"And you, General?"

"Ah. The falcon tamed. You must mean, am I happy? Sometimes things go too slowly here in the land of Inshallah, and I long for a hand grenade to stir up more action. But Selim's way works—may I be the first to admit it. It is peaceful. No more blood had to be spilled."

The immediate aftermath of Bir-Saraband's coup was well known, largely thanks to Megan's superb coverage of the situation. The Soviet embassy and everyone in it was dismissed from Kassan when Kurakin's meddling was revealed. King Nayif had renewed Revere Oil's concession, based on various escalating clauses. The Hindley incident had been thoroughly hushed up. Ahmad had been found, in the nick of time, imprisoned but unharmed, in the basement of the Army Headquarters Building. Megan had invited him to the embassy dedication, but Ahmad couldn't make it. He had final exams. As for Tamara, she had a new and busy career as Minister of Female Education in Kassan. "A demon worker," Selim had said, smiling: "she's off in England right now, recruiting teachers for the new women's university."

The next morning, en route to the airport, Selim and Megan and Jeb stopped off at the embassy to see it in the early light.

Wiggy greeted them. "Well, Jeb," he said, never at a loss for a smooth compliment, "it's a monument."

"No," said Jeb, "a beginning."

Megan's hand was in his. He squeezed it.

About the Author

Tom Murphy, a graduate of Harvard, began his career as an Intelligence Analyst for the G-2 of Berlin Command in Germany. When he returned to America, Mr. Murphy went to work in advertising, eventually becoming Vice-President and Creative Supervisor at the J. Walter Thompson Company. Currently he holds the same position at Bozell & Jacobs, and in his spare time is a dealer in art and antiques. Mr. Murphy is also the author of LILY CIGAR, AUCTION!, ASPEN INCIDENT, BALLET!, and SKY HIGH.